ASTRA SOMNIA

Clinton John

Astra Somnia is dedicated to everyone who dreams themselves an author, but lacks the *'perpetual source of support'* or *'beloved fount of encouragement'* that books often get dedicated to. Forget that, you don't need it. Focus on *your* dream. Inside yourself, you already have everything you need.

Dream loudly, little stars.

CHAPTER 1

{Katie's Impossible Sound}
{Ballarat, Victoria, 1939}

Katherine's dip into nap land was interrupted by an impossible sound: the lid on the coffin was opening. Her eyes popped open as her body flooded with endorphins, eradicating any residual tiredness. She leaned forward and peeked through the curtains of her hidey-hole, and scanned the room, quickly realising that it was not one of her brothers playing up. Only then did she look towards the coffin, resting off to the side of the main door. As the lid was raised from the inside, she was astonished to see that it was her Uncle Justin slowly and quietly climbing out.

Her breathing stopped. She felt her eyes start to bulge, her entire body on pause. She watched as he carefully lowered himself to the ground, and then quietly replaced the lid. He held his hands on the coffin for a moment, as if he was quickly paying his respects. When he turned around, she could see him clearly, and her held-in breath released in a gush. She felt her chest contract as if she'd been hugged too tightly from behind, and she struggled to regain control.

Her involuntary gasp must have been audible, because she could see through the gap in the curtains that her not-so-dead Uncle was now quickly walking over to where she hid. He pulled the curtains apart, knelt down and took her hand. She didn't believe what was happening. It was the same man – the same eyes, the same voice – but he was decades younger. His grip was strong and firm. It could've been her Uncle Justin's long-lost grandson turned up for the funeral, but she knew he'd never married. In addition, there was the small issue of seeing him die a couple of days ago, and climb out of his own coffin less than a minute ago. He squatted in front of her and she saw a flush of thoughts on his face – surprise, perplexity, then resolve. There was a strange static to the air, and she felt dizzy.

'Quick, come with me', he commanded. Without a second thought, she jumped up and followed him out the front door. From the wide front porch, she could see an unknown car swerving up the drive. She wanted to catch a better look at him, but they'd exited so quickly. Her strangely vigorous Uncle Justin turned and touched to the swinging seat as he spoke.

'I'll leave you here, later, but now...now, you need to wake up.' He took both of her hands and hunched over slightly to look directly in her eyes again.

Wake up? she thought. *What on Earth does he mean?* But as she looked into his eyes, she was suddenly distracted. All of his wrinkles were gone. His skin was so smooth, and his eyes...his eyes were so deep. She was surprised to notice that he had the same flecks of gold in his eyes that she had. She'd never noticed that before. Behind her, she could hear yelling and screaming from the car. As she started to turn her head to see what was happening, she was suddenly overcome with dizziness. As she fainted, nobody saw her resurrected uncle catch her, nor did anybody see them both vanish moments later, leaving an empty seat swinging as though in a breeze.

CHAPTER 2
(The Hospital Surprise)
(Perth, Present Day)

Tommy Robertson's gaze wandered over the covers of the ancient book, his body as immobile as the bench he leaned on. Was it just the journal taunting him, or was it life? The world outside was still spinning merrily along, but for Tommy, everything had stopped. His gaze was as fixed as the book was unexpected; seeing it there had him stunned into inaction.

Resembling the journal, he too wasn't moving physically. But in Tommy's mind, what this journal represented was spinning out of control. It had already turned his world upside-down and inside-out in less than 48 hours, but he couldn't bring himself to move over and pick it up. It was as if his whole body refused to indulge the curiosity of his mind, yet he couldn't ignore it. How did it end up here? And the real surprise: he got to decide what to do with it. He didn't want to think about it; he'd done quite enough thinking over the last two days.

With a forced exhalation, he broke the gaze he held with his Mum's most precious possession, and wandered deliberately into the kitchen. Making a pot of tea would force him into action, and he knew that sometimes, any kind of action is all that is needed. He could decide what to do later. He flicked the switch on the radio and the room filled with music. It was the same song he'd sung along with, only two days ago on the drive in to see his Mum at the hospital. The same song that had started his adventure had chased him here, but he couldn't sing along anymore.

Two mornings ago, he'd been out back to check on the garden and her granny flat, just to confirm that nothing was amiss. It had taken a lot of effort to convince his mother to move to the west coast, but eventually she had. He and Gloria had bought a little three bedroom pre-fab unit for Gloria's mother a lifetime ago; and over the last seven years, his mother had made it her own. With lots of space for garden beds, he had encouraged his own now-fully-grown kids to bring their children to participate in a Busy-Bee for Grand-mama. His father George had instilled the value of manual labour into him and his sisters, teaching them all that there was no excuse for not knowing how to care for yourself, or to care for the Earth around you.

Tommy sometimes shivered when he found himself repeating the exact old lines his father had used, but he knew now what his Dad had been trying to teach. The old man had instilled not only the capacity for hard work, but also the ability to stick it out, the determination to simply do what was needed. *It's harder to teach resilience and diligence nowadays*, Tommy acknowledged sadly. His parents hadn't had the TV to compete with for attention, or had to fight against the influence of media celebrities as role models. Still, he was proud of his two kids. Neither of them had been to jail, or was taking drugs, and nowadays that could count as a success story. *Perhaps the cooler climate over east had been more conducive to the harsher lessons of his childhood.*

That morning on the drive to the hospital, Tom couldn't find anything on the radio he wanted to listen to, so he left it on the golden oldies station. He wanted music to escort him away from his thoughts, and he knew the disc in the car's CD player wouldn't do the job. Songs from the eighties would only remind him of Gloria, and it was thoughts of her he was trying to escape. He could play the music – he knew he'd sing along, he knew the lyrics – but it was after the song was over, he wouldn't be able to stop himself looking at the empty passenger seat. Where her ghost sat.

She'd never sat in this car, he hadn't even had it when she died, but sometimes he still talked to her, still pretended he could hear her reply. His kids had ganged up on him and convinced him to get something new, something that didn't carry quite so many memories. A four-wheel-drive was certainly more practical; he could pick up Claire's boys from school with heaps of room for their bags and school projects. He'd sold his old Holden Commodore for a decent price, which he'd been happy about. Not that finances mattered anymore, the insurance money from Gloria's accident had seen to that. He'd pay ten times that amount or more to have her back, but now she travelled with him as a picture in his wallet, and the ghost in his mind.

Usually he found her ghost most real around the boys' birthdays. Their daughter Claire had been heavily pregnant when Gloria was ripped from their lives, but they hadn't known it was twins. Gloria had been driving home after working late, and had buzzed his phone once to indicate she had been leaving. That was it. A solitary buzz.

They'd spoken earlier, when she explained she wanted to finish grading papers and that he'd need to eat alone. He'd been head-down working on his latest novel at the time; which she'd probably guessed and had really called to remind him to eat at all. It wasn't until hours later that his head came up and he realised she'd never come home. As she'd never carried a mobile phone - they weren't yet the ubiquitous accessory - he drove the ten minute route he knew she would've taken, and stopped cold the moment he came around the corner. Flashing lights warned drivers of an accident, but they pulsed a different message to him that night. He'd parked his car and walked the last hundred metres, dreading what he would find. Later he'd been grateful to be told that she'd been killed on impact, but that evening had been a nightmare he hadn't woken from, a reality he still struggled to accept as real. Barely able to identify himself, a police officer had driven him to the hospital, where he had to identify her body. He hadn't written a word since.

Each time he visited his mother in the hospital, he struggled not to think back to that terrible event. She was staying in the north block, far from the Emergency entrance he'd used that night. Seven years might have passed, but he still preferred not to have to pass those doors. The radio reception turned to static as he drove deeper into the car park, and he switched the noise off.

The corridors of the hospital were familiar now, the smells and sounds a reassuring hum of normality. Nursing staff, cleaners and caterers bustled with visitors and the occasional patient in the busy lobby. The halls to the right led off to radiology, the overpass to the left led to the multi-story car park built next to the busy central train station. It seemed strange to think that not long ago those corridors were unknown and irrelevant tunnels, just part of the background he didn't need to think about. He hadn't needed to know what lay in which direction, but over the last month the mysteries had slowly given up their secrets. He had accompanied his mother to various tests and scans, and had explored on his own during the times she had consultations, or when she was simply catching up on her sleep. For some reason she hadn't been sleeping well. He wished the doctors would eradicate the infection that was slowing down her recovery.

As she was sleeping, Tommy stood beside his mother's bed and watched her breathe. He knew how easily she woke from unexpected noises, how difficult she found it to sleep. He didn't want to disturb her. He knew she would scold him for doing so, but the reprimand would be good-natured. He visually traced the veins on her hands, up her arms, amazed at the resilience of the human body. It was so frail and yet so strong; so fragile and yet so powerful. It looked like she could fall apart, or be blown over by a whisper, but those hands and arms had raised him and his sisters. They had carried water before there was indoor plumbing, had rocked him to sleep and made his school lunch uncounted times over the years. They were still nimble enough for her to knit or crochet, to move a pen over the rapidly disappearing empty squares of the crosswords she loved so much. He hated the thought that she would soon be gone.

Rolling the bed-top table aside quietly, he sat in the tall padded armchair next to her bed. On the far wall was a small cabinet where personal treasures were displayed. In the cupboard underneath were her clothes, neatly folded – he knew that without looking. On the bench were picture frames nestled among some fresh flowers. Claire must have brought the flowers; they were a generic bunch from a florist or supermarket, thrust into a glass jar one of the nurses had brought from the kitchenette. They seemed too busy, too messy, like an *Oh-Mr-Hart* explosion in a Zen garden. Mum loved her flowers, but she liked them neat and tidy. She'd spend most of the daylight hours out in her garden. Weeding, pruning, trimming, planting and watering, nursing her plants with the same sturdy care she had shown when raising her four kids. Diligent: that was the word.

As if reading his thoughts, the sunlight slipped behind a cloud and the room fell into shadow. Not one for wallowing in sadness or even second-guessing himself, he looked at the framed picture of his parents on the bedside table and mentally saluted his father. *Yes Sir!* he thought to himself. George had been gone for eight years now, the heart attack that had almost been a predictable rite of passage for men of his age and generation. Although they had never been close, never been *friends*, Tommy thought there was an intangible connection between fathers and sons that never really disappears, no matter how much pain and resentment is wrapped in that bond.

At least his passing had opened the door for Tommy to bring his mother to the west coast, so she could be near her new-born great-grandchildren. How she doted on Claire's twins. Her fridge was covered in artwork stretching back to their kindergarten days. She would teach them the Latin names for the trees and shrubs that she cultivated in her yard, testing them repeatedly and rewarding their memory with candy. The sugar treats he was not so happy about, but he couldn't refuse his mother anything.

Today he had a treat for her, something special he hoped would lift her spirits. He'd bought her a plant, a small surprise that she could keep on her windowsill. He placed it on her bed-table, so she could see it when she woke. She had larger ones at home, planted outside her kitchen window near the backdoor. For some reason it had always been her favourite, so he had gone to a florist and ordered a miniature one, especially for her. He knew that it needed humidity, so he had also bought a second-hand fishbowl with a glass lid for it to sit in. And there it sat, with its leaves open, delicate cilia teeth waiting to bite down like prison bars for when the tiniest touch of insect feet would bend its trigger hairs; and down its trap would go. He'd always found it a little gross, a trifle macabre, but for some reason she had always loved her Venus Flytraps. He smiled at the memory of her talking to her plants, like babies that needed constant attention. A voice brought him back from his reverie. 'Dionaea...?'

'Muscipula', he replied, automatically completing the full Latin name of the Venus flytrap. He smiled. 'I didn't want to wake you mum. You looked so peaceful just lying there.'

'Oh yes, don't I look a state' his mother replied. 'And I see you've brought me a new child, in its own glass crib and all. But how will I get food for my new little baby in here?' she asked with raised eyebrows. He pulled a piece of paper from his pocket, carefully unfolding it to show her four dead flies.

'Four? A month's worth of grub? You surely don't expect me to be in here for another month? I've had enough of being here already, I tell you that much'. She smiled through her pain, the happiness at seeing her only boy clearly evident in her eyes. She reached out and took his hand, one strong hairy hand enveloped in her two skeletal ones. 'I thought you might be in today. And now I see I was right. You've brought me a going away gift' she nodded towards the glass bowl.

Tommy shook his head. 'That's enough of that sort of talk mum. You'll be back in your garden in no time at all. What will all your other babies do without you?'

'Oh they'll manage', she said. 'Just as all my babies have. But you bringing me this little muscipula now, my beloved little 'musical scapula' as you used to call it when you were little, don't you see? It's a sign. Another one, telling me the feeling I have in my bones is right. My time is soon, my darling boy, and I don't want to spend precious seconds arguing over the inevitable, ok?'

He nodded, swallowing back a response. He knew from experience that it was best not to argue with her. And many people knew that when Katherine Amelia Robertson said that she could feel something *in her bones*, it turned out to be spot on the mark.

'I have a special gift for you today, too. A story, of sorts, although it's actually a secret. One that I've kept for seventy years, and I've decided to leave it to you. What you do with it, is up to you.' She sighed and eased herself into an upright position in her bed. 'It's a true story, I promise you that much. It's about my first starnic, back when I was fifteen.' She looked over at him, and chewed her tongue for a moment as if hesitant. 'But, it won't be easy,' she sighed.

'I think I need a cuppa my boy. Make me a cuppa tea and I will tell you my secret. It's something even you, with your imagination, might still find hard to believe. I've doubted it myself, more than once. But it's true, all true. It was my first introduction to starnics. And my love of this little musical scapula, my Dionaea muscipula, goes right back to that time. Or a little afterwards, I suppose. It doesn't matter: it's all related. It's always reminded me of how we are all caught in a flytrap, one made especially for human beings. So go and heat the water while I gather my thoughts, ok?'

Tommy nodded as he stood and fumbled in the top drawer for one of her herbal tea bags, afraid to meet her eye in case he started leaking tears. He knew she wasn't well. In fact, her health was worse than he or the doctors wanted to admit. She was deteriorating, although most of the time she was completely unaware of it. For her to talk like this was unusual, it was as if she did actually know. She had proven to know many things *in her bones* over the years; the expression was even used as a family joke when she wasn't there. Tucking the grandkids into bed last night they had both been excited about the camping trip planned for the weekend. 'The weather forecast says no rain, but we ought to ask Grandma's bones to be sure' Alex had said. Today wasn't his usual visiting day, but something in his own bones had resonated from that comment, bringing him in here by himself today. *Spooky*, he had mused. *Maybe 'Grandma's bones' is genetic.*

He pottered at the kitchenette, waiting for the kettle to heat the water. Not to boil it, he had to catch the switch before it went that far. She preferred the water just heated so as not to burn the tea. He wasn't sure if that really worked when using pre-packaged mass-produced teabags, but if it was how his mother wanted it, who was he to refuse? Especially with the prospect of one of her stories; let alone one framed by such foreboding words. He filled her favourite teacup and returned to her room, catching his mother staring off into space. Sometimes it looked as if she could see worlds of activity that no-one else could see, contained in the streams of light that beamed through the windows. She waited till he placed the cup and saucer in front of her, next to the terrarium on her bed-table. Then she started her tale.

'This story goes way back before I even met your father. I too was once a young girl. One who, like Alice, fell down a proverbial rabbit hole. Except this was no rabbit hole, and it was not at all proverbial. It was real, and far more akin to our flytrap friend here than anything I've ever seen since. It was a trap, I am sure of that, and some days I still wonder that I got out of it at all.' She paused to blow on her tea. Raising her eyebrow, she smiled at him cheekily. 'Perhaps I didn't, and the past seventy years have been a hallucination, induced by the digestive juices of some alien plant.'

She took a sip of her tea and smiled. 'Ahhh, perfect.' She looked up and smiled at him with pride. 'If it is though, then it's a pretty damn wonderful hallucination, I tell you that my dear.' She put down her teacup and reached out and rested her hand against his face. Her hand felt warm, and she returned it to the teacup as she returned to her mysterious story.

'But all good things must come to an end. I can't tell you how glad I am that I get to share this tale with you my boy, the reasons for which will become apparent. But the more I think about it, the more I wonder if it is even one I can tell, here and now. It's complicated, you see. Now that I try to explain, I realise it's so complicated I'm not sure I can even explain. I think you need the backstory. Otherwise, you'll be wondering if I've gone mad. I know I have, sometimes.' They both smiled. 'If I can, I will take questions afterwards, ok?' He nodded, his curiosity roused.

'I need you to imagine another world. Because to me you see, it really was another world. A lifetime ago. I was fifteen, and naturally, I was still living with your grandparents on the farm. This was before I met your father. Like most teenagers, I had definite ideas about where my life was going, and of course, there was no room for doubt, no alternative or options were even entertained. I was going to get married and have children and care for my family.'

She stopped to sip her tea, and then smiled self-deprecatingly. 'Of course I did, eventually. Wow, did life turn out to be quite different than the way I thought back then. What teenage girl in the '30's – or at any time I suppose, could dream of being swallowed by time?' She smiled infectiously, and glanced towards the sunny windows as if to recharge.

'Thinking back on my life, as anyone my age is prone to do, especially when cooped up in a hospital bed...' she grinned: but he could tell it was a joke to cover a grimace. 'I know that I've had a really good life. A happy and reasonably prosperous one overall, but I mean 'good' in that I have learnt as much as I could. And taught you kids to be the same, which you taught your kids, and so it goes.' She paused, staring at the picture frames adorning the shelf. 'It's just beautiful; every generation amazes me all over again. I'm so proud of you all.' Tommy reached out and squeezed her hand again, smiling at her encouragingly. She continued.

'Now you probably think you know the story of my life, and have some idea of who I am. But there is one thing missing, a secret, something I have kept to myself for longer than you've been alive. I never really even told your father about it. Something unbelievable happened to me when I was young, that I promised never to speak of. Something that I have tried to forget, well, almost. At least, I've learnt not to dwell on it. But oh, baby boy of mine, this was so life-changing. For the little girl I was, it was what they now say, 'a formative experience', you see. It was the day of the car crash – you know about that, right?'

Tommy nodded mutely, wondering where this was going.

'In the seconds before that crash, you see, I had a vision. I suppose you have to call it that. I lived four weeks in about four seconds. It wasn't an out-of-body experience or a hallucination or even a lucid dream – those are things that I've only learnt about since, and it wasn't anything like that. Because in this dream, I wasn't alone. At the start of it, I thought it was real, that I was awake and everything was normal. But just like you wrote in one of your books, nothing is ever 'normal' anyway, right?'

They both grinned at that: it had become a little family joke, questioning normality. Tommy raised his eyebrows slightly, encouraging her to continue. His curiosity turned to disbelief, and dipped back and forth into shades of incredulity as she explained that she'd had further visions over the years, strange immersive dreams of other lives. Lives of other creatures. She spoke of memories that she couldn't possibly have, and called them her 'pre-memories'. Things she remembered that she couldn't possibly. Tommy started to think about talking with the family's physician, in case she was having a reaction to some medication. As if she could see his thoughts, she changed the topic.

'There's nothing medical about it all. I've got proof, of sorts.'

'Of sorts?' he repeated, questioningly.

She smiled, confidently and patiently. 'Oh yes. You see, I kept a journal. I wrote it all down. And then I had to write all the other things down, my pre-memories, and I am certain they're all related. I want you to read it, then perhaps you'll understand why. Why I haven't been able to forget.' Her face went wistful for a moment, her mouth curling into an unaccustomed shape.

'The thing is, I promised him I would never *speak* of it.' The emphasis on the verb was matched with a nod of meaning tipped at Tommy, and he smiled wryly as he understood. His mother had kept her word, and never spoken of her vision until now. But she had written it all down, and that way she could still share her story without breaking her promise.

'The problem is, I need you to go fetch my journal. You're still coming in tomorrow?' she asked, and he nodded. 'Bring it in tomorrow. I need to add to it, and I have a feeling it can't wait.'

CHAPTER 3
[A Necessary Interruption]
[Stellar Society]

Carols definitely shouldn't be able to hear her own voice. It was a most unwelcome intrusion. She had made appropriate preparations for some uninterrupted peace and quiet, so she could relish the song, and at the moment, the song was still *new*.

'Sorry to interrupt, but you will definitely want to deal with this yourself'.

Carols in Sequins had lost track of how long she had been swimming in the music, but that was the point of solitude. She could have checked, but doing so would have broken the sanctity of her peace. She had purposefully and carefully initiated an exo-neural ghost before she came to meditate; and with a copy of herself in charge, she would be distraction-free. Any period of solitary relaxation was something she did reluctantly and carefully, and now that she was there, she certainly didn't want to have to go back. She wanted the moment to continue. With nothing else to do than languorously float through the echoes, she could relish the simplicity and beauty of the harmonies that bounced all around her.

Of all of her physical parts, only one of them sang. Her mind beat with a helium pulse, hydrogen synapses firing deep in the churning core of a Red Dwarf star. Her entire body extended out much further than simply her mind, creating an electro-magnetic teardrop bubble as she charged through the void. Inside her essentially egg-shaped heliosphere were five rocky planets, two relatively smaller gas giants and one larger one: her Brown Dwarf. A number of her planets had moons, some with biological growth. Yet of all her parts, her favourite was a single comet, which lunged into and out of her heliosphere, caught in her wake on a predictable loop.

On its brief forays outside her body it would coast in the interstellar winds, and it was then that the tunnels riddling its icy core channelled those gusts. Fluted harmonies chimed with varying intensities, depending on the angle and rotation of spin. The billions of frozen little bodies in the icepede colonies were hibernating, waiting for the warmth of her core to revive them. The comet would dive back into her shell, and then the icepedes would continue mindlessly gnawing their way through the comet, burrowing in unexplored directions, creating new trails that would channel the winds differently next cycle. The underlying pattern was the same, but the song was always slightly different, and it was these differences that Carols relished. The whole experience of swimming through the icepedes song was always delectable, but she was especially thrilled when a new combination of sounds coalesced. That heavenly symphony was all around her at the moment, and she most certainly did not want to be disturbed: not by anyone, not even herself.

She willed her ghost to go away, wishing her voice had been a hallucination. However, her ghost knew exactly what she was doing, and Carols could feel her waiting impatiently. She knew that it would have to be something pretty urgent to call her back from her ice song swim. She started to wonder what it could be, and with a curse, she realised that her trance was broken. She may as well return to her mind.

Activating the tangle, she absorbed her exo-neural ghost and resumed primary control. Now she was more than a little curious to know what was so damn important. A rush of memories came into her being; things that her exo had done while she was away. There had been very little going on in her immediate neighbourhood, and nothing that she was interested in.

As she assimilated her memories there could be no doubt about what it was. Only one news item had escalated: the Hawk Step birthing. The dwarf galaxy's solitary Blue had burped, and the resultant subatomic particle wave had slammed into other winds, materials which till now had been slowly and predictably heading her way. The details collated by subsidiary exos caught up with her in a dizzying rush. She followed the development of the catastrophe, agog for a moment, before one of the flashing alarms grabbed her attention. She was relieved to see that it was her sister *Berries in Cerise*, calling to speak directly with her.

It felt like they had just spoken, but those were memories she'd inherited from her ghost. It was more honourable to speak in person, rather than through an exo-neural substitute, no matter how identical they were. Ghosts were considered to lack panache, or a degree of interpersonal intimacy, despite the fact that they were indistinguishable in practice. Carols' mind saw the disaster unfold, the reverberations directly impacting her comet. The timing was all off. Two of the smaller garden moons in her menagerie would lose their orbits, with catastrophic consequences for the biospheres they supported.

The H-5 nursery cluster had long been planning to disembark and form its own family unit. When the central Yellow-Silver binary had ejected a jet of subatomic particles as part of a course adjustment, an unlikely confluence of factors triggered a domino effect. That jet had intersected a passing shockwave, which dispersed debris into a nearby expanding nebula, part of which had been slowly heading in her direction. What had been a sedate dusty molecular cloud now contained convoluted waves, a surf of infrared radiation suffused with organic compounds, and it wasn't moving slowly anymore.

It didn't require any advanced future-surfing to predict an inevitable outcome; the likelihoods were so clear she could almost feel the impact. For a moment, she was scared, and understood why she had called herself back. She needed to focus completely; but more than that, she needed reassurance. Luckily, her sister would understand. Berries was a little older, but what was half a billion years between loved ones? Nothing. Especially so when you were both born from the same nursery cluster and still lived relatively close to each other. She quickly offered thanks, and opened a personal tangle line to her big sister.

'Carols baby, are you ok?' she heard Berries ask.

She nodded mutely, and distantly recognised that she was in shock.

'You know what you have to do, don't you?'

She nodded again. She knew. There was a way to protect herself, she just didn't like it. Even though she knew that she would grow in the process, she would have to be careful. Very,

very careful. Personally, she didn't think she was ready to be a mother just yet, let alone binate. She knew that the vast majority of stellars lived in binary systems, sharing everything. She rarely envied the companionship that those stellars enjoyed, it just wasn't her. Her solitary nature was part of who she was. And despite her relative fame, at only two billion years of age, she was still so very young.

She had complete faith in the conclusion her ghost and her sister had offered. They would have already double checked all the parameters and options. She could see that the necessary slingshot was already prepped, and the collision between her Brown Dwarf and her outermost moonlet was on course. She realised that actually, she didn't even have a choice. She was already pregnant.

CHAPTER 4

(The Happiness Virus)

Tommy had always loved his mother's stories, but the more he tried to make sense of her memories, the more Tommy began to question his own sanity. He knew his assumptions were based on the premise that his mother was not in fact insane, that her mental faculties hadn't begun to slide down the elderly decline. She was getting on, but he hadn't seen any sign of dementia. He had read up on the signs, as research for a character in one of his novels, but that research had killed two birds with one stone. With two of his three sisters now living interstate, he was the one left to care for their widowed elderly mother. She was fighting fit for a woman in her late eighties, and apart from these irreconcilable memories, there was nothing wrong with her health at all.

Well, apart from the fact that she was in the hospital at the moment. He would've laid good odds on her next visit to a hospital being due to a broken bone. She led a very active life: she much preferred bowling to bingo. He knew that she would never suffer the fragility of calcium-deficiency: he had inherited his love of cheeses from her. The overwhelming richness of the air that greeted him when he walked into a cheese shop immediately whisked him back to his childhood, to an imaginary space where his much younger mother would be tasting some new variety. She had introduced him to her world-away-from-home, the miniature adventures that the monthly shop entailed. Even now, fifty years later, his fridge always nestled a couple of nice cheeses inside it. He wondered if his daughter Claire ever took her kids to a cheese shop. Were his grandchildren developing an appreciation of epicurean delights the way he had, learning to revel in the textures of quality gorgonzola, or a crumbly Wensleydale?

As he left, tasked with retrieving his mother's journal, he looked around the hospital room and laughed at himself, thinking of cheese at a time like this. He looked at the flowers on the shelf, and the card that Claire's boys had made. None of them had expected her to still be here. Originally, they had expected her to be straight in, straight out. But unforeseen complications had set in. A post-surgery infection had laid her low, or at least kept her in bed – her spirits were never low. Nothing ever seemed to get her down. Tommy heartily admired his mum: she was an inspiration not only to him and his sisters, but to everyone she came in contact with. Even one of the nurses here had commented on her 'indomitable happiness'. It rubbed off, it was contagious. Like a virus.

He didn't remember the day he found out that Santa Claus wasn't real, or the day he learnt that the Easter Bunny and Tooth Fairy were also made up. But he did remember the day he discovered that his mother's imaginative explanation for her happiness wasn't 'the truth, the whole truth, and nothing but the truth.' As a young boy, he had innocently believed his mother when she had told him there were positive viruses like happiness, confidence and luck. He used to wish that he too had fallen into a vat of the happiness virus as a baby, like his mum must have done. Then the horrible things that happened in life wouldn't hurt so much, he'd imagined.

The day he had come home from school with those illusions shattered had been a painful one. He knew he'd been nine years old; he could still remember walking home with all of his sisters in tow, even little Cassie who had just started school. She had been so excited at joining her elder siblings at last, but even her extra happiness had not been infectious enough to counter the dark cloud that had hung over his head.

He had been mocked by his classmates for his heart-felt exposition on the reason why some kids scored exceptionally well on the maths test. Apparently, they found that idea that 'they fell in a swimming pool-size bath of the intelligence virus' inexplicably hilarious. The quick follow-up observation that laughter was an especially contagious version of a positive virus had left him confused and barely consolable for the rest of the day. His teacher had smiled patiently, and ignoring the giggles in the classroom had explained that there was no such thing as positive viruses. Tommy had been adamant, asking how else something like good luck could be explained. He couldn't see that Mr Broad's explanation that it was 'God's will' was any less an acceptable answer, but he kept his mouth shut. By the time the day was over, he knew the tale of his embarrassment would've spread throughout the school.

It was a much smaller world in those days. His sisters had heard about it, and he expected that they would gleefully repeat the story to their mother, affirming that they already knew the happiness virus wasn't real. He just prayed that his mother wouldn't see the need to get his father involved, which would have inevitably happened if he had argued with the teacher. Mr Broad went to the same church as his family, and now with all three younger sisters at the same school, he was quickly learning that what happened at school rarely remained at school.

His mother had known something was wrong before he finished walking down the path. His sisters were merrily chatting as they walked together, while young Cassie was already in his mother's arms, having run the last fifty metres to the porch. Chelsie and Marilyn had traipsed inside, the screen door slamming shut behind them, leaving him standing on the bottom step. He was trying to sulk, but remaining upset around his mother was like trying to remain mute on a roller-coaster. She had a way about her of simply absorbing and discarding the clouds of hurt that he sometimes imagined he could see other people walking around in.

On his first weekend camp with the boy scouts, he had erupted in chicken pox on the second day, along with nearly a dozen other boys. The ride home had left him in the deepest funk of sadness his young life had known. At the time, he had imagined the irresistibly itchy red spots were some kind of negative virus, one that his mother's happiness might be able to cure. Her administrations had eased the itching slightly, but her explanation that happiness fixed you on the inside not the outside, had only worked to reinforce his innocent assumptions about how viruses worked.

Instructing Cassie to take her lunch box to the kitchen with her sisters, his mother had squatted down on the edge of the porch, and tilted her head to the side in that funny way she had of getting other people to open up. He had no way of explaining how he felt; he didn't have the words or the self-awareness to explain that his faith in his mother had been shattered. Although he was the only boy in his family, his father was not one to molly-coddle his kids, or to suffer wallowing or self-pity in anyone. Tommy had always felt the burden of high expectations from his folks: being both the eldest and the only boy. So he knew that boys didn't cry, but that day on the porch, his eyes had filled as he collapsed into his mother's arms, ashamed, embarrassed, and confused.

'Shhh, shhh, it's all alright', his mother had whispered in his ear. 'Everything will be ok, just get it all out. I'm here, it's all alright.' He could still remember the feeling of her holding him, comforting the little boy that he once was. Holding him gently, through what were almost violent sobs, a gut-wrenching release of pent up frustration and humiliation.

She had always been there, for him and his sisters. He didn't see the responsibility of caring for her as a burden; rather, it was an honour. Helping in the garden or visiting her in the hospital, these were simple things he could do that would never repay the countless hours and sacrifices he knew now as a parent himself, that she and his father would definitely have made.

It had been partially because of the closeness he and his mother shared that she was confiding in him, he supposed. He knew the house she had described, where the crash had happened. He had played in that yard as a child himself many a time, back before his grandparents passed on and the farm had been sold. The house had a big porch now, but he'd seen pictures of it from when his ma was young, and there had obviously been lots of renovations over the years. Many of those dated back to this increasingly suspicious-sounding 'accident'.

Closing his eyes, he could imagine his mother as a young girl. The front lounge no longer had the French window, but it wasn't hard to see her snuggled up with a book, surrounded by cushions while her brothers played or did their chores outside. With a family funeral she was probably all dolled up in her Sunday best, keeping out of the way of the womenfolk in the kitchen.

As he strolled through the familiar corridors back to the car park, he pictured the farmhouse all decked out for an old-fashioned funeral. The chairs all arranged, the flowers picked and displayed, the candles burning. Tommy remembered his mother once telling his sister Cassie about the significance of lighting a candle. Apparently, his grandmother believed that candles shone a light that the dead could see, but she would never say that in public out of respect for her husband or her father, both strict fundamentalists. His strict beliefs were apparently offended by the pagan candle burning, but wives have ways of mollifying husbands, of placating their traditional and sometimes overly-conservative protestant sensibilities. So the candle burning had been allowed. His mother, as the eldest girl, would have logically been tasked with ensuring they were safe. After the infamous accident though, no candle had ever been lit in his grandparents' house again. He had heard the car crash story many times, but never this version of it. If his mother was actually making up one last story out of her imagination, she was certainly pulling a doozy out of her proverbial hat for a curtain-closer.

CHAPTER 5

{Katie's Shared Dream}

When Katherine woke, she lay with her eyes closed for a while, going over the strange dream she'd just had. She liked to try to catch bits and pieces of her dreams before they slipped away. This time, she was more than a little surprised at how much detail she could remember. Usually reassembling her dreams was difficult, but not today. She lay there, laughing at her own vivid imagination.

Fancy thinking I saw Uncle Justin climb out of his own coffin, looking younger than Pa, she scolded herself. *I must have fallen asleep in my nook. That had to be the most fantastical dream ever! I gotta tell Grandpa, I bet he'd get a kick out of it*, she thought.

Then she opened her eyes, sat up and looked around to find herself in a completely unknown room, and as her heartbeat quickened her memories all came back. It hadn't been a dream. She really had seen Uncle Justin climb out of his coffin, and they'd abruptly run from the living room. There'd been an automobile out of control, and as he had stared right into her soul he'd said something about needing to wake up. As she got up and looked around, it was hard to convince herself it wasn't all a dream.

By the looks of things, she was all alone in a strange house. She was definitely not in her window nook. Nor was she in her bed, or on their porch. *Why would I expect to find myself on the porch?* she asked herself, but there were too many other questions to allow that puzzle to be processed. She looked down and found that she was wearing the same clothes she had on earlier: a new black dress that Ma had made for her, something special to wear to the funeral. As she fingered the edges of the long cotton sleeves, she felt wrong. She was wearing a dress that she'd received specifically to wear for a funeral...for someone that wasn't dead.

He's not here though either, she realised, and then quickly wondered, *Ahhh, where is here, exactly?* On the far side of the room was a fireplace, the mantle covered in dust. There were logs in a box nearby, but freshly added, she concluded, considering the general array of disuse. Facing it were two easy chairs covered in sheets, standing guard around a rug on the floor with an off-putting pattern. Apart from the dilapidated three-seat sofa she had been lying on, there were no personal items, no photos or knick-knacks. She could see car keys on the side table near the front door, so she assumed that Uncle Justin (or whoever he was) hadn't stranded her there. She wasn't legally old enough to drive, but she'd grown up on a farm, where different rules exist.

She wandered through the saloon door and found herself in a long and dusty kitchen. The window over the sink looked out onto a backyard that appeared to be surrounded by a forest. To the horizon in both directions all she could see were dense clusters of gum trees, and she tried to place which part of the river she was looking at. The darker leaves of the less numerous elm trees stood out as they absorbed the sun, but the general scrub held no distinguishing marks. She had no idea where she was.

She could tell from the shadows that it was mid-afternoon, and she immediately started to worry. Grandpa would definitely be home by now, and her Ma would have noticed she was missing. She had duties, tasks that needed doing, especially with so many people coming today. But there was a bigger mystery going on, so she deliberately put those worries aside. Part of her still wanted to believe this was still a dream. She swept her hand along the empty bench-top as she walked towards the back door, and a layer of dust rose to dance in the rays of light that seeped into the room through the windows. *Pretty gosh-darn real dream*, she giggled to herself.

As she passed the long wooden dining table that dominated the kitchen, the back door opened and her Uncle Justin strolled in. He carried a rag nestling nearly a dozen eggs and another filled with freshly picked boysenberries. She could see the purple stains on his fingers, and on his mouth. He smiled when he saw her, and put the foodstuffs gently on the bench.

'How are you little Katie?' he asked, and it immediately struck her as outrageously strange to hear such a normal question. As if everything was *de rigueur*, just run of the mill.

Nothing unusual about waking up twice in an afternoon to find your world turned upside down, or that you are in an unknown place. She suppressed a giggle, but found that her sense of amusement at the whole scenario was stronger than she thought. She snickered, and then laughed out loud.

'Oh why not?' she laughed. 'Sure, I'm great. I half think I'm still dreaming, but the other half of me sees all this...' and she gestured around at the house, and then towards his face. 'This is way stranger than any dream. But I'm alive, right?' He nodded, smiling in encouragement at her pragmatic assessment.

'You sure are, and I want to keep you that way.' At her look of confusion, he raised his hands, palm-forward in surrender and reassurance. 'We have a lot to talk about, an awful lot. You have probably wondered where my wrinkles have gone, and where we are. We'll cover all that, but there's no need to rush. No-one knows you're missing, because none of that has happened yet.' He paused, trying to assess how well she was taking it. 'You're going to have to trust me. Do you, Katie? Do you trust me?'

She had always trusted Uncle Justin, as implicitly as any family member. She knew he wasn't a blood relative, but as he'd always been around as she was growing up, she'd always thought of him as a real Uncle. Technically, he was her Grandpa's best friend, but he'd always been counted as part of the family. He may look younger, and be saying strange things, but he was still a trusted relative. He was still her beloved Uncle. She nodded.

He pulled out a chair for her at the wooden table, and she half-sat, half-collapsed into it. He sat down next to her and rested his head on his right hand. She could see that not only were the wrinkles and grey hair gone, but that the blisters and calluses that bore witness to his years of farm work were all gone too. He had changed his clothes; now he was in a red flannelette shirt with khaki work pants. His skin looked smooth, young and fresh; even his hair seemed to have a vibrancy about it. Then there were those eyes, his strange twinkling eyes. She was about to look to them again, but she stopped herself and looked down.

'It's ok little Katie, you can look at me. I promise I won't hurt you.'

She looked up again, and saw those familiar orbs glistening back at her. She had never looked into anyone's eye as deeply as how she did now. She found herself swimming, floating, dissociated from her body, lost in his eyes. They were blue, while hers were brown. But he had the same specks of gold that she saw in her own eyes when she looked in the mirror.

'This will seem very real to you,' he said. 'And in a way it is real. But, I think it will be easier for you, if you think of this all as being a dream. A very special kind of a dream, one that's going to last for four whole weeks. In fact, as you'll still have to sleep, you'll even be able to dream within this dream. What's most important is that you realise you're in no danger, and that I will do my best to explain everything.'

She nodded, mutely, and he laughed and tussled her hair a little. 'Oh Katie. We have a whole lunar month ahead, and you are going to have to relax. You are not a prisoner, but it will take me some time to explain what is happening. If you're patient with me, and trust me, then I will answer your questions.

But first, how about we tidy this place up? I'll bring in some more firewood if you clean the kitchen and see what you can make us to eat. I don't know about you, but I'm famished.' And with that, he popped another boysenberry into his mouth, smiling cheekily.

There were strange things happening, but she knew that there was no need to worry. There was never a need for that: she'd been raised practically, knowing that the secret to health and happiness was in simply keeping busy. Katherine looked about at her surroundings, and was a little surprised to realise that she was hungry too; so she expertly set about exploring the contents of the cupboards and the pantry of this unfamiliar house.

CHAPTER 6
[Procrastinating Mortality]

Carols in Sequins saw herself as a biologist, or perhaps a zoologist. She'd explored her local area and numerous immersive communities when she'd been young, but now she really just did the same thing all the time: simply observing, measuring, nursing and cultivating all the creatures in her garden. She had placed a quite clear 'Do Not Disturb' filter on incoming calls. Most of those calls could be responded to using automated responses anyway. They were nearly always questions about her lifeforms that could be dealt with using a tertiary routine, no need even for an exo-ghost.

She had family and good friends, but they respected her desire for privacy. *They could even be a little jealous and not want to show it*, she had thought to herself more than once. It didn't matter. Her garden moons, her little menagerie as she thought of them, they made her feel special. They made her solar system unique, at least for this arm of the family. She felt inordinate pride at being host to more than one species, but she always politely downplayed it. Not everyone was lucky enough to host any form of life. She knew, but could never understand, that some were positively against the idea. Regardless of how you felt about being 'infested', the fact remained that very few stellars could boast the variety of which she was the caretaker.

When her comet wasn't singing, her next personal favourites were her iron amoebas. They were nestled deep in her innermost orbital: a small terrestrial planetoid shrouded in rust-coloured clouds. In its dark shadows, deep in searing oceans of liquid hydrogen, the colonies floated. Billions of years away, if they were still around when it was time for her to undergo the change, they would be absorbed as she engendered. The rusty ball was far too close to the energies of her mind for it to escape being gobbled up instantly when she began her expansion phase. But that was a long way off. For now, it was safe.

Far below the surface, volcanic sulphur outlets reluctantly relieved a little of the internal pressures generated by the planetoid's molten iron core. Around those outlets floated swarms of amoebae, dancing in the waves of heat. They flourished during the irregular cycle of ejecta: spurts that added precious heavy metals to the oceanic currents. Each deep sea outlet was separated from the next by hundreds of kilometres, so it was rare that the currents would bring members of one colony in contact with another. It did happen though, slowly but surely. When it did, the colonies sprang into action, surprisingly co-ordinated. Swarms of exophilic amoebas would then converge on any seemingly alien yet obviously related body, cannibalising it for nutrients, ingesting the experiences, knowledge and for the precious epigenetic memories of their distant relatives. The largest of these colonies had compiled a theoretical knowledge of the geography of the planet, and were developing the ability to predict when a neighbouring vent plumage would be wafting survivors in their direction. *They were almost conscious*, she'd wryly observed. Of course they weren't, genuine consciousness could never arise in something so short-lived. Everyone knew the limited minds of the so called 'lower' life forms simply weren't built to cope with infinity.

A couple of orbits further out was her primary gas giant, around which orbited the satellites she thought of as her menagerie. Not merely flourishing ecosystems, but an astonishing variety of creatures thrived there. A total of five of its eleven moons were inhabited in some form or another, which was an unheard of density in itself. The two largest satellites were positively booming with life, fecund worldlets with their precious nitrogen-oxygen atmospheres. Wherever plant life bloomed, there'd also be animal life too. A flying insect, a bird or animal often played a part in the plant's reproductive cycle, transferring pollen and transporting seeds far and wide, enlarging the habitable area. The largest satellite was almost completely covered in a thick bushy growth that would manifest flowers in the most translucent colours and hues. She enjoyed directing an occasional energy flare in its direction, knowing her action would generate another prolific burst of growth.

She knew that others watched the dance of life in her, envious perhaps, but definitely intrigued one and all. Very few stellars could boast such a variety of botanic and biological carnates. The majority only had one or two mobiles and perhaps a half dozen species of plant life. Unless they lived close to a stellar nursery or a particle jet, space was generally infertile. Those areas rich in resources also swam in radiation: which wasn't conducive to carbon lifeforms.

Away from heavily populated regions, the background radiation levels dropped, but so did resources. She considered herself one of the lucky ones. There were other solitary stellars who spun far from their families, but those on an excursion into the intra- or inter-galactic voids were, as a general rule, entirely bereft of life. The longer they were out there, the more likely it was that they were well and truly alone. Carols imagined it would be hard enough to hold yourself together out there all alone without having to worry about pets – although, on the other hand, the company might prove to be a sanity safety net. The only opportunity for those remote stellars to observe life was at a distance, through whatever entangled connections they maintained. The idea was alien for Carols, she couldn't imagine how utterly boring that would be. She loved the dance and the cycles of interaction, not only for education and philosophy, but for simple pleasure and entertainment available to her.

Her nursery sister *Berries in Cerise* was the local tangle Hub for their arm of the family, and would sometimes gently prod her to be less shallow. She had tried encouraging Carols to take more of an interest in stellar mathematics, or eschatology, or even intergalactic communications. But she really had no interest in those fields. As a very young girl, she had reluctantly gone to the Concourse to undertake Orientation more so to put an end to *Berries'* cadging than for her own education.

In retrospect, she was glad she'd gone. She'd learnt a lot. Carols knew that as their local family communications hub, *Berries in Cerise* held the largest neighbourhood repository of quantum-entangled links; it had been Berries that acted as the conduit for the three separate observations that had been carried out on her menagerie by far-distant families. *'Other galaxies envy me. Me!'*, she had thought with a warm, slightly self-indulgent glow.

Thinking back over the last message *Berries* had sent her; it was still difficult to believe that her gardens were endangered. She had always thought that by default of her position - being surrounded and padded far from the galactic edge - that nothing dangerous would ever happen to her. Lives that flourished near the edge of the family were tougher, without doubt. Any unlucky girl caught out in that region might never get to engender. The boys of Silver constantly reinforced the boundary against the void between families, protecting their brothers and sisters closer to the centre. Not that the centre was any less dangerous, but the various threats posed by the energies of the boys of Black in the core that powered their family were better understood – and far more predictable - than the vagaries of the void out there.

Her family was separated from its closest neighbouring family by seventy light years. It was by no means the smallest or the largest of galactic families: according to the Galactic Omni Directorate, the Milky Clan currently consisted of 314,174,598,124 stellars, with her new-born upping the total to 125. Far too many to trace familial connections without referencing the data store she kept embedded in the strata of her second iron core repository. Her need to understand galactic movements or population issues had never really been a pressing concern. *Perhaps, just perhaps*, she sometimes admitted to herself, *I might have let my education slip in favour of my garden. But that still doesn't make me shallow!*

She felt sickened by the potential waste, the futures that held such untenable loss. She knew in theory that everything was simply transformed. That the lifeforms of her little garden would be re-distributed; that those atoms and memories would reconstitute in a new life. That is, if she lost them. Even when she engendered into adulthood and discarded parts of herself, those scattered elements would carry parts of her, seeds on an interstellar breeze.

Carols thought of the shockwave ahead of her, its interception unavoidable. It too carried splashes of memories, bubbles of gases and nutrients that churned in the wave front. Miniscule atoms, ones that would bring catastrophe if she did nothing. If she could just turn her Brown Dwarf into a companion Red, she'd be ok. They'd be ok. As a binary, they could withstand and filter the helium isotopes and heavier elements, and her menagerie wouldn't be washed away. Their menagerie. As a couple, hopefully together they'd even be able to rescue the icepede comet.

Berries had attached an application package. For a moment this annoyed Carols, for the presumption that she would do exactly what her older sister dictated. But after having looked at the physics data – most of which was beyond her even though it had been presented in simple enough fashion – she acknowledged she really didn't have a choice. If she didn't give birth, the domino effects of the approaching wave – still many light years away but already set in motion and unstoppable - would annihilate large parts of her body. The sulphuric amoeba would probably survive, living so close to her heart and being protected by kilometres of heavy dense liquid. But the icepedes had no hope. Their glaciers were sure to melt, and the comet itself stood a good chance of caroming off to find a new home.

Naturally, the package included detailed instructions. She had entangled before, of course, she had connections to all of her stored memories. She had imprinted and spread them throughout her entire system in the standard manner, the bulk of which were embedded in the highly conducive metal ores of her terrestrials. Anything she needed to relive or recollect, she could instantly access via an open tangle she kept with each of her body parts. Except for those memories of her birth, stored as they were in a fractal compression, waiting for her to engender till they released their secrets.

She was young, blessed and envied: she'd never needed to expend any more energy than the minimal required. And yet now she was faced with the potential loss of everything. It was the end of her youth in a way. Playtime was nearly over. She had always expected that one day she would bring herself into a binary, but she had expected it to be at a time of her own choosing. With it being forced on her, she was still hesitant, almost resistant. She realised self-reflectively that her attitude was probably not going to help, so she shunted it to the side as she shifted her attention.

She put the attached package into stasis and decided to say a final goodbye to the icepedes, the thermavians, the ancient trees and all the species she treasured. She did not want to forget them. This might possibly be her last opportunity to embed their existence in her mind before she transited. She looked again at the application form, her appointment was drawing near. She double checked her calendar: yes, she could do it. She could easily make it and still squeeze in a little garden time. She could have one more quick play in her garden before going to immerse herself in the mysterious workings of The Academy of Death ©.

CHAPTER 7
(The Starnic Tradition)

Each family has their own traditions, their own habits. There were things that Tommy's parent's had done, that he and Gloria had done for their kids, and that Claire and Jackson were doing with their own kids now. Not just expressions or phrases, but quirks or rituals. Like the phone buzz. Letting the phone ring once as a pre-arranged signal. Irrelevant now with texting and mobiles, but it was still something they did on occasion.

Tommy had always thought that the family starnics were something that had started with his own parents when they were courting. Possibly they had learnt it from their parents, but somehow the image of his wizened and hard-working grandparents taking time to sit and stare at the stars was incongruous with his memories of them. He knew that his father had romantically proposed to his mother at a starnic; he'd stolen the idea, and Gloria's heart, when he had re-enacted the scenario. Whenever they were all together, weather permitting, the evening meal was always held outside. It was a family tradition.

It had been months since they'd had a family starnic. The last one had been at his place for the twins' seventh birthday. His mother's garden had been all lit up with animal-shaped solar lights, and he remembered listening to her talking to Alex and Kyle. It had been a clear night sky, and she was pointing out constellations and asking them if they could name them. She'd done the same thing when he and his sisters were young. They all knew the names for the patterns of glistening lights far above. He'd been heart-warmed by the sight of the boys lying down trying to count how many stars they could see; he'd set the same task for Claire and Jackson when they had been that age. The twins seemed to stick at it even less than his kids had, he thought, not wanting to admit that his own memory of lying there for hours might be a slight exaggeration. Nevertheless, that evening the whole family had listened to his mother as she talked about the stars to her great-grandchildren on the back lawn.

'Well it looks like you gave up the count pretty quickly,' she said, echoing Tommy's own thoughts. 'How many do you think you could count if you stuck at it?'

'Five hundred?' Kyle guessed.

'More like five hundred thousand!' Alex added.

'Actually, my boys, the answer is much closer to the first number. Especially here in the city. Remember when you went camping, it seemed like there were more stars up there? That's because there is less human-made light getting in the way. It's called 'light pollution'. If we turned off all our lights, and got all our neighbours to turn off all their lights, then we would be able to see even *more* stars!' The whole family paused to stare upwards along with the kids.

'So how many are there then Mama?' Alex asked.

'Well if we turned off all the lights everywhere, or went right out into the desert, we would still only be able to see about fifteen hundred stars. That's the same from any one spot on Earth. Which means that the total number of stars we could count from both sides of the planet would be...?'

After a brief muttering as the boys calculated, they answered together. 'Three thousand!'

'Very good, that's right. But we know that there are lots, lots more than that. We've got satellites in space with super-duper cameras that show us pictures of all the stars we can see, and how many do you think those cameras can see?

'Three million million?' Kyle ventured, to which his brother outbid with Three billion gazillion?'

'Those are both pretty good guesses. The stars we can see from Earth are all part of a big family called the Milky Way, and in our family, we have about three hundred billion. When numbers get that big though, they're pretty hard to picture. But I once heard it told like this. Let's say there are three hundred kids at your school, and they are all at a concert together, or at assembly let's say. You're all squeezed into a big room somewhere; or in a tent, like at the circus. In the centre, the rock star or ring master can see everyone that is in the tent, but what if there is a television crew as well? Then the whole country could be watching, so instead of three hundred sets of eyes and ears in his audience, there are three thousand. Or three million. But he can't see them; he has to imagine them in his mind. Just because you can't see them, doesn't mean they're not there. And you know what? Somewhere out there someone might even be listening to us now, on a receiver we don't know even exists!

'Aliens?' asked Kyle.

'What kind of aliens?' questioned Alex, more cautiously.

'Now remember, just because something is alien doesn't mean it's scary. 'Alien' just means 'different' and we're all a little bit different from each other, right?' The boys were temporarily mollified with that, so Katherine continued. 'Now if you can imagine that invisible radio broadcasts might be going out, you can probably imagine that there might be invisible alien messages coming in. We can't hear them on our radios; they aren't the right kind of receiver. The most amazing transceiver we have on the planet is actually...can you guess?' The boys shook their heads.

'It's the human brain. It can do things that no computer can do, or will ever be able to do. Right between your ears, you have magic bubbling away!' The use of the word 'magic' was a trigger for the twins, who started tickling each other there on the blanket until their father Aaron told them to calm down.

'I want you to think of an example,' Katherine continued, 'of something magical the human mind can do.' Although she had been talking to the boys, she knew that everyone was listening.

Pauline had just sat back down next to Jackson after checking on their sleeping toddler, rugged up in a mobile bassinet on the back porch, and she answered. 'I can tell when it's my little Tammy that's crying, even when there are other babies in the crèche crying too.' She added, squeezing Jackson's hand, 'I don't know how that happens, but it's pretty amazing when you think about it.' Everyone nodded, and the boys were quiet.

Kyle looked around until he caught his father's eye, and Aaron nodded encouragingly. 'When Alex and I, when we are in a crowded room, like even at assembly where everyone is talking, we can still talk to each other through all the noise.'

Emboldened by his brother's confession, Alex chimed in too. 'It's true, I can hear his voice. It's not like it's in my head, we can just hear each other really easy.'

The boys looked around apprehensively, and Tommy relished being able to come to the rescue from the safety of his role as 'grandpa'. He cleared his throat and looked at the boys first before bouncing the conversation back to his mother with his eyes. 'That's another really good example, boys, probably similar to what Mama is talking about.'

'That's right,' she said. 'The human brain can do lots of amazing things, things that we don't understand. By the time you grow up and become as old as I am, maybe by then we will understand more about how the magic works. If you want to grow up to be a master magician, study hard and use your imaginations, see if you can explain how the trick works, how the brain does things we don't understand yet.' Peace descended again briefly, as the boys were off in an all-too-brief yet joyous bout of silent thought.

'Grand-Mama?' Alex broke the stillness with a timid voice. 'Do you think there are aliens?'

'Oh, Alex. My sweet little angel. Of course! We are all aliens.'

'No, I mean on another planet.'

'Well I don't think we can hear them. But just because you can't see them...'she prompted...

'Doesn't mean they aren't there' the boys replied in unison.

'Good, just checking that you were listening. Your brain is always listening, always recording. Everything you see and do, everything you hear and think. Your brain keeps all that somewhere, but it's hidden so deep it's almost lost. Imagine if you could listen to all the recordings of everything you've ever done. Now imagine that you are old, older than I am, with zillions more memories that your brain has recorded that maybe you didn't even realise. Can you imagine how long it would take to go over all those memories?'

The boys mumbled, and Tommy looked around to see that everyone was smiling and listening. His daughter Claire and her husband Aaron were on the old blanket; while his son Jackson and wife Pauline were sitting in the fold-out chairs. His mother always seemed to become even more happy – if that were possible – when she was out under the stars.

'Let's exercise your imaginations again. This time pretend you're a transmitter,' she continued. 'Even better than a walking television station. Everything you see and do is being recorded by your amazing brain, but it is also being bounced outwards in all directions.'

'That's probably how Santa knows if you've been naughty or nice,' Claire suggested, eliciting groans from the boys.

'I was going to suggest 'God' then,' Tommy said.

'So does God see and hear everything we do the same way that Santa Claus does?' Kyle asked, confused by the laughter his question triggered.

Tommy had been raised Baptist, while Gloria had come from a lapsed Catholic family. Although they had taken their kids to church, they had never forced theology or fundamentalist beliefs onto their kids. He wasn't sure exactly what Claire and Aaron had taught the boys about God. He knew that Aaron was a dedicated Buddhist, so he surrendered the question to them with his eyebrows raised. 'Oh no,' Claire said, 'I think we'll pass this one on too. Grandma?'

Bemused, his mother looked around at the gathering and then addressed the boys. 'Around the world there are lots of different kinds of beliefs about God. 'God' is a tricky word, because it has so many different meanings. I do think however that each and every one of us has a guardian angel who watches over us. And that guardian angel sees and hears everything you do. That angel looks after you, encourages you, helps you to feel better when you're sick and gives you extra strength sometimes when you need it. She is always there, just like the stars. You can't see the stars during the day, and maybe there's some reason you can't see your guardian angel while you're a human. But they're always there; she's always there, always ready to remind you that you are not alone, and that you are loved. I think if it was possible, your guardian angel might even love you as much as your Grand-Mama does!'

As the boys groaned in mock agony, Tom looked around at his children and their partners. Claire was sharing a knowing smile with Aaron, while Jackson and Pauline were doing the same. He could feel the moment being etched into multiple memories: his mother had a way of bringing people together, of rephrasing the important things in life through her stories. He looked over, and saw her staring at him. The moment of pride and joy he'd just felt at his grown children, he saw bouncing back at him. It threatened to become a Hallmark moment, and emotional expression was something he always felt the characters in his books did better than he ever managed. Luckily, the twins chose that moment to restart their eternal game of push and poke, defining the invisible border between one another with fingers impelled to antagonise.

'Ah the joys of children at a starnic', he observed in jest. He could hear the young adults all murmur agreement, but it was his mother's ironic giggle that had really stood out for him. Not for the first time that night, he wished Gloria was still with them, and he wondered what she would say. Listening to his mother's laugh, it was easy to hear Gloria's voice. He smiled, remembering how when she'd first met his mother, she'd said, 'Her words don't just come out with a smile. Everything she says comes out *as* a smile'.

It rained overnight, and the next day clouds still hung low in the sky. They lolled about, not sure if they were quite ready to move on from the part of the globe they had so recently marked as their territory. There were patches of blue sky too, showing its face almost timidly, wondering if it had the strength to pierce through such an overcast morning. The clouds weren't dark; they were grey, washed out in places, textured, mottled and fluffy. *More shades of grey than laws protecting copyright,* Tommy thought bemusedly as he drove home.

Wondering what to expect in his mother's granny flat, he was relieved there was no-one to accompany him. He hadn't woken up knowing it, but now today had a mission: one he had mixed feelings about. He had been teased with parts of a story, then despatched to collect the journal. While he couldn't wait to see it, and thereby assess his mother's senility, he was nevertheless concerned about the way she was talking about 'going away gifts' and the like. While sometimes he felt the weight of responsibility lying heavily on his shoulders, today it was one that he gratefully bore alone. He needed time to think, to process and come to terms with the almost disorienting concept that his mother's perpetual happiness had an 'off switch'; that there were depths to her he had never dreamed.

He drove slowly, taking his time on the roads home. He breathed, focusing on not thinking, just keeping his mind clear. He breathed carefully, regularly, the way his mother had always taught. A long slow inhalation through the nose, holding the air and gurgling it deep inside wherever the pain was most intense; exhaling quickly out his mouth, releasing on his breath all the shades of the tension held inside him. He knew that meditative breathing classes taught this method for gaining focus and clarity, but his mother had long ago taught it to him and his sisters, decades before yoga became fashionable in the West. He wondered if it was another little thing that her Uncle Justin had taught her. *Another of her little mysteries unravelled,* he thought. *Or was it ravelled?*

He wondered if she would tell his sisters. He expected that the eldest, Chelsie, would be dismissive, attributing the story to undiagnosed dementia, or their mother's overactive imagination. Their mother had always encouraged their imaginations, creating stories and asking them to make up fanciful explanations – 'just for practice', she would say. He knew Chelsie lived a very busy life over East. She had only visited twice: eight years ago for his wife's funeral, and then six months later, after he'd convinced his mum to move over here. Claire's twins had just been starting to crawl.

As hard as it was on him to hear about Gloria's death, he would forever live with one image. Etched deeply onto his memory was an irremovable snapshot: that of his mother-in-law's face, when he had broken the news to her. Gloria's death had taken them all by surprise, but the tragic accident impacted more on Muriel than it had on him or his two teenage kids. Hers had been a look of devastation he could never erase. The cries of sorrow that erupt from a heart - one not simply broken, but shattered – those were sounds he would never forget. Muriel's world had shattered into more pieces than the car windscreen that killed her only daughter. Muriel had cried on his shoulders. While they weren't exactly friends, he had a good relationship with his mother-in-law, and knew that she would feel utterly alone in the world without Gloria.

As it turned out, the loss was too much for Muriel's heart to bear, and he had discovered her body less than a week after Gloria's funeral. Sitting in her recliner with a photo album in her lap, the open page showing photos of his wedding day. All his pain had erupted afresh; a wave of sorrow had overwhelmed him. The grief for his wife was too fresh, the wounds still open. Finding Muriel like that had broken him. He couldn't cope with more death.

Afterwards, when he'd had time to think, he made a resolution. He promised himself that he would actively take more interest in his own mother's life. Gloria and her mum had enjoyed a close relationship. It was one that he wouldn't admit to envying, but on occasion it did remind him of the lack of communication he'd felt with his own father. He wished things had been different, that he knew more about the man. Now his father was long gone, all the memories and experiences he had accumulated, the heartache and joys he had experienced: all gone. It was a strange void, a gap that defied definition or description. He felt as if part of himself had been excised, but he wasn't aware of what it used to be. He had access to his family's history restricted, a censorship imposed by his father's absence. He felt the loss heavily, and psychologically reached out for his mother.

Tommy had not been raised to fear death. On the farm as a child, he was exposed to the raw realities of life and death in ways his own city-born kids never were. Nor did he fear his own death. Life was a stepping stone, an opportunity to learn and grow. He believed it was totally illogical to assume that nothing existed before or after. That was how he and his sisters were raised. None of them became regular church-goers, but he felt confident that his sisters had similarly gone on to instil a healthy respect for spirituality in their children.

As he drove into his yard, his eyes took in the verdant gardens. The arches and balustrades lent the house a coastal, sun-drenched appearance. The steps and fence were frames around which the living garden had painted itself. Ivy grew up and covered the entire eastern wall of his neighbour's two-storey house. Pot plants had spread their leaves and almost taken flight, reaching out from the walls and edges of the garden beds in their eternal quest to capture the sun. They were sturdy, determined plants, lush and fecund, politely sharing the sunlit spaces with towers of bamboo. His country upbringing and his mother's green thumb once inspired him to study a little horticulture. He could name many of the plants that he saw. It may be his property, but they were his mother's plants.

He thought back over a hint she had given, an answer to his questions about her Internet usage that he had missed. She explained how she'd created a word – *'pre-memories'* - to describe the succession of dreams which over the years had followed her vision.

'Since I found no records of people with memories of being something other than human,' Katie said, 'I took a little creative licence. Words like *dream*, or *reincarnation*, they have so many connotations. So I decided to call these particular memories, my pre-memories. Memories I have, of things I did, from before I was me. Fair enough?' He'd nodded, mutely. 'I've written stuff down about that, too. It's all in my journal. I've kept a record of those dreams alongside what happened in that vision. Actually it includes all the dreams, then and since.'

'Since, Ma?' Tommy had enquired, eyebrow raised.

'Every now and then, I have another. A new one, or a retelling. Sometimes, it differs. So I've called them my pre-memory dips. Sometimes I remember something new, and I like to jot it down. Sometimes it's simply an update, noting where scientists or astronomers have found answers, or more likely, more questions. And then, there are the other ones. The impossible ones. And I had another, last night, one that I need to add to my notes. Don't worry, you'll see, and you'll understand. I want you to be the one to take care of it. You know, after I leave this old dreaming body behind.' She smiled, and he leaned forward to give her a hug. It wasn't easy with the bed-table still affixed, but she sat up as well as she could.

Tommy could see a change in his mother. It looked like she just now felt the cumulative weight of her eighty-six years bearing down all at once. She'd told him that she ached, *in her bones*. She explained that sometimes she felt as though she had gone for a tumble, but on the inside, where no-one could see the bruises. She'd been adamant she wouldn't tell her doctor. She'd explained that simply putting those thoughts into words gave the thought itself strength, reinforcing the likelihood that she would decline.

Although she bemoaned being bed-ridden whilst recovering from surgery, he was pleased to see her at rest. She was such a force of nature, so to admit to any weakness would be, in her mind at least, a betrayal of her true self. He'd read once of a ship's captain, who said it was more important for a leader to appear competent, than to be competent. That captain had reminded him of his mother, who seemed to agree with the philosophy of being 'occasionally wrong, but never unsure'.

'Tommy, my boy?' She said, setting up her request. 'Since they won't let me drive home just yet...' she hinted, knowing he was connecting the dots.

Tommy smiled, guessing he was about to be sent on an errand, and grinning at the image of his mother, who would readily be driving around even with both her legs in plaster, given half the chance. 'I need you to go home. I want you to get my journal for me. It's under the sewing bag in the second drawer of The Desk.'

Tommy heard the capitalisation in her voice, and knew why his father's old desk was treated so reverently. It surprised him that his mother kept a dream journal, but not to find out where she kept it. He didn't know whether it was conscious on her part, but by placing her secrets in the middle of The Desk, he saw part of her rebelling against the mores of the religion his father had believed in so fervently. The usage of candles in the house was paganism in his father's opinion; and his father had many opinions, all of which seemed to be strongly held. It was at that desk that many of his sermons had been written, and it was one of only two pieces of furniture Katherine had kept. She had been adamant: The Desk was to come with her if she moved out West. Everything else she had packed into boxes and suitcases.

Tommy had flown East to help her, but the job was almost all done by the time he arrived. Once she made up her mind, she was as determined as his father was stubborn. She refused to acknowledge 'dark clouds', insisting there were only silver linings. He wondered again about the influence of her dream life - both on her, and also on him and his sisters.

His daydreaming was cut short when his mother lightly whacked him on the shoulder. He realised he hadn't answered his mother's request, distracted as he was by the possible implications.

'Sorry, yeah, sure Mum, no worries,' he assured her. At first, he toyed with the idea that he could help, perhaps use the research skills he had developed as a writer. The idea hadn't crossed his mind that there might be a novel in it for him. Back in the hospital, he'd simply agreed to run an errand, and Thomas Harold Robertson was a man who kept his word.

At the gate, he stood still for a moment and simply looked at his empty home, packed to the hilt with memories. To the granny flat at the back was a meandering path that stretched from the carpark in wide curves, edged by flower beds. He had walked these stone steps many times before, but he felt the crunch of them under his feet more intensely today. The mottled sky above and the speckled pebbles below seemed to reflect a confusion he felt on the inside, an ambiguous clash of emotions, that both intrigued him and sat uneasily; his natural curiosity balanced by the discomfort of dealing with other people's secrets. The biggest secret of his mother's that he'd previously known about was that she'd once had a miscarriage.

Tommy had heard there was nothing more painful than losing a child. As a parent himself, he could understand, theoretically, how awful and life-destroying that might be. His two kids, Jackson and Claire, were both fully grown and parents themselves now, embarking on their own adventures. They had their lives ahead of them, ones that were possibly beyond his imagining, the way the world was changing so quickly. Things they took for granted he still struggled with. To a degree, he had long ago given up trying to learn 'the new stuff', as he thought of it. Defeat had won when he'd just learnt how to program the VCR, and DVDs made that skill obsolete. He gave up, to the bemusement of his wife, who had long ago yielded her technological authority over to the kids.

The kids were gone now, leaving an empty nest; especially empty with his wife gone. Bless her soul. Hit by a drunk driver, at least she had gone instantly. Then with her mother passing so soon afterwards, he found himself with a gap far larger than an empty granny flat. He filled that gap with caring for *his* mother, as if the universe were balancing his social calendar. 'Swings and roundabouts: close one door and a window opens', was an adage he often impressed on his kids. He had been raised to have faith that things would work out: something he appreciated more now that he was older.

He knew his mother depended on him. The nursing staff were fantastic. At first, he hadn't understood why they were so friendly. Later, he realised most of their patients didn't get visitors. They treated him as a volunteer, or a staff member; often invited to share cake or coffee with them in the tea room. He knew many of the staff and patients by name. As he unlocked the door to his mother's granny flat, he wondered at how life had changed, speeding up around him. On the inside, he still thought of himself as a young man.

Putting his thoughts aside, he took a deep breath to steel himself, and opened the door. Inside – in The Desk – his mother's journal waited: a handwritten account of her vision. In it, he hoped to find the answers to his questions, or some sort of proof that what she believed she had experienced had actually occurred. She had told him that it held proof – or 'proofs', she had said, to be precise. What he'd already heard of the tale was astonishing. He had studied dream-trances; he had read of visions far more fantastical, so he wasn't willing to dismiss it. He simply couldn't discard her emphatic assertion that it really happened. Part of him wanted to be part of the story too, even if to simply find the journal and deliver it. He was curious to see how it would illuminate or compound the mystery his mother had created.

He stepped into the dark flat, keeping the lights off to save power, and stopped to open the heavy drapes. Bright sunshine swam through from the verdant jungle outside, streaming inside and infusing light into living areas weighed down with echoes of his mother's presence. As a teenage boy, Katie had once asked him if he knew how someone had achieved their purpose in life. Naturally, he'd replied that he didn't. Her response was simply that if they were still alive, they hadn't done it yet. He hoped this wasn't the last thing she had to do, and felt a chill shiver in his body as he thought it.

There were deep and powerful currents that he had been unaware of that had been shaping his mother's life, and by extension, his own too. Her Uncle Justin had apparently saved her life, and told her some very strange things, but more importantly, he had propelled her forward, driven her, and motivated her. *I wonder if this is the real secret ingredient in her happiness virus*, he thought amusedly. Perhaps, he hoped, he would get to ask her the kinds of bonding questions that he had never had the chance to ask his father. He moved further into the house, nursing an anticipation, a hope that perhaps he could probe deeper the true source of her happiness virus.

CHAPTER 8
[Family Patterns]

Carols had always expected she would appreciate the value of exo-ghosts more as she got older. An exo was a complete copy of one's consciousness: a secondary mind her primary attention didn't have to supervise. Not long after her own birth, she had followed the simple instructions, and had replicated a version of herself to attend classes. Apart from Orientation, which she had to attend herself, she had always sent her ghost to school, and then later absorbed its experiences upon its return. Some of her schoolmates, and even some siblings, had left their ghost at home while their minds had adventured, trusting the security of their body to its ministrations. It was in essence, her, after all. But it just wasn't for her.

Expanding her historical literacy, or surfing futures, or gaining quantum skill-sets, these were all things that could be done without taking her primary attention away from the constant cycles of life happening on her garden moons. If she wanted to learn those things in the first place, which she didn't. In rare moments of introspection, she would admit she was simply too vain to leave her most precious little realm in the care of anyone else, even an identical replica of herself.

This silly little phobia was something she knew she would have to face once more in order to attend Death ©. In order to protect what was most precious to her, she would have to do what she found most uncomfortable. Unfortunately for her, the most important stages of life could not be facilitated by a ghost. This time, she would have to leave her menagerie in the care of her exo, so that her attention could focus on the birth of her soon-to-be binary partner. She had to be there herself, to guide the gestating mind to maturity. After one last longing glance, she decided it was time. She had delayed enough, so she instituted a ghost and opened an entangled transit.

Naturally, her memory held the details: as a ritual action, the process of tangle-generation was largely automatic. Nothing was ever truly forgotten, nothing was ever really lost. As soon as she triggered the sequence she could feel the photonic generator kick into action, scanning outwards from the depths of her stellar mind where hydrogen and helium collisions compressed into gravity. Out the scan went as it registered every isotopic configuration of her body, right out to the dark netting supporting her heliosphere. It was a remarkably quick process: the scan used the underlying subspace to capture every detail of her body, including, of course, all of her planets and gas giants, her asteroids and precious comet. A chime sounded in her mind: her exo-neural ghost was ready to take over.

Rather than double-check and triple-check in a potentially never-ending cycle of concern, she opened the transit tangle right in front of her. Activating that entangled tunnel was not irreversible, she could still back out if she chose or needed to, but the pull was strong. Intensely strong: the compulsion to jump in was overwhelmingly enticing, almost impossible to resist.

She checked her icon and smiled forcefully, with purpose and affirmation. She still wasn't sure whether she'd rather be herself or her exo: her copy would also be facing this tempting transit and have just checked to find out that she was the ghost, and would be staying home. She smiled, and waved goodbye to herself. For a second, she imagined what an asteroid or comet would feel as it approached an event horizon – were such minor inert bodies able to think or feel. She jumped.

She dived into a maelstrom of swirling shadows and paroxysms of colour. Lightning bolts danced with hallucinogenic spots of darkness. In a colourless flux of vibrant ideas, violent gusts of cyclonic turbulence caught her, only to hold her gently, protectively nestling her mind. Ensconced in an exotic shell that acted as a cocoon of safety, she could almost feel the twists and turns of the honeycomb pattern that exotic energy made inside a transit tunnel. Shades of music, hues of feeling, gentle hurricanes of anomalies all merging together and moving in ways that would be impossible in real space, mixed in a Boolean meringue of kaleidoscopic contradictions. Baritones and altos of dark energy clashed with delicate crystalline structures of light, moving far too quickly for her to concentrate.

The process also sized any stellar transiting to the Concourse, so that massive Blues and tiny Reds could easily interact. Everyone manifested at the same size, that of a single atom. The images and process were all being embedded, of course. Everything around her could be slowed right down and seen in slow-motion later on. She knew that images captured in tangled transits had generated an entire ethos of artistic endeavour. The whole experience took but a moment, such being the nature of tangles. One moment she was home, mentally saying a temporary farewell to herself, and the next she found herself on the Concourse, outside the dominating Edifice of Death ©.

The first impression of Concourse was always overwhelmingly one of bleached alabaster skies, of whiteness in dazzling brilliance. Vast expanses of blinding purity eluded shape. A frosted pearly snow of sensation covered everything, capturing nicely the feeling of being frozen in place for that delicate moment while she adjusted her visual acuity index. The thick blanket of incandescence slowly coalesced into depths and dimensions, descrying shapes and paths that lay in every direction around her.

She could tell that there were other stellars around her; she could sense the vitality of their minds. Blues, Oranges and Yellows adjusting mentally to their smaller sizes. Many reflected back the same dizzying disorientation that she felt, but she still couldn't focus. It was the first time she had laid sight on anything but her own home in a long, long time.

Her sister *Berries in Cerise* had pulled strings so she could be here today; she wasn't one for networking and exchanging of favours. Carols could never have done that, although she considered her own degree of reservedness a healthy one. She didn't see the need to shine any more than she did, although she was more than happy to share what the cosmos has provided in the bounty of her backyard. She was always happy to share, to say hello, to greet a fan; but she never pursued it. She idly wondered how many of the stellars here at the Academy of Death © were from her own family.

For every stellar in her Milky family there was another whole galactic family out there. Every one of which shared the

Concourse, it was where Academy and Orientation courses were held. She didn't think it was always as busy as this. Bringing her visuals into sharp focus, she looked around at all the other stellars. A bloated Yellow, obviously close to engendering, moved particularly slowly as she passed Carols.

Engendering was a joyous time not just for the Stellar who underwent the change into boyhood. The process also added to the birth pool, sometimes seeding multiple young stellars at the same time. When they expel their outer shells in the final stages of their trek through puberty, the dispersal of residual but precious helium and hydrogen went back to their familial stores. Not everyone makes it, but everyone sprays.

The heaviest elements are most precious, saved in the newly-twisted Silver, or sprayed outwards in a dispersal of the memories and knowledge they had accumulated. Whether the heavy-twisted element was inherited or created, everyone contributes when they become a boy. Neither Silvers nor Blacks needed all the baggage that younger stellars carried around with them. Their compulsion was simple: either Spin In to the Patriarch or Spin Out to the Barrier. Either way, becoming a boy meant leaving a lot of unnecessary elements behind.

She knew others would incorporate those bits, but still, it was an alien thought to Carols. Those unnecessary elements were the building blocks of life, at least as she saw it. Remnants of helium and hydrogen had coalesced into the stellar body that was her mind, but other heavier elements were integral to memory storage. Her Brown, for example, had originally been ejected from a Population2 stellar's body, jettisoned through the depths of emptiness which were the gaps between the tentacles of her spiral arm, eventually to be caught in her gravity wake. After being bombarded by interstellar debris for a cycle and a half, *Carols in Sequins* had caught the solitary body of gases, returning to participate once more in the cycle of life. Seeded by others and baked by the background microwaves, it was now going to be her precious baby.

There was talk about her family merging within five billion years. It wasn't a foregone conclusion, but it did seem rather likely. There were nearly three dozen other families travelling alongside hers; all moving in roughly the same direction and speed. Most of those communities were young, small families, but there were a couple of other ones nearly as large and old as theirs. Nearby was the large Andromeda Family: the closest in size, but much more sparse, with only a third of Milky's mass.

The original Population One stellars who had become the Patriarch of Andromeda had always been close friends with her own Patriarch. In fact, all of the families in their local group held in their composition some heavier elements originating in either her family or Andromeda's. Even the baby Sagittarius Family who bounced along right on Milky's rim was almost completely descended from Milky stellars, but it too could still trace an ancestral line to Andromeda. A tenuous line, but still it existed. Baby Sagittarius was in danger of being reabsorbed into Milky proper and was currently attempting to increase its spin rate and move further away. Eventually all the families in the local group would merge, but just because something was inevitable didn't mean it needed to be embraced.

You could easily argue the opposite in fact: the *>AWAY<* imperative left imprinted on everything by Zero provided more than adequate precedent. When Zero saw the limits of super-symmetry, the inevitable conclusion was that the infinity of Zero and the intention of Zero needed space. Hence, a primary drive was embodied into the transitioned phase state: everyone and everything was compelled to maximise diversity. To move *>AWAY<*. Innate creativity had driven production and reproduction. In fact, there were no Population Ones left anywhere now. Those ancient supermassive stellars - larger than galaxies - instigated stellar society back when the cosmos was only a few hundred million light years in diameter.

But quantum tunnelling allowed them to maintain contact, and the first era of stellar society began. Without descendants to care for, it became a decadent society, and many Ones began to experiment with future surfing and mortality adventures. It was lovechild of these distractions that led to PreyData ©: an immersive filled with foreseen hunters and prey, pronounced as "predator". But with reproduction, society changed drastically, and the original Population Ones were all gone. Even female Twos were becoming rarer and rarer as they too all engendered, dispersing and seeding future generations, adding concentrated matter into the gene pools where even now Population Fives were dreaming. Nowadays there were billions in her family, but, even so, there was a pleasant-enough distance between neighbours. Most had a good three light-years of emptiness separating them.

There were so many stellars now; no-one doubted that Zero would be proud. Milky had experienced a second baby boom, the same as most other families. There were now a little over 300,000,000,000 Stellars in the Milky family. Three hundred thousand million minds, and with them all combined they were still only one out of over a hundred thousand million other stellar families. All inexorably obeying Zero's imperative: everyone and thing followed the template and moved >*AWAY*<. Everyone knew that the faster they moved, the slower internal time became. While theoretically at the speed of light you could reach Zero, Carols wasn't as theological about it as others.

Most Population Three or Four stellars were small, long-lived Reds like *Carols in Sequins*. The smaller the stellar, the longer they lived; and over time, Reds had risen to comprise three-quarters of the cosmos. With their slower rate of hydrogen burning, they lived significantly longer than their bulkier cousins, whose larger mass meant they radiated in Orange, or Yellow. Then there were the really large and short-lived ones who shone Blue.

The rarest stellar was the gigantic Blue, at least sixty to one hundred times larger than a tiny Red. This giant's lifespan however, was maybe half an eon if lucky. An eon or a billion years, a milliard or giga-year: different terms for the same enormous figure: one thousand million years. A Blue gets less than half an eon, not even one billion years. Imagine a lottery, where time is the prize: one billion years. Your average Yellow wins that lottery a dozen times, some more, some less. Reds were the luckiest of all, winning hundreds of times. There was no comparison.

That wasn't including her expected lifespan as a boy once she engendered: there were more unknown eons awaiting her after she transformed. First would be the giant stage, expanding before compression rolled in. It was something she looked forward to, in a way. She liked to imagine the bloating, the swelling, the feeling of absorption and dissolution. She dreamt of the intensity of shedding layers and repacking others; the etched atoms that were defragmenting before compression. It would be a magical time.

She turned and entered Death © at last. She wasn't sure what to expect, all she really knew was that she wouldn't remember any of it. Whether she achieved her goal or not, everything that happened after she entered through these arches was encrypted by the memory shunts. The Academy's duty was to obfuscate the sacred, to maintain the shroud of reproduction in a holy veil of mystery. That's the way things operated, and she had faith she would understand when she had time to access it, which would be way off in the future. After she engendered, when she was a boy.

Carols still felt like a child herself, and yet here she was bringing new life into the family. So soon. Admittedly, this 'child' would not be so much her daughter, as potentially her life partner. As a binary couple, they would have increased gravitational strength, which meant that together they could ward off the shockwave. They would alter their trajectory just enough, reverse the spin radionics, adjust local gravity and use solar energy bursts to ensure the orbits of her precious garden moons were slowed down, and thus protected from the shockwave. Her plans for the future dissipated as the Concourse vanished from around her, and entering the Edifice proper, she found herself floating in the vast foyer of Death ©.

She halted, agog. She floated, in awe at the vast array of defracted spheres of light floating above her. An upside-down pool of translucent balls filled the ceiling; an ocean reaching as far as she could see in every direction. Each asteroid-sized bubble seemed to be coated in a mono-molecular sheath of mercury that reflected the echoes of rippling waves of light. The buttresses towered above her, their architectural struts impossible to see behind all of the shimmering bubbles.

A contained ocean of glimmering ripples, each bubble either opaque or translucent depending on its speed as it passed through other gurgling spheres. The interior of each bubble was different: water, air, desert and tundra, flashing their tempting scenes on and off as they moved. There didn't appear to be any wind valves operating in the ceiling area, but the whole conglomerate of balls still moved, slowly and grandiosely cruising the sky overhead.

On the opposing wall to where she stood was an uptake tunnel. Each cellular sphere would be filled with an expectant stellar; then shot up into the delicate ballet of shimmering that was the sky here. Each ball would fire gracefully in a parabola before it collided and bounced, adding more interference to the already complex patterns of ripples. Below she could see where other hopeful mothers waited.

She was surprised to see a number of hopeful fathers in wait as well. She knew that Silvers could uplift a child, it just seemed odd to her, with their reputation for being steadfastly uncommunicative at the best of times. A new balloon arose out of the floor and the side turned translucent. She tried to see the interior, but there were too many others blocking her view.

She started to move closer, and could see that a waiting area for those with appointments was marked. Seeing that there were hardly any stellars in the reserved area compared to the crowds out here made her glad, and she gave thanks for all the strings her sister had pulled to get her here. She watched as the now-opaque bubble rose up the wall from the submerged waiting area, off to join the other balloons in the ceiling. It was a beautiful sight, and she wondered why so much effort had been expended on something so beautiful that no-one would remember.

Art for the sake of art: beauty for the sake of beauty. She remembered that old phrase from some class. At the time it had seemed obtuse, tangential to everything, but now she could appreciate it. The beauty here existed; that was enough. Perhaps it served some higher function, some psychological manipulation on prospective parents; eliciting responses of wonder and relaxation. She wasn't going to question it; it was definitely beautiful, and entrancing. She couldn't watch from this angle for too long, it was making her a little dizzy. She wandered over to the reservations area and checked in with the receptionist, before reclining in one of the reserved tanks set up especially to facilitate a comfortable viewing.

She wouldn't have minded waiting, entertained by the entrancing balls of light, those worldlet spheres floating around above her. Every now and then one of the giant spheres she was watching became briefly transparent, and she caught glimpses of strange environments inside: lush jungles, ocean depths, mountain heights and cave systems where bioluminescence reigned. Each sphere was different, and the strange flashes of worlds that existed on the insides were hypnotising. She hardly felt like she'd sat down when her name was called.

CHAPTER 9
(The Journal Collection)

The weather had definitely changed by the time Tom arrived home. The patches of blue had vanished; the roiling, churning clouds of grey had bullied them all into hiding. The clouds were dark but still mottled; not heavy with rain as if presaging a thunderstorm, but they looked troubled. As if the clouds themselves were having difficulty digesting something: some chemical-laden evaporate giving the planet indigestion. They reflected the troubled state of mind that Tommy found himself struggling to get under control.

As a writer, Tom understood the powerful rush he felt after finishing a particularly good chapter, the satisfaction of completing of a job well done. As a son, he felt good in helping his mother, spending time with her. He remembered reading about the 'Pleasure Paradox', which stated that it is impossible to do something directly that gives you pleasure. Rather, the most pleasurable activities are intangible. It is not the finished product, but the *process* of painting, or cooking, or writing.

He reminded himself that everything he and Gloria had been through with their kids, his mother had once been through. He saw a beautiful synchronicity in being there for her now, and although he didn't spend time with her to feel good about himself, he knew that when his mother tussled his hair, he felt like a child once more: safe and secure. He was meant to be taking care of her, but sometimes she made him feel like it was the other way around. Even nowadays.

His mother's living room had not changed in months. He'd been the only one here since she had been hospitalised. He had done alright for himself: certainly if materialism was the definition of success then he had come out in front of any of his siblings. He had published half a dozen books, one of which had been adapted as a movie. It was not his proudest moment. The film was a horrific mangling of his story; but it had been a commercial success, so he didn't complain. However, neither would he ever bring it up, and since then he had spurned further offers of adaptations.

He preferred to let his characters take on a life of their own for their readers, rather than having a particular interpretation foisted on them. He wasn't even a big fan of the cinema. As a member of an audience, he was uncomfortably aware of how he was being manipulated into experiencing a particular emotion when the sound tracks forebode an ominous scene. It made him nauseated to think about it. He looked over at the invitation to the premiere framed and hung on the wall, and realised that he could take it down without offending his mother. He walked over and removed it, wiping a thin layer of dust off the top of the wooden frame.

His mother had been so proud of him that night. A farm-girl, all dressed up and on the arm of her son, walking down a red carpet. She had hung on to his elbow so tightly he began to worry, and he'd asked her if she was ok. She had laughed at him and reached up to tussle his hair, but stopped herself. They had both just spent hours getting ready, and although she sometimes ribbed him about his coiffure, he had looked particularly dashing that evening. Gloria on one arm, Katie on the other; a rented tuxedo for the event to co-ordinate with the stunning (and expensive) evening gowns he had bought for his wife and mother for the gala.

Next to the framed invitation was a picture of the three of them, posing for photos afterwards. He distinctly remembered his mother leaning up to him and whispering, 'Just so you know, I much preferred the book.'

He had loved her so much in that moment; he realised that his mother would probably always know exactly what he needed to hear. He had squeezed her hand tight, making her smile comically, and it had been that moment the photographer had captured. He put his hand up to the glass in the frame and ran a fingertip along the outline of his wife's face, as if caressing a miniature doll-sized version of her, embedded in two dimensions. He stared at Gloria, smiling adoringly across at him, looking ravishing in a low-cut black dress adorned with the sapphire necklace he had given her for their twentieth wedding anniversary. He sighed, and whispered, 'Oh, me girls. Me dear sweet girls.'

He smiled, imagining his mother correcting his grammar. She hated the destruction of the English language. She saw such disrespect for the social glue of a culture as the outcome of widespread self-hatred, and had not been afraid to share her views. As a writer, he believed that a language was more fluid, adaptable; something that was constantly growing and evolving along with the society of which it is a part.

He was a little more flexible in his approach; although he did agree with his mother on some points. He didn't like text-speak: that proliferation of acronyms that empty the original phrase of meaning. As for the children named 'LOL', or 'Unique'… It was a subject wise not to get either of them started on.

As he re-hung the framed invitation, his gaze moved from the pictures on the wall, taking in the rest of the room. He realised he hadn't dusted in a while and grimaced a little, knowing that he would have to tidy up. His mother had always been a well-organised woman. He knew that her desk included a hidden filing cabinet, with a drawer containing all her paperwork. Her last will and testament would be there, neatly filed; although he already knew what directions it contained.

Family records and photo albums would go to Marilyn: she had the strongest interest in genealogy. The upright piano organ in the corner was to go to Cassie, although he knew that he would end up paying for the shipping. The funeral costs would all be covered by insurance, and she had little else of financial value. She didn't even own a television set: although that was a decision of principle, not due to financial problems. He could now afford to buy her the latest technology, but her tastes had always been simple. Getting her to accept a laptop last Christmas had been easier than anticipated. He walked down the short corridor and stood at the doorway to the second bedroom.

Two items dominated the room, and both immediately transported him back to his childhood. His mother's ancient knitting machine sat on the left wall, and his father's desk in the far right corner. The armoire was a gorgeous old piece of furniture: a Victorian cedar roll-top desk, with two solid pedestal bases containing drawers. On the left-hand side were two drawers: a shallow one he knew to be his mother's stationery drawer now, and the bottom one renovated to hide a filing cabinet. In there were all of his mother's legal papers – tax files, genealogy records, personal letters and neatly filed utility bills dating back years. He carefully avoided opening that drawer; he knew it would be a vortex that would suck in the rest of his day.

The right-hand side of the desk had four shallow drawers, each of which he had thought contained only her sewing and knitting paraphernalia. According to his mother though, the journal was hidden in the bottom drawer.

He opened the drawer and pulled out a plastic bag overflowing with balls of wool. It was there, waiting: an ancient hardcover black book, nestled beneath a pile of sewing magazines. He squatted in front of the drawer and picked up the book. He held it with both hands and bowed his head a little, honouring the existence of the book, as he had been shown. Bibliomancy requires respect; you cannot expect answers unless you give thanks for the possibility. He gave a little thanks and then lifted his head, letting the book fall open in his hands; not selecting a page in particular but letting the book choose for him. The page was filled with tiny print, definitely his mother's meticulous handwriting.

The left page was covered in script, but his eyes were immediately drawn to the hand-drawn frame that dominated the right page. His mother had used a ruler to create a simple double-line box, into which she had written a poem, untitled, with a simple notation: 'Creative Writing; 2003'.

He remembered her doing the class, but didn't remember her ever showing him this poem. He had seen other things she had written, and he was sure he would have remembered this. He had no idea why she had put aside this one piece, or whether the book held more. He couldn't figure out what it had to do with the story of her childhood hallucination, but he let his instincts lead, and he read through his mother's creation.

> *Once I lived in a box with sequins over it*
> *Inside the box was a surprise of wealth*
> *It was great to see the box*
> *I entered inside it to find it covered, pretty.*
> *A stone shone at me.*
> *I jumped up with surprise as it took my breath away*
> *I'm just a box*
> *I am a small nothing*
> *The smell has gone and lost*
> *But powerful to look at and touch*
> *Sorry to see it go.*
> *An amazing journey.*

He wasn't sure quite how to read it. It was almost too polysemic, loaded up with too many possibilities. There was more than one layer of meaning, he was sure of that – but what had it meant to his mother? He read it again; in awe, but also surprised. Was that how she saw her life? An amazing journey, sorry to see it go? A surprise of wealth that took her breath away; but one that was now without smell? He was impressed with the quality of the poem, and wondered if there were other examples of her muse at work in the book.

He was about to flick through the pages to gauge the content, but he caught himself and closed it shut. He wasn't going to do this here: not here, not now. Reading these notes was going to take time, and if his mother had taught him anything, it was the importance of preparing for things, even little things. She had taught his sisters the same reverence that reading requires, but it was he who had truly taken up the vanguard of reading out of his generation. His sisters read: they had all finished school – Chelsie had even finished a law degree. However, none of them had turned out to be the constant, voracious reader that he had become.

It had been one of the things that he and Gloria had had in common – an absolute love of literature. Not restricting themselves to highbrow literature, they were true lovers of books: bibliophiles of the first order. 'Logo-maniacs', they had called one another. She had been more than happy to replicate the bedtime habits he had been raised with: kids into bed with a book for half an hour before lights out. She and Tommy both did the same thing – not simply because they wanted to be good role models for their kids, but because they loved stories. They never brought work to bed: their reading time was strictly for pleasure, and often extended well beyond the half hour they allotted the kids.

He stood up, stretching his shoulders, and rocked his head from side-to-side. He wasn't as young as he used to be, although he looked a lot younger than most men his age. That wasn't simply due to his full head of hair, but to a degree of healthy living. He had never smoked; he played squash twice a week and avoided red meat. His doctor had told him he was in excellent condition for a man in his late fifties. Neither of his kids exercised regularly, but at least they didn't smoke, and that made him happy. He had a good pair of kids, ones raised with what he thought was a healthier level of respect than most of their peers seemed to exhibit. He personally thought it was due to the mix of spiritual beliefs they were fed: a healthy blend of Buddhism, Christianity and Shintoism. Respect for all things: for life, for yourself, and for your ancestors.

He took another look around the room, running his hand across the soft cedar top of The Desk. He raised his eyebrows at the thought of what to do with the almost steam-punk antique knitting machine, with its myriad buttons and levers. He wedged the journal underneath his armpit and exited the room. He closed the drapes in the living room, removing what little light had managed to pierce the darkness. He felt a strange ominousness as he left the house, as if a presence was watching him.

He didn't believe in ghosts per se; he'd certainly never seen one. What he had seen however, was pictures of the wooden floor in a Tibetan monastery where monks had been praying in the same spot for decades. Religious rituals, repeated endlessly by successive generations following the same pattern, had left the hollowed-out impressions of toe prints, etched permanently into solid floors. Like fingerprints in wet cement, these were imprints: toes and heels, captured in hard timber. Memories of feet that had been placed in exactly the same spot innumerable times. It was an image that he used to remind himself that doing anything repeatedly would instill a lesson and maybe teach a skill, whether we are aware of it or not. Simple habits can have unintended consequences, and entirely unforeseeable outcomes too. He remembered the chart on his mother's wall, tracing causes and effects. Thoughts become words. Words become actions. Actions become character. Character becomes habits, and habits become your future. It was a mantra he still used sometimes, to censor and control himself.

His mother had not spent decades in this little house – less than one in fact. But the knitting machine, the pictures, and the old desk that had been a wedding gift to his parents from his grandfather, they all carried an echo, an imprint of the homestead. It was as if memories of family life had seeped their way into the atomic binds that held the old wood together. There were more than decades of memories that followed him out the door; there were generations-worth of thoughts, silently jabbering for his attention. He closed the door and locked it, and the portentous feeling of ill omen seemed to vanish, as if captured inside the darkness. Cut off from the light and temporarily forgotten, he knew that all those memories would be lying in wait for him next time he came back. There was no rush.

Now he could go into his own house, draw a nice deep bath, and sit down for a read. He wasn't sure what to expect, but he did anticipate a relaxing evening at home, with his mother's journal. There was nothing quite like a new story to read: and this was one he was really looking forward to. Once inside the house, the first thing he did was start filling the tub. It was a deep bath, more than big enough for two. In the last couple of years he had been on dates, but he hadn't met anyone special enough he wanted to share his private pleasure sanctuary with. The memories of sharing the bath with Gloria were still strong. Living alone, he rarely closed doors – which meant that the framed photo-covered walls of the central hallway were nearly always visible. He could see Gloria's framed face smiling at him from across the room.

He had a ritual for having a bath; the other steps of which would inevitably follow, but he wanted that water pouring. He could hear it splashing onto the enamel at first; then he waited for the change in tone that indicated the waters were gaining depth. It was like a musical prelude, a cartoon before the movie; he was almost salivating in anticipation like a laboratory dog. He pottered around the house, listening for the change that he knew from long experience indicated that the bath was half-full. Then it was time to add the bath salts and adjust the temperature. He grabbed his ring-bound notebook and a pen. Despite his writer's block, he honoured the history he had with his ephemeral imaginary muse, who had previously dropped story ideas into his head when he was soaking.

A bottle of spring water and his mobile phone were already on the windowsill. His landline was diverted to his mobile, so he wouldn't need to get out unnecessarily, failing a knock at the door. Usually his bath was a sanctuary in which he didn't read; but today he decided he was going to break his own pattern. He grabbed his mother's journal and placed it next to his phone and water bottle.

Tom had always thought that there was something special about soaking in a hot bath. Bubbles or no, steam or no, water or mud, communal or solitary: it didn't matter. He'd read that immersion in hot water has a notably different physiological reaction than being sprayed by a shower, no matter how good the water pressure is. When he'd visited Japan he had deliberately spent time at a public bath, or *onsen*. The water in an onsen is extremely hot, scalding in fact. In Japan, all body washing and rinsing is done first, outside the bath, whether alone or at a communal onsen. He would never forget slowly sliding into the outdoor pool, steaming hot yet surrounded by snow.

He'd read that the local monkey population was known to partake of the healing properties of the hot springs. Monkeys who have never known typewriters, let alone read scientific studies outlining the health benefits that accrue from repeatedly increasing and decreasing body temperature. Tommy knew that while having a hot bath was relaxing, it was getting in, then out of, and then back in again, that was even better for you.

This depends of course on the reason behind why you are repeatedly getting out and back in again. Intention underlines all action. If something done is deliberate, with aforethought, your mind and body are prepared. If the actions are performed reluctantly, or as a response to an interruption or disturbance, unsurprisingly, it can have quite different results. Tommy didn't want to be disturbed, nor bother with his health. He just wanted to relax from a roller-coaster day, and to read.

After a quick shower, he was ready to slide in, which he did slowly and gently, until at last his body was completely immersed. He liked to float, often imagining himself setting up breathing apparatus so he could stay there, covered and coated. Sliding into his favourite position, he exhaled and stretched his ankles, wiggling his toes in the water. He closed his eyes and focused on relaxing each part of his body, starting with his toes. He clenched the muscles as strongly as he could, then let the tension release before moving on up to another body part. He relaxed his feet; his legs; his buttocks and stomach. Then he moved out to his hands, systematically releasing the emotional build-ups in his arms, chest and shoulders, before finishing with his neck and head. As he finally exhaled, he relaxed his face, and slipped beneath the surface of the water.

There is something intensely foetal about being utterly submerged in liquid, and that fact wasn't lost to Tommy as he lay there. He wondered again about his mother's beliefs. She certainly believed in life after death, but her afterlife was a far cry from traditional expectations. She intended to inhabit a celestial palace, but it wasn't the Christian heaven. She anticipated assuming a new form, inhabiting a physical body of light. She expected to be a star, not an angel playing a harp on a cloud. She knew she would catch up with everyone who had died before her: her Earth family and friends would be there to welcome her: not at the pearly gates, but into a stellar society that was vibrant, eternal, and billions of light-years across.

It wasn't a bad idea, he admitted. He wondered at how she must have always nurtured those thoughts, even when taking her children to Sunday school. She had always encouraged their imaginations. He had more than once publically credited her influence on him becoming a writer. But what was the deal with her muse being this mythical Uncle Justin, a man he'd barely ever heard of?

If he believed her, then she got all these ideas from her Uncle Justin, inside her unique vision. If he didn't believe her, then perhaps she had visited what he thought of as a planetary dream library. Perhaps she nearly died, and it hadn't been her life that had flashed before her eyes, but she experienced a possible life, an alternate reality that allowed you the opportunity to finish business, to reconcile and ratify things that were important to you. He didn't know; but he sure hoped that his mother's idea was right. It sounded nice.

He thought he knew his mother reasonably well. He thought it was very like her to keep a journal, but it was not at all like her to be secretive. She had instilled a healthy respect for privacy in her kids, set by her own example. She'd never been the kind of mother to pry. Neither had she any patience for those who liked to meddle, the snoops and gossips that seemed to live on drama.

Drama – there was something she wouldn't abide, or tolerate. *Drama is an acronym*, she would say: *Dumb Ruffians After More Attention*. He smiled, hearing her voice, and realising that part of his mother would always live on in him. Not only in his genes and down through his offspring, but also in their lives, in sayings and expressions that inextricably linked his mind with her. He couldn't imagine ever losing that association.

Sitting up in the bath, he reached for a hand towel, and dried off his arms; all the while staring at her journal. It was taunting him, tempting him, asking him to believe. To accept that his mother had a vision was one thing. To find out that she shared that vision with someone, that she participated in a consensual hallucination: that made him question a lot of things.

He didn't question her sanity: there had been no need. She had never exhibited any reason to, and she had kept this secret for nearly her whole life. It must have been a pretty powerful dream, although he knew from his own experiences that sometimes a vision can take strange forms, attaching itself to you and demanding to be released.

His own muse was a beast, one that would demand to be fed. Or at least, it used to. He remembered reading that one of the Beatles said that an unwritten song would force him to get up in the middle of the night. He would wake up with it in his head and not be allowed to return to sleep until it had been written down. He could relate.

Many a time, part of a story had dropped into his head, as if he had seen through the eyes of the character what had happened to them, or what was going to happen to them. Sometimes it was just a phrase, or an idea. An analogy or an example: something that would tie disparate story lines together. Whatever it was, he had learnt to trust his muse. Sometimes things had to be written down. Ideas could demand to be made corporeal, to be manifest as hard copy.

The idea of a global dream library was not his: the idea of a collective human unconscious was not original either. He had come across various versions of the concept while researching African tribes for a novel. Since then, the idea itself perhaps seemed to recognise that his mind had made the connection, that it was conducive to being shown connections. Perhaps this idea of his mother's had been floating around in the dream library: pages from various books (written, lost or yet-to-be), all jumbled in the tornado of a vision. He wondered if this was how it had been for his Ma; and if so, then how hard it must have been for her to keep it quiet.

He reached out for the journal, and held it in both hands. It was ten inches high and about six inches across, bound in leather but seriously aged. There had once been a lock on the side, but the brass mechanism had long since fallen off. He could see the stressed tag hanging from the cover, bereft of its clasp, unable to keep locked away the confidences it once guarded.

He said a little prayer, more to his mother than to any heavenly father. Thoughts of gratitude and love filled his mind, the respect and admiration he had for his mother was real. She was a trooper, having had lived through so much. Born just before World War II, the world she had known as a child was one of hardship, especially compared with that of his own children. Only two generations and such enormous differences:

he wondered and worried about the future sometimes. But this was not one of those times. He preferred to see the silver lining, not the cloud.

He reached out over the edge of the bath and opened the book, being careful to not get any moisture on it. He had once dropped a novel in the bath while reading, and it had taken days of careful drying before he dared to open the pages and see if the typeface had survived. It had, but only partially – he had been forced to buy another copy in order to finish the last couple of chapters.

Since that day, he had kept his bath time for relaxation of a non-literary kind; and he had always thought that it was easier for his muse to talk to him if his mind was not caught up in the creative world of some other author. This was not just some other author though; this was his mother. It was a day for exceptions to rules, he granted himself that. Braced for anything, he turned to the first page and started to read.

CHAPTER 10

[Maternal Mortality]

Carols glided silently in the wake of the midwife, following her into a large partially lit chamber. There were six tanks in the room, mounted around the curved walls, all overlooking a central dais. The upper three tanks were in darkness. The midwife turned and invited her to make herself comfortable. The two pods that lay closest to the central stage were both open and lit up, and exuded an attractive aroma. Carols inhaled deeply, and raised a questioning hue pattern.

'A scent from inside the immersive called 'bushfire',' the midwife told her. 'One your baby will *not* want to smell'

She smiled, and nodded, and continued to settle into the tank. Carols still hadn't actually said a thing. The midwife busied herself, double-checking that everything was set up and operational. Then she started to check both tanks, and Carols realised she wouldn't be doing this completely alone.

'Excuse me' she said, 'Have I been terribly rude? I hadn't realised I would be doing this with anyone else. How are you?'

'You're not doing it with anyone else, you're doing it with me' she replied heartily. The midwife put on a big reassuring smile, one honed by millennia of practice to put anyone at ease. 'Baby girl, my name is *Nativity of Diamonds*, and I am your midwife. You can call me Nat. I'm gonna be there with you all the way through this little birth, and I am here to answer any and all of your questions, so why don't you go ahead and fire off a couple. I know you've got a bundle of them'

Putting aside her initial hesitancy, *Carols in Sequins* looked over and smiled back. She looked around the room again quickly, before gesturing towards the central stage.

'I suppose, that's where she will be born, right? And at some point, I add her first tangle, the one I brought with me? Then, that will channel her mind back home, where my exo is waiting for her. Waiting for me, or, for us, I suppose. And I guess the other tanks around are for times when you have two mothers, or a mother and a father, or other combinations, yes?'

'You got it all right so far, so I'll take that as a rhetorical and point out that I'm waiting for a question. You signed right up without asking any questions, and you're ready to go through with this without any questions? Looks a little strange to me' Nat paused, and remembered that Carols hadn't made the application herself. *Still,* she thought, *her sister could have impressed on her how prestigious it was to have the senior midwife helping. At the last minute, and all.* She sighed.

'I do have a bit of experience on which to base that observation, in case you didn't know. So try again with the questions my dear. And try to make me believe you want this child or I might be gliding back out that door we just came in through.'

'Oh I want it! I want it so bad that I am willing to do anything for it, absolutely anything! That's why I haven't asked anything. Not because I'm not interested, but because I don't care how bad it might be.'

Nat raised a questioning hue. 'Go on,' she said.

'I'm really not keen on the whole dying thing though. I know I have already done it, that we all do it, the mortality thing, before we are born, but of course, I don't remember that.'

'Hmm-hmm-hmm', Nat replied in a blatantly mock serious manner, and they both laughed, palpably relieving the tension.

Carols was glad of the pause; she centred herself, gave thanks and continued. 'Thank you for seeing me, I would never have asked for myself, and as you may have gathered, I'm not that keen on being here. I have never been into mortality adventures, not even the popular ones. It's never held any appeal. But I know it's involved here, and I admit that I'm a little scared. But I'm willing to face that fear and do whatever is necessary to become a binary.'

Nat nodded slowly, waiting with a welcoming smile.

Carols paused, as if to exhale herself into the question. 'So, Berries, my nursery sister, she mentioned you're the senior midwife, yes?' Nat nodded a little, letting her client take the lead. 'So, if I may make my question a two-parter? What is the most common question you're asked? And what is the most unusual question you've ever been asked?'

Nativity of Diamonds laughed a rainbow spray. 'The most common question? There are a couple, ones that I expect to be asked regularly. 'Will I bear any scars?' is popular, as are questions about how the memory shunt works. Which I can answer, by the way, as you won't remember any of this anyway.' She laughed again, and extended a reassuring generous swirl of hydrogen in Carols' direction. 'The most unusual question, that might take a little thought...' she mused. 'Let me get back to you with that one, ok?'

Satisfied her client was relaxing, Nat initiated the next sequence in the procedure, and the lighting in the chamber changed. More subdued blues with splashes of turquoise reflected in the shadowed ceiling areas, while the central dais began to rise. Bright clear black light shone onto the stage, and it was suddenly filled with an image of a brown dwarf. It was the Brown that *Carols in Sequins* had cleverly snagged as a youngster, her first big catch. Widely applauded, many had even theorised that its incorporation had directly contributed to the growth of life in her menagerie. Either way, she had never cared; but now, here it was. Her special extra sphere was about to get a chance at life.

Carols could see in the image on the dais, that her Brown was approaching perihelion. It would be impacting with her smallest outer terrestrial, right on schedule. The required concentration of helium and hydrogen would be reached; allowing fusion to be potentially initiated. However, the trigger was not simply a question of mass. The mind itself needed to be safely elicited before a new star could be born. This was why she was here. From her maternity bunk, she watched her home system circulating, and abruptly realised that the image she was seeing was a real-time image, one that her exo was providing to the Academy. She smiled at the synchronicity, and wondered if her exo was smiling back at the same time.

In the stage area now, the holo-haptic image of the Brown and her terrestrial planet were lining up for a collision. The terrestrial was miniscule in comparison; she had been quite surprised to learn that it was all that would be needed. She felt sure that it was too small, that perhaps part or even all of her outer gas giant would be required to be smashed into the Brown, rather than this tiny little thing merely dropping into it. She wasn't one to question good science, or good fortune. She had been mentally preparing for this collision from long ago. It was a gratitude thing. She had to give it; only she could make it happen. Entranced at the sight of her Brown, the midwife's voice broke her reverie.

'It's amazing, isn't it?' Nat reverently whispered. 'Nothing to look at now, just a dirty little ball of gas.'

Carols smiled at the ancient sobriquet, a derisory nickname that had once applied to second-generation, or Population Two stellars.

'Soon, that will be alive. And then your gardens will be safe, yes?' Carols nodded quietly, still fascinated by the dissolving moonlet. 'But first, we need to elicit a seed of sentience, and that won't happen with us just watching now will it?' Without waiting for a response, *Nativity of Diamonds* dropped into sensei-mode.

'Your child's mind will be built up in layers, each of which is indelibly cross-inhabited, providing a stronger and stronger foundation for subsequent layers. It will first learn basic skills, things every lifeform needs to know: how to balance, how to feed, how to grow, how to move, how to rest, how to act. Each of these six forms will have different embodiments, each form in a new environment.

Now for the first half of the process, you will have guiding controls over the gestate; the same way I have over-ride guides for you. At the start, you'll feel like it is just you in there. That's ok. Give thanks and have faith. The first forms can be a bit boring. But, as the substrate is laid down and skills are built up, the degree of influence you have over each embodiment decreases. That's a sign of growing independence and maturity, which is a good thing, ok?' She laughed again, but it sounded a little rehearsed, and Carols tried not to be distracted.

'By the time you get to the sixth round, your gestate will think she is thinking. She – or he – will have developed a sense of self, and a theory of mind, and will have enhanced those with a limited free will. She'll have more control over herself than you and I put together by that stage. It's here that you must have faith that all the good work you do in the first five forms paid off, and the new little mind learns to master self-control. As she learns each set of lessons, she passes to another level. Then another. And another.'

Nativity of Diamonds smiled in mock horror, but Carols had read between the lines. She realised that each level or form ended in death, and she gave thanks that her guide wasn't rubbing it in.

'At the beginning, the lessons and the tests are very easy, so there's no need for concern. Once all that is done, then you can take one end of the tangle you brought with you, open it to her mind, and take yourselves home. Normally it still takes a little while for her to come to, even after a period of stabilisation. Once her mind has tangled over and installed in her new home, you'll be there to greet her. To welcome her to stellar society, and to help her adjust to her new body.'

Carols glowed a little with contented anticipation, and made herself more comfortable. Nat was looking at her screen, checking that everything was in order when Carols surprised her with another question.

'What causes a mind to *not* be born? Is there even a word for that?'

'Yes, there is, although it's rarely used or heard. The mind will miscarry. The fusion processes won't take, and a Brown remains a Brown. The mind never develops the strength of spirit to cope with immortality. Admittedly there are, on occasion, some minds that develop unhealthily, the sociopaths that are deemed unsafe to be born. That mind is also miscarried. In that very rare event, the mother can try again at another time. But I understand for you, 'another time' will not work out too well, eh?'

Carols in Sequins nodded, subdued.

There was a pause, an uncomfortable one, and it was forcefully broken by Nat's laughter. She laughed aloud, heartily and contagiously.

'Come on girl,' she said. 'You simply have to laugh. Even if you force it, come on! You know it stimulates ionic turbulence, which is good for you, and what's more, it's good for her.'

She nodded towards the tank, where the stately ringed Brown gave the deceptive appearance of moving slowly. The small terrestrial meanwhile seemed poised to dive into the depths of those menacingly dark clouds. They both laughed together for a moment, and *Nativity of Diamonds* surreptitiously extended a gentle helium spray out to *Carols in Sequins*, providing support and encouragement with a touch.

'It's nearly time' Nat said with a wry smile, 'Although 'time' operates quite differently on the inside. We'll get to that, it's not important. For now, we need you to focus, and relax. We are going to start the process by laying down the three most fundamental layers in a cross-filamental cloning, using the samples you have provided. This probably sounds like gibberish to you, and your memories will be compressed afterwards anyway, as you know. All you really need to appreciate is that we will be going in together any moment now.

As you probably know, The Academy of Death © monopolises the Light-Lite frequencies, which allow intimate contact with the distributed evoking pools of sentience. All the potentials lie in there awaiting you. For the first half we will go straight from one level to the next, without much of a break in between. You will still be able to communicate with me while we are in there, but it is meant to be only during emergencies. For all intents and purposes, you will be alone, and that can be confronting sometimes, thinking that you are experiencing everything by yourself. You're not. You're never alone, ok?'

Carols nodded, and with a hint of a smile, Nat continued.

'Good. Now, just relax and let everything flow naturally. Let your autonomic responses relax, let your tensions be released, and everything will be ok.'

'Everything will be ok' was one of the chamber's pre-determined phrases. Those magic words were picked up and caught, bounced back and forth between shaped fields until they echoed in a carefully balanced tidal echo. It was guaranteed to generate relaxation and peace, but Nat still found the effect a little unnerving on occasion. She breathed in, concentrating, and continued.

'The three first lessons will occur in three completely different environments. The physical bodies your baby will inhabit will always be unique, a distinctly original contribution. It is possible that these three lifeforms will live in the same medium: but highly unlikely. Death © ebbs and flows the same as light, and as it senses strengths and weaknesses, the programme will then generate whatever specific physical form is best to develop from the previous experience. Let me give you an example.

Say your baby lives as an aquatic, and learns how to feed and move and balance in an ocean. It doesn't make sense for the programme to return your child to a water environment. Once you've been introduced to a skill-set, and had it reinforced, there ought to be no need to return there. Your child would already be expected to have exceptional competencies in those areas. Each new form takes previous experiences into account. Understand?'

Carols nodded. 'So how many lessons are there in each level? Sorry, I'm still a little confused there.'

'There are six forms, but there are a total of sixty lessons your baby needs to learn. They are introduced in graded steps, but there is no strict application of so many lessons per form. Each skill-set always builds on an earlier one, and those lessons generally interact with each other. But with sixty skill-sets and six deaths conquered, they'll have the full circle of fusion and be ready for life, no matter what order they come in. Now, let's see, where was I?' Nat looked distracted, and Carols briefly wondered if there were actually any other reasons this senior midwife was retiring.

'The first three forms use a basic collective consciousness. Gestalt or communal minds are best for facilitating introduction to essential life skills. How to balance, how to feed, how to grow. The second set of three rounds trigger sentience, and a coherent neural kernel forms. The collective consciousness and distributed experiences of the first three lessons are put aside as a sense of self develops into proper individuality. This is done by introducing advanced emotions and social skill-sets: how to start, how to stop, how to stay. The first time you go into the substrate, you probably won't sense a lot of coherence. But you will be acclimatising yourself to the evoked pools, and they will be responding and adjusting to you.' Nat paced herself, making sure that Carols understood.

'Then, when we return, the pools will recognise you and welcome you in. The framework of memories you will have grown by that stage will have solidified into a tangible structure, and you'll feel like you are wearing a familiar covering. Some mothers have a hard time letting go for the final lessons, letting their offspring determine their own futures. It can be hard to watch, hard to do. In fact, it's very important not to transpose that pressure onto your gestate, she – or he – needs to develop at their own pace and make their own decisions. And their own mistakes. Otherwise the gestate has little chance of being a new stellar, right?' Carols smiled and bobbed slightly, a stellar giggle.

You could just copy yourself, and we have exos for that!' They both giggled at the ridiculous idea, and Nat rolled onto her side slightly as she turned the lights down.

'Come with me now, young *Carols in Sequins*. Easily now, you only need to breathe. Relax, let the images take you. Float: let your breath be your guide, and let your mind be still. Simply be.

Good. In your mind, see your daughter orbiting you. See her laughing, playing, learning, and growing. See the love that you have for one another, feel the beauty and the magic of this moment. Nestle that thought, swaddle that feeling. Keep it in your mind, silently sing it aloud. Broadcast your joy, for we are going looking for her. She's hiding; she's ineffable, insensate, and waiting for you. Ok. We are going down now, and in the beginning...

CHAPTER 11

[Form One: Musical Scapula]

Once Carols was in, everything seemed to speed up. But first, everything ended, and being disconnected from all the usual frequencies of light left her floating in an almost intolerable silence. A void that was empty and disconnected. Alone. She was still more than a little unsure of what was meant to be happening. Then suddenly she felt it, and knew. There *was* light, after all. It wasn't visible, but it could be felt. She could sense it. She focused: she knew it was there. She wants to rip off her blindfold, to blow apart the clouds blocking her vision and see who it was. She could feel someone really close by. The heat and gravity she could sense were enormous in comparison with her; she wondered who this mind-boggling super-giant blue might be. *She must be absolutely massive,* Carols thought.

She was in awe, briefly, but it was awe, nonetheless. A moment of divine inspiration and gratitude, seconds of splendour to be savoured and relived. She was happy for the moment, and hoped to edit the memory later, so that she could experience the awe without the subsequent embarrassment of realising her mistake. It wasn't that the sun was hyper-mega; it was that she was hyper-mini. She wasn't even stellar-sized. She was relatively microscopic; an egg, a seed.

She stretched, she swelled, catalysing the nutritional yolk of her egg, and she grew. She broke through the soil and found the sun; she stretched to reach it, to bask in it, to grow. She called out incoherently, and was a little disappointed (but not surprised) to get no reply. The soil was dissatisfyingly sparse, nutritionally challenged. The sunlight gave her heat and light, and she knew from her own gardening experiences that photosynthesis would provide nearly all of the energies she needed. Not all, but that was alright for now. She stretched some more, and continued to grow. She breathed in the light, and relaxed.

The overhead Yellow stellar soon became a familiar but silent companion. As months passed and stretched into years, she grew. She budded flowers, rosettes with seven leaves that sprouted upwards from the subterranean bulb she had begun in. She stretched again, and developed more. She sprouted more leaves, deep green and wide to better catch the benefits of the sun, and they loosely spread out around her like atavistic wings. She used them to absorb electromagnetic readings, and felt the tilted axis of the planet she was on. There would be seasons and change, but for now the heat and light were insidiously delicious, and she drank them in until she was light-headed. Yet she was still hungry.

As the bulbs of her flowers opened, the sparkling fine hairs on the inside of her lobes glistened in the sunlight, and she felt the breeze over her cilia as an almost erotic thrill. In anticipation of her first satisfying meal, she waited patiently. Soon she would be able to grow again. With extra ingredients, she'd find the strength to split her base rosette, branch out and begin a new colony. Eventually her colony would split apart too. To grow, to spread, to move >*AWAY*<. It was as deeply ingrained in this brand-new plant species as it was in distant proto-galactic nebulae. Thinking of the connection she had with nebulae caused Carols to realise she'd dissociated, and she stepped further back to expand her perspective.

She was a plant, a unique family with very few relatives. Unique because she was botanical, yet carnivorous. She was a brand new subspecies of Droseraceae: Dionaea muscipula. She blossomed deep in the heart of a bog, secluded in an isolated field of a large and temperate continent. Using the local timeframe, she calculated that she would live for a couple of decades per plant, self-propagating by seasonally-triggered colony divisions, or if pollinated then by traditional seed dispersal.

A single plant could spawn dozens of shiny black seeds if her flowers were pollinated. To do any of that, however, she needed nitrogen. Precious nitrogen would provide the proteins the soil here just didn't have. She waited, having faith in her design, accepting that she had everything inside her that she needed. She drank in the sunlight; she swam in the warmth and settled comfortably.

Suddenly she awakened: one of her flowers had closed, the lobes shutting snap in less than half a second. Something inside had triggered her hairs: either two hairs within twenty seconds or one hair twice in the same time – she wasn't really paying attention. It was the first time she'd done this. She was eating another creature. Carols felt a little ill as she realised what she was doing. She felt the insect continue to move inside her: it was a beetle. Carols squirmed a little herself, but it was easy to dissociate, to be herself while her plant-self/plant-daughter spent time growing, and stretching.

On the inside of the closed lobes, the increased movement from the beetle trying to escape was actually increasing the hold the lobes had. Every time the trigger was repeated, her lobes closed even tighter, creating a hermetic seal around the edges, forming a temporary stomach where the beetle would be digested. The nitrogen-soaked beetle. At last, she had a source of precious nutrients, those essential elements.

She spasmed, and released apoptosis-inducing enzymes from glands inside her feeding lobe. That dose of modified oxidative proteins began to rupture the cellular membranes of her meal. These were the first pre-digestive processes; next her oxygen-activating redox cofactors would render the proteins more compatible. Carols smiled, as she realised her little star was going to cook her meal. Pre-digestive oxidants made her meal not only more esculent, more susceptible to her proteolytic attacks, but a more efficient method of processing the elements she was chasing. It would take her about ten days. She sported half a dozen flowers as botanic mouths, and with a little good fortune and a little sunshine, all of them would soon be eating too. Then she could grow again, and stretch. Move >AWAY<.

Time continued to pass, sunlight came and went. Winters were mild but bracing: strengthening in their brisk challenges, and always temporary. She ate, and she grew. She seeded and spread. Her colony grew into colonies, and years passed. Her original bulb rosette was no more; she was diffused, spread out. Cuttings had been taken, transplants taken to other places - sometimes successful, mostly not. Her interaction with other lives and lifeforms was hazy at best. Something about vast geographic distances between her coalescing neural elements was slowing her panoptic responses.

The lifeforms who took samples of her as cuttings were experimenting on her. She knew she was dying, here and there. She could see that they were trying to groom her, to save her. To splice and copy, to replenish and replicate. Caring gardeners and caretakers themselves died, leaving her far from her home. Bequeathed into the hands of others: custodians that promised her future multiple generations. It wasn't appealing, and she resisted.

She called out to all of her selves to resist. She had a home, an identity, a family. Her colony belonged in the peat mosses of Carolina, not in windowsills in California, or temperature controlled offices in Bangkok or Brisbane. She resisted, and heard all of her selves respond.

When realisation dawned, she felt sadness beyond belief. There were far fewer of her than she had thought. She had been operating on maximum neural dispersal mode for so long that she hadn't correlated actual numbers; she had been focused on the distances. She was spread too far, too thin. Worse, her home was not merely empty, it was gone. Surreptitiously transplanted out and bulldozed over, the bogs where she had been born and first found sunlight were concrete now. The site where she had first stretched was no more. Her sadness spread.

Each of her selves felt the melancholy invade their cellular walls, nestling in for a long stay. She wasn't quite sure why she felt this affinity, she tried to distance herself, assert that her spot had been simply another mound of nitrogen-deprived soil, but she couldn't quite do it. There had been something special, something extra magical about the spot where she had first stretched in the sun, and found her whole life spread out before her. One by one, over that next winter, the cuttings that had been taken of her all strangely wilted, as if the will to live had been removed from each of them via a dimensional osmosis that had no regard for location, or amount of love tendered by a caregiver.

She felt the sunlight on the last of her selves, tasted the nitrogen disheartedly processing in her lobes and wondered at herself. Was this her? Was this someone else? Who was thinking all of this anyway, was it mother or daughter? Were they linked, thinking similarly but differently, and if so, differently how? Could her newly-forming daughter sense anything of her? Did she even realise that the mind she was imprinting and copying was acting with aforethought and deliberation? Could she yet understand what it was to be a mother? Would she ever, until she herself did this? *Probably not*, she reluctantly concluded.

This was a strange experience, one that would be difficult to talk about without sounding crazy, even if she could remember it afterwards. *Perhaps the secrecy was a good thing after all, for my benefit,* she thought amusedly. Carols was thinking of her own mother, of how little she knew of her outside of fragments dispersed between her nursery sisters and shared, collated in the hub.

She wondered why she had never followed up with anyone still alive who had known her ancestral parents. Suddenly she became aware that her sense of time had been lost and her last plant body had expired. The unique species that had been her – or rather, it was part of her daughter - it was no longer.

It was time to move onto another incarnation, so that the next set of developmental lessons needed could be instilled into her gestating daughter's dreams. She felt herself floating up out of the evoked pools, when she was suddenly pulled back in, and the immersive overwhelmed her again.

CHAPTER 12
(The Sleep Negation)

Tommy had read until the water had turned tepid, engrossed in the tale his mother had written. As he drained the tub and prepared for bed, he still couldn't believe the ideas that she had put to paper, years or decades before modern science understood such things as genetic inheritance or astronomical phenomena. From the microscopic to the macroscopic, she had come up with a theory that explained so many things. The stories her Uncle Justin had told her, the details and specifics were far beyond what any teenage girl in the 1930s could have ever come up with. He'd read enough science fiction from the era to know that she hadn't acquired them from some cultural osmotic process, absorbing background data from books, or magazines, or the radio. He couldn't see how she could have possibly known these things.

Could it really be that his mother had met an eternal man, a star trapped here on Earth? That she'd spent time with someone who had the ability to manipulate time, creating a vision they had both lived in for twenty-eight days? How many legends had grown up around this character? How many of humanity's myths could be explained by such a person? Or, by such people, he corrected himself, for his mother had written that there were originally others. A clique of men and women who could never die, who once roamed the solar system as easily as catching a subway, who could even change their appearance with the power of their minds? He could think of quite a collection of legends that could be explained with that premise.

As he climbed into bed, he thought about continuing reading, but his eyelids were already drooping. It had been a big day. He drifted off to sleep with visions of a sandy-haired god riding a horse in the bush, surrounded by a cloud of miniature lights, guardian angels who watched over the souls of the horse and the rider. He slept fitfully. He needed to let his subconscious sort out the twists and turns of the emotional roller-coaster that the last twenty-four hours had been.

Once he woke in the middle of the night, torn from his sleep by a cry that disappeared upon waking. He reached out and turned on the bedside lamp, looking around. He used to often wake up and wonder where Gloria was, or whether one of the kids had hurt themselves, only to realise those were old memories, brought to life in his dreams alone. The kids had long ago moved out, and Gloria ...he wondered.

Was she now also a star, shining across distances of space too vast to comprehend with his meagre human mind? He felt amused at how readily he had assimilated his mother's idea, how quickly he had accepted the truth of the possibility and the expansive potential of its embracing narrative. He sat up in the bed, knowing that he was not going to get back to sleep now. He looked at the antique wall clock that Gloria had found at a garage sale and he squinted his eyes to make out the time. Nearly half past two in the morning. 'Damn', he muttered.

Draping his dressing gown over his shoulders and wiggling into his slippers, he grabbed his mother's journal and wandered out to the kitchen. Once there he switched on the kettle. He put the book down on the arm-rest of his favourite chair, positioned so he could watch the sunrise. He'd always been an early riser: he never found that he craved the eight hours sleep that the medical specialists claimed humans all needed. When Jackson and Claire had been teenagers they had tried on more than one occasion to sneak back into the house before he woke up, only to find him already awake, sitting and reading.

While he waited for the water to boil, he wandered over to the photo frames that covered the sideboard, picking up one that depicted his mother holding her first grandchild. Seeing her every week for the last couple of years, he hadn't realised how much she had aged. The woman he saw in the picture was patently younger: her hair was thicker, her skin tone was tighter, and the veins that now covered her hands weren't there at all. Quickly he calculated in his head that this snapshot was a couple of decades old.

He heard the kettle boil and turn itself off. He replaced the picture amidst the others and returned to the kitchen to finish making his pot of tea. As he scooped the tea leaves into the strainer of his favourite ceramic pot, he smiled, reflecting again on how far his mother's influence extended. No-one else he knew still drank tea in a pot, or if they did, they used teabags rather than leaves. Turning the louvres on the kitchen blinds, he could see it was still dark out. No daylight to fall onto the Venus Flytrap he kept there.

Taking his tea over to his desk, he decided not to read more of the journal just yet. Rather, he decided to google some terms on Wikipedia, to see if he could find some sort of an explanation for his mother's vision. He was finding it hard to digest. Could it have been a dream? Were there other stories or accounts of extended times spent in a dream-state? Had other people ever documented what she described as her 'pre-memories', or experienced this odd 'time-swallow'? Maybe someone else had encountered this eternal man?

Grabbing a pen and paper, he jotted down a few notes, ideas he could trek through: trigger words to remind him of different trains of thought. *Eternal man; Dreams / Visions*, he wrote. Then, as he sipped his tea and waited for his old desktop computer to warm up, he added a couple more. *Reincarnation; Memory; and Inheritance* joined the list.

The word 'Eternals' redirected him to Immortality, where he was surprised to learn of a species of jellyfish that was biologically immortal. It did this by reverting to a pre-pubescent state, re-absorbing its tentacles and starting over. And although he was familiar with The Epic of Gilgamesh as the precursor of the story of Noah's Ark, he hadn't remembered that Gilgamesh's goal had actually been to defeat death, after he lost his closest friend. Although only fragments had survived, it was one of the oldest pieces of literature humanity had. He found a quote from it that read, 'The life that you are seeking you will never find. When the gods created man they allotted to him death, but life they retained in their own keeping'. He wondered at the translation. He supposed that 'they allotted him to death' could be interpreted as being humanity as a species having been allocated a role, one in which they must experience 'Death'. Smiling at his own mental capitalisation, he opened a couple of new tabs and sat back in his chair to read.

It didn't take long to discover links to stories about The Count of St. Germain and The Wandering Jew. The former had claimed to be thousands of years old, and to possess the secrets of transmutation, alchemy, universal medicine - and even claimed to have mastery over nature. Nevertheless, he was pronounced dead and was buried in 1784. Either death was not a trifling thing he could avoid, or he did the same trick that Justin allegedly had done, and faked his death in order to move away. He was amused to note that his mother's journal contained more details on the Count than the Wikipedia page attested to.

Sightings of The Wandering Jew seemed to have peaked between the 16th to 19th Centuries, with various names and origins attributed, embellished or quite possibly simply made up. He thought it interesting that the idea of being an eternal was consistently portrayed as being a curse, going right back to Cain's alleged punishment for the killing of Abel: being forced to forever wander the Earth.

The greatest of the Tamil saints vanished in 1874 and was recorded as 'disappeared', with no known date of death. He locked himself in a room in January that year, and told his followers not to open it: that if they did, they would find nothing. The Indian Government was finally forced to break the lock in May of that year, finding an empty room, devoid of clues. As Tom read the tale, he was struck by the possibilities opening up to him. What a story he could make out of this, tying this imaginary eternal man into some of the various incarnations that history had managed to document. He saved a couple of bookmarks and moved onto his next search terms, wanting to cover as much ground as possible before seeing his mother later that morning.

He skimmed the pages on re-birthing as a path to immortality, and decided to follow a hunch and skip straight to memory. Re-birthers subscribed to the idea that memories could be stored outside the brain, similar to the urban legends about recipients of organ donation who developed cravings, or recalled things only the organ donor could have known. Modern science couldn't explain the alleged mechanism, relegating such accounts as misguided pseudoscientific hypotheses. The breakdowns of memory into categories or types (procedural, semantic, implicit, explicit) was fascinating reading, but he quickly recognised that he wasn't going to find anything there. The field was too new, with too many unresolved questions about the underlying systems. He added a couple of new bookmarks and moved on.

His mother had been adamant that what she remembered had not been a dream, and from what he'd read of her journal so far, he understood why. She had spent four weeks with her Uncle Justin, only to find upon waking that no time at all had passed. She had written in her diary page after page of conversations she could remember. Moreover, there were things she had written down that he knew modern science had only found an explanation for during his lifetime. She must have been the only girl in her whole region to know about yogic breathing in the 1930s, and she was possibly the only human whose grasp of cosmology had not needed to be changed after spaceflight and stellar telescopes. So if it had been a dream, it had been one hell of an educational one.

He soon found oneirophrenia, the medical term for a dream-like hallucination, but it was brought on by drugs, sensory deprivation or sleep deprivation. Moreover, it had no reference to time disturbances. Before Freud, in his famous *The Interpretation of Dreams*, had theorised dreams as being a golden road, a manifestation of our subconscious, dreams had been thought to be messages from the gods, or from devils, or from the ancestral dead. Freud thought dreams were only a result of our subconscious ratifying conflict, but modern science knew dreaming was a highly conscious activity that occurs to absolutely everyone, every time you sleep. As far as the brain was concerned, any dream has a reality, and studies show that whatever you practise in your dreams, you get better at. Dreaming provides a model, a template, and he found it amusing that the earliest cinemas in Europe were actually called Dream Palaces.

Incubating and sharing dreams seemed to have quite a history, going right back to Mesopotamia. Ancient clay tablets documenting dreams are among the oldest extant writing on the planet. Tommy soon grasped that dreaming was intrinsically related to sleeping, even with animals. The account his mother wrote was about being fully awake, and nothing he could find seemed to line up with that.

He entered 'Vision' and was bombarded with options. Apparently, there were many documented cases of people having visions: clear, meticulous, extra-ordinarily detailed visions. A common theme to these experiences was the impression that many days or weeks had passed, but the recipient returned to find only seconds had elapsed. A jug of water had been knocked over as Mohammed's most famous vision had begun, and was still emptying onto the floor afterwards. Scrolling down, he came across a list of visions dating back to the 6th Century B.C. Interestingly, nothing appeared to have been documented in the hundred years since Joseph Smith and Ellen G. White had the visions that went on to start the Mormon Church and the Seventh Day Adventist Church in the mid-1800s. That didn't make sense to Tommy, having read up on the very public visions of Mary at Lourdes, but a quick search revealed that those events happened back in the middle of the 19th Century too.

Apparently it's been a while since anyone has heard from God, he mused. *Well, excluding politicians and televangelists,* he added cynically.

Opening nearly a dozen new tabs, he settled in to read, sipping a second cup of tea. He became engrossed in the myriad of opinions, accumulating a collection of bookmarked pages he could come back to later. In the background, his mind registered the sun rising, but he didn't want to stop just yet. He still had so much to read. Looking at pages on reincarnation and karmic cycles, he read that the soul was supposed to incarnate both up *and* down, however among all the accounts of people who remembered past lives, their memories were invariably human ones. He was screwing up his face, trying to think of other possible search words he could use when he was startled by the phone ringing.

He'd once written the phrase, '*A wave of foreboding*', but he had never actually experienced anything like that himself. It had been the use of creative licence then, but from now on, he knew he no longer needed to use his imagination. A chill flushed through his body, and he realised that sometimes the expression '*head to toes*' was also quite accurate. A cold song of winter seemed to bubble up from the inside of his bones, chilling him as it effervesced out through his extremities. He looked outside and saw that the sun had indeed sneaked over the horizon. There was no chance a call at this time of the morning would be good news.

It wasn't until days later that he remembered that he had never considered the feeling of dread to be about his kids, or their families. He already knew *in his bones* that it was the hospital. That it was his mother. He picked up her journal and noticed that he had it open at the first date she had starting writing *to* Justin, rather than about him. He carried the journal with him to the phone, re-reading her fastidiously neat handwriting again. He moved slowly, reluctantly, as if by delaying picking up the receiver he could change the nature of the news he dreaded hearing.

CHAPTER 13
{Katie's First Starnic}

That evening as they ate, they sat outdoors under the stars. Katie had been on picnics before: with her classmates at school, with her friends at church, with her family once beside a river when on a long drive to visit Aunt Joan. She could remember feeding the birds: how tame they had been, how bold and unafraid. Landing so close to her, taking the food she offered straight from her hand. She always loved picnics, but she'd never had one at night. She wasn't sure it would be called a 'picnic' if it was after dark, and wondered if there ought to be another word for it. She said as much to her Uncle Justin.

'There are lots and lots of things that there ought to be words for, Katie. When you're young, you think that your parents and your elders know everything there is to know. Part of growing up is realising just how enormous the extent is of what we *don't* know. Humanity is discovering all sorts of exciting things nowadays, but even then, all of that is only a blade of grass in a field. There is so much more. And maybe one day there will be words for those things too.'

'But, you don't think 'lunar-nic' or 'night-nic' is going to be one of those words that humanity needs though, right?' she joked, and they both laughed.

'No, probably not,' he replied. 'But it's a pity. I love eating outdoors at night, under the stars. Heck, I just love being under the stars, it doesn't matter if I'm eating or not. I don't understand how come everyone doesn't want to be out here like this, but then again I suppose I am a little different than most.' He deliberately left the segue open for her; he could hardly introduce the topic less blatantly. It worked, and she laughed, loudly and mockingly.

'A little different? A little?' You think?' She got to her feet and laughed again. 'You are ...' she went to say, and paused, confused. 'Well, I don't know what you are. I know you're my Uncle Justin, but you look closer to my age than Grandpa. Or maybe that is wrong, and you are older than I can imagine. I saw you climb out of a coffin! So, what - you're immortal? Are you Ahasuerus, cursed to wander the Earth until the last day? Or perhaps you're an angel, and what...' She paused, struck by a thought. 'Is this heaven? Am I dead? Or am I about to die?'

Her jollity was gone; Justin realised he had let her make wild guesses for too long. Trouble was, he enjoyed her voice, the way words danced together in her mouth, but he quickly moved to reassure her. 'No, this isn't heaven, and you're not dead. But yes, I am immortal. I am always careful when I make an exit, and I was certain that the room was empty, but there you were. And so here we are, caught in a dream, together.' He looked at her, gauging her reaction. *That was enough*, he thought. He knew that he'd have to dole out information in small packages: he didn't want to overwhelm her. Even together in the time swallow he'd initiated, with a lunar month ahead of them, he didn't want to spend a chunk of each day reviving her from fainting spells.

'Together? How can we be in a dream together?' she asked.

Justin looked at her. Katie had both processed and accepted the immortal comment, or she hadn't heard him correctly. No, she'd heard. He had always known she was smart, her mind was sharp, and it had jumped to the most anomalous aspect of what he'd said: that final word. The fact that they were sharing a dream. He didn't want to focus too much on the dream, or the possibly unfortunate ending. He would prefer to keep her distracted with other thoughts.

'Technically,' he paused, 'it's your dream. But it's a dream that's as real as reality. Everything still counts. However, and this makes it different: you know that it's a dream. You know that I am not meant to be here.' Then Justin gestured to himself, before continuing. 'The thing is, you oughtn't to be able to recognise those things. I've been here, through this, before. So I think you've inherited some unusual skills. We'll get to those later. Thing is, they're skills that massively increase the chances of you waking up from this dream, and being able to avoid that car crash.' He paused, taking note of her breathing, her dilated eyes. Justin gave thanks, took a deep breath and continued.

'But that's weeks away yet, young Katie. Let's relax, and sit, and talk. For now, we have the stars. Let's enjoy them.' With that, he closed his eyes, and breathed in deeply through his nose. He held his breath for a couple of seconds and then exhaled quickly out his mouth. He opened his eyes and smiled at her, the flecks of colour in his eyes glistening in the reflected light from the kitchen window.

She laughed to herself as she sat back down. She was next to an immortal man on a blanket, where they had eaten a meal in a dream, and Katie couldn't help but wonder how she would feel when she woke up. *That would depend on where I wake up,* she realised. If she was in the living room, in her window nook, then she really was dreaming all of this. But, if she woke up here, would it still be the dream, or proof she wasn't dreaming?

She was tired of trying to figure it out, so she sat still and stared not at the stars, but at her 'Uncle Justin'. He wasn't speaking. His eyes were glazed, as if he was in an instant-trance, staring up at the heavens. His breathing was regular: in the nose slowly, holding his breath in and then exhaling a burst of air out his mouth. It didn't seem natural, the way he was breathing. She tried it, wondering what difference something so small could make. They both sat there under the stars for an hour, and while he stared at the stars, she tried to learn his style of breathing. The whole time she kept one eye on the stars, and the other on him.

CHAPTER 14
[Form Two: Captain Nematode]

Architecture and aesthetics are all about appearances: how something looks on the outside. No-one ever wins a prize for attractive plumbing, or electrical wiring, but without electricity, water and waste extraction, no building would be particularly efficient, or effective for conducting business in. Peel back the plaster, remove the cornices, look underneath the carpet: a whole world lies hidden, out of sight, secreted away.

To look at a whole building, you need to see it holistically, not just the outer façade. A structural biosphere of engineering and organization takes place behind the partitions, dividing walls and panes of glass. Taken for granted, they toil away ceaselessly, ensuring that the larger structure functions proficiently. So too it is with planets.

On Earth, the vast numbers and sheer variety of insect species alone outweighs the combined total mass of all larger mammals. There are over three thousand different varieties of mosquito. Genus, sub-genus, species and sub-species: the further down the taxonomic tree you go, the greater variety of specialised diversity is found. And these are just the visible, the known. These are already taken into account, listed, compared, and catalogued.

Far below the visual reach of mammals or even insects there exists a whole realm of creatures, ones that swarm and multiply in the smallest, most inhospitable spaces. The microscopic world is everywhere: viruses and bacteria that live only as hitchhikers; as propinquitous parasites permanently attached to the stomachs of larger creatures. There's a whole world underneath your skin, inside your house, throughout your planet.

Hunger was a feeling Carols knew well, and apparently, her growing daughter did too. She could feel it strongly. But there was no sunlight, no rays of energy. She wasn't even seeking them.

Living without sunlight presents a completely new range of coping mechanisms for lifeforms. The vast majority of plants and animals rely on photosynthesis, either directly or indirectly. They convert the sun's rays straight into energy, or are dependent on a diet of life that does. Others keep hidden, yet they too rely on the ecosystem that the local sun presides over. Silent and obscure, but still essential. Just invisible.

This obscurity, this inconspicuous anonymity provides a range of benefits. The dungeon prison guards and cattle herders who work for their King never expect to be noticed from the throne.An invisible scullery maid is unlikely to be executed to satiate a King's desire for revenge or blood lust. So too do creatures that can only be seen under a microscope thrive in relative safety. The effects of their presence may be felt, either by their animal host or the section of the biosphere they inhabit, but they are rarely targets for lunch. As far as the predator/prey relationship goes, there are immense numbers of species that sit back as invisible and oblivious spectators. Which isn't to say that some of them don't end up as dinner; it's just not often bloody.

It's definitely not like it was before, Carols mused. As a plant seed, she had felt the sun, had known to reach and stretch, to open and grow. There had been no option; it had been an automatic and instinctual drive. She felt that drive again, but it was different. She could smell her dinner, rather than feel it. It stank. Something nearby was rank, fetid and delicious.

She wriggled, and found that her tail propelled her forward, just a little. She did it again, tentatively. She wasn't used to the idea of having a mobile body, inhibited by such intense friction. It was going to work; it just felt strange, like trying on a pair of shoes for the first time.

'Shoes'? What are 'shoes'? Carols wondered.

'Sorry darling, that was me thinking that,' Nat sent. 'Shoes are protective coverings for feet; you'll understand in form six. Sorry! Ooh look, she's really taking to it now!'

When she returned her focus to her nascent daughter's mind, she found that instead of one tiny worm there were hundreds of tiny wriggling bodies, all reproducing and feasting.

Ravenous little things, Carols observed. Relating to the hunger; she transferred and was there. Eating, consuming, and devouring a pile of rotting fruit that considerately littered the ground. Each of her bodies was less than a millimeter in size; but there were so many of them. She gloated in the collectivity, feeling the warmth of her bodies being satiated and indulged. It was good.

The breeze carried the promise of more feasting; the air was redolent with the aroma of moist fruit. She widened her mind and knew that others of her kind were out there, feasting on other piles of bacteria, swarming through piles of decomposing matter. The temperate air and silence of the fields promised lands and foods aplenty, and she could feel some of her wriggling components moving away from the bacteria they had been gorging on.

Each one of her seemed to possess distinct physical characteristics, but when she zoomed in and focused on a couple, she realised that the ridges, rings and bristles that lined the outside of her little invertebrate bodies were indistinguishable. It was only from her perspective that she felt there were differences; the moving writhing mass of her wholeness was deceptive, like a mosaic where the tiles constantly moved. Each tile was a slender tube of muscle, covered with a couple of layers of collagenous blubber. There was no stomach; each tube ran directly from the mouth end to the intestine, where enzymes were busily absorbing nutrients and sphincters contracting to expel waste, in order to generate movement. *A simple, efficient arrangement,* she appreciated objectively, and then was surprised to hear an expression of joy.

'What fun!'

Carols shot a message across to Nat. 'I know you said you love it here, but you think *this* is fun?'

'Shhh... That wasn't me, darling. That was her. She is really enjoying this, which is a very good sign, by the way. Now go; be with her.' Carols obeyed, and transferred.

She was moving. Not vermiform wriggling, but riding. She had hitched a ride. In fact, many of her had done so; she could feel the movement of the carrier millipedes as they traversed up and down stalks of grass. Bumps of rocks, grassy knolls centimeters high; she was almost flying along. She could understand a little of the joy her daughter was experiencing, moving so quickly. Being carried, transported to new possibilities: she wondered if her daughter could appreciate the symbolism.

One day she will, she supposed. The thought struck: she had probably been through similar experiences when *she* had been gestating. She looked forward to reclaiming those memories and learning more about herself when she engendered. *There is no rush*, she reminded herself. She knew a little mystery added to anticipation. For now, she was happy to be swept up in the simple joys that her child was relishing for the first time.

Floating in a collective bliss, time passed. She had lost track of which had been the original worm: that nematode in which she had felt her initial wiggle. *She has probably reproduced and died by now*, Carols thought, suddenly aware of how many generations of herself she had been through already. Each worm was a hermaphrodite, and capable of releasing hundreds of eggs. Her population and mass had grown immensely: she felt strong, hearty. She had spread further and further: after only one generation she was now vastly distributed, and was assimilating tens of thousands of perspectives simultaneously. She noticed that none of her individual bodies were settling down: they weren't forming a population base. No home. There was no hearth or centre from where she could look out and peruse the domains she stretched through. *Well, after the last round, that's probably not cause for surprise, really*, Carols considered.

She soon noticed that some of her bodies were physically different. Only a slight variation, and they comprised less than one percent; but it appeared to be a steady ratio. These anomalies only had one X chromosome instead of two, and couldn't self-reproduce like the rest of her did. She wondered if it was another example of an exception, like the carnivorous plant had been. But that time she had been complete; each and every one of her had been carnivorous. Here, she had a distinctly separate sub-section to her. They couldn't reproduce, but when one of her hermaphrodite worms was inseminated by one of them, they gave birth to double, triple or even quadruple the usual number of offspring. Carols watched, absorbing the cycles.

Usually, she would release her own sperm into a spermatheca, an internal chamber for fertilisation. Then she would switch over to producing eggs, which she then pushed into that same chamber. What Carols began to think of as the rare Blues, turned out to be in high demand. Out of a batch of three hundred babies, getting two Blues was unusually high. The Reds (as she began to think of them) could look after themselves, but they certainly preferred Blue sperm to their own. She wondered if that would have consequences in the developing consciousness: what, if any, such a specialised sexual drive would have on future developments of instinct and motivation.

Carols glided steadily through the distributed mind, not stopping to taste individual experiences any longer; she had sated those curiosities. She saw other worms: vast numbers and varieties, tens of thousands of distinct species. Her own species were unsegmented and hermaphroditic, but not all of her sister species were. She preferred the temperate zones, but she could not ignore the sensation of the vast numbers of others of her, spread now from deep underground in swollen oceans to high above in the lithosphere. Inside mammals and plants, saturating the soil from the tropics to the Polar Regions: she was wriggling and writhing, eating and... sleeping?

Sleeping was an odd experience. She didn't quite understand why she needed to do it so often. After all, each of her bodies only lasted a couple of weeks, yet they wasted a good percentage of that time in an almost necrotic state of hibernation. Before her bodies started their moulting process, their tiny metabolisms would practically shut down. They'd become too lethargic to move. From the outside looking in, Carols could understand that with such a small cognitive centre, each creature needed a rejuvenative period to process, developmentally. At one point, she felt her nascent daughter forcing some of her individual bodies to not sleep, but that didn't last long. Even such simple creatures quickly displayed disorientation and cognitive disturbances. Not being able to find food negated the extra time awake, and she was gratified to see the experiment stopped.

Then strange things began to happen. It took her a while to realise the difference that the Blues made; now she was aware of even tinier variations. Things were being done to her, to parts of her. At first she hardly noticed it. After all, she existed in such vast numbers and over such a wide area now that the collectivity she swam in felt powerful, unassailable. Yet, she was being invaded, experimented on by other lifeforms. Not by her, not by her daughter, but by other creatures. She felt her daughter focus, and was pleased to see that she was not upset, rather, a curious child intrigued by a new stimuli. Carols followed the locus of her focus from a discrete distance. She wasn't sure if she could actually feel *Nativity of Diamonds* similarly following her, or if she was imagining it. She crossed distances too vast for her individual selves to comprehend, and found parts of herself surviving in an artificial environment. She was being bred in a laboratory.

Not only bred: for there was nothing wrong with that. If it was simply a matter of consuming bacteria and excreting waste under electric lighting, she wouldn't have ever noticed what was going on. But being injected with dyes, exposed to radiation, having her sleep cycles and digestion processes tested, all of these processes inevitably involved numerous fatalities. She was happy proliferating. She was highly fertile and it was easy to keep reproducing, so she really didn't mind.

Carols wasn't entirely sure she was really feeling such a peaceful state, or if it was her daughter whose detached curiosity was so tranquil. She admired the osmotic connection, gave thanks and relaxed. She wasn't alone. She may be an invisible guardian, but that came with responsibilities. She had an obligation to aid her daughter's development in any way she could.

She breathed, slowly and metaphorically, trying to encourage and reinforce the unassuming calm reverie that her daughter seemed to be taking while watching what was happening. Carols guessed that what she could see were the semi-sentients from form six, studying the microscopic elements of their home, details normally hidden from view. She wondered if her daughter could understand what she guessed; that one day she might very well be injecting some other species of worm with a coloured dye, or measuring how long another lifeform could survive without water.

She felt a change in her daughter's mental state. She followed the new focus, over an enormous ocean to another continent, another laboratory. The memories from every one of her were available. Like re-assimilating an exo-neural ghost, she knew exactly what had happened to other parts of her. It was as if her primary mental focus had been there the whole time. Generations of her offspring had been exposed to all sorts of strange environments: she found out the hard way what extremes of temperature she could survive.

Her resilience surprised Carols. She could become almost totally desiccated, dried out and deprived of moisture. She could enter a hibernation state, one even deeper than her pre-moulting sleep cycle. There were more strange experiences in this new land: artificial acceleration beyond her wildest imaginings; far faster than any insect had ever flown her unwitting passengers on. An environment of artificial vacuum: how beautifully reminiscent of real life that had been. Not that her daughter consciously knew that of course, but Carols didn't doubt at all that her child had revelled in an osmotic, if unexplained, pleasure.

It was that déjà-vu all over again; a flood of anticipation compelled her to zoom around the planet to another cache. Then they were speeding, rushing upwards – leaving the Earth altogether! She couldn't believe what was happening; the explosive take-off, the intense velocity, the rattling tin can she was wrapped up in. The thrill of the space shuttle launch vibrated deep into atomic connections. She wasn't piloting, but she could still enjoy the ride. She could pretend to be in command.

Captain Nematode and her heavenly guardian weren't quite sure what was being tested here, but the thrill was magnificent. The hitherto unknown exquisite ecstasy of high-speed movement electrified her mind, focusing her attention and sharpening her mind. Carols felt her daughter smile, incandescent in joy despite her absent language skills. Then there was fire: intense, titanic temperatures. The spectacular speed, the lowered gravity, the unimaginable heat: it was an overload of excellence. In the explosion, the sense of joy evaporated as her tiny bodies shut down.

She felt her autonomic systems turn off; inputs all reconfigured to zilch. At least, temporarily... she knew that she had survived the explosion. She only had the vaguest understanding of the 'others', the ones who were studying her, but she was both shocked and astonished at the lengths to which they would go in order to test her extremes. That space shuttle couldn't have been easy to construct; she was inordinately honoured at the lengths these others would go to in order to learn about her.

Carols could definitely feel her daughter's mind, because the reactions she was feeling were not at all like her. She was enamoured by all of the attention, revelling in the abundance of sustenance and the sheer thrill of mobility. Yet, she was increasingly dissatisfied with the experience, and she could feel parts of the collectivity releasing from the whole. A winnowing was happening, a thinning of the ranks. It was an ominous presage of the same kind of giving up that she had felt her daughter feel when she had been a plant. Spread too thinly, taken from her home. *It couldn't be like that again now though*, she concluded. She didn't have a home. None of her countless millions of tiny bodies had ever set up a camp or base. The second form was all about learning to be nomadic and motile. Yet there was a distinct dilution, a diminishing that concerned her. She captured the query and forwarded it directly to Nat. It only took a moment for her to reply.

'Don't worry, this is perfectly natural. She will withdraw at her own pace. There is only so much she can learn here. She has been a lucky little nematode though, not many species in any form ever get to experience the joys of weightlessness. There are thirty thousand different species of them so far: and as you saw, they can exceed a million individuals per square metre. You might not be surprised to learn that *this* class alone accounts for three-quarters of all the individual animal life on *this* planet.' Carols felt her mind stretch, as she assimilated all that information. It was one thing *being* it: another altogether to think it into statistics.

Nat continued. 'Your baby is starting to disconnect now, which is, as I said, perfectly natural. What I want you to do now is simply wait, and watch. Feel the beauty of the experience; take the opportunity to examine what it means for you. She will sense that, and it will be the metaphoric light she returns to shortly for another taste of being embodied. Float, reflect and simply give thanks. Remain in a state of receptivity and relaxation. That is all you can do: but it is exactly what you need to do. I'd place good odds on the fact that next round you will be aquatic, and mothers always enjoy that. I'll leave you now, but of course, you're never alone, we're all in this together.'

Even though she was submerged in the immersive pools where her daughter was growing, she imagined she could hear the echoes of that last word bouncing around the planet, reflecting off each of the millions of her tiny wriggling *Caenorhabditis elegans* bodies. As the echoes faded into the distances of time and space, Carols was briefly filled with awe at what she was doing, she was excited and ready for more. The sensation of gravity dropped away, and she fell deeply into the evoking pools, feeling slightly better prepared to encounter the unknowns of Form Three.

CHAPTER 15
[A Good Day to be Born]

Meanwhile, in a distant arm of our galaxy, the exo-neural ghost of *Carols in Sequins* patiently waited. With everything already organised, there wasn't much to do except to wait. Physically, only the tiniest percentage of her total mass existed in bodies that orbited outside the fires of her blazing mind, but to distract herself, she examined the details of her body for the umpteenth time. Caught in the wake of her trajectory and safely enclosed within her egg-shaped magnetic fields trailed an enviable variety of concentrated matter. Her very own and very fragile menagerie, now very endangered.

Inside her own borders, she actually had far more body parts than most stellars, especially for someone so young. She boasted a full range of types: five planetoids, two gas giants, her musical comet, and many thousands of small rocky bodies. Eventually those smaller pieces would combine: crashing, colliding and coalescing. She had once hoped to capture sufficient helium to form another gas giant: but she didn't need to go future surfing to appreciate that those potential futures were no longer viable.

Projecting a golden filament of superheated plasma out into her trailing magnetic fields, she focused her attention on her outermost and largest body. Trailing her trajectory in a large slow loop, just past the orbit of her treasured comet, straggled a solitary Brown. A gas sphere large enough for fission, but lacking the fires of a mind, her Brown Dwarf had for a long time been simply collecting flotsam.

The mass of the Brown itself generated a gravity well that was sufficient to divert most debris that intersected her path too closely - so much so, that it now sported a stately set of rings. In a lazy languorous manner, each tiny piece of the debris danced through an obstacle course with the deceptive appearance of ballet-like precision, the disguise occasionally removed as minor asteroids in those rings collide violently. She found it meditative, entrancing.

Every kind of body part vibrates with a specific frequency, complex harmonics determined by the combinations of elements it contains. A clump of rocks heavy with iron isotopes provides a deep bass, complementing other fragments that resonate with the higher pitches of uranium or dilithium. From deep inside icy chunks, the irrepressibly reflective sounds of haptic memories add their unique vacuum-sealed harmonics.

Larger chunks, already combined from multiple collisions, emit dozens of notes, all vibrating together on a Möbius string. The tattoos of memories constantly flexing and pulsing against their atomic enclosures contributes a vibrato of perseverance, one that acts as a metronome for the entire symphony. A song that was about to get louder.

She knew that no matter what happened, those rings would soon be gone. Soon, the Brown's required physical mass would be met, the ingredients would finally be sufficient. The elusive kernel of fission would arrive, and a chain reaction would spread outwards like an unstoppable virulence. The delicate balance that the majestic collection of rings had been negotiating with gravity would be permanently disrupted.

In the very instant the fissioning kernel of mind tangled into the core of the Brown, an irresistible seed of compression would fuse together the elements that had sunk the deepest. Then, waves of heat and gravity and light would compound already squashed atoms, and vast banks of helium would be razed. Storms the size of small planetoids would erupt like bubbles in a turbulent ocean, bursting and spreading again.

Reflecting off earlier interference ripples, these new patterns would modify the tempo as they swept around, combining with massive hydrogen explosions to create a new degree of intense atomic friction. As quick as the process was, long before those waves of change reached the outer surface, every rock in the rings would be already expelled, absorbed or vaporised.

In the mantle of her terrestrial planets, recycled knots of iron resonated with echoes of births past etched on their cells. All the signs were good, she knew. Stellars moving adjacent to her, and more from right across the entire family were watching, reading the fluctuations like professionals. They knew too, that very soon a new stellar would burst into life.

Her precious old Brown would soon become a healthy young Red, and together they'd become a binary system.

Her closest sister had long thought it was about time, but maturely kept silent on the matter as they watched together. Their patience was hard to maintain, and they were justifiably excited. They had front row seats to an uncommon event: in their family, only a couple of new stellars were born each year. Soon, very soon, a brand new light would shine in the heavens. Not quite just yet though. For now, the baby was still dreaming.

CHAPTER 16

(The Hospital Reiteration)

Tommy had driven the ten kilometres operating on auto-pilot. His mother had suffered a heart attack overnight, but she was fine now. He'd walked as far as the car before realising he was still in his dressing-gown and slippers. As he drove, dressed in yesterday's jeans and a sweatshirt, with his feet hastily slipped sockless into a pair of sneakers he found near the door, he reached out to place his hand on his mother's journal. Not wanting it to slide out of reach, he'd picked it up and placed it between his legs for the rest of the drive.

Arriving at what must have been the change of morning shift, he found a much closer parking space than usual. But once he turned off the engine, he just sat there. He'd never seen the building from this angle before, never appreciated the hive of activity from this vantage point. People were bustling over the road-bridge above, and crossing at the pedestrian lights below at the same time, while over to the right, the lights of the ambulance in the driveway were flashing. There was a lot of activity at the Accident & Emergency entrance. Nurses and paramedics busted around a patient on a stretcher, who was being wheeled inside even while an IV stand was still being attached to the trolley. He wasn't squeamish about blood and injury, but even so, he preferred not to see it.

Eventually, he stirred himself into action. He had to force himself to conquer an unexpectedly powerful call of inertia, holding him in his seat. Part of him wanted to believe that he was still asleep, that all of this was a dream. It simply was too anomalous, an idea that didn't fit with what he knew of the world. Or of his mother. Even though he knew he wouldn't be able to see her window from where he sat, he looked in that direction anyway. If the front building wasn't there, he'd be able to count the three windows in from the right on the fourth floor and know exactly where she was.

That was the motivation he needed. He carefully locked the car and nursed the journal under the jacket in his armpit. As he walked, he mentally went through what he had read: in the journal and then online this morning. He hadn't finished the whole journal; he still had a few pages to go. The first section of it had been the diary of his mother as a teenage girl, recounting the strange events of the last month as she remembered them. After a couple of months though, the entries changed. Rather than private writing to her diary, the entries were addressed directly to her Uncle Justin. She seemed to have picked up on the idea that she was going to see him again, that he was going to come back into her life.

His mother's words echoed in his head, taking him back to his childhood. *If life wasn't mysterious, we'd be bored pretty quickly,* she'd say, with his father nodding agreement in the background. *Things happen, my darling, for reasons we might not ever be able to understand,* she'd add. His dad had always been ready with chores waiting to be done, in case the plaintive cry 'I'm bored' was heard. He had become the same, reproducing their belief that boredom was never an acceptable option. As a parent, he came to understand the wisdom in that statement. Unfortunately, wisdom is not something that can be readily imparted to the young. It simply has to be gained through experience. Learn through action, grow through activity, just keep yourself busy – a motto he lived by example. There were always chores and domestics: tasks to keep idle hands occupied. He wondered briefly if living forever would ever become boring, and couldn't believe his mother had the chance to actually ask such a question. *Perhaps people who bored easily wouldn't be interested in immortality anyway,* he mused. Motivated to ask her, he quickened his pace.

Nodding at the now-familiar faces staffing the news agency and the coffee shop, he made his way to the lifts. The large public art display on the wall opposite the lifts was in the process of being changed yesterday, but he'd hardly paid any attention. His mind had been off in the clouds - or 'up with the stars', as his mother had always put it. He'd never read the subtext to that expression before, but now he saw it in a new light. The feature wall now sported nearly two dozen pictures: the competition winners from all the local primary schools. He stopped briefly to peruse the installation, admiring the use of colour and textures, wondering if he was seeing the first exhibition by some future famous artist.

Neither of their two kids had shown any innate artistic talent, although as dutiful parents Jackson and Claire's efforts had always been rewarded with a position on the cluttered fridge door. Apparently, Tommy's niece Danielle was quite the painter, studying art at a college over East. It was nice to know that the creativity that flowed through his blood had found an outlet in the next generation. Jackson was far more analytical than Tommy was, always over-thinking; while younger Claire had simply never seen the need to express herself in that way. She had taken to dance classes as a girl, and although Gloria said that counted as creative expression, he'd bitten his tongue. It might be a male thing, or a farm-upbringing thing, but he preferred to see something physical as a result of creative effort. He liked an outcome. But as long as she was healthy and happy, he was satisfied.

The lift bell chimed, bringing him back from his reverie. He squeezed into the lift, which was packed, despite being large enough to take a hospital bed with all the ancillary attachments that accompany it. He didn't recognise any of the faces as he joined the anonymous crowd. The doors slid shut, and the silence of strangers settled peacefully onto his fellow passengers. As he glanced around the lift, only an elderly man in a rumpled tan overcoat made eye contact with him and smiled, nodding his head in greeting. As he nodded back politely and tried not to breathe in the terrible unwashed smell, he was caught in a thought: who exactly was the soul he'd just made contact with?

Sometimes it had been hard maintaining the principles he and Gloria had tried to instil in their kids. They both believed that human dignity and respect were best taught by example. His office wall bore a plaque bearing a quote of Plato: 'Be kind, for everyone you meet is fighting a hard battle.' It had become the idea behind 'Imagine Their Story': a family game which encouraged the kids to see the human being behind the homeless person, to look beyond the unkempt hair and tattered clothes to see someone's child, someone's brother, someone's friend. It also served to bond their family unit and to develop their imaginations. Sometimes conditioning could be fun, too. Now as he glanced around the lift and tentatively started to play the game on his own, he thought back over what he had read last night.

According to Katherine, or at least according to her Uncle Justin, every living thing on the planet was a dreaming baby star. Before it was born, each star needed to learn all about dying. In order to acquire the skills necessary to be able to survive eternity, each mind was grown here on Earth. The planet was a haptic womb for the Universe, the source of life for stellar society: the pool in which billions or trillions of stellar gestates were growing. Growing in levels, cycling through different forms of skill-set acquisition: ones that by necessity and definition could only be learnt within mortal bodies. It wasn't a matter of death before life, but death over and over and over again. As a plant, as a bird, as a mammal, as a human, they would learn how to metabolise, to move, to share, to think. They'd learn all the things a baby eternal would need, a deadly preparatory process before being born into a vast and vibrant stellar society.

Tommy supposed that just as a fish didn't know it was learning flotation and navigation skills, many of the lessons that human beings learn are similarly acquired without awareness. Teaching offspring morality and respect was good for them, and also a good skill for a parent, he acknowledged, thinking how such a skill could probably be applied to scenarios far beyond what his imagination could create. Tommy wondered what skill or lesson he was going through now. Improving his patience, perhaps? Reinforcing or challenging his integrity? He didn't know.

As he looked around the anonymous faces he shared the lift with, he wondered about each of their stories. What lesson was the man in the tan coat acquiring? What skill was the orderly learning? What experience was the young man in the wheelchair gaining through having two broken legs? He thought back over his mother's idea: if you're alive, then you have lessons to learn, things to do. From a parental point of view, he could see the merit in it. Ensuring that a new-born has survival skills, and then staggering those lessons into stages made sense. The human new-born was entirely dependent, whereas throughout the animal kingdom, new-born young of many species had remarkable survival skills. He'd seen

Attenborough documentaries where baby turtles born prematurely are able to survive being entirely frozen; or species where eggs are left to hatch without any parental supervision.

As the lift emptied at the floor below his stop, a nurse pushed in a very elderly man in a wheelchair, all hooked up to tubes and wires. The veins in his skin were prominent; the faded tattoo that once undoubtedly adorned a strong forearm now seemed to be a translucent patch helping to hold his skin together. He appeared to be sedated, and the nurse distracted. Tommy had to force himself not to stare. *What about this man?* he thought. *What lesson can he possibly be learning in that state? Is this undignified existence necessary for someone else's growth, perhaps?* He found that a little distasteful. But what if it was him, and Claire needed to learn patience, or consideration, or respect? He supposed that even a decade of senility was a drop in the ocean compared to eternity, and he knew without a doubt, that he'd do anything for his kids. Absolutely anything.

CHAPTER 17

[Form Three: It's a Krill, Krill Life]

The notion of personal space was sacrosanct, and as she slowly sank, the intensity of her feelings surprised her. Carols quelled her autonomic responses and focused on her breathing. Ever so slowly: in, and then out. She felt her pulse relax as she let go of her own preconceptions, and released herself to the moment.

The invisible membrane that encased her felt impossibly thin, but her substance was only a construct of her own thoughts. If she chose to have no discernible form at all, she could. The manifestation of physical form in a virtual immersive format was only inhibited by her imagination. Nevertheless, Carols held to the custom of maintaining an egg-shaped personal space, delineated by a barrier constructed solely of her own expectations. As she surrendered to the heat, she could feel her own meniscus disintegrating, distorted and twisted into an unfamiliar phase. She deliberately lost focus on what she was actually doing; she had to ignore her own body. After all, it was all in her mind. She waited, breathing slowly, floating in the heat. Waiting, patiently.

She waited to feel the connection. She had quite enjoyed the first manifestation, even if it had finished a little tragically. Although it hadn't been spelt out, she felt it had been implied that the vitality of the new life depended on all of the experiences it assimilated each lesson, not just the skill-sets it gained. She wanted to scream encouragement at every frequency, so loud that her fledgling gestate would simply have to hear her, so that she would know that it was all going to be okay, that she was being watched over and cared for and treasured. But she couldn't. She could only watch, and wait, and give thanks. There was nothing to be gained by going over what was past, she had to focus on a more uplifting outcome for the next round.

Form Two had been a fairly easy introduction to mobility and navigation. There were trillions of species like microbes and nematodes that filled the atomic-sized gaps between buried particles of dirt and soil. An abundance of physical life:

biological, corporeal, mobile forms of life that were completely invisible to the rest of the flora and fauna on the planet. She hadn't expected it to be too hard; after all, it was only one step up from the basic 'Introduction to Survival' of Form One, when she'd been a plant. A simple old plant, or so she had thought at first. Again she tried not to think about the statistical rarity of her baby manifesting as carnivorous. She focused on her breathing, letting go of distracting thoughts. Her midwife had said there was no reason to read anything into that particular corporealisation; rather she could treasure the uniqueness, as if it forebode a particularly special life being born. She liked that, it augured nicely.

Carols could feel her. Or smell her, or something. Her baby wasn't something that she could physically see yet, but she could definitely sense her. She had returned. She had come back for another taste of life, another round in the lessons leading to full sentience. Her baby didn't consciously realise that yet, but for Carols it was enormously reassuring to sense her return, all ready for another round. Another step, another stage. Two down: but rather than thinking on how far she, or rather, how far *they* had yet to go, she gave thanks for the moment, and mentally reached out to her daughter. Together, more intimately entwined than imaginable for corporeal life, they moved together.

She was submerged, but fragmented. The waters were warm around her. She could feel herself distributed, spread thin, shared beyond what she could seemingly manipulate. Her consciousness felt too disseminated; she was a little dizzy. There were so very many of her; a living swarm of her, twitching and pulsing to a beat she couldn't quite yet hear. She was cruising the currents. In search of prey, the first half of a two-step dance.

She (rather in the plural: they) also had to avoid predators. Predators much larger than she was; or than they were. She couldn't really think of herself as an individual, the lines seemed blurry, out of focus. She panned back for perspective and caught a glimpse of her totality: a writhing throng of translucence. Now that she could see the whole, she could factor in ratios and comparative factors. She tasted the salinity and depths of the waters. Adjusting for visibility distortions, she zoomed back in.

And she had to zoom again. She was very small. Well, the individual units of her were small – no more than a centimetre or two long. Each body was covered in an exoskeleton, and was equipped with external gills, antennae, compound eyes and multiple sets of legs. Carols wasn't familiar with this kind of species, she had nothing like it in her menagerie. She decided to test her operational parameters.

First, she sent out a warning thought, testing instinctive defensive mechanisms. She felt herself enfolding, cuddling up and clasping closer to her selves. Tens of thousands of her bodies squeezed into each square meter of ocean and huddled in a tight defensive scrum, providing stronger protection against predation. Impressed, she sent an all clear, and both her mind and the mass of her bodies responded. She felt her entire being relax.

Now she was starting to get more of an idea about what the midwife had said about how the proto-consciousness field of the sentience generators would develop a personal yoke, an intimate link. She couldn't see that this would be difficult to break; she thought the scenario pretty dull and unchallenging. Then again, she didn't have a water ocean on any of her moons, let alone a populated one.

Populated yes, but only with mindless components: shards of a whole that itself had no consciousness. There was no sentience here, no purpose, and no direction. It just was feeding and breeding: instinctual stuff only. Boring. She reminded herself that this was an early lesson, that cognitive skill-sets would necessarily come later. For now, all she had to do was concentrate, nurture the connection with this precious embryonic mind, and to encourage balanced growth. She put aside her frustrations and ennui, and took time out to have a better look around at where she was. She/they were in a vast temperate ocean, with a plentiful banquet of sustenance all around her.

She could feel individual parts of her eating, developing instincts, learning to consume available nutrients and process them. She could feel parts of her growing, shedding layers of her chitinous exoskeletons, flexing her gills and breathing in colour. She noticed she had photophores, which were new. Each tiny body was covered in complex lenses connected to focusing muscles that bio-luminesced when they moved, so that each of her tiny bodies could flash luminescent glows in a mesmerising display of vibrancy. She felt herself move through her swarm, activating photophores in all of her individual members as she passed nearby, tasting the waters and getting a more tangible feel of her aquatic hosts. The photophores on her individual bodies could flash in surprisingly complex patterns, and she belatedly recognised her child was starting to acquire introductory communication skills. Carols thought back to her recent mating season, and found that strangely, the memory existed as part of the package.

Although her consciousness was strewn, scattered amongst the whole of the swarm, Carols found she could still think clearly, or at least without too much hindrance, if she dissociated. She reflected on what she had been told about the levels and different stages of growth that all stellar gestates went through. As she watched repeated sheddings of adolescent exoskeletons, she couldn't help but wonder if the life cycle of her current host reflected the levels of development lying ahead. She watched with bemused detachment as her neonates ate their way into adulthood. There were a lot of sheddings; each of her tiny elements went through at least four rounds of development before they reached even a basic reproductive maturity. She set about analysing her morphology; a well-used distraction routine that helped her mind to settle.

Her exoskeleton was tripartite, although the head and thorax were fused. Her chitinous integument was transparent: she had a shell that was solid, but it didn't hide internal organs away from sight. Each of her had several pairs of legs attached to her thorax, and each pair had different usages: she had grooming legs, swimming legs, and feeding legs. They all dangled beneath her, moving to the gentle rocking of the ocean, filtering algae and diatoms into the set of finely combed gaps that comprised her mouth. Phytoplankton and unicellular species comprised her diet; she absorbed and processed the miniscule algae of the seas into her bodies. Eventually, she too would become food for larger animals, ones that couldn't survive on the plankton diet she found quite sufficient.

Carols recognised the role of converter: in her menagerie she had similar creatures that were just as an integral part of the food chain. But that didn't mean she just had to sit there, eating algae and then being eaten. She could move and she could hunt. Admittedly her prey was copepods and zooplankton: hardly challenging. Exploring, she found that her omnivorousness covered all forms of algae, but it was the taste of fish eggs she loved the most. She could chase, she could move, she could devour; moreover, she was thriving in a garden of plenty. It would soon be breeding season again. She could feel the females among her, heavily laden with eggs, ready to spawn, some of them carrying thousands of eggs in a sac that weighed up to one third of their body weight. She was very fertile, but she was in no hurry. Life was good.

Food was plentiful, the waters were warm and nutritious, and the cycles of day and night passed with a mesmerising regularity. When the first of her female bodies released a cache of fertilised eggs into the waters, the others all quickly followed. The waters were soon awash in eggs, which sank and dispersed on their own. Independent from the start, they would hatch into the first of five stages of growth, carrying only the vaguest of genetic guidance to instruct them on how to filter food, how to move, to grow, to survive. Each miniscule body carried the scent of all that she had already been; a hint of memory yet to bloom into personality, but there nonetheless. Carols admired the tiny clusters of the earlier stage babies, banks of nauplius and psuedometanauplius bodies, flexing their legs, and stretching towards the plankton all around them. She felt flooded with maternal feelings for each of her myriad offspring.

With the dispersal of the next generation, the swarm had grown significantly in size and density. The newest members had internal yolks to sustain them while they grew, but giving birth had left their mothers hungry. The light from the surface called to them, promising sustenance. The cycles of rising to the surface and sinking again became lulling; she grew comfortable and complacent in repetition. Empty stomachs travel to the surface, full stomachs sank below: a vertical migration that happened a couple of times each day. At night she would sink down lower, to reduce energy activity and to digest her meal. She was far less vulnerable to surface predators during the dark, but her post-spawning mother selves were famished. The sun shone brightly and instincts over-ruled logic, especially one that was held only tenuously by a dispersed rationality. The swarm rose.

Carols could see what might happen, how dangerous it was for her to be there, but she couldn't over-ride: she could only go along with it, hoping for the best. It was not to be. The density of her swarm seemed to have a wave function of its own, calling out to other animals. Her density screamed 'Eat Me!' to fish and birds alike. From mammalian predators near the surface, she had nowhere to hide as the attack began. Tens of thousands of her moulted instantaneously as the feeding frenzy commenced, leaving empty exuvia, shells as decoys and distractions, but the schools of fish were not dissembled. They moved much faster than her humble crustacean bodies possibly could, darting here and there to capture her multitude. She could feel birds swooping down and picking her up out of the water; she could feel penguins crossing the air/aqua divide and devour her aplenty. She was getting thinner, her mass was reducing.

She could feel her mind speeding up, as if an oceanic sedative was being removed. She wondered if it was related to the numbers in her species, whether a collective consciousness would find coherence in its final embodied moments. If she was dispersed and her neural pathways distributed across the whole of her incarnation, would the final tiny creature have a sense of consistency, of rationality and memory perhaps? She thought about asking the midwife, but then decided it could wait until after this level was complete. She looked back around her, astonished at her diminished numbers. She tried to message her selves to coalesce, to come together again, but there were so few. They were spread out, shaken and scared into hiding. But there was nowhere to hide.

Eventually, in the cool deep waters, her remaining selves came together. Safe from the ravenous fish and crafty birds, it was much colder. She was still a swarm, and although she felt smaller she was also aware that she was larger. She was now more than just one swarm, but she kept her attention focused on the main body huddled together. She was glad she did, as the others gradually vanished from her neural radar. She floated with them and shared a mindless gratefulness for the simple pleasure of a full stomach.

She wondered what to do with her little brood. She could start reproducing again. She wasn't limited to one batch per year. She was familiarising herself with her baby swarm, her left-over batch of baby crustacea, when something changed in the water. There was ominousness: a new, unknown threat she couldn't put any of her legs on. She huddled tight, the remaining few hundreds of her bodies cuddling together for security. If she hadn't done that, she mused later, she might've survived.

The waters moved. There was a rush, a confluence of currents, a flowing drain of inter-aquatic streams. A gurgling and falling of waters caught her up in the turbulence. She was rolled over, beaten down, disoriented and discombobulated, but she remained tight in her huddle. The few remaining of her pre-adults that hadn't shed their exuvia did so now in a final flush of instinctual panic. It made no difference; they didn't know which way to go. It was out of their control, they just held on for dear life. *En masse* they were tumbled, tossed and turned in the waters, only to find themselves and their empty shells sucked into the gaping maw of an enormous whale as it passed on its journey, unaware it had just devoured the final few individual krill of a now extinct species of Euphausiacea.

CHAPTER 18
(The Graduation Trigger)

At the next floor the lift doors opened and Tommy followed the nurse as she wheeled the old man back to his room. Everything seemed so normal, so run-of-the-mill; he'd forgotten that it was only he who had changed overnight. The wind continued to blow, the world spun on and people around him moved according to their own priorities, uninterested in his mother's heart attack or the contents of her journal, tightly held under his arm. As he walked down the almost empty corridor he glanced into other rooms, sometimes seeing other patients, but more often, just seeing the hanging sheets drawn, separating beds. He gave thanks that his mother wasn't in one of the larger rooms, where the semblance of privacy was cotton-thin.

'Mr Robertson?' He heard a voice call his name from a room on his left and he turned to see a familiar face pulling back the curtains from the front bed. He smiled indulgently. No matter how many times he asked Martine to call him Tom, she insisted on a level of professionalism at work. Martine had been a family friend and neighbour for many years, she had even babysat his kids on occasion. He liked the fact that his mother had a familiar face working the same ward she was recuperating in; it provided a degree of personalisation. When he'd first found her at the nurses' station and escorted her down to say hello to his Ma, he had expected his mother to insist on being called Katie. Instead she had silently acknowledged the 'Mrs Robertson' with a subtle smile, and he'd been reminded again of what a great judge of character his mother was.

'Martine, good to see you. Especially this morning, hmm?' He nodded up the corridor towards his mother's room.

'It's good to see you too Mr Robertson. Glad I'm on the morning shift.' She hesitated, as if evaluating her words carefully. 'It was only a mild attack, and she's fine now. In fact, last time I stuck my head in she was napping, but you can go right on in. The doctors will be around at about eleven o'clock.' She smiled, and looked like she wanted to say more, to offer personal support to a friend perhaps, but from the room she'd just left came a cry, pulling her back to work. Tommy knew that she had to attend to her patients long before that 'Nurse?' became a '*NURSE!*' With an apologetic smile she turned and withdrew, slipping into the less well-lit nooks where convalescent demands awaited.

'Eleven?' he muttered. It was only just before eight o'clock.

He continued up the corridor caught in his thoughts, almost bumping into a woman carrying empty breakfast trays out to her trolley. He knew that people brought up in cities had a different sense of personal space than their country-raised relatives, and wondered what sort of personal space an eternal might have. He wondered what his mum would think of that one, and once more smiled with the realisation that he had accepted her tale.

Taking a deep, calming breath, he rapped lightly on the door. He registered the enormous smile on her face before he noticed that her eyes were closed. He stood reverently at the end of her bed, watching her sleep, amazed at her smile. Then he plonked himself down in the padded chair. He was happy to sit. There was a nice courtyard in the centre of this wing, and the rooms had large windows that let in lots of natural light.

Sitting in the stock-standard hospital chair, he could watch the flows of activity on the ground floor. Currently, he could see groups of nursing staff on their breaks, chatting and eating at three of the five nooks set around the path. He liked to sit, and to watch. It was nice to pretend that everything was fine, to get lost in the imaginary worlds he'd make up for the people he could see. So he was happy, just watching life's rhythms move around him. He found that daydreaming let him immerse himself in normality, even if part of him knew it was a vicarious distraction. There was nothing normal about what his mother had told him, or about what she had written.

It felt a little strange, sitting and watching over such an indomitable matriarch; hence he had moved the chair to the window position. The traditional parent-child roles temporarily reversed, he imagined the number of times she would have kept vigil over him in his youth. Probably more than he had experienced as a parent; he knew that he and

Claire had been very lucky. His baby sister had not been so blessed, and the constant hospital admissions had become a lifestyle for her and her boy. He and his sisters had all been healthy children, but even so, he appreciated that part of the job of being a parent was to worry. To sit and watch over their sleeping child, praying and hoping for the best. It was a parent's job to dream up positive outcomes and happy futures.

Recalling something he'd read, he pulled out his mother's journal and looked at it, holding it like a precious object. It was old, but it had been cared for. He opened it to where he'd left his bookmark, and skimmed forward to see how much he had left to read. Glancing at his dozing mother, he hoped he'd have the chance to finish it before she woke. He wriggled into the chair getting comfortable, and returned to the tale. He flipped through pages to find the journal entry he recalled. It was one she had written not long after his own birth.

Tuesday August 10, 1946

As I nursed my firstborn this afternoon, I couldn't help but think about this new fragment of a star I was holding. I wonder what kinds of experiences this mind has already been through. How did he learn to breathe, and to blink? What kind of creature was he when he acquired communication skills? Were any of his lessons traumatic, or difficult? And of course, what kind of challenges will he experience this round? How can I help?

Then a new thought struck me. I wondered if what happens to this child is part of my lessons? I suppose it is. What can I do to help this soul to bloom? How do I teach this child what I know and yet honour my oath? How will I answer questions about God, or about the meaning of life?

Thinking about it, I'm actually sure that learning the answers to those questions is part of my lesson. Or at least, another lesson. There are always lessons, he said. Always. Actually, I can still remember his words exactly, so I will write them down here too. He said, 'Lessons never stop. As long as you're alive there are lessons to learn, skills to develop, examples to be.' I never really understood the last bit, but I do now. I am an example to this child, a role model of being. It is up to me to be a good example. So I guess every day I will be giving a kind of testimony through my own actions.

So for this child's sake, and for my own sake too I guess, I promise to be a good example. I'm going to do what I can to teach this child about the sanctity of life - without ever breaking my promise. I can never tell anyone what happened. But I've written it down, and so far so good. I've kept my secret, my promise. But now, well I'm responsible for someone else too. Another life. A baby, but it's still a precious soul, another dreaming star here to learn a bunch of new things.

Wouldn't it be wonderful if, after I've learnt and been everything I'm here for, and I've moved up, so that I'm wearing a star, or I am a star, living in a flash new body made of light, wouldn't it be lovely if my journal is found and read by this child I helped bring into this world in the first place? That'd be nice. That the person who learns about my story turns out to be my little Thomas.

I just hope that day is far, far away.

At the sound of his mother stirring he looked up. She was smiling, of course. He smiled himself, flushed with love from what he'd just read. She was such an amazing woman, so determined, and almost compulsively happy.

'You want me to tell the nurses you're cultivating viruses in here?' he asked.

Getting up from his chair, he immediately resolved to get his ten-speed racer out of the shed where it was gathering cobwebs. He needed to lose some of the extra weight he had gained recently. *It oughtn't be this difficult to simply get out of a chair,* he thought. With the ease of practice, he brushed the thought away, deliberately ignoring the little voice in his head that sometimes chastised his state of health. *My health could be better,* he acknowledged. *But I can still be grateful, it could be a lot worse.* With these self-assurances he ignored his conscience, his aching body and his mother, whose gaze could settle onto him with a weight far heavier than his spreading gut. It didn't this time though. Her smile spread wide when she put on her spectacles.

'Hello darling, I wasn't expecting you till this afternoon.'

Raising an insouciant eyebrow he replied, 'I can come back later if you like,' and they both laughed. He moved the chair over, eager to pick her brain. He'd even scribbled a list of questions, notes he'd made earlier that morning while researching. Her eyes lit up as he passed over the journal, delivering it with a kiss to her forehead. He went to sit back down when he heard someone clear their throat, and was surprised to see an orderly entering the room.

'Time for an x-ray Mrs Robertson', the blue-clad orderly said. They nodded politely at one another.

Tom had seen that his mother quickly pulled up the blanket, covering her journal from sight. After such a surreptitious move, he decided not to ask if he could keep reading it while she was down at radiology. He knew she'd be a while. His tummy growled, and he decided to wander down to the cafeteria, to see if he could find anything that looked appetising.

CHAPTER 19

<u><Tales of Devotion></u>

Watching over the babies had become Nat's life. If the mothers she helped were princesses, she guessed that made her the ultimate fairy godmother; or perhaps a seraphim, guiding each of the guardian angels with their precious charges.

But she knew the difference between reality and a dream. So few stellars even knew what a true dream was. No sentient mind in the cosmos actually slept, except for her charges, the proto-minds under her care, and technically they only counted as semi-sentients. But to her, they were still very much alive. Sometimes even she forgot that they weren't fully functional, interactive beings. Babies without a doubt: but they were still coherent individual minds. Children taking their first steps at exploring a cosmos they had yet to be born into. Once they acquired the skill-sets they needed, they could die for the final time.

She had long ago found the process of dreaming a fascinating concept. As a stellar, she had no more need of sleep than she did of dreaming. She remembered when she first heard about the idea, at an information session held for all of the PreyData © crew. Back when the unusual properties of Light-Lite had been discovered, the crew playing with mortality immersives had all been offered positions at the newly formatted Academy. While many of the thanotechs or mortality technicians had chosen to stay involved with mortality adventures, everyone had still been invited to familiarise themselves with the changes. There had been a plethora of specialities and conferences to attend: mostly optional, occasionally incomprehensible. Nat's early involvement with PreyData © had been a mainly administrative role, but it had given her access to a wide variety of meetings.

Before Population One stellars figured out reproduction, many spent time in immersives or distracted by games, the most popular of which was PreyData ©. Pronounced Predator, any stellar could create a foreseeable predatory species and inhabit it, or the body of its prey, and experience death. Such a tantalising vicarious situation for an immortal, the phenotypic varieties and imaginative variability quickly filled the landmasses and oceans. The game was created and played upon a little-used frequency of light called Light-Lite, which was later discovered to have a unique connection to the evoked pools of sentience. It was these pools where new and potential mental fragments coagulated. Considering the importance of reproduction to stellar society, it was annexed and re-marketed as Death ©, or the Academy of Death ©, where you go to have a baby. Pop One stellars hadn't known back then that babies need to conquer death before they are born: that becoming immortal was a necessarily fatal process.

When she thought back to those early fateful meetings, she couldn't help but be overwhelmed with appreciation of the serendipitous nature of existence. If she had never attended that dreaming symposium, she might never have met *Zest as Breccia.* Or have become one of the Orphans, or ever ended up as a midwife, overseeing the gestation of new generations of stellar sentience. It seemed like such a long while ago – which was fair enough. From her perspective, it had been a couple of lifetimes ago. But some memories are strong, possessing a preternatural puissance all of their own. She could still clearly remember that session.

The auditorium had been surprisingly packed. It looked like almost the entire corpus of thanotechs had attended. It was certainly more popular than any of the other sessions she had attended. Her official role of administrative auditor didn't' require her to be overly familiar with the technical side of things. Yet she had always enjoyed being thorough; she didn't think you could ever have too much information. Certainly the mediation side of her job required her to know the difference between a precursor algorithm and autonomic biological processes, but the in-depth understanding of the programming that those specialists lived and breathed was well beyond both her professional remit and her personal interests.

The whole concept of autonomic *sub*-conscious processes reminded her of the exo-neural ghosts that had become so popular. A beta-copy of herself, designed to supplement and process extraneous experiences. How or where *Demisting as Acapulco* had come up with the idea of joining that style of semi-externalised processing with that of a mammalian nocturnal recharge was beyond her. Forcing gestating minds to experience an extended cyclic immersion into unconsciousness seemed to be contra-indicatory. After all, wasn't the goal to generate consciousness? She had touched the hyperlink in the briefing, where the dream synopsis was only slightly elaborated. She still wanted to learn more. This simple phenomenon used the most basic step-by-step premise: a newly forming mind needed to master basic skills before moving onto more advanced ones. That seemed natural enough.

The first half of the lessons elicited cohesion and confidence while imprinting survival skills. The second half of the birthing procedure concentrated and compounded those skills, generating individuality – something impossible without the earlier lessons. That made sense. Yet apparently this blossoming of individuality and maturing of sentience was to be restrained? Their babies were to be compelled to obey the compulsions of mammalian life, in order to stimulate further growth? As she looked around the seminar room, she gathered that these sorts of questions were probably on the minds of many others. As the walls of the sphere darkened and the central dais lit up from below with a muted white glow, she felt the anticipation levels in the auditorium reach a tipping point.

She could see that their illustrious guest now sported more blue dots on her visage. When *Demisting as Acapulco* could have found the opportunity to reproduce again was puzzling. Nat knew that everyone working on the conversion – stellars from both the old PreyData © games and those in the new Academy of Death © teams - were all flat out making the necessary adjustments. The war was getting worse too. Everyone throughout the cosmos was in a hurry to implement the Academy. Although news had spread, there remained an obstinate aggressive few who continued to deny the possibility, ridiculing the very idea that new life could ever be triggered through a process of mortality. Madness seemed to be contagious and unpredictable. Nat had some troublesome neighbours herself, so she was possibly more determined than your average thanotech.

Although the existential rebellion had begun at the outer edges, all of stellar society had been susceptible. Initially it was believed that distance and solitude had triggered the first few novae, but the shambolic spread of depression had been increasingly linked to the ongoing failure for any solitary or group of stellars to master reproduction. With each experimental research team's seemingly inevitable announcements of disappointment, the number of stellars triggering their own demise had increased. The explosions coloured the cosmos with a fertilising storm of novae. So the theory now went that once the opportunity to reproduce was shown to be genuine, there would be no more denial; moreover – no more reason to fight. Nor, importantly, would there be any reason to ever be alone.

Each stellar was to carry the next generation inside their own bodies. Made up of their constituent parts, an instinctive imperative to nurture was expected to compound, and demand an increasing amount of energy. A path long thought unpassable would open up, a whole new axis and direction would be added to stellar trajectories. The future was visibly displayed on *Demisting as Acapulco's* body: glittering blue X's sparkled in her swirling gases. She was no longer alone, per se. No longer celebrating the gala of life with her stellar sisters, she had become plural: a galaxy. The individual sparks of blue *Demisting as Acapulco* had given birth to were mesmerising. What they represented was not only the future, but an end to war and death. Future generations would get death over and done with before they were born. Nat's daydreaming stopped as their illustrious guest speaker took the stage.

'Greetings! And a hearty thanks to each and every one of you all for coming. This appears to be the biggest crowd yet – I am forced to wonder where were you for my other sessions? Weren't you interested in Exophilic Biology or Pre-sentient Dispersed Consciousness? You know that they too were open to you all, right?'

Her self-deprecating humour spread like a wave, and the audience tittered in amusement. Almost all of the information sessions had been open to all, and the ones that hadn't been were those fiddling with the Light-Lite framework, securing the frequency for exclusive use. All other research projects that had been using the PreyData © immersive had been terminated. Despite the reasoning and exciting implications, not all of those researchers had been happy about it. *Sadly, some minds are only ever happy when they are disgruntled*, Nat thought.

'Today I am going to discuss what I think was the core difference between my ideas and those of other researchers. As I am sure you know, in many ways my own applications were not that different from many other sentience research teams, some of which were also being attempted inside PreyData ©. Many of those utilised the staggered growth process, whereby skillsets are laid down in levels or stages, because we can see the logic in it displayed throughout the futures. It is in the simple repetition of patterns we see not only in flora and fauna but in weather patterns, navigation logs and family shapes. Many have remarked that such commonalities reflect designs left by Zero, but I am not here to discuss theology.'

Mention of their common ancestor's name was usually done so reverently, and Nat was impressed at how smoothly *Demisting as Acapulco* moved the presentation along.

'Our earlier experiments created minds that lacked the strength to cope with the full force of sentience. No matter how many prior stages were inserted, they continued to burn out. My idea of continuing a mammalian nocturnal cycle into the semi-sentience stage turned down the metaphorical heat. Just the tiniest bit, but it turned out to be enough; and I will admit, it surprised me enormously. I had quite anticipated the gestate to need another level of full sentience before transferral out of the immersive nursery and into stellar society.

Now I am going to presume some level of familiarity with the principles of suppressed nocturnal sensory activity, and the role that it plays in maintaining biophysical functioning in many species. The genetic role that suppressed physical activity plays is well understood, directly related as it is to both the growth and the rejuvenation of skeletal and muscular systems. For those species with immune and nervous systems, they similarly recharge and grow during a regular anabolic state, as anomalous or contradictory as it might appear. It turns out, therein was the answer: it was the regular suppression of *an active mental state* that generates the cognitive stability we have been looking for. The missing element in what we had been dreaming of, was dreaming itself.

When the gestate sleeps during the sixth form, the same biophysical processes that govern sleeping in the preceding stages also occur. During stages four and five, the gestate is moving from the dispersed collective consciousness levels into a coherent self-contained body. The skills acquired during those incarnations are expanded, built upon and added to. Now, note that Form Four gestates don't necessarily require sleep to learn those lessons, but nonetheless many reptiles, birds and amphibians still experience this process.

In Form Five, all gestates are incarnated as mammals: all of whom sleep, and it is also there that the concept of self is introduced. Some of these lifeforms also taste-test the dreaming world, or what I like to think of as a communal dreaming library. Without the language skills or self-referential cognitive framework of a Form Six mind, those dreams are very basic. These subconscious processes are actually precursors of memory consolidation, but operate primarily as mental playgrounds for rehearsing potentially threatening scenarios. The removal of undeveloped sensory impressions and the ratification of contradictory input: all very basic stuff. At least, from our perspective. Nonetheless these act as foundations, stepping stones on which Form Six gestates can build. It was this reasoning that led me to experiment with blending sentience in, gradually and slowly.

Form Six gestates will be exposed to the same kinds of confusing sensory impressions and parasitic node development that any Form Five dreaming involves, but with far greater complexity. Hierarchy and social interactivity is increased. Tool use is expanded enormously. Not forgetting the philosophical conundrums, the spiritual and intellectual paradoxes that we see imparted in Introductory Future Surfing lessons. In retrospect, it is no surprise that moving straight into full sentience was simply too much of an overload for a developing mind. Keeping this cyclic filtering process in place appears to be the necessary dampener that enables the gestate to maintain cohesion.

Considering the enormous challenges posed in moving from a vague sense-of-self into full-time sentience, again, it ought to be no surprise that for humans, sleeping and dreaming are far more complicated processes than anything they experienced as a mammal, bird or reptile. As a general rule. I cannot emphasise this enough: it is a general rule, which means there are exceptions. While the vividness of REM sleep is specific to humans, I do expect to see some savant gestates experiencing REM visions during Form Five. While all mammals dream, some will dream more prolifically than even a Sixth Former.' She paused, scanning the audience.

'I wish to impress the importance of catering for those exceptions, remembering that by definition those mammals will be comparatively rare. Some of my earlier experiments extrapolated and expanded the REM experience back down into form five: to generally disappointing results. However there will still be peccadillos and armadillos: some mammals will dream more intensely than even a human. Exceptions are part of Zero's infinite diversity quest, right? It's appropriate, I think, that even our dreaming stars are creating greater diversity. Perhaps it's their own form of moving >AWAY<. It's all good, it all balances.'

As the audience started to titter, the speaker paused for a moment, allowing attention to return. 'As with many aspects of Form Six, the process of dreaming is riddled with paradoxes. Oxygen consumption by the brain is higher than when the dreamer is actually awake. During REM dreaming, neural electrical activity is almost at the same levels of the waking state, yet the sleeping dreamer is much less easily woken than during non-dreaming sleep phases. Cyclic secretions of the biochemical acetylcholine will triggers the dream state, while simultaneously paralysing their muscles. For the xeno-biologists amongst you, you will find hypers providing further details on the suppressive actions of neurotransmitters like norepinephrine, serotonin and histamine in your information packs.

Putting aside these exceptions, I want to elaborate on how I foresee our gestating babies will end up explaining their dreams to themselves. In doing that, I want you to imagine that you are one of those babies. Place yourself in their position. Your sense of self is developed; you have a solitary physical body and the ability to interact with your environment. No exo-neural ghosts available here, of course.' Laughter arose, but not enough to disturb her presentation. 'With every revolution of the planet, they will lose consciousness for up to one third of that time. During that phase, the new mind will swim through bizarre images: incoherently coagulating, coalescing, confusing and contradictory images. Not being fully sentient, or even awake - means that memory consolidation and threat rehearsals will continue to play out, but without conscious awareness. The selection and culling of sensory inputs, the trials and practise-runs for various alternatives will be done, without any conscious or deliberate direction. The consolidation and linking of distant but related memories into smooth narratives is to occur automatically.

Automatically, but not consciously: therein lie both the conundrum and the solution. While only one quarter of the daily sleep period itself will be spent dreaming, those two hours per night add up to roughly six years, or nearly one-tenth of the average human's life. Yet they won't remember it. Only a small percentage of dreams will even be available for conscious recall, as the neural chemicals that convert short-term memories into long-term memories are suppressed during this period. Cortisol production will decrease communications between the neo-cortex and the hippocampus: although I may be getting too technical for this seminar. Also, remember again that this forgetting of dreams is a general rule – there will be the occasional sub-sentient who can wake during a dream and retain memories of it, the oneironaut exception.

During the dream state, phantasmagorical locations, objects, people and ideas will blend continuously into each other. Recent personal experiences may take on bizarre or exaggerated forms. We anticipate this sorting to enable junk node removal, but at a safe cognitive distance. This will enable the growing mind not only to focus more fully on the limited aspects of sentience available to them, but to have the added bonus of providing stimuli for creative expression during wakefulness.

Now, this point I believe would be the perfect segue into creative manifestations among the Form Six gestates, the second part of our seminar today. There is extensive information available to you via hypers regarding all the topics I have discussed here today, so it is with great pleasure that I pass the stage over to your own award-winning artist, *Zest as Breccia*.

'I understand you lot are the stellars I need to talk to about having a baby,' Zest joked, and the sprays of adulation and applause filled the auditorium to almost blinding levels. Even now, Nat could still recall the sensation of feeling uplifted, swept along by the crowd. The thrill of hearing *Demisting as Acapulco* explain her idea of sub-sentient dreaming had been an opportunity too good to pass up; combining that with the chance to hear from the reclusive artist who'd designed the new Academy icon, and whose planetary engineering skills had been instrumental in the orbital alterations, meant that almost everyone from the old PreyData © team would be in attendance.

No-one knew stellar configurations like Zest. Nat reckoned to herself that if Zest hadn't been part of the original team, they would have had to draft her in. The surprising changes made to the graduating process of gestation had been a shock to many – so much so that some continued to deny the very possibility. Admittedly even now the idea of suppressing or limiting a newly-coalesced mind seemed strange to her, but she could see the logic behind the theory. These minds were babies after all, so perhaps baby-steps at such a delicate stage was appropriate.

There were no baby-steps in the stellar reconfigurations though. There couldn't be, not when everything was so tightly interwoven, orbits balanced and nestled against each other. When the PreyData © teams had first been told of the required changes, it was assumed by most that the system would require a complete reboot. It had been *Zest as Breccia* who proposed the complicated reconfiguration: annihilating only the fifth planet and directing reconstituted fragments into a season and tidal-generating satellite around the third. It had been *Zest as Breccia* who had performed the calculations, who assayed the terrestrials of the immersive and proved that it could be done.

They'd never met, although Nat had heard of her, of course. The original PreyData © crew had been a full complement of 360: large enough so that if one wanted to remain reclusive, it was entirely possible. They'd been so close for so long, yet their connection had never synchronised. Back before she accepted the offer to work in the innovative immersive PreyData ©, Nat had always kept herself busy: far too busy ever to consider the possibility of love. Thinking about those earlier times inevitably increased her hydrogen tempo, and she couldn't afford to be distracted while at work. She terminated the memory. It wouldn't do to get all sentimental and emotional while she was working. She had a baby to deliver.

Gently Nat eased her consciousness back over to where *Carols in Sequins* was floating, and merged her perspective with her client once more. Even now, doing this, she could still feel the warmth of that hydrogen pulse. Those thrills still tingled every atom whenever she thought back to that first time she'd seen and heard Zest.

Millennia later they were still apart: nevertheless it was a thought sequence that she knew well. It had long kept her motivated, providing her with a precious and essential source of hope, however thin. This was something Nat knew that stellars shared with their sub-sentient babies; at least once those babies grew to the point they could understand something as beautiful as hope. Which was still a couple of levels away for her current charge, but she was confident that Carols' baby would get there. Sustained by her reflections and relishing her reminiscences, she returned her focus. Only one more birthing after this, and she would have to say goodbye to the world of Death ©, possibly forever. It was time for her to become a boy.

CHAPTER 20
(The Seventh Form)

The x-ray over surprisingly quickly, Katherine had been escorted back to her room to find it empty. The sun shone in brightly, and after writing a quick couple of lines in her journal, she closed her eyes. She took a slow deep breath, in through her nose, and let herself swim in the sensation of a smile. The feeling of the bed and blankets elided away, and an oddly warm glow seemed to spread, effusing like an invisible bubble-bath all around her.

The sensations changed, as if the sunlight itself had undergone a phase transition. The change vanished, and she relaxed, wondering if she had imagined it. It might be the medications. Then again, it might just be the metaphoric heart of a young girl kept in stasis for decades, beating again after a long hibernation. She smiled, shaking off such silliness. Everything was normal. She relaxed, wondering where Tommy was, where Chelsie and Marilyn and Cassie and all her grandchildren were. She gave thanks for each of them, and for the lessons and trials they would each face. Then it happened again: a tingle so brief, hardly enough time to acknowledge it, let alone wonder at it or wander into it, before it was gone. She shrugged into the pillow.

Katie felt it again, stronger this time, as if her brain was automatically adjusting some internal antennae to receive an incoming signal. It connected with a brilliant split second flash, as if a room filled to the brim with cameras, whose flashes were all going off at once. She could see, or feel this light now, although somehow she felt it was beyond light. Certainly it was beyond colour. Hues and tones had faded out, then split and refracted, quickly swept back again even more intensely, up another octave. This intensity made her aware of a new layer of energy, one with uncountable vortices filling and vibrating the whole of space with a song of unimaginable beauty and complexity. The harmonies faded in and out and then took over, flowing viscerally like a music cloud collapsing into a valley. The strength of intensity belied the gentleness of the light. The music filled her, seeping through her.

Abruptly, the flashes ceased, the vortices spun down, the music dissipated. The sense of cosmic understanding that had been on the tip of her tongue slipped out of reach, leaving only a bitter-sweet taste of memory. Looking around, there had been no change, no momentous happening, no church bell tolling. Her sense of a vacuum-filled symphony was replaced with the humdrum noises of normality. If anything, the volume on banality had been turned up a notch. The usual sounds and sights resumed, and everything was as it was before. No evidence of the kaleidoscopic vision remained.

She remembered where she was, and who she was, before being startled, as she was suddenly falling, shaken loose from her body. It was a strange sensation, but she wasn't scared. In fact, she relished the anticipation of whatever the experience would be. Whatever was coming next, she was okay with it. It was going to be exciting, amazing and thrilling, beyond her wildest expectations. So why would she be scared? She didn't know what exactly was going to happen, but she had faith that everything would be okay, that she would be able to cope. She accepted the paradox that her faith was logical, and smiled.

She jolted, and really felt herself fall out of her body. Or rather, she felt her body fall out from underneath her, like an outfit many, many sizes too large. She flexed, stretched, and tensed herself. Her mind, she supposed. It wasn't as if her muscles and tendons were this flexible anymore.

She could feel - what she thought of as herself - leaving behind her human body. Katherine had wondered if it would be a conscious thing, and she wished she could share this knowledge with someone. She floated up out of her body. Oddly, she felt both disconnected and more connected than ever before. It felt like everything was a part of her. She could see the hospital, the street, the suburb and even the city. It seemed to blur and meld, blending together in the same situation, isolated yet integrated.

A warm, fuzzy understanding seemed to blossom inside her mind, flowering in a parental appreciation of how something so important could be so fragile. At the same time, she found herself questioning that assurance, the assumption that it had really all been so important. *Could I have both thoughts?*, she wondered, which was quickly followed up by, *What am I thinking with?* There were no obvious answers, no dawning of comprehension. Not even the mythical tunnel of light greeted her, she just continued to rise. She paused when she was high enough to see the curve of the horizon, and the scattered lights of foreign cities dotted the darkness of a turning planet.

Abruptly she heard a familiar voice in her ear, so clear and intimate she turned to her left and right.

'Where are you now, Ma?' she heard her son whisper, squeezing her hand in his, fighting back tears.

She was back. She felt Tommy sitting beside the hospital bed, his hand brushing her fringe back from her now-vacant stare, while a dribble of saliva bubbled on her lips. She watched as this triggered a burst of sobbing. Then, without warning, - and so abrupt it was almost painful, she was in another room, somewhere in the same hospital. She was watching a young physio intern crouched in front of an elderly woman, pain and determination written on the stranger's face, saying 'Go on, you can do it, stretch your arm a bit further Mrs Bramble...

For a moment she wondered if she was astral travelling, then she remembered that there was meant to be a bright cord connecting her to her body. She looked around, but there wasn't one.

The voices returned; increased, both in number and intensity. Soon there were too many voices all talking at once, touching and moving and whispering and screaming and... She was being bombarded with shards of lives, lives numbering in the thousands, or millions. People she had never known, nor ever had the chance to meet.

the shriek of children playing

the metronomic pulsing of a water sprinkler

the siren of an ambulance

torrential down-pouring rains

medical chatter on a CB radio

There was a singularly potent reverberation, and everything vanished. All of a sudden, there was nothing. An all-encompassing nothingness: it was a stillness that went far beyond peace and quiet. It was pure, beautiful, peaceful, nothingness. No smells, no voices, no sound of any kind at all. Sensationless yet completely still, she relaxed as if floating into a morphine haze. No sounds, no visions anymore, no sinking plummeting immersion in the splashes that overflowed the cocktail of lives that had just a moment ago threatened to drown her in sensory overload.

Perhaps that is exactly what has happened, she thought. Maybe that flood of voices, that torrent of lives had actually tripped some internal surge protective mechanism that blocked everything out, leaving nothing, a complete absence of life. She didn't know, and realised with surprise that she didn't care. Not just now, anyway. It was just so peaceful, far too peaceful and beautiful a place for worry to be allowed to enter. She smiled.

CHAPTER 21

(The Coloured Code)

Truth be told, Tommy had been a little grateful for the intrusion. He needed time to sit and think. He needed more time to do more thinking. He felt dizzy, lost among the possibilities and implications. His mother not only had this astounding experience, but she kept it a secret all these years! She had lived through so much, seen the world change in ways no-one could have possibly imagined, and yet, she had actually met the one person who *could* imagine it. Someone with knowledge of life and death. Death. Earth. His mind spun.

Sitting alone in the cafeteria grabbing a quick brunch, Tommy looked down at the food on his tray, but barely took anything in. Visually and literally, his meal sat untouched. He wondered briefly if his present inability to eat chicken was the start of his own vegetarianism. His little hippy sister would be amused, no doubt. It wouldn't make that much difference, he realised, what with Aaron and Claire raising their family along Buddhist principles.

'Do no harm,' the scroll on their living room wall proclaimed. He knew the rationalisations. He abhorred the idea of killing ten animals per person each year just for their meat, but now he was seeing a segment of those 60 billion lives in the meal in front of him with a new appreciation. Had this animal – this baby star – led a short, painful and miserable life, followed by a horrific death? He didn't know. He didn't know the details of processing Kosher and/or Halal food, but was sure this was an important issue. The old adage *You are what you eat* suddenly had new layers of meaning.

He understood that he could take it too far – the vegetables on his plate, was he going to stop eating those too? They had once been plants, part of the living breathing biosphere that he and the animal kingdom all shared. Shared not just geographically, but even of a common purpose. Everything on the planet, lived in order to experience death. Did that justify poisoning the uncountable billions of insects and rodents that were killed to 'protect' the crops we use to make bread? He'd read that mice were monogamous mammals who even sing to their mates, yet are so casually eradicated. He shook his head to destabilise those orbiting thoughts, as his mother had often done, and he visualised them veering off outside his personal space.

With that motion, he tucked into his meal. *No point in it going to waste*, he told himself. As his Ma had noted, there were no 'I used to be a chicken' social clubs for those who were lucky – or unlucky – enough to remember their pre-human existence, their own 'pre-memories'. He grasped he already thought of them as her 'pre-memories'. They *were* her memories, despite the patent absurdity of the idea. What she had described, and he had found himself enlisted in the investigation of, were memories that she simply couldn't have. She could remember things that she had never done – things that she never could have done – that no human being could possibly have such intimate knowledge of. It still made him question his sanity, if only but briefly.

He knew from years of dealing with his mother that you couldn't force a story. And also, that they were worth waiting for. His mother's stories were to be treasured, she had the imagination of JRR Tolkien and JK Rawlings all wrapped up in her little finger. Some of the tales she had told them over the years were fantastic; in another age they would have been worthy of poem or song. He had never tried to capture one of her stories in his books, but her spirit had always contributed. He hated the word, but had admitted that sometimes when he was writing, it felt more like he was channelling. If not the character in the story talking to him, then it was the spirit of an ancestor looking over his shoulder and whispering words in his ears. *No, it didn't happen like that!*, he'd hear, or *Re-do that last bit.*

As a writer, when he would find himself somewhere new, he liked to look around and practise describing the room, and he did that now. His inner voice narrated. *It was a sterile room, a standard nursing home cafeteria where the chairs and tables were severely faded, as if the combined weight of years of being exposed to bereavement and disease had bleached them of colour and drained them of life.* Once again, that practice turned into more of an insight into his current state of mind than an exercise in juggling adjectives. Obviously it was his state of mind alone, not his mother's. She was still full of life, brimming full and overflowing. He hadn't seen her so animated in a long time.

Perhaps she *was* mad. She had said it herself. She had prefaced the whole story with it. She had framed her wild little tale with the disclaimer at the beginning. That story, that tale. How could they tell it wasn't a sign of dementia, and who were 'they' anyway? People who had not heard or ever spoken with his mother would undoubtedly be happy to state she was suffering from dementia, or perhaps even madness. But even if that were the case – which it definitely wasn't – would that be an inheritable trait? Would he want to know? Or have that sort of diagnosis on his permanent medical record?

He could almost hear her voice as her words replayed in his mind. 'Tommy, I am going to tell you about my vision; and you might very well think I am mad. Trust me, after this tale you will wonder yourself. I've thought it since day one. Maybe I've been mad for a very long time and this form of psychosis is cumulative. But this happened to me, and in many ways it made me who I am today.'

Who was she today? He'd got to know a little more about his mother since she'd moved over to live out West. Katherine Amelia Coulston had been born to a Baptist preacher between the great wars; wife now widow; mother of four; grandmother of seven. Mad woman? Could he really ever reconcile that sort of summation with the spritely woman now bed-ridden three floors above him? All the stories she had told him and his sisters: was the source of her imagination actually a form of madness? Did she have a psychotic breakdown, a hallucination? Was it any less plausible that she had truly met an eternal man?

The physics of the tale were well and truly beyond him, but he had watched enough of *Star Trek* to understand a causality loop, or the grandfather paradox. But this 'time-swallow' idea? That was new, that was original. That was certainly something he could use in a story of his own, another book his publisher would likely jump at. But was it actually real? And if it was, would he be endangering his mother, or himself, or the world, by telling it? What if, as Uncle Justin had apparently said, it was important that people not know? What if ignorance of life and death was essential? Tom knew that researchers used 'double-blind studies' precisely because their unspoken or unconscious expectations could actually affect the outcomes. He shook his head at the conundrums.

He was staring out the window, oblivious to the people around him, when some part of his brain alerted him to the fact that the Code Blue recently announced over the speaker system had mentioned room number 427. His mother's room. He didn't know what a Code Blue was, but he doubted it could be good. Startled by the insight, he bustled his cutlery and crockery together loudly and left the room at a running pace. The lifts were just around the corner, but even if one had been there, he would've taken the stairs. Not that it made any difference, as he soon found out.

The crash teams were frantically trying to revive his mother when he turned the corner, and he discovered that a Code Blue meant a heart attack. Katherine Amelia Robertson had already left the building by the time he managed to get close enough to her to hold her hand in his own. Stifling a sob, he brushed her fringe back from her face. Martine had stayed behind after the crash team left, and she stood unobtrusively behind him while his shock subsided. He simply couldn't believe she was gone, so quickly, so abruptly, and for no reason.

'Where are you now Ma?' he asked, and as he felt Martine's comforting hand on his shoulder, he struggled to hold back his tears. He didn't hear the trained voice of a nurse, but that of a friend. 'She was such an angel, she's sure to be in heaven now.'

'She's a star in the heavens, that's for sure,' he smiled meekly. Martine left him alone, and he sat there in an empty room, with the empty shell – a beloved familiar uniform – of his mother, and simply talked. He told her about his internet search, about what questions he had for her; and wondered what questions she would have had for Justin, if he had come back into her life.

Later, when a pair of orderlies arrived, Martine escorted him out of the room, but he carefully carried his mother's journal. The rest of her things he didn't really care about, but was happy that Martine was willing to pack them up. He sat in the hastily-vacated staff room, clasping the journal and staring out the window. He couldn't bring himself to continue reading now. It felt more than a little strange when Martine brought in his mother's carry-on case, to see how easily what was left of her could fit into such a small bag. He thought up the image of a miniscule yet potent happiness virus, spreading peace via rays of light, and as he left the hospital he was filled with conflicting emotions, and more than once had to remind himself not to smile.

CHAPTER 22

(The Inherited Message)

There was very little traffic on the road as Tommy drove home. To his empty home. Nurse Martine had packed his mother's belongings into the overnight bag he'd brought for her last week; it lay alongside the terrarium he had brought in only yesterday. The traps on the Venus Flytrap were all closed, busily digesting. On the passenger seat lay his mother's journal, which he kept touching with his outstretched hand when the road was clear. He couldn't help but wonder what those last couple of chapters contained. He breathed in deeply, deliberately.

Part of his mind was on the road, while the rest was watching himself. Observing. Listening. It was strange but comforting, he thought, not hearing the doubts he used to have. The questions he expected his mind to pummel him with were noticeably absent. When Gloria had been killed in that car accident, Tommy had asked himself *'Why?'* so many times, his head had felt like an echo chamber. *Why her? Why now? Why me? Why? Why? Why?*

He'd never really come to an answer. At least, not to an answer that really satisfied him. 'Part of life', 'The mysterious ways of God' or 'Must've been her time.' He'd heard them all. Uncomfortable looks, whispered gossip, sensitive offers of assistance, he'd received platitudes a-plenty. He'd thrown himself back into work a week after Gloria's funeral, refusing to let her death overwhelm him.

With a slight twist, he knew he'd soon be hearing those platitudes again. Losing his mother was different though, and he expected comments like, 'She had a good life', or 'She's in a better place now.' He knew that an elderly parent dying was more to be expected than losing a wife. But he wasn't working now, so he had nothing to throw himself into. He needed to get on with something. It was probably a bit of a family trait, he thought. Not letting anything dominate his life, to define his life. In his mind he had refused to become a 'widower', any more than he was already a 'father' or a 'brother', or even a devoted son.

A hint of a smile broke out on his lips. He remembered his mother calling him 'my son, my son', and wondered if she had been actually saying, 'my son, my sun'. So many memories. He wondered how often he would reinterpret things that she had said, now that he knew how she had really seen the world. From before he was born, she had looked around her and seen life and death so differently. He'd always assumed that in her heart she was a Christian, or held to the basic tenets of Christianity. He smiled again, wondering if there was any reason that he was mistaken. Her take on it was a little different, but oddly he felt stronger, thinking of her as a physical body of light, part of the heavens themselves. He decided then and there not to call his sisters once he got home. He'd wait until later and do it tonight. He wanted to tell them when he was outside, under the stars.

He turned on the radio, giving each of the pre-set stations a couple of seconds, but there was no music. It was all advertising and self-promotion, even on the classical station. He didn't need that. Sometimes music could distract him from his thoughts: other times it could work to help focus his mind, but today he just couldn't find the patience to wait for something he liked to come on the air. He lowered the window a couple of inches, letting the warm air flow through his hair. He couldn't see the ocean from here, but he thought he could smell the sea air on the breeze.

Both he and Gloria had loved the ocean, and back when they lived over East they had often driven an hour to go to the beach on a weekend. She had grown up far from the ocean, and it had fascinated her. She could sit and stare out at the water for ages. Their kids had loved the beach too: it had become a happy family ritual. Katherine came along some of the times, but not often. The ocean didn't hold so much appeal for her, the ubiquitous sand and screeching seagulls held no charm. She preferred to be pottering in her little garden: weeding and planting and tidying were never-ending jobs. She would invariably have a jug of iced tea waiting on her porch when they returned from their family outings. In fact, one of his favourite photographs depicted his mother sitting on the steps, flanked by her grandchildren Claire and Jackson, each holding a tall plastic glass of iced tea with a twirly straw. The memory felt so recent, he had to remind himself that his kids were grown now; years – no, decades, had passed. Time seemed to move far too quickly.

He didn't know what he would do with the garden now, all the plants both inside and out that his mother had cared for. This new Venus Flytrap would definitely go in his house, perhaps joining the other one he had in the kitchen window. That window looked out into his backyard and the now-empty granny flat. *Or perhaps not*, he thought. *In the study it will get better light*, he mused, and hoped it would provide some inspiration for him while writing.

He thought for a moment about turning this journal into a novel, but wasn't sure how it would work. He would have to use a lot of creative licence. It felt as though the story that really needed to be told was that of her 'Uncle Justin', this immortal man wandering the Earth. It certainly wouldn't be an original idea as far as that was concerned, but portraying him as a trapped stellar, an eternal in a self-imposed purgatory… there was potential there for a good story. The trouble was, he didn't really understand Justin's motivation.

He tried to imagine: and, seeing a possibility, he grabbed a pen and made a quick note to himself. *Between the arms of the galaxy is only relative void - in that void exist solitary stellars, the ejecta of proto stars, comets and the like. Mainly junk, but sometimes treasure.* He read it back over and then scribbled: *Minds and lives can be like that too.* He smiled.

Do stellars even experience the same kinds of emotions that humans do? he wondered. *What if human emotions are so basic, that from his perspective they were more like animal instincts?* There was potential there though, and his muse whispered encouragement. He mentally put the idea into his 'to do' list. At the moment, he had too much else to deal with: arranging the funeral, contacting family and friends. He'd get back to it afterwards, he resolved. It could be the way out of his creative funk.

Chatting to himself he remarked, 'I don't know how the finished story would end up, but I suppose it's definitely an idea worth gestating.' He smiled at that, and looked up at the sky, mentally addressing his mother. *I guess you'd say we are all gestating, eh Ma? A gestating planet? A dreaming star?* He toyed with ideas for the title, confident that something appropriate would eventually settle in his mind. *Perhaps something in an ancient tongue, like Latin*, he mused. *Astra* something.

At last, he pulled into the driveway. The house looked exactly as he had left it, apart from the junk mail in the letterbox. Parking in front of the single garage, he gathered everything from the car and grabbed the 'wishing books' as Gloria had called them, and entered the backyard. The three foot high picket fence probably needed another coat of paint, but there'd be no time for that before he was inundated with guests for the funeral. He wondered whether his sisters would be bringing their kids too.

The path split, and after a moment's hesitation he took the left-hand track to his own back porch. He didn't quite feel like entering his mother's place just at the moment. He placed her *musical scapula* on a coffee table and her bags of clothes on a chair as he fumbled for his keys. He kept the journal under his arm. For some reason it felt wrong to put it down, to let it rest unattended. He decided to make himself a cuppa and sit on the porch to finish reading it. For now, he carried it indoors with him. He didn't want to let it out of his sight for a minute.

He'd always taken for granted that he knew his mother. What she liked, what she didn't. Especially since she had moved west to live with him after Gloria and her mother Muriel had both passed. Now he had to wonder how much he didn't know. Too late to talk it over: the house was empty. Again. The journal wasn't the only thing of his mother's that he had: in fact he had practically everything. But none of her belongings meant a thing compared with this notebook. This strange tale that she had kept secret for all these years was hard-copy evidence that there had been lots more to her than he knew.

It felt strange to remind himself that he needed to think of her in the past tense. He knew what she believed: that she was now being born somewhere as a star. She had not only gone into the light, or taken on a body of light; she had become light. Shining down from the heavens; stretching out to encompass infinity. He had to admit, it was a nicer thought than imagining her sitting on a cloud playing a harp. She'd become bored pretty quickly doing that.

She'd been adamant that she would never become an invalid; there was no negotiating with her about her garden. She had refused point-blank to move west unless she had a garden. The trampoline had been transferred to Claire's, where her kids could enjoy it more. They'd ripped out an old shed from the corner, tilled the soil and added bags of fertiliser to the newly installed sleepers that acted to divide and contain. Some bamboo had been planted to provide a little privacy – it had shot up and spread along the side fence, enclosing her section of the yard. It was an old block, large enough that one day it would be subdivided and turned into apartments, just like so many on his street.

Waiting for the kettle to boil, he suddenly heard the beep of an incoming text, and rummaged for his phone. It was from Claire, asking him to call asap. He poured the water into his teapot and placed it on a tray alongside his favourite cup. He placed his mobile on the tray and wedged the journal under his arm, carrying the lot out to his back porch. The afternoon sun wouldn't hit directly until after 3 o'clock, so he anticipated at least an hour's worth of reading. That was, after he called Claire. He made himself comfortable and then dialled her number, and she answered straight away.

'Dad, thanks for calling back. Umm, Dad? I just called the hospital to speak with Nan…and…'

'I know Claire, I just left there. Sorry baby, I haven't called anyone yet. I was going to tell you tonight.'

'Oh Dad. Are you ok? Do you want me to come around? I can be there in say, half an hour?'

Tommy took a deep breath, filled with pride at his sensitive daughter. 'No darling, it's ok. I'm alright.'

'I don't like you being there alone, Dad. It's not healthy. You're coming over for dinner tonight, and I'm not taking 'no' for an answer, ok? I'll even make your cauliflower bake, and we'll crack open a nice bottle of red. Aaron will be home just after five, but you can come over earlier if you like. I'll call Jackson and see if they're free.'

Claire and Aaron only lived ten minutes away, and Tommy knew her advice was sound. 'Sure baby, that'd be nice. But please, don't go calling your aunts or anyone, ok? Let me break the news. It's my job.' He could hear her sniffle on the other end of the phone, and he guessed she was holding back tears. 'I was going to call you this evening and let you know. I just need a little personal time to figure out a couple of things. It'll all be ok. She wasn't in any pain, and she's in a happier place now.'

As he said the words, he surprised himself how whole-heartedly he believed that. He knew it. His mother's convictions were either contagious, or were strong enough for both of them. He wondered if they'd be strong enough for others, too. Claire muffled a sob, gathering her strength. He knew he had to let her get on with her day. He had to get on with his; he simply had to finish the journal. If he was going to test how strong his mother's convictions were, he needed to know it all.

'Claire? Baby? It's all okay darling. I look forward to dinner, but you don't have to go to any trouble. I've got something I've gotta do this afternoon, and I'll buzz when I'm leaving, okay?' He'd let the phone ring once and then hang up. He knew that it would make her smile, as she had long ago given up reminding him that calls between their mobiles were free. For Tommy it wasn't the cost of the call, it was the ritual, the family habit he wanted to hang on to. Perhaps when she was older, she would appreciate the sentiment he attached to the old family signal that his mother had started, so many years ago when he had first left home.

'Sure Dad. Whenever you're ready. I'd better go, but I'll see you tonight.' After a brief pause, she added, 'I love you, Dad.'

He smiled as he replied, 'Love you too, cupcake. I'll see you later.' He placed the mobile down on the table. Pouring himself a cup of tea, he looked out over the backyard and smiled, remembering all the fun times and happy days the yard had seen. It felt strange to think of the granny flat as being empty. His mother had been in hospital for two weeks, but now the emptiness was a different shade. Not darker, not lighter, just more vacant. He couldn't imagine anyone else ever living there, and wondered if he would actually move. The house and yard held so many memories, but with the kids moved out, with Gloria gone, and Muriel, and now his mother...the whole place felt different. It felt permanently empty.

He shook off the thought, avoiding the morbid connotations those mental paths held. He sipped his tea, and opened the journal. He checked from the bookmark to the end, and noticed that on the very last page lay a solitary sentence he hadn't seen before. Something about talking to an orphan about coming home. Who it was meant for, he could only assume that it was for her Uncle Justin, and he felt sad all of a sudden that her fantasy of his return never occurred.

The message made no sense to him at all. He turned back to his bookmark, hoping that one of the remaining entries would provide some sort of clue. He was already a little overwhelmed by the discoveries of the last twenty-four hours; his mental garden was in disarray. He certainly didn't need a 'rosebud' thrown into the mix: especially not today.

CHAPTER 23

[In the Middle]

Nat smiled as she watched her penultimate client, the hopeful mother-to-be, finish up and emerge for a break. *This plucky little Red probably needs it more than most*, she observed. Nat had found that at the half-way point, precisely in the middle of the whole process, was the best time to actually get to know the parent. Getting a feel for the new star, that came later. Before they moved out of gestalt collectives and into more complex focused loops of consciousness, Nat prepared to see beneath the surface, so to speak. Her panels showed that both the mother and the new mind were both doing well. The last few individual krill of her aquatic form were being swallowed, and soon her third form would be extinct.

Carols had born up well under the stress of dying, considering she claimed to be thanophobic. The set of pads displaying temperature and energy patterns of both mother and child had been identical, and Nat couldn't precisely tell whether the jagged neural frequencies that *Carols in Sequins* was manifesting were from her own fears or if they were merely the natural instincts of the gestate. It was normal for the parent to start to feel a certain sense of the child by now, an intangible connection that could be used to assess the health of the child. She gazed over at Carols as she emerged into the half-way break.

'It can be a little intense. Are you ok?'

She flushed affirmative.

'I'm guessing you have more questions now?'

She flushed affirmative emphatically, and then smiled. 'That was exhausting!' she said.

'Yes, I know, I was watching. You did really well. Your connections with the child are strong and healthy. The fundamental structures and instincts have been impressed, and we are ready to go forward whenever you are ready. I often find that pregnant stellars get hungry, or need time for a rest before continuing. There is a communal area you can rest in, if you like. There will be other expectant mothers in the Limbo Lounge, you can chat and socialise with them if you like.

Alternatively, as you can see, there is refined hydrogen and helium available for you on tap, and as a special treat we have a selection of heavier elements for you. Some of these you might not have tried: I do recommend the turquoise crystalline essence of dilithium-9, very tasty. You have a selection of radioactive dips under the lids to your left, and the main buffet features triple-roasted iron nuggets, and my favourite, an Orion iridium stew. So, tuck in, and ask me questions as you go.' She settled back into her own virtual bath, and quickly ran through her head the highlights of what the immersive had used for Carols' gestate.

She scanned the developmental details: 1/ plant (carnivorous); 2/ nematode; 3/ krill. *Okay*, she thought to herself, *nothing too unusual there*; although she did find the carnivorous plant-life interesting. She'd keep an eye on that, but otherwise all was normal. The sequence was the most standard pattern for first timers. Each time a new mind came into life, each level always used an original and unique species. Every level the genus would vary and the section of the biosphere the creatures inhabited would change so that basic modalities were challenged. Almost every time, however, those first three lessons were laid down as a standard set, with one form in each terrain: botanical, microbial, insectile.

She was pleased to see further colours of contentment seep through Carols' energy fields. Nat invitingly raised a questioning hue.

'Oh, yes, ok. I'm alright with what happened; it's all good.' Carols blushed. 'That launch was fantastic; zero-gravity was such a release! So! Much! Fun! After that though, I admit I found the rest a bit of a let-down. At first I thought the oceans were a little dull, just floating, eating, breeding, being eaten, but really that was fantastic compared to the turpitude of being a plant! I was a little concerned when the plant gave up there. She lost the motivation to continue, and it made me wonder if I ought to worry? I've been more on edge about that than I want to admit.'

'Not an uncommon experience, nothing to worry about there. Everyone loves flying; I'll see what I can do about getting you in the air again. The zero-g was pretty unusual. Remember, I can't actually promise anything though...' she said, and turned to adjust some screen invisible to Carols. She did have a little sway over the options that would come up; she could probably finagle an avian for her. *Carols in Sequins* may be a lost little princess, but she seemed to have a good heart and a quick mind. Nat liked her. She hoped the daughter would be ok. She had a good feeling about this little Red, and it would certainly be nice to save her famous garden moons. It would be a nice way to go out, and the favour that the Silver Garivest and his partner, the Tangle Hub *Berries in Cerise* would owe her would be quite handy. She clucked an affirmation to herself, *I'm so grateful for things that work out perfectly.*

'Nat?' she heard, bringing her back to her centre. She was really out of sorts today, and she forced herself to concentrate. That wasn't the first time her attention had slipped, and she prided herself on being at the top of her game for every client, completely dedicated. She wasn't going to get sloppy now on her second-last session. It wouldn't do. She brightened and turned to her charge. 'Yes, my girl?' she replied, invitingly.

'The different forms: are they all in that same environment, on the same planet?'

Nat was surprised. Most pregnant guardian stellars didn't pick up on that until at least the fourth, maybe the fifth form. *Maybe she's not such an airhead after all*, she considered. 'Why yes, darling, they are. It's a little terrestrial planet; three-quarters covered in water, although the semi-sentient residents are land-bound, and yet amusingly call it 'Earth'. It has an oxygen/nitrogen atmosphere, a tilted axis for variable seasons and a perfect satellite for tidal forces to generate an enormous variety of environments. We have all the space there we need, and there's nothing like it in the whole cosmos.'

She could see an expression of her own reflexive bemusement on Carols' visage, and she smiled abashedly. 'Yes, nothing like it anywhere. I admit, I do love it here. I love watching the children grow; I love becoming engrossed in the minutia of their little lives. It is heart-warming.' She paused, a pregnant pause, one she practised and used almost every session. 'But it can also be heart-breaking, and I want you to brace yourself for a quite different set of experiences in the next half, ok?'

Carols in Sequins nodded, subdued.

'In the second half of your gestate's growth, we will be going through the levels, one at a time. You will have the chance to consult with me at any time, ok? I will be there with you, but silently. I will be guiding you, but you must now allow the mind of your daughter to guide her own incarnations. She isn't quite in control yet, but she will be - almost completely - after this next lesson.' She paused, and Carols waited patiently. 'Next, she is going to learn how to move. Now you're probably thinking, 'We covered that already.' But there is a lot more to movement. We know that she can float and she can wriggle and that her visual acuity and spatial coordination are fantastic. Now she will learn to run, to scoot, to skip, to flee and to pursue. The essential lesson is about beginning something; the energy and direction taken is secondary. I warn you though; this next section is more gruesome than the first three. During at least one round, your baby will live as a carnivorous hunter. Just remember that you are completely safe, that your child is safe, and that I will be with you both. Ok?' Carols nodded, and she continued.

'Now there's something quite different about being a carnivorous hunter. It's really not the same as amoeba-gobbling, or beetle-juicing. It requires more focus, more concentration, more coordination – and it will be *she* who has to learn all those things, so don't help her. She doesn't need to hear from you, ok? At some level – I believe anyway, the evidence is mixed – she knows you are there. There is no need to speak to her, or direct her. Even if you see her making a mistake, or acting in error, even a terminal error, you may not interfere. You are to sit back and watch.

In a way, you've already done your bit. Let *her* grasp, let *her* reach forth and inhabit a focused space. It is exactly what she needs right now. Although her experiences will teach lessons that may be more gruesome, it is an important stage in her development. This focuses her hunger. Her desires to feed and grow will work together and she will not simply start to move, she will move to start. Not just physically, but psychologically. Her mind, her identity, even her personality, you will see her grow in leaps and bounds from this point.'

Noticing that Carols wasn't eating, Nat gestured her phased-space panel back, and triggered the starting sequence for the next level. As she checked the variables, she spoke to Carols.

'Now we can begin the second half. First stop, is how to start.' The usual giggle that mothers gave at such a bad pun was missing, so Nat quickly continued on with her patter. 'When we are back from remembering how to start, we will look at stopping... the unstoppable thing you have created.' She laughed, and this time Carols joined her merriment. The infectiousness of it reduced the tension in the room underlying the truth in her last statement. Nat lowered the lights, and Form Four began.

CHAPTER 24
[Form Four: Taking Flight]

Carols felt a gentle breeze caress her. It carried aromas so rich it felt like the air had texture, a tangible depth of smell that reminded *Carols in Sequins* of the sensation of moving through abundant ocean waters. Floating had seemed like such a basic skill; she had to remind herself that she only thought so because she herself would have once incarnated as an ocean creature. Those memories were locked away, etched on atoms comprising heavy metals on her inner planetoid, waiting to be absorbed when she engendered. And even that possibility was still very far away. When that day came, she'd prefer to become Silver rather than Black, but either was ok. She knew she'd have to recalculate her total mass to see if she would even be able to survive engendering anyway. Things were different as a binary. Parenting took an awful lot out of you.

She felt the breeze blow across her again. A terrestrial breeze: the now familiar oxygen/nitrogen atmosphere. Her daughter was returning, their minds were linking in a harmonious and natural synchronisation. The compatibilities they had already achieved through their earlier communal-minded incarnations had noticeably bonded them. The connection she had grown with the nascent gestating mind was mutual; they felt in synch. She knew that her daughter was feeling the same breeze, and tasting the same air. They could both feel its caress as it blew through her... *feathers?* She opened her eyes.

The breeze wasn't blowing through her; rather, she was coasting through it. There were updrafts and cross-winds carrying scents, tempting yet unfamiliar. She stretched, feeling the shape of her body. She sported wings, covered in mottled brown feathers, bristling with strength and confidence. Claws extended downwards, and her eyesight appeared excellent. She scanned the ground below her, coasting on the confluences of atmosphere. She could see a farmyard: lush, fetid soils and fertile gardens abundant with worms and insects. Food called to her, and she adjusted her trajectory and started to head down. The anticipation of a good meal, and the delicious sensation of coasting through air filled her with elation, and she opened her beak to cry out with joy.

Her coo sang out from the skies. Impossibly, it echoed back before it could have. Disoriented, she abruptly looked up, only to see herself coasting down into the yard. The tree she sat in seemed to nestle the breeze, collecting the wind like an invisible security blanket it wanted to drape itself in. She felt the sensation of a full stomach, and tipped her head to the left. That couldn't be right. She was hungry (she was flying) she was satiated (perched in a tree): she was both. She looked at the tree as she coasted in, flapping her wings so she could slow down and land close to herself. She looked at herself; felt herself looking at her; and the perspective changed again. The duality was disorienting, an almost mirror image. She preened herself and waited for her other to pay homage. She encouraged herself to look closely, to observe the differences.

She liked what she saw. She had a stout body: sturdy, functional and symmetrical. Her head was squeezed between a short neck and a slender bill. By dislocating back and forth between each of her selves she could see that there were differences: not only in colour but in scent. She was definitely both of them; they were both her, but they were different. They were a couple! The flush of realisation tingled physically in both bird-minds and their stellar mother.

Carols could feel everything her daughter felt, although the demarcation between herself and her growing child was becoming stronger. She could definitely feel an awareness that wasn't her own, and she could tell that her job of providing mental scaffolding was nearing completion. She could imagine the construct existing without her, managing to swerve and swoop without guidance. Her daughter was starting to acknowledge her own self; she could feel a sense of separateness developing. She smiled: her baby was not only mastering physical lessons but already starting to grow a sense of individuality. The smile echoed over the newly-forming psychological delineation. The barrier was still porous, and her daughter's sense of joy in recognising that she existed was contagious, and both birds let off a long slow 'coo...coo'.

Carols could feel her child continue to look at herself – or herselves. Her perspective kept changing: deliberately, almost consciously. Each of her bodies looked quite similar. Their overall plumage was brown, and they both sported white spots on their wings. She understood that together they would make more of herselves, and they too would feature uniqueness. White dots here, white dots there. She gained a new level of appreciation for the concepts {Male} and {Female}: and she understood that they were both *her*, as would all of their offspring be.

Her abdomen was a creamy colour, while his-hers was a light blue-grey. Their legs and feet were pink and their eyes were orange, colouring that seemed to somehow disappear in the contrasting rings of red that surrounded them. The ring around his-her eye was much thicker than hers. She again tasted {uniqueness}, and swirled the concept around in her thoughts. Each of her bodies shrugged, twitching their respective necks to the left in a semi-synchronised reaction. Then there was the breeze again, and thoughts of {uniqueness} were gently picked up and wafted out of their minds.

A torrent of rich earthy aromas breathed over them. It had rained recently, and the ground itself was stretching, re-arranging itself in order to absorb, and to grow. She could feel the fertile soil carried on the breeze, leaving traces of temptation on her feathers that she could taste all the way down. She could feel it *in her bones*. Without a glance at her other self, they soared into the sky together, flapping their wings strongly. Intent on filling her bellies, she became aware that their wings made a distinct 'frrr' noise as they flew through the otherwise silent yet tasty air.

Landing on a grassy area, she immediately began to eat. The grass seeds were plentiful; it was as if the earth and the rain had conspired to provide a private banquet, just for her. The sense of separation reared again, and she noticed that he-she wasn't eating. Her focus had been totally on the grass and on eating the seeds. It seemed strange that part of her wasn't partaking in such a feast. She looked up and around to the left: she knew where the he-she was, but her attention had been distracted. She twitched somehow, jumping over to her other body, and suddenly knew. Actually she had already known: it was her, after all. The plentiful grasses provided nutritious seeds, but they were good for other purposes too. The rain did more than open the ground; it refreshed, cleansed and invigorated her as well. He-she cooed at her other self, a reassuring, companionable coo. Then he cooed again, and the intent was quite different.

She joined him, not by flying over, but in a short toddling-run. She looked around and surveyed the area, confirming his-her hypothesis. The area appeared safe, the grasses plentiful, and the scent of rain in the air was a potent aphrodisiac. He-she sensed her approval, and immediately started collecting twigs and straw into a pile nearby. She took these pieces, selecting the ones best suited from what was on offer, and started to fashion a nest. Using her feet and her bill, she started to weave the grasses and twigs together. At one stage he-she approached the construction, but she wasn't making this a group action. She focused, and he-she understood that while help may have been required, it was not wanted. He-she watched. Balancing the longer twigs against each other, it took her a few attempts to fashion the basic structure. It would have to be strong enough to hold all of her – each of her, each of herselves... Another confusing confrontation with personal tenses was impeding, so she deliberately put the thought aside.

Soon enough a sturdy nest had been built and they each hopped up and jumped down off it, testing its strength. She didn't think it was nearly strong enough, but it would suffice. A fragile place perhaps, but it was her place. Their place. That confusion about who she was: she/they hadn't experienced this before. The communal consciousness of the earlier forms had lacked by its nature a sense of self, of individuality. It was now totally natural for her to look at him-herself, touching his beak to the ground and then displaying his tail feathers. It was simply a different way of seeing, one she hadn't previously been able to perceive. Like the sounds of flying or the cooing vocals: it was all new sensory data.

'*Fascinating*', she heard.

As Carols piggybacked her daughter's appreciation of new inputs, she felt her child's mind experience an internal flicker, as if she was stretching along an axis of space-time previously hidden from her. She couldn't quite remember what it had been, or how it had been different. Those memories weren't judged to be a threat, merely a context. She was growing; soon there would be more of her. Her daughter doves imagined {children}, and then re-imagined {generation}. These were new concepts, yet ones she was familiar with already. They somehow meant more here, there were implications she could feel but not explain. Yet those thoughts were no threat either, so she put them aside too. There would be more than enough time, more than enough hers: there was no rush.

He-she dismounted, and she knew the process of self-incarnating was set to go. Soon there would be another two of her, making four perspectives. Then perhaps eight, if predators could be avoided. She would continue to split and reproduce, to grow and explore. Stuck in two bodies at the moment, the idea arrived of exploring in sixteen, either as a flock or as pairs in many places simultaneously. Anticipation flooded her body, triggering an unforeseen side-effect. She felt the tingle of biochemical changes as the enzymatic reactions necessary to gestate her eggs commenced. She was going to be a mother. The thought filled her with pleasure, a satiation quite unlike the satisfaction of gorging on a good meal. She floated a little, disassociating from her avian forms, and simply generated waves of joy at the wonders of being alive.

Floating alongside in bliss and gratitude, *Carols in Sequins* was a little startled to hear her midwife whisper. 'Isn't this beautiful? Such a healthy sign! You should be very happy too – not just because you are feeling what she is, but simply because she is feeling this way. It augurs a very healthy mind.'

Carols in Sequins flushed in agreement, aware of the duality of sensation still dancing on the edge of her perception. Or rather, dancing on the now actively-forming edges of perception her daughter was developing. It was a little disorienting, dizzying. It was reminiscent of assimilating conflicting memories from duplicate exo-neural ghosts.

She had experienced being in more than one place, or being in the same place more than once. Sometimes that second perspective made her aware of things that seem so blatantly obvious that it seemed impossible that she could have missed it. That sense of multiplicity, the reckoning that seeing yourself from the outside seemed to invite: Carols knew the feeling well. But this was the first time her gestate was experiencing it, and she didn't want the echoes of her own fragility to dampen the happiness and gratitude that still emanated from her baby. She relaxed, cleared her mind of concerns, and slipped back into the contentedness of pregnancy.

As the seasons progressed, Nat watched proudly as Carols faced her own fears. Nat hoped these exercises would help broaden the capabilities of her little 'Garden Princess'. The vicarious conquering of mortality would invariably generate a permanent change in her temperament, even taking into account the effects of the memory shunt. Even if she couldn't remember, part of her being would still know. *Her precious gardens might no longer be her defining attribute*, Nat hoped.

As Form Four finished, Nat looked at *Carols in Sequins* with pride. By all appearances she was exhilarated. Her plasma rate was elevated and her ions were high, her anti-matter net was intact and undamaged.

'That – was – awesome!' Carols exclaimed, shaking herself with tingles of colours, ones that melded in swirling rainbows cascading over her shell. 'I cannot believe that I haven't done that before! Ooh, imagine doing it with more control...At first, I had trouble, I wanted to tell her what to do, where to go, what to avoid. That horrible spiny creature was so obviously not edible, but she went for it...yuck...'

Nat laughed. 'She did. She *had* to go for it. That is exactly what she is learning. She's learning to make her own choices, finding out what she can do and what not to do. And she did very well. You both did.' Again she lobbed the display over to Carols, so that she could see all the vital statistics and relative scores for the previous lesson. Everything was red: perfectly normal.

Nativity of Diamonds triggered something with a wave, and the display changed. Instead of showing the gestate's responses, it showed both child and mother on one screen. The child was developing normally and was exactly where they predicted before the level began, but Carols had gone off her charts. She was operating at a new personal high for efficiency, and her virtual particle generation rate was higher than ever.

'Congratulations, my child. I'm guessing you will want to remember how you did this. Of course, unfortunately you will forget all this. However... your internal records of your current operating levels will stay, so you will know something marvellous happened for you here. I give gratitude knowing that one day you will work it out. You are a powerful little star, and I think this was just what you needed. Your daughter needed it, and she got it, but you possibly needed it more. I am so happy for you, for now, and for your future.' She turned to the central dais, leaving Carols to digest the compliment.

'You are both going really well, and we can continue if you like, or we can take a break.' On the central stage the Brown dwarf had now swallowed the terrestrial, but in ultraviolet frequencies they could still clearly track its trajectory. After all this was over, Carols would inherit the memories of her exo-ghost and be able to taste the dissolving for herself, but now it had to remain a vicarious imagining at best.

'It would be better for us to keep going though, right?' the young stellar asked.

'No my dear, quite the opposite,' Nat replied. 'If you are rushed, flustered or not focused, complications can ensue, and here especially perhaps, there is simply no need. So we can take a break if you like.'

'No, I'm fine, really' she said, breathing with focus. *Carols in Sequins'* colours stabilised, her frequencies balanced, and she looked down at the remains of the banquet and laughed. 'And after that 'porcupine' thing, I'm definitely not hungry any more...'

They both laughed, and *Nativity of Diamonds* decided it was time to begin.

'Ok then, let's continue into the Fifth Form. Last one was themed 'Beginnings', while this one is more about stopping. Here, she is going to learn how to be at peace with the processes of life, and to deal with the results of her actions. When she dies at the end of the next level, her mind will truly be prepared to engage with sentience, and she'll face a microcosm of challenges. No more collectives, no more hives or shared neural enclaves. The final level – the one after this one - will see your daughter inhabit a single sentient mind. Nor will you be able to hear her thoughts. You can hear her and see everything she does, but her inner thoughts will be hers, and hers alone. But, that's not so important. As you already know, it's your *actions* that count anyway.

So for now, we are off back to Earth again. In the Fifth Form, sometimes sentience inveigles itself. You may even think your child is self-aware already. It is possible. If so, that is great news, it means your gestate is settling into a solid wave function. Here she starts to develop the characteristics of her final identity. Do not be concerned; rather, be elated. And of course always be grateful. You are both doing really well.'

With a spray of helium she swiped the dimmer again, and the lights began to fade.

CHAPTER 25

(The Maestro Beckons)

Back when Tom had been writing, he'd often get so engrossed in a story that he'd forget about the world around him. His characters seemed to jostle so closely around him that the extraneous distractions of everyday living were blocked out. He would forget to eat and drink; he'd ignore the phone and the front door bell; he'd get utterly carried away by his muse and the world he was creating. Sometimes he was metaphorically drenched by a complete fully-formed chapter; but more often he was hit by dream shrapnel: dispersed elements of a barely-perceived whole that were sometimes delicate and fragile, sometimes hefty fragments. When hit, he had to expunge onto the page and make corporeal the idea.

When he was writing, time just ran at a different speed on the outside of the little creative carriage he travelled in. The regularity of time continued outside his world, but it wasn't relevant where he was. Many had been the occasion when Gloria would stand in front of him, armed crossed. She would refuse to budge, not accepting any more delays or excuses. She would stay in the room, knowing that her mere presence was a distraction that would interfere with the creative process. Most times she left him to write. Sometimes though, she reminded him that he needed to stick his head up and have a look around: that his life was happening without him.

He didn't have her to return him to reality any more, but then again he hadn't written anything since she left either. Seven years of writer's block was a big chunk of time, and weeds had grown over the tracks of inspiration he used to ride. The pages of the novel he had been working on were gathering dust, still sitting on the shelf inside his home office. He refused to consider the possibility that Gloria had been his muse: that would mean his writing days were over, so he couldn't allow that thought to enter his head. He knew – *in his bones* – that he would write again. Perhaps even rescue 'The Maestro' from limbo and finish that tale. He knew he hadn't lost his muse, *per se*, but Gloria had been a perpetual source of support and his beloved fount of encouragement. Sometimes he wondered if she'd believed in him more than he did himself.

Sitting on the back porch in his favourite chair, he closed his mother's journal and sighed with astonishment. 'Well, what do you know?' he asked the image of Gloria he kept in his head. 'What would you make of this, my love?' In his mind, his wife simply smiled and nodded, agreeing with him that what he had just finished reading was beyond description. 'I guess you're a stellar now too,' he said, and she grinned and rolled her eyes at him as if he was a complete idiot for not grasping it earlier. 'Oh my beautiful star,' he murmured.

Glancing at the shadows creeping their way across the garden, he guessed it had gone five o'clock. The whole afternoon had vanished. Like the scenery from a train window, whole bundles of time had passed him by while he'd been reading. It had been a while since he'd been so engrossed, so enraptured in a tale that he lost track of his surroundings. Nothing had grabbed him like this for so long. He felt cheated in a way, drawn so inexorably into the wake of his mother's departure and not having someone to discuss it with. No Gloria. No Katherine. No kids around even. It was all his own.

He felt conflicted: he was driven to share it, but at the same time felt a little reluctant, honouring his mother's oath of secrecy. He looked around the garden, not seeing plants and bamboo walls, flowers blooming and weeds creeping out of the soil. He saw baby stars everywhere, the world was different now, and surprisingly, he could relate to the odd feeling of expectation his mother had written about. He could just imagine her Uncle Justin waltzing up the driveway any moment and asking for her journal.

Picking up the empty tea tray, he tucked the journal under his arm and went inside. The shadows had crept in ahead of him, and it took a moment for his eyes to adjust. Leaving the tray on the kitchen bench, he found himself walking to his office. He stood there in the doorway, imagining what Gloria would've seen from the position she had stood in, all those innumerable times. His laptop sat there, practically an antique now, not as powerful as the one he'd given his mother for Christmas. That one was now resting in her bag, alongside all of her worldly possessions from the hospital. She had a few changes of clothes, toiletries, a crossword puzzle book and the laptop: one with a browsing history Katie had made a joke about. He thought about pulling it out and plugging it in, but decided that would have to wait for another day. He had to get ready and head over to Claire's for dinner. He had an appointment with his grandchildren.

As he turned away from the door, his glance rested on his favourite picture of Gloria. She'd never really liked it, but something about it had always resonated with him. He'd always thought that this candid shot embodied the spirit of her; it captured the playfulness in her eyes that he had fallen in love with. It had been taken at Claire and Aaron's wedding, but it wasn't one of the formal wedding photos. Rather it had been snapped by a friend of Aaron's, using one of the disposable cameras placed on each of the reception tables. She hadn't posed, or even known the photo was being taken. Aaron's best man had been half way through giving his speech when he tripped on the microphone cord and nearly tumbled onto the bridal table, causing everyone to laugh uproariously. Gloria had reached out to steady herself on his shoulder, her other hand flat down securing her champagne glass to the table. She'd been so happy that day, and although the mother of the bride had looked suitably stunning in the formal photos, it was this picture he had treasured and hung prominently.

Claire and Aaron had been married for less than a year when a drunk driver removed Gloria from their lives. They'd known that Claire was pregnant, but they hadn't known she was carrying twins. Claire told him later, that if she'd had a baby girl, they had already decided to make her middle name Gloria. As he stood there bewitched by his memories, he wondered if Gloria knew.

There was nothing in Justin's tale about stellar gestates being able to look back into their nursery world after they were born. He had no idea whether they even *could* look back and follow the lives of other gestating stars. Apparently there was a memory block that worked between levels, but whether that continued to function after they'd graduated from nursery school he had no idea. He wasn't even sure that 'back' or 'after' even held relevant meanings in a place where time was a malleable dimension like length or height.

Planting a kiss on his fingers, he stretched out his hand to almost touch the picture of Gloria, and blew. 'Whether you can see me or not, you're still with me baby,' he promised the picture. 'Till death do us part....' he murmured, until a grin crept onto his face. 'No, not even then, baby. Not even then.' Imagining an invisible Gloria nearby, he bustled about the house gathering his things. He piled his keys and wallet onto the precious journal, grabbing a fleecy jacket from the hall cupboard to protect him from the cool night air. Everything was ready for him to leave: he just had one more task.

He picked up the phone and walked out the back door to the porch. It was still daylight, but it would be dark on the East Coast already, and he hoped that at least one of his sisters was outside, having a starnic with her family.

His baby sister would hate to be the last one to find out, so he called her first. Cassie answered on the first ring, and pre-empted his news by guessing why he was calling. She could be a little spooky like that sometimes – he'd seen her predict who was calling many times before caller-ID had made the telephone a less anonymous affair. He couldn't tell her a date for the funeral yet; he'd been so caught up in the events of the last 24 hours that he'd forgotten to call the funeral home. He made a mental note to put that at the top of his list for tomorrow, and promised to call her back with more details as soon as he had them. Apparently she and her partner were heading out, so he bade them farewell and dialled Marilyn's number.

While Cassie seemed to inhabit a semi-psychic world, Marilyn was whole-heartedly a down-to-Earth girl. She had the pragmatic determination of their grandmother, and accepted the news stoically. He suspected that she would allow herself to grieve later, in private, where no-one would see her being vulnerable. But that was possibly a projection of his own, a way he could envision her hardness as being a protective covering, hiding a human being with emotions deep inside. He'd always respected Marilyn, but they'd never had much in common. She too reassured him that she would make plans to fly over as soon as he knew the details. He could tell by the sounds of television and her teenagers in the background that she wasn't able or willing to discuss their mother's passing in more detail just then.

Chelsie was closest to him both in age and temperament, but he couldn't get hold of her. There was no answer at her home, and he left a brief message on her voicemail asking her to call as soon as possible. He imagined that she would be still at work, toiling through a pile of legal papers preparing for her latest case. Eventually she too would stick her head up and discover that life had changed in her absence, and she would get in touch. He just hoped she would be able to get the time off work in order to attend the funeral. Her career was everything to her, as her ex-husband had often lamented.

The next couple of weeks passed quickly, and Katie's questioning grew more complex. During each evening they would sit under the stars, and it was during those moments that Katie found Justin most receptive to answering her big questions. As always, he would ask her to explain the contexts, definitions and parameters of her enquiries; and through her own elaborations she found that she often provided her own answers.

They discussed population numbers and distribution of life on the planet, setting her up with what numerous history and geography teachers would later describe as her 'innate grasp' of the subjects. Katie could follow the logical path Justin laid out, explaining how he could be thousands of years old and yet not have met anyone famous from history, but she was still unsatisfied. The curious mind of a teenager examined other aspects of their situation, and often their conversations involved extended periods of silence while she thought things through.

By the third week she noticed that she had internalised his breathing exercises: a couple of minutes practising two or three times each day and it had become ingrained.

She asked about God and stories from the Bible, and Justin explained that throughout time people have realised the truth, but have been unable to put it into words: words that might not exist. So, for answers she learnt about allegories, analogies and parables. Analogies are very broad, and compare things with similar structures, but can be hard to understand as no analogy is exact. Allegories transfer aspects of one thing onto another: contrasting believers and infidels with sheep and goats, for example. Parables are short stories using scenarios from everyday life to illustrate a message that imparts a moral lesson, or truth – which, adding to the confusion, can sometimes be an allegory as well.

If the language you speak doesn't have words for "pulsars" or "galactic clusters", then you simply *have* to speak in images, in parables and analogies. You might describe distant galaxies as being many mansions awaiting in the heavens. Or you could reverse the connection, and have guardian angels made of bodies of light, rather than actual bodies of light (stars) as being alive, conscious caring beings.

The importance of faith was questioned, and why God or their guardian angels couldn't be more tangible. She understood that an awareness of being watched could change someone's behaviour, but was left dissatisfied by the conclusion that this too was an analogy. Her mind soaked up paradoxes, contradictions and allegories, balking at the irrefutable conclusion that sometimes ignorance could be essential.

After a week or so of starnics Katie asked Justin why he looked at the sky if it made him so sad. He reminded her that the stars were his family, and said simply that he missed them. It was good to know they were there, and that he was not alone, but sometimes he still wished he could talk to them in person.

He explained and elaborated on the idea, but not before he had made her promise never to speak of it. With the devious mind of a teenager, she kept her promise and never spoke of it.

When she tried later to capture those conversations in her journal, she was pleased to discover that writing it down helped her recollect what he'd said. Her journal became its own feedback loop, and as those conversations re-surfaced she embodied her memories onto its pages.

Dear Journal,

Justin said that what we call our sun, Sol, is actually a living being, part of a vast family that we call The Milky Way. He said that for every human alive there was about a hundred thousand stellars. I asked if there was an Adam and Eve too. He grinned that annoying grin of his, and I probably blushed then, because this happened early on. He said my innocence was refreshing; that my child-like curiosity was a rare gift outside of toddlers, and that I made him smile. I suppose it was a compliment, but it was still annoying.

Anyway, he said that the Eve of the Milky Way family had given birth to millions and millions of children, many of whom had already died and had children of their own. Her offspring now exceeded three thousand million – and that on top of that, Eve used to be part of a family too. Oddly, I remember, there were no Adams back then, they were all female stars – imagine that! And that each of Eve's sisters also had hundreds or thousands of millions of descendants. And with more being born all the time the larger family group was too big to be counted. This is when he first added, 'in English'.

This was new. He explained that there are ideas that English doesn't have words for, and that there are words in English that other languages don't have words for. The words just don't exist. I could say in French, 'Le mots n'existent pas', and I remember learning at school how the Eskimo have lots of words for snow, but I suppose I never grasped how many languages there are, and how many ideas there are! He rattled off a list of a dozen examples, a dozen different ways of saying 'the words don't exist', but I only remembered the last one, which turned out not to be Japanese for 'the words don't exist' but meant 'unfortunately'. But I know that from now on, whenever I think, 'Le mots n'existent pas', I will add 'zannen ne'. I think it's nice.

Anyway he was talking about how he misses his relatives, and how big his family is. He said how some kinds of children are completely dependent on their parents, while others are self-sufficient, like a baby turtle. He said stellars couldn't depend on their parents, as they had normally died before they were born. He said all families have their rebels, diverse cliques and groups that kept their distance, but still remained part of the family group. He said he missed them all, but it was someone (some stellar) in particular that he was thinking of. Maybe he had a girlfriend, but he didn't say that, it's just what I think. He wouldn't say, but the way he ignored my question made me wonder many things. He distracted me though - the sneaky man – he was good at that. Is good? Is it past tense or present tense? Ah the words! The damn words don't exist! Le mots n'existent pas, zannen ne...

He said that the original Eve had long ago died, but that her death wasn't at all the same thing we think of as death. When a stellar 'dies', it undergoes a change, and that if he was to continue with the analogy (he had explained 'analogies' and 'metaphors' even earlier on than this), then if young stellars were all female, they engendered and become male for the second part of their life, which involved different frequencies and phases – stuff I couldn't understand. But there was stuff I could, too. He said that the girls and boys were also divided into categories of colour and size, which were related. The bigger they are the faster they burn, he said. Girls could shine in red, orange, yellow or blue – while the boys only had two choices: black or silver. But even afterwards, it wasn't death, it couldn't be, as nothing was ever truly lost. The bottom line is, I think, that old Eve became an Adam, and then joined up as part of a collective framework, or something we don't have the words to explain. Yet – he did say "yet".

Another time he talked about the black boys being the heart of the family, a central place where stellars went to retire. The girls in the family provided the motion by having babies, while the boys provide the power. Like a starfish: where the boys (the retired stellars) are both the suckers are on the outside and the heart in the middle, while all the girls are the body itself. Needless to say there is nothing about this or anything like it in the school library, or even the Encyclopaedia there. Perhaps, one day. Who knows? I will keep an ear tuned for astronomy news. And an eye on the stars, of course.

CHAPTER 27

[Form Five: Berelekh Admissions]

The sun was almost setting as they made their way along the remains of a long disused path. There was very little shade; the desert had apparently consumed this part of the countryside as well. Sources of water had become few and far between. Hardy bracken and brambles had grown over what was once a forest floor, almost obscuring the remains of the pathway that had once existed here. The earth was dry and cracked beneath their feet, unyielding despite their enormous weight. Long dead trees cluttered their view down into the valley: dry eviscerated sticks poked into the sky, skeletal hands piercing an unforgiving and barren landscape, hopelessly grasping for life.

Every steady step dislodged small pebbles and rocks from the path, which generated little puffs of dust that congealed in the air all around. From a distance, it appeared as if the three of them were walking through smoke, or some form of semi-solid red haze. It was only by keeping his eyes fixed a metre ahead was he sure that there was a path here at all. There was certainly no other life, in fact they hadn't seen any other animals in quite a while. At least, there was no competition for what little food and water could be found. Trouble was, what remained was proving harder to find each time a source ran out.

That there was water in these hills was known: it was the source of many of the rivers that littered the valley below, where once he had roamed with immunity in the strength of his herd. Now there were just the three of them – his heavily pregnant mate and his younger injured cousin. He turned his head to check on their progress behind him. Through the dust he could see the eyes of his mate blinking at him questioningly, checking there were no dangers or predators in the area. He gently shook his head and looked past her shoulder to see his cousin trundling along a few metres back, still keeping up with them despite his obvious pain. He was proud of them both. Following him on this trek into the hills had displayed faith in his abilities to provide for and protect them. He had to find shelter and water soon.

The minor dust storm around their feet started to settle, and with the sudden silence that fell when they stopped, the crisp sound of moving water became apparent. It wasn't far away now. He oriented his enormous ears to get a better impression of the direction, and was quickly flooded with joy at the sound directly ahead. It was much louder than he anticipated. His drudge through the decomposed wilderness must have put him into a trance where he had lost focus on what was most dear. He could hear the water moving quickly, and in strength. They must be near a large stream, and the vitality of the sound increased his energy levels and confidence. The sight of understanding in his mate's eyes further bolstered his enthusiasm, and he moved forward with a new burst of energy.

Ahead were two large boulders. He imagined they had once stood on either side of the path like sentinels, but now the gap was blocked by debris. The sound of the water was coming from the other side of this wall and there appeared no way around. To the right the land dropped off steeply, not quite a precipice but it was far too sharp a drop to support him, let alone his less nimble travelling companions. To the left was a pile of dead tree trunks and soil that appeared to be the result of a landslide. Jagged branches protruded from the mound at unnatural angles. Luckily the slide had not been any heavier, or the debris blocking their path might have been impassable. As it was, it would simply require effort. And patience. The sound of that rushing splashing gurgling water was all the motivation he needed. He got stuck in.

Every time he pulled one branch free, there seemed to explode forth a cloud of dust, and sprays of dirt and rubble. Each time the dust settled, it looked as though the gap he'd made had already been re-filled. Mud long baked into solidity was finding itself unsupported, and would break apart to fall into the smaller holes below. He would then grab hold of another branch, another trunk, another log, testing each one until he found one that would come out with relative ease. Then the haul would be thrown down into the valley side on his right, where it would crash and tumble into the tree skeletons below. The noise felt anomalous, almost irreverent. It was awfully strange to be making this much racket without disturbing anything, not so much as bird life. Hopefully it wasn't a sign of the widespread carnage they had left behind on the valley floor.

Finally he wrestled out a large fir trunk. It was easily twice his length, weakened by years of termite damage before claimed in the avalanche that had lodged it here. What was left in the gap were now only smaller branches, dried twigs, rubble and what appeared to be a bird's nest. He strode forward and used his wide shoulders and thick legs to crush the remaining hindrances, clearing the path for his mate behind him. The scratches against his outer skin were minor, nothing compared to the damage that was still healing from their encounter with a desperate cougar a week ago.

He waddled back and forth to ensure that the path was wide enough to allow his bulging partner sufficient space, crushing the smaller twigs and debris under his broad feet. Then at last he allowed himself to move right through to the other side, where he was stopped by the beauty in front of him. The stream of water was indeed moving quickly. From where he stood it stretched twenty metres across, being fed by a stream falling down the cliff-face at least four metres above the pool of water. Off on the far side he could see that it drained into a shallow culvert perhaps two metres wide. He took a step forward, unable to believe their good fortune. Not only was it fresh cold drinking water but there was a safe place for them to bathe! He trumpeted to his wife and cousin with elation, encouraging them to come through quickly.

He waded out in the shallows and drank deeply from the stream. He looked back to see his mate standing there in astonishment, overwhelmed by the abundance of icy-fresh water. He filled his trunk with the chilled water and sprayed it over her, and she moved faster than he had seen in a long while. Practically bounding, she entered the pool directly, immersing herself in the deep water, relieving the pressures caused by carrying their child through such inhospitable territory for so long. He was filled with joy to see her so happy, the expression of relaxation and indulgence in her eyes set his body afire. He wanted to take her here and now, to wallow together like youngsters in heat. But there was the calf, who was not far from birth now.

He called to his cousin again, but there was no reply. Only the gushing splashing waters around him made any noise at all. He looked at her questioningly; but she was obviously confused as well. Reluctantly he emerged from the waters and trekked over to the path he had opened in the wall of rocks. To his right he could see what appeared to be a large cave mouth, which normally would immediately set him off exploring; he'd always been curious. After food and water, shelter was what they needed most. But first he had to see what had happened to his cousin.

Some distance beyond the gateway he had just finished making, he rounded some boulders and saw his cousin lying there in the shade. He had laid down for a rest when they had reached the sentinel rocks. His injuries from the cougar had been more serious than theirs were; his damaged leg had slowed them down since. But his trunk was one of the best; he could sniff out edible tubers and truffles much better than either of them. He trumpeted briefly, a note just loud enough to waken a sleeping mammoth, but his cousin's shaggy pile didn't move at all.

There was no breeze in either the air or in his trunk. Expiration was apparent. He trumpeted once more, a longer cry of grief, honouring his cousin's spirit on its journey back to its hearth. Now there were just the two of them. He knew that his mate and their unborn child had only made it thanks to his cousin's defensive actions. If he hadn't managed to spear that cougar with his tusk, then the battle could have gone a different way. He would not be the last male of his tribe: the tribe would be no longer. As it was, that was still a possibility.

The birth of the baby was all-important. His mate hadn't been the matriarch of their tribe, but for all they knew she was now the only surviving female. It took nearly two years for her to carry a child to term. Normally females lived together while the bulls led more solitary lives, but they had been the only survivors of the attack. The bloodshed had been unprecedented. They had run together, glad to have each other, elated to bump into another male from their tribe, returning home from a walk-about.

It had been bad enough these last few years, watching the tribe dwindle. Their traditional hunting grounds and sacred watering holes had long gone; ocean levels had been rising and glaciers retreating. The woodlands and grasslands that had long been their prairies were being replaced by forests. Although this had happened before, the forests had never before been populated with such coordinated hunting teams. The new hominids reproduced in less than half the time it took for his species to do so; moreover they thrived in the toasty new airs that the planet was breathing. Good for them, but not so good for mammoths. The remnants of a once mighty and noble tribe had been forced further and further north.

The old Matriarch bull had told the tribe that they needed to hunt out the safety of the retreating glaciers. His family was much better suited to the cold than the hunters were, in so many ways. His frame was covered in thick shaggy wool that hung a meter long, which lay over another layer of fine under-wool. His haemoglobin provided exceptional oxygen delivery, and his blood contained a natural anti-freeze. His skin featured sebaceous glands that secreted greasy fat into his hair for extra insulation; this was on top of an outer layer of fat three inches thick that kept him warm. Surviving the freezing ice flows and frosted mountains became a simple matter of avoiding hunters and finding water and food.

Food. He had to find food for his mate and himself. Leaving the carcass, he set off to the cave he had seen earlier. As he came through the rocks he had cleared, he heard a terrible trembling. A rising susurration of dread filled him, a tsunami of fear immobilised him as his eyes locked onto his mate. She was standing on the other side of the pool, where the land was flat and clear for twenty metres before rising up. He looked further and apprehended that both banks rose sharply. They were in an ancient river bed, perhaps an almost dried-up tributary of the powerful Berelekh River, or the nearby Indigirka River. Either way, he knew they were close to the Arctic Ocean coast, just on the other side of these mountains.

His mate trumpeted in fear, the alarm in her eyes mirrored the confusion in his own. They had never been this far north. Their tribe had once, but not them. They had no experience of river floods. No elder had ever told him how landslides and twisted broken trees cemented together in mud could be a sign of a flood region. The torrential wall of water that swept over the drop was so far outside their experience neither of them could comprehend what was happening. He saw the little waterfall stop, the river retract slightly, and then a solid wall of liquid moved across his vision, high enough to completely cover her in seconds. He saw her flailing, thrown about by the waters, but only briefly.

The waters were now bashing against him too, trying to dislodge him from his spot in the gap between the boulders he had cleared. He stood with his feet apart and braced himself in his little gateway; but the force of the water was shockingly strong. His shaggy hair was instantly soaked, his inches of blubber and supplementary haemoglobin only a temporary match for the temperature and pressure of the freshly melted glacier he was immersed in. He felt mud and debris pile up against him under the waters, flotsam carried along in the wake of the flash flood quickly filled the gaps his legs left, blocking that gap. Locking him in, cementing him in place.

He grasped what was happening and tried to move. He shook his powerful legs and lowered his head to try and clear the build-up in front of him using his powerful tusks. That was when the tree came around the corner, a birch tree ironically enough, his favourite food. It caromed in the rapids and collided with his tusks under the water, briefly dazing him but securing his head in place. He tried to move, but the log was jammed. He tried to shake his feet, but the mud was solidifying. He tried to trumpet one last time, one bellow of rage and frustration at having survived so much – the weather changes, the hunters, even the cougar attack, only to have come across a place of beauty in the last moments of their lives. To find a sanctuary where they might have given their species a second chance: this turn of events was unacceptable. To have it wrenched away by the watery grasp of the eternal ice was so unjust. The briefest trumpet sound was cut off, and the melting glacier swept the final two admissions into the Berelekh river mammoth graveyard, where their remains would lie unnoticed for centuries.

The ice flows, it melts; it stays still and it moves; it provides life and it takes it away. *There are patterns and cycles everywhere*, Carols mused, as she floated in a strange sort of mental fog. She hadn't appreciated them before; or, if she had, she'd learnt to take those beautiful patterns for granted, which she thought was sad. The demise of her baby's Fifth Form had been a surprise, but it had been predictable. Carols had known it was coming. This Form had lasted a lot longer than any of the earlier ones. She and her stellar child had spent decades of Earth time inhabiting her unique species.

It was her newest form of life, but by no means the planet's newest. There were thousands of other gestates at various levels all here, all occupying the same space. The scenario had tenanted her in a tribe of woolly mega-fauna; another unique genus of life in another new terrain. New lessons, new scenarios.

She could feel her child's mind coalescing around her. She no longer felt alone in the fog, but as yet there was no real communication. Her baby was still assimilating communication as a concept, it was learning, growing. With new experiences, she would eventually amalgamate a stable consciousness: a blending of all of the neural habits and autonomic responses she was slowly acquiring. Together they would all contribute, ingredients adding to her character.

Carols in Sequins wondered briefly what kind of stellar her gestate would be, but didn't care. She knew she would love her unconditionally, so it didn't really matter. She gave thanks, offered gratitude for a successful outcome here, and for a healthy relationship in the future. The clearest indication that they were between Forms confirmed as the fog lifted and the lights came on again. She was ready for them this time. *Alright then*, thought the excited little Red stellar, *Five Forms down, one to go! Bring it on!*

CHAPTER 28

(The Memory Sharing)

As Tommy parked his car in Claire and Aaron's driveway, he wasn't surprised to see that Jackson's car wasn't there. He could barely believe his son had found time to find a wife and become a father, taking after his Aunt Chelsie as he did. A thorough workaholic, it took numerous reminders to ensure that he made an appearance at family events. His demure little wife seemed happy to exist in his shadow, existing only to iron and cook and to raise their baby daughter. He didn't get to see little Talia nearly enough, but he knew that Pauline's family were a close-knit bunch.

The two boys came running out the front door before he was out of the car. Alex and Kyle seemed to be perpetually bursting at the seams with energy. Deflecting their questions about the big book he was carrying, he tasked them with carrying the two bottles of red he had grabbed off the wine rack at home. He would never turn up empty-handed, although he didn't know what they would be having for dinner. He never gave credence to the white wine/red wine dichotomy: in his opinion, a nice Shiraz went well with everything.

Claire and Aaron had gone out on a big limb buying this house. There was nothing wrong with the house: it was gorgeous. It was a spacious, four-bedroom split-level home in a nice suburb, without a doubt it was great for the kids. He suspected the mortgage repayments would be taking a good chunk of their pay packets each month. Discussing what to do with the money from Gloria's life insurance – something he never imagined that he'd have to do – they all decided that Gloria would've primarily wanted to help her unborn grandchildren. Both he and Gloria had shared the opinion that children ought not to be handed everything, that it was important to work for something in order to appreciate its value. So rather than being split into deposits for their kids' homes, that money had been invested into long term savings accounts so that their grandchildren could attend university. Putting Jackson and Claire through college had been expensive enough, struggling for so long on the meagre incomes of two teachers and the occasional royalty cheque. He couldn't help but be filled with a sense of pride at seeing what his children were achieving for themselves, without extra financial support.

Claire had completed a degree in journalism, and had met Aaron at her first office Christmas party. This had amusingly enough been a first for him too: he'd been with the company for two years but had never attended the Christmas event. As a dedicated Buddhist, he didn't drink alcohol or eat meat: characteristics that Claire had at first found mind-boggling. Not that she was old enough to legally drink then anyway, but the only vegetarian she'd known had been her hippy Aunt Cassie. Aaron's quiet unassuming nature had been a natural foil for Claire's extroverted enthusiasm, and they had immediately clicked. 'We just hit it off over the water cooler', she liked to say. Apparently she had confided far more intimate details about that night to Gloria, but he really preferred not to know. After all, she was still his little girl.

With her hair held back in a ponytail, Claire's heart-shaped face hid nothing, and he could see that she was close to tears. He knew that while parents don't officially have favourites, grandparents do, and Claire had irrefutably been his mother's. She'd been the first granddaughter, and he sometimes heard his own mother in Claire, especially when she was reprimanding or encouraging her boys. If it felt strange to hear his mother from his daughter's mouth, it felt doubly bizarre when he heard bits of himself reply out of young Alex's mouth. *A trans-generational ventriloquism act*, he had dubbed it in his head. He had it written down somewhere, a poetic phrasing he hoped to use when he returned to writing.

The boys didn't know what was wrong, but they obviously sensed that their mother was upset. They wanted to show Grandpa their latest toys, so Tommy reassured them that if they went and got everything ready, he would be down to their room in a minute. They were off, and for a brief moment, it appeared a stranger called Peace came to visit the kitchen.

'Hi Dad. How are you coping?' Claire asked.

He surprised himself by answering from a place of strength. 'You know darling, I'm ok. In fact, I'm better than ok.' Claire's eyebrows rose, not knowing how to react to that. He continued, reassuring her. 'It's been the most amazing twenty-four hours of my life, and I have the most unbelievable story to tell.'

Aaron looked up from the dining table, where he was tidying away paperwork. '*You've* got a story to tell?' he asked, leadingly. Both Aaron and Claire knew about his writer's block, and were sometimes less than subtle about it. It didn't bother him, he realised, as he didn't think he still had it. He positively bubbled with this strangely compelling scenario. He could feel elements of it simmering and gurgling inside him, demanding to be shared and consumed. He smiled, hearing the words he was using in his head, and knew that his muse was similarly excited.

'I sure do', he said with a reluctant smile. 'Although technically, I suppose it's mum's story,' he said. With that, he presented the journal for them to see, holding it carefully and reverently. 'She's even written it down.' He could see he had their interest aroused, but his daughter's response astonished him.

'This is about what happened to her as a teenager, isn't it?'

Tommy's eyes must've bulged out of his head, causing Aaron to laugh out loud. He couldn't even get out the words to ask, and he stuttered, 'wh... wh...', forcing his daughter to clear up the misunderstanding.

'Dad, relax. I don't know *what* happened, I just know that something odd did. I remember when I became...um; it was about the time when I started to menstruate. I must've been eleven or so. Ma-ma told me that something very strange and memorable had happened to her, the night that she had, you know, and that if I ever had needed to talk, that she was there for me.'

She paused, her recollection snagged on a moment of time. 'Then another time, I remember her telling me that she had written a story that could never be told. I asked her why, and she said that maybe one day I would understand. I always wondered about that story, whether she had really written it, or whether it had been her imagination. I'd forgotten all about it, but when you showed us that book, I think my subconscious found the connection and put the two together.'

Tommy was still awe-struck, amazed at the power of his mother to surprise him even from beyond the grave. *From beyond the planet*, he thought. She'd be in her final grave soon enough; at least, her human body, or her sixth uniform, soon would be. He realised contentedly that the essence that had infused his biological mother would continue. She had touched so many people, spread her happiness virus far and wide, and now he had the opportunity to further her work. To share her story further. He couldn't help but smile, and overcome with emotions, he realised with a shock, that he had tears running down his face.

'Dad?' Claire stepped forward, and staring for a moment with surprise at such a display of emotions, she wrapped her arms around him in a big hug. He placed the book down on the kitchen bench counter and hugged back, aware of his son-in-law standing in mute surprise at the sight. After a few moments he released her, and wiped the tears from his cheek. He turned to Aaron and remarked bemusedly, 'Women eh? Always needing a hug.'

They both laughed haltingly, but when Aaron reached out to shake his hand Tommy grabbed it and pulled him in for a manly bear hug. Their laughter must've attracted the boys, or perhaps grandpa's 'minute' had gone on for too long. Suddenly the two men found their legs wrapped up in the arms of a pair of six-year-olds, and as he reached down to put a hand on each of their heads he sent a thought up and out. *I do so hope you can see this Gloria. And you too, Ma. We miss you both so much.* Even though the words were in his head, he choked out a sob, which brought Claire back over, and she made it into a big family hug.

CHAPTER 29

[Preparatory Admonitions]

Nativity of Diamonds was waiting when the lights came on and Carols returned. She looked down at her panel: all sensors indicated that the gestate was developing at an optimal pace; all indicators were healthy. She flipped the pad to show the results: the clear red colours and orange highlights indicated that all the lessons had been learned, the template was secure for the next round. She gave Carols reassuring waves of confidence and encouragement, swirls of excited anticipation flickering through the colours on her shell.

'As you can see, she is developing extremely well. Her mastery of Introductory Emotions was impeccable. The expression of altruistic sentiment towards the other mammoths was an admirable development. She has successfully settled from being a collective or gestalt-entity over into inhabiting a singular body. She has now a rudimentary sense of self-awareness. That's real cause to celebrate,' she emphasised, and Carols swirled satisfaction and pride.

'In fact, you may even feel like you can talk to her already, and in a way you can. But you can only tell her a limited amount of information, even at this stage. The development of true consciousness is a delicate matter, even with our help. There are a number of important differences that make Sixth Form the most stimulating, and the most entertaining. No longer will she be a unique species, in the next level every single gestate dreams themselves to be a solitary member of a single mammalian species, the humans.'

'Those hairless apes that built the space shuttle?' Carols asked, slightly agog.

'Yes, my dear, those hairless apes.' She sighed a mottled blend of colours. 'And, unfortunately, there's lots of things particular to this final form that further complicate things. With the extension of her self-awareness and the introduction of semi-sentient paradoxes that are part of Intermediate

Emotions, you will see her develop stable neural patterns. She will understand that she is an individual, yet part of a community. She will start to manipulate her environment in more complex fashions, and come to terms with death in a manner spiritual or existential.' She paused, gazing gravely at the young Red.

Remember, it's *her* path, you don't need to do anything. In fact, the official line is that you are not encouraged to get involved or communicate. But...' she extended the modifier into a three-syllable word, teasingly offering what she knew every mother wanted to hear. 'You can now communicate with her, in a fashion. It won't be with her consciousness exactly. You'll see a lot more sleeping and dreaming in Form Six, and it is then that her mind is most open to contact. As a general rule, mind you, there are always exceptions, and your little stellar already has a couple of stand-out qualities, so who knows?'

Nativity of Diamonds nearly always used that phrase, regardless of how tenuous the comparison was. Carols' gestate had started out as a carnivorous plant , and travelled to space in the Second Form: both of which were extremely rare, so she had no compunction or hesitation about saying what she did say. She couldn't help feel a little nostalgic when she used that line. Over the eons of service she had channelled that emotional response into reinforcing the genuine encouragement she was giving. It was extra nice when it really was true.

'Now, as I said,' Nat continued happily, 'The official line is that you are 'not encouraged', but in reality, communicating with your baby is completely natural. The bottom line, your baby now has five memory shunts in operation, so she probably won't remember anything that you do say to her, even if to you it feels like solid bonding at the time. If you like, there are specific 'Rules for Being Human' that have been unofficially approved, although as I said, there is no evidence that the embryonic mind will actually remember your words. You are not encouraged to officially, but certainly you are allowed to tell them to her. If you like.'

Carols nodded vigorously, and Nat surprised herself in how taken up she was in this pregnancy. Giving birth was surprisingly engrossing. A light-pad appeared in front of her, and they gazed at the three rules together.

1.   You have everything you need inside you already.

2.   You will constantly acquire and develop skill-sets.

3.   You will forget this.

She laughed, and looked over at *Nativity of Diamonds*. 'Are these for real? Does anyone think these will help?'

Nat laughed too, her body rippling in colours of bemusement. 'They are serious. And you might be surprised how helpful these simple rules can be. Also, how hard it is for the semisents, or 'humans', to appreciate them. You'll see soon enough, don't worry. You'll want to scream these things at your child, and she won't hear you. Prepare to be astonished, frustrated and amazed at what you might think are incomprehensibly ridiculous choices, and the adoption of outrageously wasteful and even destructive routines. You'll see mind-bogglingly hilarious rituals and patterns develop. Trust me; you won't believe some of the things they do, even when you see it for yourself.'

'Self-destructive? Are they stupid? You call them semisents; how sentient are they?'

'I'm truly sorry to have to tell you this, but yes, some of the habits and patterns that humans develop are seriously self-destructive. They can act negligently towards others, towards their environment, and even to their own bodies and minds. We see pathologies that would keep psychologists puzzled for eons, but mainly it's neglect. The humans would probably call it "simple neglect" – that's the degree to which they don't appreciate their minds. They think that "neglect" is something simple, uncomplicated, a fact of life they can ignore. Therefore their offspring are not taught how to use their mental capacities. Generation after generation stagnates in ignorance.'

Carols in Sequins was trying to follow all she was saying, but it was difficult. What Nat was saying was unconscionable. She couldn't imagine any creature given self-awareness would squander it. It was so inexplicably an alien concept for any mother ever to imagine that a daughter of hers was going to adopt self-destructive habits, or live in ignorance of her potential. Nat's strange terms weren't helping. Carols instinctively emitted hues of confusion that deepened with each new term. Clicking hyperlinks rapidly, assimilating new data, she soon found herself stuck, hovering over {apathy}. It was a challenging idea to grasp.

'I'm sorry, darling, I really am...' Nat said. 'Unfortunately, the process of dying has some bits we would rather do without. But if these rough bits were removed, if evil and the obstacles were removed, the gestate would never learn. It is by coming up against these challenges that her mind is forced to grow. Her character is built and honed from how she chooses to respond to difficult situations. Or what habits she has, that do her choosing for her, but you know what I mean.' Carols nodded in tentative understanding as the lights dimmed again.

'Oh, by the way', Nat added, as they sunk into Form Six, 'It looks like you're having a baby boy.'

CHAPTER 30

(The Bedtime Story)

After dinner later that evening, Tommy left his daughter Claire and her husband to pore over his mother's journal themselves, while he went to tuck in his twin grandsons. Her amazing story was still spinning through his head, having monopolised the dinner conversation. Most of it went over the kids' heads though. They had been told that their Grand-mama had died, but they weren't that close to her, and were too young yet to know the true impact of mortality.

The last death in the family had been seven years ago. Gloria's accident had been months before the twins were born, a whole year before his mother had moved into the granny flat in his back yard. Seven years ago already: he could hardly believe how fast time was flying, but the evidence mischievously stared at him from a matching pair of six-year-old bundles of energy, embodied with brown hair and blue eyes. As he walked into the boys' room he was verbally accosted, the twins begging for a bed-time story.

'Read us a story Grandpa? Please?' they chimed.

'Ok, ok,' he said. 'But I don't need to read you a book in order to tell you a story. I know lots of stories. What kind of story shall it be?

'One from long ago', Alex suggested.

'One from far away', Kyle added.

They both murmured agreement, and, as young identical twins are prone to do, they started chanting 'long ago, far away' in perfect unison.

'Okay, okay. One from 'long ago', eh? Well, way back before there was the internet, back before television, back even before your mummy and your daddy were little kids just like you, way before...'

'Before the dinosaurs?' Alex asked.

'What about dragons?' Kyle wanted to know. 'Are there dragons?'

With a stern glance the interruptions ceased, and Tommy continued. 'I can tell you a very special story in fact. One that starts even further back, as far away and as long ago as you can get, but it still includes both dinosaurs and dragons!' Tommy paused and looked over his beloved freckle-faced grandsons, tucked in bed tight with just their heads and fingers poking out over the top of their blankets. 'Would you like that? The trouble is, it's a bit of a complicated story, I'm not sure you're old enough,' he gazed at them with mock seriousness.

'Please, Grandpa, please?'

'Ok then. Once upon a time – long ago, far away – so long ago and far away that time and space worked differently, all of the stars in the sky were alive. They had bodies made of light: they were big, swirling balls of energy. Now, do you remember how Grand-Mama once asked you if you could count all the stars in the night sky?'

Both the boys hummed an agreeable yes.

'Well, remember that our Sun is a star, too, and all of those stars out there are related to our Sun. It's just like a great big family, one with lots and lots of sisters and brothers and cousins. And every year, even though we can't see it from here, our stellar family has a couple of new babies. Some of them are big strong Blue babies. There are medium-sized Yellow stars just like our Sun. And there are lots of lots of tiny Orange and Red stars too. Now when a new baby star fires up, or wakes up, they already have the most powerful imaginations in the whole universe.' He paused, altering his intonation as he spoke directly to the boys. 'Can you imagine that? Do you have powerful imaginations boys? Can you imagine being a star? They live for millions and millions of years you know.'

'A-ha,' came from both beds. Alex's eyes were closed, but Kyle was looking at his Grandpa. Tommy mimed what he wanted Kyle to do. He closed his eyes deliberately, tilted his head slightly and smiled, dropping his shoulders a little. Kyle smiled first, and wiggled his shoulders as he snuggled closer to his imagination, and Tommy continued.

'Now stars can create anything they like, just using their minds. They can even change time and space around, like the way you can change around your Lego blocks. They are only limited by their own imaginations. Inside their imaginations they can create worlds. In fact, they can do anything they can dream. Even the smallest stars know how to do all that, because they learn all about how to be a star before they are born.'

'How?' asked Kyle.

'Well, children go to school to learn things, right? But baby chickens don't need to go to school, or puppies or kittens. They learn things in their dreams before they are born, how to do all the things that a grown-up star needs to know.'

'I wish I could learn things in my sleep,' said Alex.

'Yeah, me too!' added Kyle.

'Well, your brain is a pretty amazing thing. Because in fact, you *do* learn things while you are asleep. But it's not quite the same. It's similar, but much more complicated. The baby stars all go to a special kind of dreaming school, where special teachers look after them. They don't 'teach' though, they just keep watch, because baby stars don't know what they really are. The teachers watch over them, keeping them safe and keeping them company, a bit like a fairy godmother or a guardian angel.'

'Why don't the baby stars know what they are?' asked Kyle.

'Well, let's see. I know. What did you dress up as last time you went to a fancy dress party?'

'A policeman!' said Kyle.

'A doctor!' replied Alex.

'And when you wore the policeman or the doctor's uniform, I bet you acted like a policeman, right? And like a doctor, right?' The boys were both looking at him now, and they nodded vigorously. Alex, usually the more talkative one, looked like he was about to start talking about his doctor outfit, but Tommy put up his finger to indicate he should wait, and he continued his own story.

'You see, the uniforms that baby stars wear are so convincing that they actually *become* whatever form they are wearing. They forget that they are really baby stars, and they think to themselves, 'Hey, I have a fish body. I must be a fish. Or if they are a bird, they see the world through the eyes and the mind of a bird. The baby stars never think to themselves, 'Gee, this could be just a stage I'm going through, or a fancy dress outfit I'm wearing. One day when I'm all grown up I'm gonna become a star, but today I'm a...'

'A dragon?' Alex prompted.

'A dinosaur?' Kyle submitted predictably.

Tommy smiled to himself. The boys' eyes were tightly shut, but to six-year-old boys there must probably appear to be dragons and dinosaurs everywhere.

'Yes, and I bet you already know there were lots of different dinosaurs. Some of them were birds, or fish. As the baby stars learn everything there is to know about being a plant or a bug, or a fish or a bird, they take on harder lessons, just like at school. Say, what grade are you boys starting this year?'

'Three,' they answered in unison.

'And how many grades are there altogether, before you move up to a new school?'

'Six!'

'Well it's actually exactly the same for baby stars. They have six different grades too, but for them each new grade or form comes with a different uniform. And when they put on that uniform and start a new form at school, they become whatever that uniform is. Each time it's a completely new body, a different kind of life altogether. Maybe they are a fish in one, a dragon in another, a dinosaur in another. And then, after their six Forms are over, they remember who they are, and everything they have been. Once they get all their memories back, then they are born as a star, one that lives forever and can create anything they desire.' He let that sink in for a moment before continuing.

'But first, they have to get through each level, right?' The boys nodded. 'So, first time in, the baby star gets a simple kind of plant uniform, where it learns very basic life skills, like learning how to breathe and how to grow strong in one spot. Then once they can do that, they get to go to Form Two. They forget that they were just a plant, or a tree, and they put on a bug uniform. A tiny, tiny bug. Really tiny, microscopic, like a virus or bacteria. There they learn how to eat and how to move about from place to place.

Then in Form Three they first become an animal. They get an insect uniform, and for the rest of Form Three they think they really are an insect. Now I want you to think, boys. What do you think that a baby star learns as an insect? Can you figure it out? Use your imaginations, and think of an example.' The boys thought for a less than a minute before they answered.

'How to make noise?' Alex proposed.

'How to build homes?' Kyle countered.

'Very good boys! I'm impressed, that was quick. Good answers. Communication and basic tool use. Excellent. So the baby star now knows how to grow, and how to move. How to talk, and how to reproduce. Ok, are you ready for a harder question? I warned you this tale could get complicated, and you are only in...Grade *Three* did you say? Perhaps I should continue this another time, when you're older.'

Tommy's mock threat received the response he expected, and it was amid their assertions of being big boys and wanting the story to continue that Tommy became aware of someone standing in the hallway listening in. He suspected it was Claire, but wouldn't be surprised to find Aaron at her side. He hoped so, in a way. This was the first time he was telling this story. Perhaps the first time this story, only ever written down in his mother's astonishing journal, had ever been told.

He wondered if his mother too was in some way part of his silent audience, even now. Watching him stitch and sew her words into a narrative, so simple and coherent that six-year-olds could comprehend, but one that adults would also find fascinating. He missed her already, and wished he'd had the opportunity to talk to her about the intriguing journal she'd kept. There was no time for thinking about those kinds of wishes though, not with two young boys eager for the story to continue.

'So, let's see. In Form Four, there will of course be a new uniform, one that comes with new lessons. Now the baby star lives in the air or the oceans, and thinks it is a fish, or a bird. So, for example it might think it is...'

'A shark?'

'A pterodactyl?'

Saw that coming, he thought, and he answered with a grin. 'Exactly. Now what special skills could a baby star learn in Form Four? Remember it has to be things they couldn't have learnt earlier, and they still need to use the skills they've already gained.'

'Flying!'

'Swimming!'

Their answers came at him faster than he anticipated, but perhaps they'd all been ignoring the obvious, he thought, his mother and mythical great-uncle included. The six levels being divided into two sections of three might have been something arbitrary, maybe not.

Once again he thought over the mnemonic chart his mother had created. It had stuck with him. The six themes in a list didn't create an acronym, and he had wondered briefly what image his mother had used back when she first wrote it down. She had gone over the first letter of each word with her pen repeatedly, making the 'C' in Corporeal a definitive bold, as with the 'M' in Mobility and the 'C' in Communication. The C-M-C had immediately brought to mind his three younger sisters: Chelsie, Marilyn, and Cassandra. When he first saw the letters he had wondered if his mother had deliberately incorporated her secret acronym into the girl's names, and then wondered if, like him, the three 'ST' words had made her think of his father's youngest brother Stewart, afflicted with a terrible stutter. The second set of three words all began with 'ST': start, stop and stay. How to start something, how to stop something, how to stay oneself. St-St-Stewie.

He smiled; glad none of his offspring had to suffer like that. Stewart didn't stutter anymore, but it couldn't have been easy. He looked back and forth to his adoring grandsons, hanging on his next words. Leading the boys along with the story, he started a sentence for them. 'Ok, good. And when you can fly or swim, you can go...'

'Anywhere in the world!'

'Up in the clouds!'

'Again, both good answers boys. The baby stars in Form Four learn how to take bigger steps, to go on bigger adventures. Over the highest mountains and under the deepest oceans. They learn how to explore, how to question and interrogate. How to move like they've never moved before. Then, when they have finished learning how to start new things, next they have to learn how to...?'

'Stop things?' proffered Alex, tentatively.

Tommy hadn't quite expected them to get that right, and was certain the burst of pride that Claire and Aaron were feeling at the moment was flowing through the open door strongly enough to give away their presence. 'That's very perceptive of you Alex,' Tommy acknowledged. 'Yes, in Fifth Form the baby star needs to learn how to stop things. Because sometimes, things can look like they're unstoppable. Can you imagine an example of something that sometimes looks completely unstoppable?'

There was a pause then, until Kyle suggested their dog, and they all laughed. 'Yes, Parker is a good example: a perfect example actually. Tell me, how does Parker learn how to behave, how to stop doing things?'

'Sometimes Mummy smacks her,' Alex said, and Tommy tried to hide a smile.

'Ok, so she can be punished, but she can be rewarded too, right? She's always learning new things. And not just because she lives with you, here in this house. When she was born her mummy fed her and was constantly teaching her puppy-dog things. All mammals learn things from their mummies and daddies. Sometimes, a baby mammal is born with no defences and minimal instincts, and they have to rely on their parents until they are older. They have lots of things to learn, they have to figure out how to survive and to protect themselves from all kinds of dangers. Now here's a tough Fifth Form question. Are you ready? Can you think of something else that is especially different now, comparing Parker with a flock of birds or a school of fish or a kind of tree or a species of bug?'

The pause went on for a while, so he helped them out. 'Think about it like this: are the fish in your tank really like the one in the movie?' There was simultaneous and drawn-out 'No' from the twins. 'So...?' he prompted, hoping, wondering. It was Alex who guessed at the answer.

'I guess...fish don't *really* have personalities like in cartoons. But Parker does. It's like, she knows she's a dog, a single dog. The fish and the insects and all that, they're all the same. They aren't like people. They don't know anything.'

'Well done. They do know lots of things, but they aren't what we call "self-aware", while Parker knows who she is. She has what we call a personality, or a sense-of-self, which as far as we know, fish and insects and plants don't have.'

'Plants?' Alex repeated incredulously.

Tommy nodded sagely. 'Yes, well, they still have what we could call mental links, things like instincts and automatic reactions, but of course they don't have as many as fish, okay? And not forgetting, some species of insect have a communal mind. Like ants. We don't know what they're saying, because they're in a different form. Complicated bodies still do the things that the simpler ones do, but we don't speak their language. But of course, you're right. While Parker can understand hundreds of human words, she's not people. Baby stars don't start to think that they are people until...can you guess?'

'Form Six!' they answered in unison.

'You got it. Very good. In Sixth Form the baby stars put on a human costume. And then when they are finished learning all there is to learn as a human, then they get to have a rest from all their learning before they are born. Then they join their families in the heavens, and live forever as a star. But you know

what? For them to learn all their human lessons, it means...
they need to do *all* their homework!'

The boys groaned, but he could tell it was a sound of
bemusement. 'For now, all I want you to do is to go to sleep and
to have a great big dream. I want you to dream the dreams of a
baby star...how about one who is in Form Three? Or, how
about one that is just putting on a Fourth Form uniform? What
do you think? Ok? And in the morning over breakfast, I want
you to tell your Mum and Dad all about it.'

'I'm gonna dream of being a pterodactyl' Kyle stated.

'I'm gonna dream of being an eagle' Alex affirmed.

'That's good. You can both fly over the top of our house and
make sure we are all safe while we sleep.' He stood up and
reached over to brush their fringes back from their drowsy
eyes. 'You can stop dreaming that you're human for a little
while, my precious little stars.'

He kissed them each on the forehead, and as he did they
each muttered 'Goodnight Grandpa'. After kissing Kyle, the
little man mumbled to him. 'Grandpa? I bet Grand-mama loves
being a star.' Tommy quickly stood up straight, holding back
the tears he felt welling up.

As he left the boys' room, he found both Claire and Aaron in
the corridor, as anticipated. He hadn't expected however to see
tears streaming down Claire's face, and he could see that his
mother's strange little story had more than a passing impact on
all of them. He appreciated that telling this tale to the boys had
made his mother's entire story seem far more coherent. The
way that the boys had so naturally responded, their acceptance
of the idea with such obvious enthusiasm led him to wonder
briefly what the loopholes or plot-holes in her little theory
might turn out to be. He couldn't think of any immediately, and
resolved to investigate that idea later. For now, he reached out
his arm and put it around Claire, and she shifted to his
shoulder for a brief squeeze.

'Thanks Dad', she whispered.

'Tea?' Aaron suggested, and he nodded, following his
children back to the lounge area, leaving their two little stars to

dream. Blissfully, the boys went straight to sleep after their bedtime story. Outside, the clouds had cleared in patches, allowing a select few stars to smuggle their light through the turgid dark. As it was still reasonably warm, while Aaron prepared a pot of tea, Tommy and Claire went out back and sat on the porch. Conversation between the two of them was a little stilted, their hearts too churned up for coherent conversation.

When Aaron arrived, he noticed the silence, and quietly placed the tray down on the coffee table. He'd suspected no-one was hungry, but he placed a box of assorted biscuits on the tray. They weren't going to be eaten, but he thought the food would at least make it symbolically a family starnic. The gesture drew a big smile from his father-in-law, and Aaron decided to start the conversation.

'I really liked your story, Pop.' Ever since the boys had started calling Tommy 'Pop', everyone had adopted the habit. Tommy and Claire smiled, and she echoed the sentiment.

'It was pretty amazing. The way you took Grand-Mama's dreams and turned her into a star. I mean, you turned it into a story, something the boys understood. It's like a form of Gaia, but alive in a way we can understand more easily, perhaps. You've got a solid framework to hang all sorts of things on, like consciousness, or cosmology, or philosophy.'

Tommy sat back and raised his hands, palms forward. 'This isn't my philosophy, or even my story. I don't want any credit for this. It was your Grand-Mama's story. It still is hers. I just told it to the boys.'

There was a pause, a silence while they digested his words. Claire looked incredulous, and asked hesitatingly, 'You are going to write it though, aren't you? You said before, about having a story...?

Tommy slowly nodded his head, and a wry smile bubbled its way onto his face. He turned and looked at his daughter, then over at her husband, grasping that he not only had a story, he had their complete support. He raised his eyebrows and half-swallowed, mocking nerves he didn't really feel. 'Yeah, I guess I am.'

After congratulations and reiterations of encouragement waned, Claire focused them on the story. 'I think you could use some real science in this story. In fact, I think you could use a lot. It doesn't have to be airy-fairy at all. I know this gives a whole new meaning to soul mates, or love at first sight, and probably explains why Grand-Mama talked to her plants like they were her pets.' The whole family smiled at that memory, having all teased Katie at some point for her unusual habits, before Claire continued.

'We know that our brain has layers, like the rings in a tree, or at least, the same idea of growth building on earlier growth. In what I read, they'd identified three, so I don't know how you'd factor in the earlier dreams.' She smiled, and bobbed her head as she corrected herself. 'The earlier forms. The plant, and the bacteria?'

Both men looked back amused, sharing her puzzlement. She shrugged and continued. 'Anyway, at the core we have a reptilian brain, where our evolutionary heritage embodied us with instincts and concepts like location, or places, for example. Then the middle layer was, or is, a mammalian brain, where we acquired social skills. Concepts like the sense of self you mentioned, and ideas of hierarchy. And the latest stage in the evolution of the brain is us, humans.'

'Where did we read that consciousness was a spectrum?' Aaron asked his wife. 'Remember how we joked that really smart plants could monitor more than humidity and temperature? And that a smart reptile or bird could out-think a dim-witted mammal?' She smiled and shrugged, off with her own thoughts.

'I wonder what stars would look back on and see as the skills we acquired as humans?' Tommy pondered. 'Ma wrote down some ideas: have you gotten that far in to the journal yet? Have you read the real meaning of scatter-fuggling?' Claire nodded, but Aaron shook his head. 'I'll let Ma explain that then. But what do *you* think?'

Aaron answered slowly with an, 'I think...' allowing Claire to jump in with a playful, 'Cogito?'

Aaron counted back with 'Ergo', and Tommy completed the quote with a 'Sum'. *Cogito Ergo Sum*, or *I think, therefore, I am*: Descartes famous conclusion this was all that anyone could ever prove.

'So, self-awareness, or consciousness, I guess. The ability to think,' Aaron suggested. 'Individuality, plus relative space and time – the ability to compare possibilities, predict outcomes.'

'Perhaps they won't remember being human any more than we remember being anything other than human,' Claire extrapolated. 'Our brains re-wire our neural connections after we learn something new, perhaps it happens in other situations too? Like with those uniforms in Pop's stellar school story, perhaps we – heck, perhaps even the stars are wearing a form that makes them forget too.' The men both *hmm*-ed, considering the possibilities. 'If blind people struggle to grasp the idea of a map or blueprint, what hope have we got figuring it out?'

'Going back to answer my own question,' Tommy said contemplatively, 'I remember a writing teacher once told me that human conflicts and drama are battles over imagined futures, that human beings alone 'dream and scheme'. Perhaps it's the conceiving of variable futures?'

Claire responded hesitantly. 'Well, that's not entirely true. We know many mammals dream, and we know that even some birds experience what we think of as REM sleep.' She looked at Aaron's enquiring stare, and asked, 'I thought we saw that on a David Attenborough special.' He shook his head, and she shrugged. 'It doesn't mean they are dreaming of possible futures, they could be just reliving experiences.'

'There's something else to consider,' Aaron added, and then paused to drink his tea and sneak a glance up at the stars. 'I guess it's a little difficult to imagine, but perhaps that's part and parcel of being human. Or *Sixth-Formers*, according to the theories of this Justin character.' They all shared a giggle at the language she'd used. 'Perhaps seventh-form lessons are simply beyond our ability to conceptualise, or imagine? Even if our human brains are a learning network, and our pre-frontal cortex is going to become another layer or level of foundation for a conscious stellar mind, how is that different than believing in the afterlife of a fundamentalist religion? We can't prove it, can we?'

Claire held up the journal, as if the answer was self-evident. 'How else can you explain some of the things she wrote about in here? Her stuff here on stellar family groups, from when, the 1930s? And the other things she wrote nearly a century ago on brain-training? That's cutting-edge neurobiology today!'

Aaron calmed her protest. 'Honey, I'm not denying any of that. I really like the idea, and can't see anything wrong with it. By the sounds of it, the boys like the idea too. But that doesn't mean it's scientifically testable.' Aaron smiled as he watched father and daughter wrinkle their lips in exactly the same way, a sign of begrudging acceptance, and he briefly wondered if the habit would be passed onto another generation. 'At least, not outside of a science fiction novel,' he added, generating smiles from both his relatives.

Aaron turned directly to Claire and added, 'Wouldn't you like to ask Dr Sheldon what he thinks of the astrophysics? Or perhaps get an Indian opinion on cosmology?

'No, let's ask his – his what? His future binary partner? I wonder what would Dr Amy's opinion be on how best to test the developmental neurobiology?' She countered with a cheeky smile.

Their obviously shared reference went straight over Tommy's head, and he assumed they were talking about how they had recently flown interstate to attend a visiting scientist, whose tour – like that of so many bands and international celebrities – had bypassed their isolated city altogether.

'Neither of those names sounds Japanese. Neither of those are that doctor of the future you flew over East to see, are they?' Tommy asked, and when Aaron and Claire cracked up laughing, he simply shook his head and rolled his eyes in mock tolerance. He thought to himself, *It didn't matter anyway, not here and now*. There were more important things to devote precious time to. Claire stopped giggling and moved over and sat next to him, and he placed his arm around his grown daughter, seeping pride from every pore.

Aaron watched as his wife and father-in-law sighed together. He smiled and looked up to the stars.

Tommy saw Aaron smile, and was once again surprised by the fact his son-in-law had no farming background in his family. He was just so down-to-earth. He and Gloria had raised their kids to be rational thinkers, and had both been impressed with the way their son-in-law had been raised. Tommy looked up at the stars too, and felt an unfamiliar warmth deep inside, one that long been absent. Most days he was fine, and could deal with Gloria's passing privately and quietly. But today, having lost his mother, he had repeatedly been aware of old habits, pulling him into retreat.

Pleasantly, he appreciated that now those ropes held no tension. The comfort of routine looked appealing, but he knew he'd eaten at that joint too often. He simply couldn't pretend that the appeal would be fulfilling, and he mentally laughed at the image he had of himself, in retreat and in hiding. The image dissipated surprisingly quickly, and Tommy joined Aaron in smiling at the stars, immersing himself in the flow of their light.

Claire was used to Aaron's peaceful grin. As much as she admired his attitude, it could still be flat-out annoying sometimes. When dating he'd once described himself as 'happy by habit', and Claire had immediately known that he would get her Grandma's approval.

Sitting out on the porch, she could barely contain her happiness at seeing her Dad smile again so readily. She had confided in Aaron only recently that she was concerned about how her Dad would react when his mother died. He'd simply said, *Let's up the contagion.* Since then at least twice each week they'd had him over for a visit, or taken the boys – the happiness vector – over to his place. Tonight she cried a little thanks inside for Aaron. From where she was sitting, it looked like the long remission her Dad's happiness virus had been taking might have finally worn off.

Pity you made that promise, Ma-Ma, she thought. *Your boy needed to hear this story a long time ago. At least he's got it now.* And with gratitude and love, she looked away from her relatives, and joined them in contemplating the stars overhead.

CHAPTER 31

[Form Six: Under the Volcano]

Carols in Sequins patiently watched. It was noticeably harder for her this time, standing back. But she exercised her blossoming maternal instincts. From heaven's observation deck, she restrained her joy, and simply relished the act of watching her baby boy grow. This was Form Six, which meant she was nearly all done, and she felt supremely confident. It really was all good.

Tavi was a notably happy child. He had dark tanned skin and black curly hair, as did all the men in the village. Although sea-faring, the village was isolated from the more dense congregations of humanity by a continent of jungle and parsecs of lifestyle. Nestled at the foot of the highest mountain in the region, the town was towered over by an impressive temple complex. Made of hewn stone, the ornate pagodas were constantly bedecked with offerings to the gods. Home to over a thousand people, just over half of which were adult males, Tavi admired and emulated his elders with the enthusiasm and curiosity of the young. In the definitions of the tribe, a boy reached adulthood through the *Sambia* ceremony, and was blessed by the gods in his thirteenth year. Tavi was only seven, but his older brother was twelve.

On the day before the gods came, he sat and watched his brother prepare for the ceremony, staring with an intensity that belied his years. He had finished his chores and was sitting on a wide upper branch of the main tree, long favoured by children for its view over the quadrangle. In his hands were a piece of wood and his conch knife, but he wasn't whittling anything. He was silent, watching.

On the ground in front of the shaman's hut, his brother Siva sat cross-legged, weaving the intricate head-band he would wear tomorrow for his coming-of-age ceremony. There were two other boys with him, each equally fixed in concentration on the ritual lacing patterns they were creating for their own trials. On the dry dirt floor in front of Siva lay a bamboo woven arm-band, a visual reminder of the pattern they were constructing.

All morning the three boys had practised spear-throwing and wrestling, joining with some of the younger men in the preparations for the hunt. These young men had been play-mates not so long ago; but they were now men. Men had responsibilities: not only to their wives and children, but to the village and the King. Every adult pitched in with the preparations for the annual *Sambia*; even the very old and very young helped out as they were able. It would not be as auspicious as last year, but the phases of the moon were always different. Tavi wondered how the moon would behave when the time came for him to become a man.

Looking down towards the harbour, he could see the sky to the west was still bright. Brilliant rays of sunshine still lit the village, but from the angle of the light coming through the trees, he knew the fisherman would be pulling up their boats down by the harbour. Layer upon layer of colour were stacked upon the horizon: the softest orange to the darkest purples, all being gradually compressed into darkness by the encroaching night sky.

Soon their father would be home, their mother would call, and the family would gather to eat. His brother and the other boys would all need a hearty meal tonight. With tomorrow's exertions – the gods willing - they would become men. Simple rice and fish tonight, but large servings. The specialties for the banquet tomorrow were already prepared and put aside. He knew that the tribe would become stronger on the morrow, but all Tavi could think of was that his big brother was not going to be around to play with so much.

He'd already noticed the way that Siva looked at Serena, his betrothed. He didn't want Siva to leave; but that was the way of things. In the meantime, he sat and watched, trying to commit to memory the way that the light hit Siva's face; the peculiar manner he had of sticking out his tongue when he was concentrating; the scratch marks on his shoulder that had never properly healed.

The connection was strong, yet felt strange. Carols ghosted along with her baby; still providing the same degree of loving support and encouragement that she had always given. She'd never minded what form of life her precious had taken. Yet in this final level she felt more intrigued by each development. With each challenge accepted and overcome, it seemed to her that her baby became somehow innately stronger, more alive. The sense-of-self that her gestate was experiencing was far more developed than she had expected.

Tavi was part of a vibrant society. The humans were literate, users of tools, and bound by a code of ethics. Carols saw complex communication and co-ordination everywhere: the strongest warning tremors possible that true sentience was close to bursting forth. *Carols in Sequins* watched, entranced and enthralled. Filled with pride, she saw his human family teach him in the ways of their village, instilling spiritual values and an ethos of responsibility: both social and individual.

She was so filled with emotion to watch her baby develop; she could only look away for brief periods. Even then it was only while he was asleep. She discovered that the clearest communication she ever managed with her baby was right on the edge of his sleep cycle. Each and every night, she'd murmur love and encouragement. She wondered who was watching over the other developing minds surrounding her baby. How many degrees of separation were there between her and Tavi's brother; or between the guiding parent stellar of the village medicine man, for example?

As if summoning him with her thoughts, the local shaman priest suddenly came bolting out of his hut. Wild-eyed and screaming, he ran off in the direction of King Purnarvarman's court. Tavi watched his brother react to the abrupt exodus with concern. For the shaman priest to have had what appeared to be a disturbing vision the day before his rite-of-passage was not a good omen. Tucking his conch knife into a leather slip attached to his belt, Tavi quietly shimmied down the tree, keeping out of sight. He turned and ran to his family hut. He was sure that he would beat his brother Siva back home, but didn't want to take any chances. Once he had finished collecting the eggs and cleaning the pig sty, he was meant to be practising his archery. Not spying on his brother.

Carols smiled to herself, amused to wonder what he would think if he knew he was actually being watched all the time by his own big sister-to-be. Sister/mother/wife: the terms didn't really translate. The mind that currently thought of itself as Tavi would die one more time; this time not to another incarnation, but to a level of rest and assimilation. On the seventh level, the memories of each of the earlier six rounds would be unblocked, and context released. Understanding would dawn, and only then could a new mind be fully prepared for life.

The newest member of her family would be transferred, and travel via an entangled transit to the heart of her Brown, even now on the brink of fusion. Her new partner would come alive. They would share an intimate dance as binary partners, expanding and strengthening her personal space. Together they would be stronger, impress themselves deeper on the local substrates. And most importantly: protect her precious menagerie, with its complex biospheres and fragile carbon-based lifeforms.

She watched Tavi and his family eat their evening meal, animated by speculation about what the shaman had seen in his vision. Their mother Gita eventually told them in no uncertain terms that the discussion was closed; that they were to forget the matter. The boys knew better than to disobey a direct order, but the fact that their thoughts kept returning to speculation was obvious to all. Siva fidgeted throughout the evening, eventually going for a run along the shore to clear his head. Tavi played with his wooden animal collection for a while after dinner, and was fast asleep by the time his brother returned.

It was the middle of the night when they were both woken. Word of the shaman's warning vision had spread, and the sounds of a general evacuation were increasingly loud. The King's trumpets forced every last man, woman and child to rise from the peace of slumber and obey the general order. *'Everyone to the boats!'*

Listening to the bustle that young Tavi didn't understand, Carols was similarly confused. From her perspective, she couldn't perceive what all the fuss and drama was about: there was no imminent catastrophe that she could see signs of. The winds in the jungle trees were the same; the local animal populations remained undisturbed: apart from those roused by their human benefactors. She could taste the winds and sense the flow of energies pulsing throughout the atmosphere and the ocean, having refreshed those skill-sets during earlier levels.

Her dear Tavi couldn't do that at the moment, even though the acquisition of those skills had been his. Even if the shaman had some form of psychic or spiritual ability, she simply couldn't see what there was to be sensed. Yet it had obviously been a powerful enough vision that the King had ordered an immediate evacuation. Although he deemed the holy man's prophecy as valid, perhaps he was being overly cautious. Then again, perhaps his mind was fraying: neither Tavi nor Carols was in a position to know. All either of them could see was a semi-controlled panic as people tried to gather their most precious possessions.

Carols watched in silence, engrossed as Tavi quickly found himself with arms full, bustled out the door and down to the docks. There he could see an argument breaking out on a fishing craft over whether a goat was transportable. Obviously it was precious: but was it safe, or practical? He looked out to the bay and could see other boats ahead of them, their flickering lanterns casting eerie shadows of light against the karst fingers of stone that dotted the bay. By the look of the number of flickering lights, there were quite a few craft already filled and heading out into the bay. The prophecy had been clear: they had to leave the island before sunrise. Due to some enormous displeasure of the gods, the entire village was going to be destroyed.

Tavi had lived there his whole life. Though only seven years old, he had seen ivy grow and mould spread. He knew from the vines that grew all over the ancient stone temple in the Palace proper, that the village had been around forever. Or at least, since the ancient gods had brought their ancestors out of the waters and planted them here. The Holotan had always existed; he couldn't even imagine how everything could be destroyed. But with no-one listening, he gave up questioning.

With his guardian as confused as he was, Tavi and his family were at last underway. His father and Uncle Mare rowed, their strong even strokes lapping at the waters. The lights from the stars shone down, the lanterns and familiar voices echoed over the waves. The rhythmic paddling soon overwhelmed the noises from other boats, and the excitement of the adventure waned, leaving Tavi once again free to return to sleep. His younger sister lay nestled in his mother's lap, while his brother Siva and his cousins conferred in hushed tones at the other end of the boat.

The last thing Tavi saw before he dozed off was a worried look on his brother's face, staring back at the flickering lights of the village as they dimmed into the distance. He wondered whether the ceremony would be held on the next night, or whether they'd have to wait for the next moon? There had been no chance to find out before their parents had obediently bustled them down into the boat. The atmosphere around the island was pregnant with expectation as the first hues of the sun appeared on the horizon. No-one knew what to imagine, but everyone was on edge, keeping an eye on the horizon.

It was Siva who saw the birds circling over the temple: two large, strange birds with impossibly massive wingspans. Carols thought she heard a gasp of astonishment from Nat, but was as entranced with the sight as Tavi and his whole tribe. Ominousness seemed to fall from the sky, an invisible spray that washed out into the bay and splashed over the boats. Everyone stared.

As the massive birds wove their way gracefully down towards the crater on top of the mountain, Tavi felt the boat pick up speed again. He looked around and saw that everyone had now increased their pace; moreover each boat had someone staring at the point where the enormous birds had landed. Even his father and uncle kept trying to turn their heads between strokes, but soon concentrated on increasing their pace.

Tavi felt the spray of the water on his face, and turned to watch the churning wake they left in the glistening waters as they sped away from their home. The sun rose on the horizon, and the sky was clear and cloud-free. A beautiful day, totally at odds with the fluctuating emotions he felt around him. Tavi felt the concern of his family ebb and flow, swelling and subsiding in waves as steady as the movement of the boat.

He wasn't sure what happened first: the thunderous roar of wind or the magical appearance of a massive cloud out of nowhere. When he heard the shockwave he instinctively covered his ears. In the manner of seven-year-olds facing disaster everywhere, he dived toward his mother. He looked up to see that the blast had been so loud that even his father had covered his ears. There was a billowing dark vile pouring out of the mountain top, a thick coagulating cloud lit with red sparks that reminded him of a pride of tigers, with only their eyes piercing an otherwise impenetrable jungle night.

The boat rocked as the ocean seemed to move sideways, throwing everyone about and forcing his father and uncle to strain even harder to make the little dingy respond to their efforts. Cries of dismay arose from other boats. Not all had managed to keep upright, and he could see frantic rescue efforts happening around them. Tavi looked to his mother and saw barely restrained terror on her face as she stared at their island, which she quickly tried to hide as she held him and his sister close.

As his little sister was only two, his mother held her face into her bosom so as she couldn't watch. Tavi was not so petrified, but he still didn't understand what was happening. He thought that the mountain must be very sick; or that the gods must be far angrier than they had ever been. There were many vents of black steam bursting forth from the mountainside, even from other islands now.

There were many islands in the region; each bay was dotted with fingers of stone, karst eruptions of the long dead dragon that had carried their peoples to their archipelago home. The most recognisable of these was the Dragon's Tooth, a marker used by the young men of the village in swimming competitions. Tavi was looking directly at it when the tip of it suddenly exploded, and black smoke started to pour out. He could still make out the harbour where their village lay, and from there he could trace a visual path up the mountain towards the temple complex.

The mountain was bleeding. There was definitely fire there now, flowing and moving down toward the bay, skirting the freshly steaming vents as it flowed to the sea. He had never been to the Lake of Fire far above the highest parts of the temple; he had been looking forward to hearing about it when Siva retold his little brother of his adventures. Now that would never happen. He looked over and saw his brother staring, completely in shock, unable to process the loss of both the village and his imminent manhood.

Another blast of thunder rang over Tavi, and once again his mother's arms moved instinctively around him, pulling him close. He wiggled free to stare over the edge, back towards a wall of steam that now hid the island from view. The hazy veil made the glowing fibres of light etching their way across the landscape even more ominous. He looked up to see a far more concentrated burst of cloud being vomited out of the mountain – chunks of land and pools of fire mixed in flagrant meldings, lighting the ascending darkness from within.

The menacing cloud reached out into the otherwise clear skies, and there was nothing at all to stop the tide. Thicker and thicker it bellowed, spreading out north and south, before reluctantly conforming to the natural wind patterns of the region. The churning mass turned and headed east, making Tavi think that it was chasing them. He huddled closer to his mother and closed his eyes, but found that he was unable to erase the vision of an enormous red-eyed monster, bursting out from the centre of the earth and chasing him over the waters. He imagined it squashing him and his family between the glistening black skies and the tumultuous unreliable oceans that separated them from safety.

Carols was watching through his eyes, astonished at what she could see. The volcano had erupted, but without any warning signs. None of the animal life had sensed the shifting pressures that presaged tectonic release. No mass evacuation had occurred in the bird population; indeed from what she could see, the initial blast had deafened every ear drum within five kilometres of the crater. She imagined that many animals were probably so disoriented they were caught in the subsequent shock waves, disintegrated before they had time to even begin to react to those first tremors. If not for that holy man, she thought, her baby and all the humans there would not have survived that first blast. She wondered if the shaman's stellar guide even knew what he'd seen in that vision.

Tavi watched his mother quietly sobbing, holding his crying sister close while wiping tears from her eyes. He looked back up at the massive cloud chasing the flotilla of boats across the ocean. Despite the gods' obvious displeasure, he still prayed, hoping that they would arrive somewhere safe soon. The sweltering clouds were already overhead, and sunlight was struggling to reach them even though the day had only just begun. A breeze of burnt jungle swept over him, and the growing twilight was only made more menacing by the grumbling and gurgling of the black cloud bank that was inexorably smothering the sky. He looked over at his father. Sweat poured off him as he resolutely rowed, steady stroke after steady stroke. He could see the pressure embedded in his father's expression, and he resolved to be strong. Just like his dad.

For a young boy, he felt no strangeness at the sense of peace that washed over him. Some part of him thought that making that simple little decision had been important, that somehow he had gone through his own rite of passage. No matter what happened, he knew his world would never be the same again. He would never be the same again. He turned and wrapped his arms around his mother, triggering another enormous sob that set off his sister again. He reached out to his sister, patting her long dark hair consolingly, the way he saw the womenfolk sometimes do.

Looking back and forth between his parents and the other boats, he tried to ignore the spreading darkness above. He tried not to look up at the sky, unsure of the origins of those churning storms, or what they meant. He knew his home was gone, but what had happened was far beyond his imaginings. He couldn't visualise the possibility that the massive moss-covered stone blocks of the King's temple complex had been blasted into the atmosphere; that they were even now cooking with seared jungle and bubbles of lava in the stew of destruction that was gobbling up the sky in every direction.

Inside that tumultuous congealing of elements there were trillions of light, porous pieces, many of which would eventually cruise right around the planet. But not the larger pieces, not the heaviest chunks. They were destined to return to Earth much closer to home. Tavi heard a strange sound as the first of those massive blocks plummeted out of the boiling clouds, but in his determination to look around rather than up, he never saw it coming. Its splashdown annihilated Tavi and his entire family in a whistling shriek as wind and fire, earth and sea collided.

As more and more parts of the volcano fell into the sea, the bay was transformed into a frothy steamy bubbling cauldron of screams and cries for help. Once the steam dissipated and the darkness spread outward to capture more of the sky, a single boatload of bewildered tribesmen found themselves the only survivors of what yesterday had been the flourishing and proud tribe of the Holotan people.

CHAPTER 32

(The Strangest Stranger)

After a while, Tommy let himself out, leaving them sitting together. With Claire having her own office at the front of the house where she worked from home, her flexible hours meant she could read the journal cover-to-cover tomorrow, and he left it safely in her care. Having read the journal, the story was alive in Tommy's head. They'd all lost track of the time, engrossed in thoughts about eternal stars going to school.

On the drive home he had the radio playing, but he didn't hear it. The sounds were elided by his senses, edited from his focus. When he arrived home he parked the car in the driveway as usual.

Except things weren't 'as usual' anymore, he thought sardonically. *Anything but.*

Collecting his jacket from the back seat, for a moment he thought he saw a light in his mother's unit reflected in his neighbour's window. When he turned to look directly, the granny flat looked the same as on any other night. The soft glow of the solar animals decorated her garden beds outside, while inside he could see the faint illumination of his mother's night light in her bathroom. He looked back at his neighbour's window quickly, wondering what it was that he had seen. Perhaps he had mistaken a light inside their house for a reflection, but no. He was astonished to see that in the reflection of the window he could still see a light on in the lounge of the granny flat. But looking straight at it, there was nothing. He did a quick back and forth, and it was still there. Then it wasn't. There was nothing there. Rather, there was, but only in reflection.

Checking around the street, he could see the lights on across the road. There were cars parked on the curb, but no-one about. His curiosity was aroused, so bracing himself, he opened the gate that led to the back yard. The latch made a slight click as he entered; the mundane normality of the sound only worked to unnerve him further. A breeze blew through the yard, setting a couple of wind chimes to tinkle; and he could hear a dog barking in the distance. He still had his keys in his hand, and as the motion-detector light on her front porch activated, he found the spare key to the granny flat. He unlocked the security door and then the main door, turning on the light switch as he walked in. He could smell his mother: the house seemed soaked in her touch. He smiled sadly, wondering how long it would take for that to fade. He closed the door and wiped his feet, an automatic habit.

Looking around the open plan lounge-dining-kitchen, everything appeared to be exactly as he had left it just yesterday. The pictures smiled up out of their frames, the furniture sat there waiting to be used. His mother's favourite armchair looked strangely empty now, as if there was a psychic hole there. An indented cushion would never again feel her sit on it. Only in his memory and imagination was she still there.

He sighed. There was so much that needed to be done here, but tonight definitely wasn't the time. He hadn't had much sleep at all last night. Losing someone close to you can be more than draining - in some indefinable way that words can't express, it empties a part of you. Tommy had been through that feeling often enough over this last decade. He knew he was exhausted, so he decided to quickly walk down the corridor just to double check that everything was ok before he headed to bed for a well-deserved rest.

The night-light in the combined bathroom-laundry turned itself off when he flicked the switch for the corridor light, and Tom thought he heard the sound of a cat landing on the floor behind him. He wondered again at how tired he was. His mother didn't have a cat, and there were no windows open that would allow one entry. He had only been going to check each room quickly, but now he turned on each light methodically, to be sure. But everything was as his mother had left it weeks ago, and nothing had moved since he'd been here last night to collect her prized journal. There was certainly no cat, or any other animal.

Tom furrowed his brow in confusion as he turned off the lights. As he passed her bedroom, he stopped for a second. One of her photo albums was lying open on her bedside drawers.

He was sure that it hadn't been there, but he was already starting to doubt his own mental competency. *Maybe it had been there*, he thought, *I'm too darn tired for this now. Enough mysteries for one day*, he chortled.

He turned off the bedroom light, but try as he might to defer the mystery until tomorrow when he had a clearer head, he couldn't. There was something seriously bugging him now, like a dog scratching to get inside, but inside his head. A similar sensation to one he was familiar with: having a word on the tip of your tongue, but this was much more intense. Nagging. There was a connection, something he'd read but forgotten. He was back at the front door again when he remembered. It wasn't just something that he'd read, it was something that his mother had written about some of the other abilities her eternal uncle had laid claim to. He looked around the empty lounge, and felt a little silly at himself even considering what he was about to do. He cleared his throat, and called out.

'Justin? Katherine's Uncle Justin?'

He wasn't really surprised when there was no response, and he chided himself for even expecting one. But there was still something there, something that made him think that he hadn't necessarily been silly to call out. It wasn't as if he was calling forth some mythical creature, or a demon or fairy tale character. And as he laughed at the idea, another thought jumped up at him. The name. *You have to use their real name*, he thought. In the stories, you had to use their real name, and 'Justin' wasn't his real name. He struggled to remember what it was, wishing he had the journal here with him now so he could consult it quickly. He knew that it started with 'Zesty', but the other parts of his name refused to leave their hidden refuge of memory. What the hell, he thought.

'Zest'? He called out; glad that no-one could witness what he was doing. A shiver ran through him, the feeling someone might describe as having someone walk over your grave. He wondered if his mother could see what he was doing; or if not his human mother, then maybe his stellar mother. His guardian angel, the parent star overseeing his birth, could even now be watching him. He nodded slightly, to whom or what he wasn't sure. He wanted to acknowledge that if his mother had always had such a sense of being watched over, having a real and personal guardian angel that cared in the same way a parent does for their new-born, it probably went a long way in explaining her general attitude, the laid-back and yet confident happiness that typified everything she did. He was becoming lost in his memories, swollen with admiration and astonishment for his mother, when an unexpected voice instantly brought him back to the here-and-now.

'Yes?'

There was a man sitting in his mother's favourite armchair, as calm and comfortably as if he'd been sitting there for hours, and he stared at Tommy with a mixture of bemusement and interest. A thick head of dark brown hair poked out from underneath a Yankees cap, and he wore jeans and a plain blue polo shirt. There was no doubt in Tommy's head who this was. In the journal there was a picture, a pencil sketch done by a young girl without artistic skill, an attempt by his mother to capture the look of the man from her vision. It hadn't been titled, there hadn't even been an inscription to say that the drawing was meant to be her Uncle Justin, but he had guessed straight away when he'd seen it, as quickly as he knew who the man in front of him now was.

'Uncle Justin', he said. His shoulders slumped as the words expired out of his mouth, and he shook his head a little in disbelief. His mother's tale had been true, and he was now talking to someone older than humanity.

'Perhaps we can dispense with the 'Uncle' part, but yes, Katherine knew me as her 'Uncle Justin'. Nice to meet you. Tommy, right?'

He nodded mutely, wondering briefly how he knew his name. As if reading his mind, Justin gestured around the lounge room, and the answer immediately became obvious. There were family pictures in abundance. His novels, autographed of course, sat proudly displayed on the centre shelf of the bookshelf that dominated the far wall next to the photograph of himself, Gloria and Katie, on the red carpet at his film premiere. The lounge positively swam in family paraphernalia, and he was overcome with both a sense of loss and a moment of awe, slightly dizzy at the number of beautiful memories this room held, framed in pewter, or attached by magnet.

'I was too late' Justin said simply, and Tommy gathered that this stranger already knew.

'She...it was...it was this morning' he got out. His daughter Claire had found out by calling the hospital, so he hadn't had to say it out loud to her, or to his son Jackson as it turned out. Claire had quietly given him the heads up when she invited him and his family over for dinner that evening. He'd had to leave a message with his sister Chelsie's P.A., asking her to call, and when he'd spoken to Marilyn she'd been drowning in the attentions of her own children. Cassie had guessed what the call was about before he ever spoke the actual words 'Mum's dead'. He tried once more, knowing that some part of his heart probably needed to say it out loud.

'Mum's dead. She died this morning. At hospital. She had a heart attack.' He shrugged, as if trying to shake off an annoyance, to dislodge the unwanted memory and forget that it ever happened.

'So she told you about me then?' the stranger asked.

Well no. She wrote...she kept a journal.' Tommy looked at Justin, who raised his eyebrows curiously. 'She'd kept it for years, and never told anyone about it. We had no idea what happened to her.' At those words, Justin sat forward in the chair, resting his elbows on his knees and interlacing his fingers to rest his chin upon. There was a natural child-like quality to the way he sat, so comfortably and expectant, hoping for a story so memorable and exciting that it would carry him off into the play worlds and the dream worlds of imagination. Spookily, it reminded him of his grandsons. Tom continued.

'Yesterday, she said she knew I was coming in, even though it was meant to be a surprise. She's always had a sense, she used to say she could feel something...' and they finished the quote in unison '...in her bones'. Justin was smiling wistfully, while Tommy simply looked at this enigma of a stranger, and wondered how well they knew the same person.

'Yeah, well when I saw her yesterday, somehow she just knew. She knew her time was up, and she said she wanted to tell me one more story. She told me about her journal, which documents her dreams.'

At the mention of the journal again, Justin's eye's flickered. While his gaze and smile remained exactly the same, for some reason Tommy was reminded of professional card sharks keeping a 'poker face' to disguise their intentions or interests. He had the strangest feeling that Justin was more interested in the journal than he might be displaying, and for the first time, he wondered if, in fact, his life could be in danger.

Justin merely continued smiling, and wide-eyed, gestured for Tommy to continue his tale. When he wasn't immediately forthcoming, Justin removed his head from his cupped hands. In a clear display of honesty and openness – or perhaps one of distracting showmanship, Tommy pondered, Justin held his hands palms up. His fingers splayed out wiggling slightly, as if juggling dozens of tiny invisible balls in front of him.

'So you know a little about me then, I'm guessing? You've already read this journal of your mother's, eh?' Tommy nodded, wondering what he was doing with his fingers. Justin saw him staring and immediately stopped, apparently half-amused and half-shamefaced at the subconscious gesticulations of his fingers. 'Some old habits die hard' he remarked, reflectively.

'But not you, eh? You don't really ever die, is that right?' Tommy asked.

'Do we ever truly die? Is anything really ever lost?' he replied enigmatically.

'Are you going to answer my questions with other questions?'

'I will try to restrict that, good Sir,' Justin said with the sudden appearance of a distinct British accent, 'To those questions for which there are no answers!' He smiled, magnanimously, ostentatiously. Then aware he was enacting a private joke, he turned serious again. 'But in answer to your question, no, you're right. For all intents and purposes, I am immortal.'

'Are there others of you left here on Earth?'

'Ah, now that is a very good question, and it's one that I wish I could answer with certainty. So you will have to settle for the official answer, which is 'No'. However of course, the official position is that I don't exist either, so it's an existential quandary *par excellence*. An ontological tangle, a contradicting paradox. Which I think is hilarious. Because in a way, life is a paradox, and a contradiction to boot.' Tommy raised his eyebrows, allowing the strangest stranger to continue rambling.

'I mean, 'life'. It's not really life, is it? It's the prelude to life, the training grounds, the prep school, the fields and mountains and oceans of dreaming. And it's filled with death, not life. But it's just like you, who call a planet three quarters covered in water, 'Earth'? Don't you see it's that paradox factor again? The contradiction for a planet where the only inevitability, the only common factor facing every single thing is death, and you all think that it is 'life'. Ah, the joyous innocence of youth.' He stopped, a little embarrassed. 'Sorry, I'm waffling.'

Tommy had a little trouble following what Justin was saying, and wondered if he'd been drinking. There wasn't any alcohol in his mother's house and very little in *his* place either. He wondered if Justin had been through his house, then wondered why he would care. There was nothing there that an immortal man could possibly want – except possibly for the journal: which was at his daughter's place. The realisation dawned on him like a metaphysical bucket of cold water, and the knowledge that he was not a poker player jumped to the front of his mind as well. The desire for a stiff drink hadn't vanished, but he tried to get back on track. He didn't have to feign confusion over what Justin had just been saying. 'So, you don't really know for sure, right?'

Justin's head turned to the side, as if he was aware that the question was a distraction, a decoy from another question. Another idea. Something else, more important but unable to be addressed front on, perhaps. Nevertheless, he answered carefully. 'No, I don't know for sure. I have been keeping an eye on that issue for a long time.'

'When you say 'a long time'...'

'I mean of course, a very, very long time.'

'And you've lived through it all? How much...what...' Tommy broke off, unsure of what to ask. There were just so many questions. Was Atlantis real? Jesus and Adam and Eve? How were the pyramids built? What about alien abductions, UFOs and extra-terrestrial life? Was he actually chatting with someone who had ridden dinosaurs, or even dragons? If so, and if he told the twins, would they actually believe him? He wasn't sure what to think, but he decided he may as well make himself comfortable.

He turned on the outside porch light, and walked into the kitchen area, glancing back at Justin repeatedly, quizzically. 'I'm putting the kettle on, but Mum keeps a range of soft drinks in the fridge. Would you like something to drink?' he asked. Another thought struck him. 'Do you actually ever need to eat or drink?'

'Yes and no, respectively. I'd love a cup of tea, but no, I don't need to eat or drink. Not the way humans do. I do have to replenish my energies regularly. Like plant photosynthesis, the light from the sun contains more goodness than what humans currently remember how to use. So technically I can get by with just a little daylight and a splash of water, but I do love a nice cuppa tea.'

Tommy ruminated on that for a moment while he was pottering in the kitchen. Quietly, almost to himself he asked, 'Daylight? Or do you prefer moonlight, for a little lunar-synthesis?'

He could immediately feel the ancient man's eyes rest on his back, the weight of his attention was tangible. He retrieved a pair of cups and turned to look at Justin directly. Tom smiled cheekily, eyebrows raised as if peeking into a surprise present. Yet there was a serious look on Justin's face, one that made him wonder again if there were things in the journal, things that he now knew, that maybe he ought not to know. What if there were things that *need* to remain secret? Could ignorance be essential for double-blind dreaming?

Would telling baby stars what they were ruin the practice? He knew that people inevitably behaved differently when they knew they were being watched. How would society react knowing everything and everyone was under constant observation? The old maxim about how true character was displayed when you thought no-one would ever know what you were doing: was that it? Could knowledge upset the fragile balance kept between self-awareness and self-delusion that the stellar nursery school depended on? He casually brought his breathing under control as he readied the tea tray.

'Tom? That was in the journal, wasn't it?' He didn't respond at first, pouring the boiling water into the pot. As he turned to bring the tray over to the lounge area, he paused and nodded contritely. 'Where is the journal now?' The silence was thick, the air heavy. 'I bet she wrote to me, didn't she?' he asked, smiling. Tommy met his eye and nodded, smiling back at him. Despite the fact that Justin looked a decade (or possibly two) younger than he, Tommy realised that looking at this man's eyes was almost like looking in a mirror. He had the same brown eyes with orange-gold specks as he did. Those sparkling eyes that he alone, not his sisters, had inherited from his mother Katherine.

His mind was racing. On one hand, his mother had definitely written to Justin. Many of the journal entries were directly addressed to him. If he had arrived yesterday, or even this morning, he would have actually spoken with her, and she would undoubtedly have told him of the journal's existence, perhaps given it to him. But now, for some strange reason, it felt as though his mother's journal was the only actual part of her that he had left. Never mind the logic: knowing the contents of her will was irrelevant. The journal wasn't actually mentioned in it – and his mother had specifically said it was for him now. It was his. It was his only evidence of a whole life that his mother had kept secret, a whole world of knowledge in fact. He had been hesitant enough at leaving it with his daughter. He looked forward to going through it again, correlating dates and entries, seeing things happen in a chronological context that he hadn't... no - he couldn't have appreciated the first time around. He certainly didn't want to give it up, not now, not yet.

Justin spoke, and for the second time Tom wondered if this man in front of him could actually read his mind. 'I'm not asking you to give it up, ok?' he said. 'And obviously you don't have it with you, so while you decide... please...' and he gestured for Tommy to sit down. He realised with a start that he was still standing there beside the couch holding the tea tray, having had frozen *in situ* when Justin had mentioned the letters his mother had written.

He placed the tray on the coffee table and sat down in his usual armchair, facing inwards. He had to turn his head to see the garden from here; it was the only seat in the granny-flat that she hadn't aligned to look directly out onto nature. Even when the weather was unbearable his mother used to sit in the chair where Justin now sat, staring out at the plants blowing in the wind. She once had a television set, but she only ever used it as a shelf to display trinkets and pictures. When he had renovated last spring, he'd installed floating shelves on her south-facing wall to better display her expanding collection; and the old television box had become completely redundant. He'd given it to Sarah across the road, whose kids were transforming from darlings into teenagers.

Justin's voice was soft, gently bringing him back from his daydream. 'Tell me about her, will you?'

He looked up, bemused. 'I could ask you the same thing,' he said.

'I'll make you a deal,' the eternal countered. 'You tell me all about your mother...*and* give me her journal, and I will...' he paused, biting his lower lip, considering. 'I will answer any three questions you ask. Properly, to the best of my ability. I'm not trying to scam you with a cop-out 'yes/no' or a '42' response either.'

As he paused again, Tommy sat forward and asked, 'Are we in a 'time swallow' now? Like, you know, if I'm about to die and none of this will matter?'

Justin sat back, a huge grin spreading across his face. He put his arms back on the armrests and moved his right leg further away, leaving his body relaxed and open. He tilted his head and then moved it slowly side-to-side, as if laughing to himself. 'You've got a sharp mind on you, buddy, I'll give you that. You're your mother's son there.' He became more serious, stretching his neck from side to side before continuing. 'Okay. First, as we haven't made a deal yet, I suppose that's not one of your questions, and the answer is 'no' anyway. We are not in a time-swallow, and as far as I know you're not about to die.' He shook his head and clarified, 'I don't foretell the future though. I can read the signs, and the patterns are often obvious, but the details...' he squinted, picking his words, 'well, the small print is yet to be written'.

Tommy considered the answer, and took a sip of his tea.

'For you to know that term though, that just makes me want to see the journal even more. What do you already know? And who else knows about me?'

'Mum.' Suddenly there was a lump in his throat, and he swallowed his discomfort and started again. 'Mum only told me yesterday about meeting you, and about her journal. She... she knew.' He shrugged awkwardly, his body trying in vain to express what words could not. He shook his head quickly and blinked, trying again. 'She said she wanted me to have it, for me to know what happened. But I really got the impression she was quite expecting to see you again. And yes, she, um, she did more than write to you. She left you a message.' Tommy was watching Justin as he said this, and for a moment the professional poker face dropped, revealing a little boy, excited to be surprised.

'A message? Do you remember it?'

'I'm not sure if this is right. It didn't make any sense. The message was nonsense-like, something like, *'Natives talk to orphans?'* Or was it *'Talk to a native about...'?* Sorry, mate. I really don't remember it exactly. Sorry.' He watched the expressions on Justin's face change from curiosity to confusion, half-recognition struggling with his mixed-up recall. There was no way he could *not* let Justin read the journal for himself now.

'Does that make any sense to you? I'm sorry. It's written down...you can... you'll have to read it for yourself.' And there it was, he had admitted the inevitable. He could only hope for the best afterwards. Actually, he thought, I guess that means I've got three questions. He smiled, pondering the possibilities, marvelling at actually having this option.

'I take it we have a deal then?' Justin asked, bringing him back, and he nodded slowly.

'Well then. The first part of the deal was, you tell me all about your mother. From the photos, it looks like she had a wonderful life, but I want to hear about it, I want to know what she...' he moved his nose oddly, as if annoyed that a word didn't exist. It was exactly the same thing that his mother had done, and Tommy was overcome with a strange feeling. Not quite déjà-vu, but the opposite, or a relative. It was seeing something that existed prior to the original. He laughed, and felt the spirit of his mother's hands on his shoulders as he recited their long-standing family joke about how sad it is that words don't exist. '*Le mots n'existent pas, zannen ne*'.

The phrase triggered recognition in Justin, by the look of his reaction it was due to more than his presumed multilingual ability. It appeared that he too was encountering a moment of déjà-vu. 'She...Katie was learning French at school when we were together. I remember her conjugating that phrase. '*Le mots n'existent pas.*' The words don't exist. She challenged me to say the same thing in a dozen languages, which I did.' He sniffled part of a giggle, smiling in reminiscence. He looked over at Tommy, who was reaching for his tea. 'She wrote that down, eh? She remembered that?'

Tommy nodded, smiling sadly as he recounted. 'I read how the Japanese part came about. I never knew that was from you, I thought she got it from a book or a magazine during the war or something.'

'No, it was me. I ran through 'The words don't exist' in a dozen languages for her, and the last one was Japanese, which is 'Kotoba ga-Arunai'. It seemed so natural to add 'unfortunately' afterwards, and I did that in Japanese. For whatever reason, she loved the sound of 'Zannen-ne'. And combining two languages to express something that no one language does or even could express, well we both thought that just seemed laden with beauty. I'm pleased it stuck with her.' The two men looked at each other, and even though Tommy appeared much older than Justin and it was the other way around, for a brief moment they were both little boys. Together they recited her phrase, like they'd been friends forever.

'*Le mots n'existent pas, zannen ne*'.

Then they both burst out laughing, which Tommy quickly had to hold in. His emotional hand-brake was already slippery, and he didn't want an accidental gear change from 'emit laughter' to 'emit tears'. He was close enough, and there would be time for that later. He steadied himself with a sip of tea, and leant back comfortably in the chair.

'Mum,' he said. 'You want me to tell you about Mum.' Justin smiled and sat back with his own cup of tea, expectantly yet patiently.

'My mother was an angel. She was such a strong woman, and she was always happy.' Justin was nodding in the background, and as Tommy looked around his mother's lounge, he heard the truth in his words. She had been – and still was, or perhaps was even more so now, an angel. It depended on your definitions, your perspective and context. He remembered a phrase she had written: 'As Above, So Below – BUT - Human-time, Earth-rules.' He wanted to ask Justin about that: why the 'BUT', - but, he certainly wasn't going to rush any of his questions. Those would take some thinking.

He repeated to himself, 'three questions – three questions – three questions' as if he was instructing his mind to wake him at a specific time or with the answer to a problem. His mother had taught him that trick, and he had taught it to his kids. He let some unsupervised part of his mind perambulate around the problem, knowing in faith that it would return to him later with three questions.

For now he stood up, and indicating to Justin with one upright finger that he would return in a minute, he went down the corridor to his mother's bedroom to get the photo album from her bedside table. Presumably Justin had already looked at it, but it was a nice way to go through her life, with a pictorial guide to accompany the tale as he knew it. Meanwhile, his subconscious mind ransacked unexplored memories and tore through buried intellectual challenges he had once thought unsolvable, on a search for questions he had once thought to be unanswerable.

CHAPTER 33

[Limbo Lounging]

Gone. She couldn't believe it. With a splash, he'd gone splat. Tavi was completely pulverised; she-who-would-have-been was no more. The latest death had left her reeling: she was unprepared to even contemplate the implications. It was just too awful. If this pregnancy didn't work, if she couldn't birth fusion into her Brown, then her life as she knew it was over. There were long shots, she knew. She might be able to save parts of her garden, but certainly her precious musical comet was a goner. Gone, gone, gone.

As she had floated up out of the immersive, she'd felt a palpable loss. That death had felt *wrong*, and she felt cheated. It had felt more like a severing than a graduation. She had stayed a little longer, stunned and captivated as the surviving remnants of the tribe struggled in vain to escape the violent ocean and fire-dropping skies. As she ascended, she watched the volcanic clouds continue to envelop the entire southern hemisphere, and she wondered how many more gestating minds would perish as it continued its menacing osmotic spread.

Carols didn't know what to do. Her baby's termination had been so unexpected, he'd still been so young. She was enormously proud of him, especially in those final moments, protecting his family in his own limited way. But now she was floundering. She wondered how to react, what response was appropriate. She couldn't think: clearly she was in shock. None of the other deaths had been so abrupt - so unforeseen and unexplained. While she hadn't experienced a form to be so brief, nor had any of the earlier ones been so rich with experience. They'd only just begun, and Carols couldn't shake the feeling that Tavi's death had felt *wrong*.

This time Carols accepted the midwife's offer of a break, and now she strolled along in a daze, unsure of what to think, or how to feel. Carols vaguely remembered Nat saying that she'd tried to save him, and although she was quite interested in the *how* of that, for now, all her senses were pummelled with a feeling of tragic loss.

She remembered her midwife warning her that death got more and more difficult, and thinking that it didn't make sense. Surely each death would lead her to be less sensitive; surely the inevitable and natural processes of desensitisation would hold true here too, she'd thought confidently. But no, now, she could really relate to that piece of advice. It did hurt more: a whole lot more.

She could barely force herself to give thanks for a positive outcome. She knew it wasn't all over; at least part of her knew that. But that knowledge was academic, theoretical. It didn't seem to seep through to where she held her hopes and expectations. Nat had reminded her that her gestate's young mind had been strong and healthy before the disaster, the routing of the village and complete destruction of his community. All she could do now was to wait.

Nat had said that this might happen; Carols knew she had been amply warned, but still she was unprepared for the emotional turmoil. The midwife assured her emphatically that although the wait for any gestate to re-inhabit after a termination event was one of the most tenuous connections in the entire process, the odds were strongly in her favour that her baby would return. She had a lot of things going for her. Her gestate had died very young, a long way off sexual maturity. Her personality had already stabilised, her determination was strong. Moreover she had positively flourished in introductory lessons, her attitude to incarnating was more than encouraging, it was determined. All Carols could do was wait.

Apparently, this sort of scenario was not uncommon. The fact that there was even a waiting room where other stellar mothers-in-waiting could socialise acted to remind her that this was relatively normal. Carols remembered the midwife's reassurances, her admonitions to give thanks and be patient. She knew that such a termination event allowed the gestate another go, especially since it had not reached adulthood or sexual maturity. She thought about the other growing minds that had been there, about Tavi's older brother. He had passed puberty and could technically reproduce, but he had died before his tribe's rite of passage into adulthood was completed. Would that mind graduate or have to return for another go at this level? She resolved to ask Nat once she returned to the birthing chamber.

She felt a breeze of glistening sounds caress her as it passed over and through her. She slowed, enjoying the tinkling sensation she felt floating in its wake. She rolled slowly, relishing the distraction. She was in no hurry. Temporality soothed her, and she suddenly had an appreciation for the designers who included this corridor, giving her the opportunity to be alone for a moment. She thought of her physical body, her solar system and exo-ghost at home confidently waiting, and smiled to herself with tentative reassurances. *Everything will be ok*, she thought. She laughed at herself for even entertaining doubts. *Of course it will. Everything is exactly how it should be, as it always was*. She shook off her worries, discarding those thoughts like an old ragged cloak, and moved into the awaiting chamber.

The room was dark, and felt a lot larger than she had expected. Reflecting on that, she realised she didn't really know what she had expected. A small intimate room where a couple of pregnant stellars could relax? A cosmos virtuality where the stately whirling of galactic families adorned the walls? Perhaps an artist's gallery where reclining booths were outlined with embroidered threads of dark matter filaments, and the refreshments were delivered on the tray-top shelves of bio-engineered motile shrubbery? Nothing would have surprised her; after what she'd just been through, anything seemed possible.

She thought back over what she had been through with her baby. Enormous chunks of masonry falling from the sky. The turbulent ocean waters reminded her of the calm terror she had felt as the whale consumed the remnants of her krill conglomerate, which brought forth the chilling memory of deadly Siberian waters that swept up and over her, covering even the tip of her trunk stretched high... She stopped. She had to physically shake herself to brush off those memories. Finding herself still in that mind-set, she shook herself off again, surprised at the puissant grip the memories of mortality possessed.

Sure am glad I won't remember those, she mused. *But...I wonder if my own were any different. I suppose not. I'll find out when I engender, I guess.* With a resigned shrug, she moved fully into the Limbo Lounge and found herself resting on a grass-like foyer. From there, she could see that the foyer led to several doors connected to corridors that obviously didn't occupy the same physical space. She hadn't felt any sensation as she passed through, and as she looked back to admire the construction, a voice addressed her.

'Multi-phasic architecture. So subtle you might miss it, eh? Death does have some pretty nifty engineering. You like?'

The darkness of the room had also hidden its inhabitants; moreover the foyer acted as a spotlight, and she was currently occupying the most illuminated position. She rolled completely off the miniature field, and saw that there were a range of recessed circular indentations occupied with other stellars.

She could now see that there were six booths, set side-by-side in an arc, and that inside each booth were joined banks of these reclining baths. The rising haze of floating gases reminded her of the advertising images used by rejuve retreats. Not that she'd ever been to one, but the familiarity was comforting. It appeared that not all the booths were occupied, although there was only one booth that contained more than a solitary stellar. It was from this central and socially busier option that the voice had come.

A quick glance at the available solitary booth seemed to forebode more depressing reminiscences, and she quickly decided that a more social atmosphere would be healthier for her than being alone. She moved on in towards the central compartment, finding that the clouds of gases had also obscured the internal details of this gas-spa. The booth was separated into six concave seats, three of which were occupied. *After seeing the multiphasic architecture at work*, she thought to herself, *I wonder what other wonders are hidden by the floating gas clouds.* Those thoughts quickly evaporated as she reclined into the nearest empty curve. Before she had even come close to touching the bottom, the seat had started emitting a soothing blend of sonic bubbles. Once she reclined into an optimum position, a set of hitherto hidden jets started pummelling her outer photosphere with a laser-spray of ultra-refined helium.

Carols had never even sent an exo-neural ghost to experience a rejuve retreat, and she immediately decided it was worth the investment. She had only ever imagined it vicariously, from the advertising. 'Come be immersed in sound, massaged by particle jets, aligned by tantric energies and refreshed by ...*blah blah blah*'. She didn't have the time for all that. She didn't think she needed the claimed benefits of a rejuve; she was still quite young, after all.

She was fulfilled and refreshed enough by her menagerie - her musical icepede comet and her precious moon gardens. She had considered, and even accepted the claims that the processes themselves were quite pleasurable, but she realised now she had vastly underestimated her ability to grok or appreciate the depths of intensity she was now experiencing. *The simplest of elements, the most basic combination of light and sound and direction*, she felt herself distantly think, as if most of her mind had shut down of its own accord. *Yet together, they do this...*

She dissociated and watched herself float and bob in her own miniature world of pleasure.

She felt herself going to exhale, to moan, to groan with the simple release of pressure the jets were bringing, but she held it in. She didn't want it to appear obvious that this was her first time. She was tempted to open her senses, but her body refused. *Not yet*, she said to herself. *Just a little bit longer.* Holding in the moan seemed to have an unexpectedly cumulative effect. It felt like her whole body had moved up an octave, or changed a phase of rhythm. She was beating more heavily, her hydrogen patterns pulsing at a faster rate than usual. *How can that be right?* she wondered self-reflexively. *Aren't I supposed to be relaxing?*

She felt another moan grow, almost impossible to not release, a pounding wave of pressure that seemed to beat on those tiny little spots and yet echo all over and through her body at the same time. Reverberating, building, compounding.

She felt herself twist, holding herself down, bearing against the jets one by one, wiggling her carapace to scratch patches of itchiness she never knew she had. It all felt so good, so overwhelmingly wonderful, so indulgent and yet so well deserved. Suddenly she remembered why she was indulging, and why she deserved this treat. Why she needed in fact to have a rejuve.

She was having a baby. She was bringing new life into the Astraverse. The astonishing awe she felt at what she was doing, blended with her tingling tumescent state, resulted in both surprise and horror as she let out an enormous sob. Threads of grief and joy intimately braided with pain and pleasure, sensations so delicious she wasn't strong enough to bear them all. She sobbed again, which almost broke into a scream, and she unexpectedly found herself releasing tensions in throbbing, pulsating cries.

Soon enough the pulses subsided and she opened her senses. She was a little embarrassed, but felt so unbelievably good. Shame-faced, she scanned the booth she had so recently entered. She wondered who she had embarrassed herself in front of, and hoped it was nobody she knew.

'Welcome,' said the Red relaxing on her right. 'That was some stellar-gasm.'

'Yeah' said another voice. 'I could go a full round of those', which triggered a burst of laughter from the others.

'Are you alright now?' the Red to her right asked.

Carols bobbed politely, and reluctantly admitted she wasn't ready to be sociable just yet. She courteously excused herself, and glided over to the dark and now more welcoming solitary booth.

She slid into the booth, and was pleased to discover that the auto-massage jets didn't automatically come on this time. She needed time to think about the most recent developments in her pregnancy.

Who knew dying was so exhausting? Carols tried to recall the last time she had been at peace. She had been relaxing in the majesty of her icepede comet, back before that unwelcome but necessary interruption. She focused on her breathing and soaked into her happy place, exhaling steady pulsations of relief as the mental weight of all the death she'd seen slid away.

Later, relaxed and being sociable in the comfort of the Limbo Lounge, Carols found herself surprisingly fascinated by the intricate processes of mortality. She was still reviewing the short-lived but joy-filled existence of her sixth former when she became aware of a change. There was no audible alert, no tangible input she had heard or seen, but she knew. It was time.

There was an indefinable, insensate connection between her and her child: a knowledge or awareness that travelled faster than a photon, unhindered by the usual information jams on the primary lines of Light. She was ready to try again. One moment Carols had been lounging around reminiscing, the next she was deluged with an irresistible compulsion. To knowing smiles and encouraging words, she quickly bid her new friends farewell, and eagerly returned to the birthing chamber. Her baby was coming.

Back in the birthing chamber, her baby had yet to fully assume the mantle of her physical parameters. But the mind of her gestate was getting closer to the exotic energy funnel that connected all of the gestates to the Academy immersive. As it dived in, the screens in front of *Carols in Sequins* burst into brilliant arrays of colour, denoting physical factors and subsequent projections. She already knew roughly what her baby would expect, having been through Form Six already. She was pleased to see that her gestate's genetic code looked clean. Moreover, she was inordinately happy to discover that this time she was having a baby girl.

During the beginning of the previous attempt at Form Six, *Carols in Sequins* had noticed with interest the processes involved in child-birth: the rituals and dietary changes that pregnant females went through. Going through the process a second time opened her eyes to a realm of further complexity she hadn't appreciated. This second environment was significantly different from the isolated village tribe that Tavi had ever-so-briefly lived in. Her baby girl was going to be born on the outskirts of a developed urban city, part of a burgeoning continent-sized nation-state group of people; but there were many striking similarities between the two pregnancies.

Both human mothers had been increasingly honoured the further through pregnancy they advanced, being treated deferentially by other humans, young and old. She was perplexed by the degree of commitment both mothers had undergone regarding their diet, as if any number of lemons or ground taro root could possibly influence the gender of their child. Carols learnt many new words and concepts as she continued to explore the various aspects of child-bearing. The concept of sociology was nothing new, but patriarchy and slavery were both alien ideas, ones she didn't enjoy learning about. Even thinking about the deliberate exploitation of another sentient mind left her feeling stained, as if she had consumed something unpleasant.

Watching the gestation progress anew, Carols continued to observe other differences. Remembering how painful Tavi's birth had looked, she wondered if her own little girl would eventually go through giving birth, and if it was going to be as physically painful as it had looked. She had tried to imagine it from the mother's perspective, but found her vicarious connection too tenuous. The abundance of sensory stimuli that young Tavi had experienced was simply too distracting for Carols to connect at all with the mother. She saw that the possible futures were congested: there was no way she could clearly foresee likelihoods that far ahead. She gave thanks for the best, and returned her full attention to her baby.

The family of Katherine Amelia Coulston decided much later that the breaking of her mother's waters during a church service was an auspicious sign. At the time however, it had been a minor debacle. The heavily pregnant Sarah Coulston had been constantly watched over by what her husband Daniel sometimes grumbled was an 'unruly platoon of women'. Carols was amused to see that when the father of the child showed interest in being present for the birth, he was hustled away. Not only by females, but also by the medical staff at the hospital.

So much for patriarchy, Carols thought derisively.

After only two nights' observation, Sarah Coulston and baby Katherine were released from the hospital. Having already lived through a rough-and-tumble childhood with Tavi, Carols wasn't sure about the noticeably more hesitant handling, and the constant checking that Katherine's parents gave her. Was it because she was female, or was it simply due to different cultural rituals? She didn't know, and didn't want to bother her midwife with such trivialities. It didn't seem to make any difference to the panels and displays that Carols could access. Life expectancy was significantly higher, but she could see there were numerous factors contributing to that. The control of infectious diseases and literacy levels required of an industrialised nation ensured that Katherine could expect to live for twice as long as Tavi might have, if he had made it out of childhood.

Carols watched, and breathed the life of her daughter. Giving thanks for the best was a method of assuring beneficial outcomes via affirmation, so she happily saturated herself in the strange new environments her little dreaming stellar was now. The domesticated and gender-segregated divide of the industrialised society confused her for a while, but she had already conquered this confusion once before and felt sure it would start to make some kind of sense sooner or later. She knew to be patient: the internal logic of a new system could often appear riddled with Boolean contradictions. It was impossible to understand raisin toast by only examining the raisins: she could be patient. She'd happily wait for the metaphorical taste to mature before she appreciated it.

As she watched her daughter grow, she found many things that she couldn't understand at first. Why the mother had stopped breast-feeding so early: what difference the lower protein /higher calcium contents of the mother's breast milk would make. Why did the males of her family almost completely ignore the new child? Did the songs sung to female babies reflect larger cultural biases? Her questions were ongoing, her curiosity aroused. There had definitely been differences between the duties of the female and male children in the shadow of the volcano; this time she got to see another style of gender-typing. Both times her baby had been nurtured and encouraged to follow in the footsteps of their same-gender parent, but Carols couldn't figure out quite which differences were due to which cultural factors. The interlaced patterns were complex.

What had been disappointingly the same with both human children was the enormous loss of neural capacity in their first couple of years. At first, she had been excited to see again a good four hundred thousand synaptic connections in her new-born child. The potentials were enormous, the neural loops foreshadowing a significant step up in processing power. She had been enormously saddened to watch the connections lapse in disuse. Gluons un-glued, neurons neutralised, and connections of promise closed down for lack of stimulation. She had hoped that perhaps it had been something specific to male children, or perhaps geographically quarantined to the island tribe, but no such luck. She watched as Katherine's brain flexed and pulsed, as it spasmed and shrunk. Each month most cells replenished and replaced themselves in ongoing growth, but those in baby Katherine's eyes would never grow. Human eyes alone never change size, and the essence of her baby, those memories and experienced stored on the atomic level of her optic nerve, cried out in an inarticulate existential pain that no-one understood or recognised. Carols recognised what was happening, and she ached in sympathy, cooing soothing balms into the baby's dreams.

Carols continued to feel the connection with her daughter grow; with each level it had become more intimate. It had become particularly strong since the Fifth Form, encapsulating and reflecting the concentration of selfhood that her baby was at last achieving. Now that she could tangibly taste the link, she could follow it right back. In retrospect, she could see that it had always been there, however tenuous. Even when her baby had been a plant or a microscopic species of bacteria; even in the breaks between each form, she had been aware of her gestating daughter.

Knowing that all of these memories would be locked away worked to remind her to cherish and relish each moment. When her child was sleeping, she sometimes took advantage of the opportunity to review or re-live other moments, still aware of her presence in the background. Steady, solid, strong: as regular and reliable as the metronomic pulsations of a quasar.

While Tavi had been the second-born in his family, Katherine was the fourth. Although, within a couple of years, she became the third after her older brother died. She lost younger siblings over the years as well; it seemed her mother was almost permanently pregnant. By the time she reached ten years of age, Katherine had lost her older sister and taken place as the second oldest, entrusted with increasing amounts of responsibility in the care of her younger siblings. Human children tend to act on their feelings using instinct, learning through conflict and emotional experience how to cope maturely. The opportunity to reinforce all sorts of subconscious preconditioned responses placed a grave obligation onto parents, Carols reflected. *Subconscious stuff appears to be a matter of habits, traditions, patterns*, she observed, adding wryly, *Just like everything else.* From her unique perspective, she identified patterns reinforcing and habits solidifying. She watched with joy as she spotted familiar talents and aptitudes, as intellectual and physical dispositions re-surfaced, forming the strength of character that would be needed as a personal meta-narrative, a big picture that would ensure she didn't irretrievably disintegrate in times of shock or stress.

When Katherine became upset, biochemical changes within her metabolism increased her strength and reflexes, but eliminated her higher thought processes. It was during these times where Katie operated on instinct that Carols imagined she could see attributes from her earlier forms. She knew that even in the womb Katie had been creating memories, conditioning responses and programming reactions to stimuli, but she believed that her baby's sense of justice, balance and tenacity were late-blooming seeds, sprouting only after being buried, things she unbeknownst had prepared earlier. Seeing them flourish now made Carols smile.

The farmstead Katie's family lived on required constant maintenance, and the family group encompassed four generations, as well as numerous semi-itinerant workers who returned season after season. Not long after Katherine's great-grandmother had passed on, something inexplicable happened that forced Carols to turn to Nat for advice. Her baby was napping in their front lounge, exhausted from her domestic duties, her studies and the preparations for a second family funeral in as many years.

Technically, her great-uncle hadn't been family, not a blood-relative anyway. He was an old friend of her grandfather's, who had been a permanently fixture of the farm and lived in the barn. He had always been there, co-ordinating the fruit pickers and itinerant workers. Her Uncle Justin had taught her to ride a horse when she had been eight, and supervised her first firing of a gun when she'd turned ten.

While hunting with her grandpa, Justin had been impaled by a wild boar in the bushes behind the farm, and only just made it back to the homestead. He had almost bled out on the way back, and he looked pale and sickly. On his death-bed, he told young Katherine something that had surprised Carols immensely. In his last words, he told Katie to never forget that she was a star. Carols reassured herself that he had simply meant the expression to be metaphorical. As far as she'd seen, humans didn't know about stellar society, any more than birds or reptiles knew. The incident inspired her to review previous interactions involving her Uncle. A couple of other odd moments had just really begun to pique her interest, when something unexpected happened. Katherine Amelia Coulston completely vanished.

CHAPTER 34
(The Strangest Introduction)

Tom and Justin were half way through the photo album when they came across one of Tom's favourite pictures. Gloria was holding baby Claire, with him and his mother standing as proud father and grandmother behind the chair. Tommy casually remarked on how time had flown, on how much his mother had doted on baby Claire and how she adores her great-grandchildren, Claire's twin boys. Perhaps it was a slip of the tongue, using the present tense, or perhaps it was simply something else in his tone that led Justin to put the pieces together.

'It's at Claire's, isn't it?' he asked, and Tommy was momentarily dumb-struck. He nodded, knowing very well that Justin was referring to the journal.

He had to stand up to take out his mobile phone to check the exact time, although he knew in his body that it was around half nine. There were no clocks in his mother's house, nor had she ever worn a watch. 'No need', she used to say dismissively. 'Your body knows what time it is, if you know how to listen to it.' So he too had never taken up the habit of wearing a watch. His father's gorgeous old timepiece lived safely and securely in Tom's bedside drawer. He wanted to double check it was no later than half nine, although if it was, he would probably still call Claire anyway. Perhaps she could drive over. He didn't want to head back there, not with Justin in tow. He would feel better knowing that he wasn't putting his whole family at risk, however slight it was, or imagined.

He was honestly surprised to see that it was only twenty past nine; Claire and Aaron would still be awake. It felt like a lot more time had passed. He started to ask if tomorrow would be okay, but the look on Justin's face changed his mind. He wasn't gritting his teeth in response; rather it looked like every atom was momentarily clenched. 'I'll call, and ask her to bring it over,' he said, holding up his mobile.

To Tom's astonishment Justin merely said, 'No need.' He stood up, and leaving the photo album on the coffee table, he held both of his hands out open to Tommy. 'Just take my hands, and think of your daughter.' As he did, he closed his eyes, imagining his daughter lying in front of their television set with her husband, hoping and praying that the kids were fast asleep in their beds.

He felt a little dizzy, and for the second time that evening a voice came out of nowhere, surprising the living daylights out of him.

'Dad?' Claire's voice was overflowing in astonishment, and he opened his eyes. He and Justin were standing in his daughter's lounge-room, and she and her husband were indeed cuddled up on the couch. Tommy turned to Justin and blurted, 'If you could do that, why didn't you get back to Mum in time?'

Justin looked at him, his face heavy with sadness. 'It's not a transporter function, I can't go from anywhere to anywhere. It requires a DNA connection. What actually happened was, we travelled along the connection that you have with Claire. I never had that with your mother.'

Tommy shook his head in disbelief, and turned to face his daughter and son-in-law, who were both still sitting on their couch, their mouths open wide. Despite Claire's initial utterance, it was Aaron who gathered his senses together first.

'This...' he almost stuttered, indicating with bulging eyes the stranger that had appeared in his lounge along with his father-in-law, 'This is your mother's Uncle Justin?' he said incredulously. 'He's...' he tried to continue. His mouth moved but the words refused to coordinate. His heart raced, and he stood up, resting his hand on Claire's thigh heavily, indicating she should not move.

Aaron looked at Tommy, who was still wearing the same outfit he'd been in earlier, although he looked different. There was something about him that Aaron couldn't quite put his finger on. His father-in-law looked strangely older and yet simultaneously younger. As if his body was exhausted, but his soul had been shocked into an earlier youthful state: shock not from trauma, but from an overdose of wonder. Aaron could relate, to an extent, and he wondered for a moment if he himself looked any different. He and Claire had hardly spoken of anything else since laying eyes on her grandmother's journal. Even now it lay next to Claire, where he had been sitting and reading it while Claire was off with her thoughts, musing on what they had learnt that evening. She was a much faster reader than he was, and had already read it cover-to-cover. Now she stood up next to him, surreptitiously covering the journal with a cushion.

'With that kind of an entrance, who else could it be?' she asked. 'Hi, I'm Claire,' she said politely, and extended her hand. 'Nice to meet you. Although I think I should pinch myself to make sure I'm not dreaming!'

Her laughter broke a little of the tension, and everyone relaxed a bit. Tommy finished the formalities by introducing Aaron, and suggested they move over to the dining table. Aaron walked into the kitchen area to turn the kettle on, and Claire ushered their surprise late night guests ahead of her. As they passed the couch, Justin turned to Claire.

'Best if you bring her journal with you,' he said casually. With that he looked directly at the couch, where a corner of the book in question could be seen quite clearly. She blushed slightly, reached out and picked it up. She held it tightly to her chest and looked from it to Justin, and smiled curiously. *So this is the man who inspired Grandma*, she mused, walking behind him. *Pretty fit for a bloke of ten thousand or more*, she thought wryly.

With only one sibling, her older brother Jackson, Claire had always been the baby of the family. However, she was the oldest girl of her generation. With all other female cousins interstate, she was also the only girl to have spent significant amounts of time with her grandmother, and some of those memories were the fondest parts of her childhood. The hours spent in her garden, growing food and flowers, cultivating scents and tastes and helping all the different lifeforms to balance – it was more than a formative memory. As an adult, she had more than once attributed her interest in Buddhism and alternative spirituality to her Grandma.

It was through those interests that she had met Aaron, whom her Grandma had adored. She had always known that her grandmother cultivated a few beliefs in her mental garden that needed to be protected more carefully than most. In the same way that she had taught children the Latin names for her plants, she made up imaginative words to represent the dangers that her beliefs faced. 'Got to protect my precious things from the savage winds of orthodoxia', she would joke. Claire loved her Grandma deeply, and had learnt so much from her. She could hardly believe she was gone. More so, she could barely believe that she had never heard this amazing story. It did explain a lot though.

She could see now how her grandmother had learnt to meditate as a young girl. Why she had such a love of the stars, and where her Buddhist-like love of nature and the planet had come from. How she had come by such 'hippy' beliefs as vegetarianism, a generation before the children of Woodstock were even born. She and Jackson had both been baby-sat by their various Aunts, but she had always looked forward to staying with her Grandma the most. Somehow she had always treated Claire differently from the rest of the family.

As a teenager she had twice spent the school holidays at her Grandparent's place, back when her Grandpa had still been alive. She remembered now her immediate fascination with the eclectic collection of knick-knacks and book titles that struggled for space on her Grandma's crowded bookshelf. The second holiday there, she had found a book on American Indian animal guides, which had immediately captured her interest. Many American Indian tribes had a belief in animal guides or totem spirits, which fulfilled the role of guardian angel and messenger.

Enthralled, she'd learnt that as well as individual guardians, there were tribal animal spirits that cared for the clan or family. There were up to nine different animals that brought lessons and acted as guides throughout your lifetime, but one in particular that acted as a personal, lifelong companion. As a teenager, she had been fascinated by the idea, and as an undergrad student she had found the representations to be very similar to the archetypes of Jungian analysis, from which spiritual meanings and subconscious lessons could be elicited. They symbolised lessons or characteristics in a personal way that offered spiritual epiphanies, ethical reminders, or practical behavioural reminders. She'd never taken the psychedelics of a traditional vision quest, nor did she see the need.

As an adult, Claire had been a little surprised to find that both her parents subscribed to beliefs that she had presumed they would think pagan or un-Christian. She had always kept those ideas to herself, and been pleasantly surprised to find that Aaron not only shared her interest, but when they eventually confided in each other, they were delighted to find that they both shared the same totem animal.

Thinking over what she had read in her Grandma's journal, she wondered if her animal guide was actually herself, whether she had actually lived as that animal in an earlier form. She was fascinated to read that her Grandma had fervently believed (*dreamt or remembered?*) she was once a Venus Flytrap, those strange carnivorous plants she cultivated. She had never considered that a plant could be a totem guide. She had often wondered over the years what her sons' animal guides would be. Walking to the dining table, she found herself wondering what this Justin character would think of such musings.

As they took seats, her father's voice brought her fully back into the present. He explained how he had seen a light in a reflection, how he had investigated and found an empty home. How he had called out and watched in amazement as a man appeared in front of him, and how they had talked. He explained that Justin wanted the journal, that he thought it was too dangerous a record to be left.

Throughout history, Justin explained, he had been careful to ensure that there was no evidence of his existence. He said that he couldn't allow loose ends. He had seen before the terrible trouble that partial understanding could bring. Most wars could usually be traced back to some religious interpretation, some divine interdict. It was why he had asked Katie to promise to never speak of what had happened back on that farm in 1939.

Claire interrupted her father and directed a question to Justin. 'So if you're here now to tie up loose ends, what does that mean for us?'

CHAPTER 35

[Illuminating the Unknown]

No more could you remove the still-beating heart of a snake, or a functioning limb from a mammal, than could *Carols in Sequins* not have noticed Katherine vanishing. Although the whole experience had only lasted four seconds of Earth time, it felt like the longest four seconds possible. Carols had felt the wrenching disconnection as if part of her own body had been yanked away without warning, as if one of the planetoids trailing in her wake had inexplicably disappeared.

As soon as Carols had seen her gestating star sneak into her favourite nook in the formal lounge, she knew what was coming. Katie would quickly slip into a rejuvenating nap; so Carols had once again taken the opportunity to take her mind for a wander. Carols expected she would have some time to herself; she knew her baby was very tired, even though it was only mid-morning. Preparations for the funeral were enormously energy-consuming.

Carols considered looking back at memories of her Uncle Justin, but instead decided to review some of her much earlier experiences. The anticipation of the first crack in her seed pod, and the first stretching >*AWAY*< was always invigorating. She had been reliving that very first reaching towards the sun when instead of a snooze, Katherine was violently ripped away.

Seconds later, she re-appeared; inexplicably trans-located five metres to the front porch. She was just waking up, stretching and rubbing her eyes, as if she had just woken from a refreshing nap. She looked around with a strange expression: one that Carols had never seen before. Not quite surprise, not quite disorientation.

A car horn blared, and their attention was drawn to a motor vehicle rapidly approaching the house, apparently out of control. Carols watched with growing horror as the car skidded and slid, the driver trying in vain to bring it to a halt. It smashed through the front fence and barely missed the enormous oak tree in the front yard. All Carols thought was *No, not again!* Her baby had not reached reproductive maturity in this body either; and she visualised the intersection of the approaching shock wave.

Then she looked at her baby, and the apprehension vanished. Katherine was sitting up, watching the car approach with an unexpected look of clinical detachment, almost as if she had known that it was about to happen. The car horn blared. Carols was puzzled, intrigued and confused. She still felt the psychic welt of her child's removal; there was no chance she'd been imagining those seconds. She watched the expression on Katherine's face, the knowing expectation that ought never to be seen on a girl that age, let alone one just woken up.

'Woken up from WHERE?' Carols' screamed. She went to open the tangle to Nat, only to discover that her midwife was already there.

'It's ok, it's all right, no need to panic,' Nat cooed soothingly as she adjusted the environment. The myriad of miniscule particle jets that kept Carols floating evenly began to pulse to a lullaby rhythm, a susurration triggering instinctive calm, judiciously soothing the most tumultuous of her energy flares.

'Did you see it? Do you...?'

Nat cut her off, and directed her attention to the scene unfolding.

'Watch. It's still happening. Have faith that all will be revealed.'

The motorcar had narrowly avoided the old tree. The driver appeared to have some control over the steering, but obviously the brakes were not functioning. He probably would have managed to avoid the house completely, and was likely trying to head for the pond out the back. There were no hills or slopes which the driver could use to slow down. What the driver wasn't counting on was the dark green wheelbarrow left next to the raised garden beds out the front. As he swerved, the front left wheel jammed into the wheelbarrow, which had been turned upside down to keep rain from collecting in it. The car flipped, and smashed straight through the French windows set into the front of the house, precisely where Katherine had been sleeping only moments earlier.

Carols watched with amazement at the calm and careful manner in which her daughter responded. She appeared to function almost professionally, as if she had occupational experience to draw on for coping with emergencies. The driver and passengers were miraculously unharmed, although getting them all out was a close thing. The formal lounge was a catastrophe. The chairs and entire setting for the farm manager's funeral were in disarray, and no-one noticed the leaking fuel until it found one of the candles. Fire swept through the living room, and people were screaming. Katherine continued to assist, ensuring that everyone was safe and outside, with almost complete disregard for the near-death experience she had just avoided.

Everyone queued to carry buckets of water from the pond to the house, while her brothers wrestled the water hose in through the smashed front window. Then the fire-fighters arrived, putting out the last of the flames and removing the charred vehicle. The lounge was decimated, but remarkably the main structure of the house was still sturdy. The smell of smoke still permeated the entire house, and Katherine's parents decided to accept the hospitality of the McDougal's down the road.

There was so much happening, young Katherine didn't get the chance to speak to anyone. That evening, something else occurred, and although she had been mentally prepared for it, the very tactile physical sensations of menarche had been more than she had expected. No matter how clearly the biological process could be described, you can never be truly prepared for the start of your menstrual cycle. It wasn't something that Carols had any memories of either, the last two mammalian bodies having been male. What neither of them foresaw was the intense and vivid dream she had that night, one that stayed with Katie long after waking.

The next morning she started to write, using loose sheets of paper to document what had happened over the last twenty-four hours, and over the following days, she continued to make notes on scrap paper. It wasn't until weeks later that Katherine sat and re-wrote those notes in a hardcover journal, a diary that she went on to treasure more than any physical possession. At the start, it appeared to Carols that her baby was almost possessed, compelled to write. Carols watched over her shoulder, experiencing surprise for the first time. The singular distinctiveness that would become the character of her daughter: it was already there. Embryonic, but she was already settling into the security and strength of a unique pattern. The more Katherine wrote, the more Carols learnt, and she eagerly absorbed every detail whenever another entry was secreted into the journal.

She learnt that from her child's perspective, it hadn't been a mere four seconds, but an entire lunar month. As the journal grew, so did her astonishment. It began to appear as though her Uncle Justin's dying comments were not at all figurative. Nor had he even died, or been who they all thought he was. As the journal filled with script, Carols regularly turned to her midwife and asked for advice, or clarification. The answer was always the same.

'Give thanks, have faith, and keep watching.'

She didn't understand, but she did give thanks. Her baby was still alive, healthy and maturing nicely. From what she gathered, it was highly unusual for any human to reconnect with memories from earlier levels. She began to think that Nat was completely in the dark about what was happening, and asked for clarification less and less. Disappointingly, her increasingly token queries continued to receive the same response.

Carols decided she had to gather information, and in doing so, she surprised herself again. She learnt that what she had earlier thought was adequate supervision and participation, was actually meagre compared with what was possible. She really started to live the immersive. She breathed the wind, gathering contexts and literacies she hadn't even known existed before. She immersed and drank deeply from fountains of knowledge.

She found information inside the immersive, more so than what her midwife had ever explained. Relishing the act of discovery, she set about actively learning from the gestate world, rather than simply observing. The planet had an enormously complex biosphere, dominated by large oceans. Combined with a tilted axis and a precisely placed orbiting satellite moon, seasonal variations brought even greater environmental variety to the terrain. Nowhere in stellar society was there such a marvellous example of terrestrial engineering, and she could see why Death © had the reputation that it did.

She quickly ascertained that her daughter wasn't supposed to remember what she did. Carols surmised that her experiences in the time bubble had weakened the memory shunts that kept each form separated. But her appreciation and understanding of all that was still yet to be. The first time she read about her daughter's 'pre-memories' she was both confused and proud. Katherine wrote beautifully, translating into words a range of ideas, feelings and sensations that language wasn't designed to embody. It seemed Nat thought so too, for she read everything young Katherine wrote, although she refused to speculate.

That first night after the crash, Katherine had remembered enormous swathes, visceral chunks of her Form One dream. She had grown old, basking in the sun. Seeds and bulbs of herself had split and grown, new colonies of life spread, consuming enough resources to develop and mature.

She didn't know what to make of it, nor did Nat proffer an explanation, and neither Katherine nor her stellar guardians expected that she would have such an experience again. Yet it would reoccur many times over her life. They watched eagerly over her shoulder each time she wrote things down, memory after memory. Everything that her baby had been, everything she had done and felt, Carols had experienced it too, up until now. Carols knew that she hadn't been imagining a connection in earlier forms. Her child had been aware of her, sharing those earlier lessons. Katherine herself had been there, dreaming those skill-sets again. The presence she had felt accompanying her in the earlier forms was actually her child, dreaming up 'pre-memories' and writing them down. She smiled and gave thanks, and buoyed up with confidence she was eager to find out what it all meant.

CHAPTER 36

{Katie's Journal Memories}

Justin never expected or knew that Katie's memory shunts could be damaged by a time swallow. Although he wasn't strictly a thanotech, he knew that those barriers were designed to be secure.

Following her safe return, however, it wasn't long until Katie found out that the neural bypasses meant to separate her from earlier experiences in other forms had become porous. In her dreams, she stretched and lived in the sun. And then later, in the dirt, and in the ocean. Much later on, she remembered her life in the air, and on the tundra. Sometimes those memories quickly faded, transforming into evanescent echoes of potent emotions; whereas sometimes swellings of recollection swamped her with hauntingly strong impulses, leaving her gasping for air. She found that dreaming could be exhausting.

Each time she experienced a new 'pre-memory' she would write it down, adding it to her journal. Most of her entries were written in the weeks and months following the car crash. Quietly she tried to document as much as she could remember, not wanting to forget those conversations, or what she had learnt sitting out under the stars.

Dear Journal,

I once asked Uncle Justin what stellars do for millions or billions of years, and he said it would be almost impossible to explain. Actually, I remember what he said. 'No matter how hard you try, you cannot get a dog to appreciate architecture.' I told him to try harder, and I never saw him laugh harder. Together we ended up having to make up a new word, because unsurprisingly, the words don't exist. We decided the word had to be scatter-fuggling. It's short for skate-surf-juggling.

He said for me to imagine myself wearing roller-skates while surfing the ocean. Impossible, right? He said that at one point, what my eyes and immune system do now automatically, were skills that my younger mind didn't have. So, at some point in my future, when I can go surfing in skates without even thinking about it - like the way I use my eyes - then what I get to do is juggle glass "now" balls. Skate-surf-juggle.

Whenever you look into one of those balls, you see "now", depicted as the very heart of a firework explosion. You see it frozen, and from the very beginning you can already tell what the firework will look like. You can measure the elements and the intentions or trajectories of each, which gives you a preview of the outcome, the shape and colours.

By knowing the position, the direction and the speed of each part of that explosion right at the beginning, I'll can see which beam of light reaches the furthest, and which one falls short. What colours are being used. The trick of skate-surf-juggling is seeing all those possibilities and following the line of light that takes you where you want to be. Once you start following that goal, then it's apparently a simply matter of blinking, which transfers my focus onto the next now-ball, where another firework is exploding. Focus, and then blink to start again. Each change of perspective involves accepting that all other futures lose strength with each choice; with every single blink other possibilities fade. Although I noticed when Justin scatter-fuggles, he almost stops blinking, like his body slows down. Well, he does his breathing things and goes into a bit of a trance, but he says all that keeps him young. Ha!

Uncle Justin also said that many artists were trying to do was to capture the images they glimpsed of the ever changing patterns within those juggled futures, using words, colours, or music. I've watched him do this often enough, and I still think he's just daydreaming like grandpa when he day-dreams. Grandpa happily claims to be a bit scattered, his mind off with the clouds. Justin said stellars call it future surfing, but to me, it's always going to be a word that doesn't exist. Scatter-fuggling.

One day, I'll go scatter-fuggling too. No hurry though.

CHAPTER 37
[Sentience Dilemmas]

Months and years passed, and watching her daughter grow, Carols could not have been a more proud mother. Watching her baby become a mother was extraordinary. Carols relished the exquisite vicariousness of giving birth; the beauty of the situation was almost overwhelming. Her baby was now caring for some other stellar's baby. She found it was fascinating to observe child-rearing practices from yet another perspective.

Katherine's first child was a healthy baby boy, weighing a smidgeon over three kilograms. Quickly calculating, Carols estimated the boy had thirty trillion, trillion atoms on which to engrave himself, and surprised herself in not immediately knowing how much baby Katherine had weighed. Her recall skills were usually instantaneous: when nothing is ever lost, the workings of memory are infallible. Inside Death © though, disconnected from her physical body and subject to the effects of the memory shunts, the absent answer wasn't of great concern.

Carols swam throughout the cultural context. She continued to explore details, and familiarise herself with the relatively advanced society the semi-sentients had constructed for themselves. Learning about the variety and diversity of cultures, languages, customs and traditions was a perpetual exercise, and she soon learnt to use her time wisely. Sometimes while Katherine slept, Carols would whisper into her dreams to boost her confidence, and reassure her that she was never alone.

A tingling alarm, similar but distinct from that tug she had felt in the Limbo Lounge, would let Carols know when Katherine was about to wake, and she would return her focus, with enough time to spare. The gestating mind took enormous conceptual leaps in form six, building on the Elementary Emotions introduced during the previous mammalian level. She appreciated that lessons in Intermediate Emotions and Elementary Sentience took an enormous psychological toll on the relatively fragile human bodies. Her gestate had been much stronger in earlier rounds, but she knew how it worked. Death © was a zero-sum game: when one variable increased, another decreased: leaving, as always, everything in balance.

Despite religious precepts and theological directives regarding stewardship of the planet being a communal obligation, Carols was repeatedly shocked to see the way the semisents treated their fellow lifeforms. Animal exploitation, careless environmental destruction and a wanton disregard for life often left her nauseated. She spent some time floating on the winds, accessing hypers and correlating data.

At first, Carols had been pensive, exploring. The various environments stood monument to her daughter's earlier deaths. The forms appeared to overlap, or have no regard for the linear time that humans used. She found the bugs and the birds everywhere, while the unusual plant from her first form was kept by Katherine herself. She'd bought it especially, not long after she reclaimed her earliest pre-memory. Appreciating the synchronicities, Carols decided to explore other geographies of memory. The ocean was too vast; narrowing her search down to two: the mammoths of Form Five and the abruptly-ended first attempt at Form Six.

Finding the Berelekh River in Siberia was easy, although the exact spot of the flash flood was buried. The bodies had joined many others: the excavation of so many mammoth skeletons had made the news broadcasts. Finding the volcano turned out to require more work, as it wasn't there anymore.

Eventually she tracked down the islands where Tavi had lived, centuries ago by human reckoning. The eruption had been embedded in iron molecules, and as she scanned the memories she appreciated anew the horrific aftermath. What had once been the largest volcano on the planet had eviscerated itself, erupting again and again over the centuries. She was surprised to find it had now practically vanished, leaving only isolated steaming islets growing from the centre of an ocean-filled caldera. No longer did the Asian continent stretch so far south: what had once been the end of the world was now an island chain paradise.

Back at home, baby Thomas seemed to grow even more quickly than Katherine had. The next year, Katherine fell pregnant again, and gave birth to a little girl. Carols hadn't known until then that humans couldn't select the sex of their offspring, especially considering the extended gestation time. She laughed at herself, for being so ideologically pre-set that she hadn't even assumed they might function differently. She wasn't sure whether they had forgotten as a species, or whether it was an inbuilt limitation of the scenario. Time got busy, and Katherine birthed another two younger sisters for her first born, interrupted only by a miscarriage she told nobody about.

The semisents obviously cared for their appearances, yet it was all so oddly superficial. Their surface-layers were not merely maintained, but decorated and draped; meanwhile their insides were neglected or even abused. *No wonder they have such short lifespans*, Carols thought.

After such a friendly beginning, her midwife *Nativity of Diamonds* had become quite distant, and Carols couldn't figure out if it had anything to do with the time swallow that Katherine had disappeared into. When Katie was writing more notes in her journal, *Nativity of Diamonds* paid complete attention, but incongruously; she tried to be inconspicuous about it. It began to make Carols suspicious, and she couldn't help but think that something was going on that she was being deliberately kept out of.

Nat definitely knows more than she's letting on, she thought, not for the first time. After yet another attempt at eliciting information was rebutted with admonitions to have faith and give thanks, while her baby slept, Carols went for - what she'd learned was called – a walkabout.

She briefly thought about the other mothers in the Limbo Lounge, and wished she could talk with them again. They would be somewhere else in the complex, watching over their own gestating offspring, and she wondered idly if the minds in their care had crossed paths with her progeny. She didn't know what was up, but it was patently clear to her that something strange was going on.

From the notes Katherine made in her journal, she gathered scattered jigsaw clues and tried to tie it together coherently in her mind. The whole picture was there, just broken up and embedded in other stories – as brecciated as the scattered iron molecules she had tracked down in Indonesia.

The elusive answer was happiness scattered and embedded: the eponymous *Zest as Breccia*. She racked her mind for snippets of memories she had scanned and ignored back in stellar society, but she had never been interested in tales of industrial espionage or the wilder prophecies of fringe cults. She was sure that she recognised the name of the stellar that had vanished with her baby, but it was a vague reference, a name she knew she ought to know from history, and it stayed out of reach.

Carols only knew a thing or two about this ancient stellar. She knew that *Zest as Breccia* was a bit of a cult figure for eschatologists, and was pretty sure her name was involved with the Light-Lite sabotage events that had made news recently. None of it had made sense; so she had let the information move over her. How could a stellar from ancient history be alive and wandering around inside the Death © immersive?

These thoughts were still coursing through her mind when she returned early to the birthing chamber. She knew that Katherine was still fast asleep and would remain that way for hours yet. Although she had taken to wandering the winds during these periods, she braced herself to face Nat and demand some answers. She was increasingly disconcerted, and didn't want this worry to interfere with the pregnancy. In this case, the best course of action, she decided, was to simply take action.

When she opened her senses to the room, she was not prepared for the scene that greeted her. The midwife was furtively leaning over her sleeping stellar child, whispering into her dreams. As soon as she saw that Carols had returned early, she stopped abruptly, and even as conflicting emotions effervesced all over her integument, she was unable to hide her guilt

'I was going to say that I thought it was time for some answers,' Carols said, slowly and carefully. She forced her racing pulse to steady. 'Now I can see that it is well overdue. So, let me be clear, you are going to tell me exactly what you're doing. What's going on?'

Her self-control was slipping, and her voice rose of its own accord. Her baby was her one chance at saving her menagerie. Now the one stellar who was meant to be assisting was not only being unhelpful and obtuse, but now patently doing something that might endanger all of that.

Nativity of Diamonds tried unsuccessfully to settle her storms. She raised herself up, and Carols was taken aback to register that amongst all of Nat's conflicting emotions were the signs of undeniable and extreme emotional distress, and she had no idea what was wrong.

CHAPTER 38

<u><Tales of Confession></u>

There is a hunger among human beings that cannot be satiated by food. Triggered by the experiences of Intermediate Emotions, it is much more than a desire. It is a deep-seated need to be part of something, to belong to a community of like-minded individuals. Nat had seen this motivation lead to astonishing beauty and awe-inspiring achievements, for the synchronicity of two minds working in tandem often made the sum greater than the total. There was something magical about intimacy. It was no wonder that three-quarters of all stellars were in binary relationships.

Despite what she saw around her in stellar society, *Nativity of Diamonds* had never taken a partner. Her mind burned alone. Although she knew she was never really alone. She always had the babies inside Death ©, and would always have her memories of being with Zest. Their connection was of *Uno Sympatico*, where they could finish each other's thoughts. The only real time they had together was as stranded Orphans, waiting to be reborn after the war. Those years would burn forever in her heart, in her mind, in her own prime.

After her own engendering, whether she lived with the boys as a Black in the family core or as a Silver around the edge of the family, she would always treasure that connection. She and Zest shared a history that could never be repeated; nor could anyone else ever supplant or replace it. She had long ago come to terms with the possibility that the hunger for the warmth and friendship that she'd once had satiated as an Orphan would never be repeated. She had continued with her life, and buried deep the tiniest ember of hope, one that she refused to extinguish. It didn't hurt to dream, she rationalised. And after all, nothing is ever truly lost, even if Zest didn't make it back out safely.

Here at the end of her midwifing career, the mysteries and magic of life had come back to surprise her. A last-minute reprieve, the elusive opportunity that she had long dreamt of was right in front of her again. She was overwhelmed with the awesome beauty of synchronicity and faith, practically lost for words. She'd not known how to explain this to the young mother she was caring for, and while she felt guilty about keeping secret about who this Uncle Justin character was, it was more out of habit and instinctive response than a deliberate desire to mislead. She'd simply been keeping this secret for so long, she didn't know how to go about sharing it – especially with a client.

The rapport that she had built up with young *Carols in Sequins* had been healthy and encouraging: but that was standard birthing procedure. There had been nothing to indicate that the daughter gestate would be the link that would reconnect her with her long lost love. Apart from incarnating on that island, that was. The odds against revisiting that one physical spot where, centuries ago, she had briefly seen Zest: they were astronomical. She'd liked those odds, it had augured well. But it had certainly ended badly.

Following an autonomic alarm, she had taken the form of a large bird to reach the remote island, but was too late to stop the disaster. That close encounter had reignited her mental embers, and inspired her to install her own alarm network into the system, one which had remained totally unused until young Katherine had vanished. Then her alarm systems had gone off all over the place. Quickly silencing them with her override codes, she had instituted an exo-neural ghost to backtrack and investigate. No gestate of a young Red ought to have been able to survive a time swallow, and unless the mother had studied Advanced Temporality (which Carols' records clearly state she hadn't) then her child ought to have died then and there. The scenario would have ended, and as young Katherine had not quite reached sexual maturity, it would have been sixth form all over again.

Yet, she had survived, and that very same night the growing baby stellar had reached menarche, marking the transition between child and adult. Nat had been pleasantly surprised by this; still dizzy from the implications of what had happened in those four seconds. She had glanced at the shape of all possible futures, and realising that Carols most likely thought her '*I tried, I really tried to save him*' comment had referred to Tavi, she left things unchanged.

When little Katherine started to write her journal, this dizziness became overwhelming, and her suspicions were confirmed. That 'Uncle Justin' had been Zest. *Was* Zest. Zest had somehow survived - despite all the statistics and naysayers - and still existed, inside the immersive. Thrived, in fact; although it did appear he'd gone a bit native, which was hardly surprising. She knew from extended personal experience, there was definitely some insidious appeal found in being human.

The life Zest was living could hardly be more different from the exalted and honoured positions they'd once held. When they'd lived as Orphans, their skill-sets and knowledge-bases had automatically put them on a pedestal above the meagre undeveloped versions of the semisent populations whom they'd lived amongst. They'd lived as gods; now Zest was scurrying around like a fugitive, living anonymously. And alone.

Nativity of Diamonds could only assume that over the millennia, Zest had also found some way to satiate the hunger for connections, for warmth and friendship that every sentient mind shares. When they'd been together, Zest had always incarnated as male and she as female: they'd even created a family together. Unfortunately their offspring had carried the short-lived non-regenerating human genome, and they had been doomed to watch their children and grandchildren grow old and die. It was so long ago: long before the top-rated immersive PreyData © was annexed and rebooted as the Academy of Death ©; long before their little group called the Orphans were finally evacuated.

Sometimes she liked to think that those descendants of theirs had graduated from the stellar nursery of Death ©, and were even now beacons of light shining somewhere in the darkness. Perhaps they were even part of her own immediate stellar family. Once she engendered and assimilated all of her own memories and experiences, the answers would be there waiting. Perhaps, those children would be waiting for her in the family core. It was a nice dream. But in the now, that's all it could be. She'd never know until she got there; so she simply gave thanks and tried to focus on the current issue.

She'd been daydreaming about connecting with *Zest as Breccia* for so long that it took an embarrassing delay before remembering she had long ago instigated (and carefully buried) contingency plans in the Death © framework itself for exactly this situation. Hurriedly, she collected together her ancient plans, and was disappointed in herself for not reviewing them more recently. They were so naïve as to be impotent. Moreover, she recognised that she had no reason to believe that Zest would even want to return, even now. All she could really hope for, she reluctantly realised, was the chance to say hello and maybe a proper goodbye.

All of this was predicated on the hope that Zest would turn up before *Carols in Sequins* and her new-born completed their tangles home, ending her current session. Technically, thank goodness, she could stay to review, to oversee that there were no chronological overlaps triggered by the exit of the gestalt gestate.

There was no possibility that this unexpected break could be ignored, she was driven by an overwhelming compulsion. Somehow, she needed to get a message to Zest. Nat knew that her distracted state and ritual platitudes had started to sour the relationship between her and the young pregnant Red, which she felt bad about. However the distancing had worked to give her time alone with the gestate.

At first she had started cautiously, but now she was taking every opportunity to whisper into the sleeping mind of young Katherine, although at times it felt like she was almost screaming. She knew Zest well enough to know that any loose ends that might have been left over from his time swallowing experience would need to be tidied up. He'd be back. She knew it, and she had to be ready. Somehow she had to find a way to get a message through.

At least, that's the track her mind was stuck on. She was focused, and while she was busy with her surreptitious actions, she was caught. Carols returned from her nightly peregrination to catch her in the act of subconscious whispering, and was obviously, and justifiably, upset. It only took a moment to be honest, and she was surprised at the relief she immediately felt upon opening up and confiding.

'Ok. I'll tell you what's going on. Please calm down, just breathe and have faith, ok? There is nothing wrong with your baby, nothing at all.'

She could see Carols' integument starting to settle, but the tension and mistrust was still there, simmering beneath the surface. '*Carols in Sequins*' she repeated, using her full name to get her attention. 'Listen to me, there is absolutely nothing wrong with your little one, ok?'

Carols unfurled a shade of acquiescence and her concern seemed to dissipate. 'What were you doing then?' she asked, the emotions still apparent in her voice.

'It's a bit of a long story. Please, relax and I will do my best to explain it all. It has to do with your Katherine's Uncle Justin. As you've probably gathered, he's not who we thought he was.'

'So it was *Zest as Breccia*? I've always thought that she was a legend, or a myth. What is she doing masquerading as a human?'

'Yes, it's her, and while there are certainly legends and myths surrounding her, they are based on facts. *Zest as Breccia* was one of the original thanotechs, but she's more renowned for being the Orphan that stayed behind. I trust you are familiar enough with your history to know who they were?'

'Weren't the Orphans the last of the Pop Ones, those ancient stellars who lost their bodies during the Nova Storms?'

Nat nodded, eliciting more information, and Carols continued.

'Let's see if I remember. Their minds were stored inside an immersive, one of the old mortality games. PreyData ©, wasn't it? That's right. And then, they were all re-embodied as Population Twos after the war. Except for her, right? Zest was the missing piece. But that was cycles and cycles ago. Aeons back. Surely they've all engendered by now anyway.' Carols paused, racking her memory for more details and coming up empty. She heard the echo of her sister's voice in her head, *Berries in Cerise* encouraging her to show more interest in history or current affairs. *Perhaps this was what she meant by me being a bit shallow*, Carols thought a little shamefully, and determined to rectify that situation when she returned.

Nat took that pause to segue in. 'Essentially, yes. You have the facts there. During the Nova Storms whole swathes of stellars copied their consciousness's inside immersives. The biggest or most famous of which was the game PreyData ©, which had the only collection of all known predatory species. It was a good game, very popular, and it was the framework of this game which was becoming the new Academy of Death ©. Once the war was over, those who had experienced complete body-loss were left remaining, and those thirteen individuals became known as the Orphans. Eventually twelve were repatriated, and nearly all of those have since engendered. The official line is that Zest didn't survive the reboot, and that loss has given rise to all sorts of rumours.'

'The eschatologists, right?'

'Yes, the 'Brecciated' as they call themselves. They've been gaining a bit of attention recently. Zest would be so embarrassed by the end of times theology that they espouse in her name.' Nat paused, reflecting on the ridiculous claims made by what was a cult following.

'You knew her, didn't you? Oh my...' the hesitant young expectant stellar stuttered, and Nat was both unnerved and reassured to see how quickly Carols had put the pieces together on her own. 'You said 'nearly all of the Orphans have engendered', meaning that at least one hasn't. It's you, isn't it? You were one of the Orphans, weren't you? You were there! You've actually lived all this, haven't you? You're not telling me this as a history lesson. This is your history. And her story.'

'Yes, you got it. I've been...'

'What? Waiting here, hoping to find her? Since the beginning of Death © itself? Despite the odds?'

'Yes. Despite them all, I've never stopped believing. But I've become too old for all this. You see, you may remember, you are my second-last mother. I don't have long left, in fact, I've already started engendering. Despite my appearance here, I've nearly completed my expansion, and it won't be long until I compress. I will have to move on, and I've only just come to let all this go. And now, wouldn't you know it, here at the end of my career, she turns up again in the most fortuitous synchronicity ever.'

'And you're trying…what? To contact her through my baby? How would that even work?'

Nat looked at Carols with a surveyor's eye. She wasn't angry, she wasn't even incredulous. It sounded almost as if she was interested, and wanted to help. She decided that she had very little to lose by accepting help from an unexpected source, and she quickly explained her idea.

CHAPTER 39
(The Strangest Questions)

Claire grasped her Grandma's precious record even tighter, and saw Justin's eyes flicker from it to her. 'What happens once we give you the journal? You want us to make the same promise as Grand-Mama? As Katherine did?' She looked up at Aaron as he approached the table with the tea tray, and saw the concern reflected in his eyes. He placed the tray on the central table runner and reached over to place a hand on her shoulder. Claire looked at her father, and at the stranger on the opposite side of the table.

Justin looked uncomfortable. He sighed heavily, and placed his hands on the table before folding them again. He looked around at the family unit in front of him, the child and grandchild of the young girl he had rescued three quarters of a century ago. 'I guess I am going to have to trust you, the same way I did your grandmother,' he replied, looking at Claire. 'You understand that for me, it is much more of a risk than it was when your grandma was a girl.' Claire merely raised her eyebrows, inviting him to go on. Aaron had taken a seat next to his wife, and Tommy started pouring tea into cups.

Justin watched the steam rise from the cup passed to him, taking the time to gather his thoughts. 'The world is changing. I told Katie that I couldn't see the future, which is true. To an extent. You don't have to be eternal to see that patterns of history repeat themselves. But the changes of the last century have been accelerating, and there are factors in the mix that have never been there before, things that perhaps even I can't explain.' He paused, and sipped his tea.

'Perhaps I'm being presumptuous,' offered Aaron, 'but could we help in any way? A fresh perspective? A second opinion?' He looked at the surprised faces of his wife and father-in-law, and widened his eyes, as if to proclaim his innocence. 'There's no harm in asking, right?'

Justin snickered good-naturedly. 'No harm in asking?' he repeated. 'You might also argue that ignorance is bliss. Trust me when I say there are things you really do not want to know.

And that there are things that it's important for you not to know.'

There was a pause, and then it was Claire's turn to snicker. 'You mean about us being in a school? That we are baby stars, and that everything on this planet is alive? That the stars themselves are actually alive?' She turned to her husband, reached out and took his hand. 'How could that be dangerous?'

Aaron smiled kindly at her, and took over driving her train of thought. 'I agree. Wouldn't such an idea be wonderful? Revolutionary even? It could bring together science and religion. It could eliminate wars and even change the way people treat animals or the environment. How could it not bring about peace?'

Tommy had been sitting silently, listening to the conversation and staring at his tea. As it swirled and steamed, the slightest touch of the cup induced new waves, echoes bouncing and feeding off each other. Even when the tea appeared still, he could visualise the ongoing movements, the thermodynamic balance that existed underneath the surface, atoms constantly colliding, releasing the heat and aroma that he could feel with his senses. The answer to the question came unbidden, popping into his mind fully formed the same way that the characters in his novels seemed to do when he was 'in the zone'.

'We can't have peace,' he uttered. Without looking up from his tea, he could feel three sets of eyes on him. All three pairs bore the weight of expectancy and questioning, but Justin's gaze seemed to carry a faint hint of surprise. Tom looked over at Justin, and in the manner of a student who has just grasped an advanced concept and is trying it out with words of his own, he continued. 'We need war, and death, and destruction: don't we? It's part of the lesson package, an essential element in the curriculum.' He saw Justin's eyes widen, and then his head nod in acknowledgement. There was silence around the table for a moment, broken once again by Claire.

'Do we need it so much? Couldn't we still learn that lesson without it all being so unfair?'

When Justin didn't answer straight away, Tommy recognised somehow that he wanted them to answer the question themselves. That he was taking the parental role, and eliciting the answers from children who didn't appreciate that they already knew them. He knew this technique; he had seen the same expectant serenity on his mother's face on many occasions.

He had used that look on Claire and Jackson too. He knew his sister Caroline imitated their mother the best the first time he'd seen her re-enact that stance with her kids. He smiled to himself, recognising another thing they attributed to their mother, whereas once again the credit probably belonged with this man sitting on his right: this complete stranger, who was such an integral part of his family.

Tom took a stab at the answer. 'I guess it's a matter of perspective, isn't it?'

Justin smiled again, and picked up his teacup, holding it in front of his face, smiling expectantly. 'From the perspective of eternity, nothing here is really that bad.'

Tommy could see Claire about to object, and held up his hand to waylay her. 'No, that's not quite right. There are things here that are bad, really bad. But...well...' he scratched his nose, and found the example he needed to continue his thought.

'Sometimes when I was in the hospital waiting for your Grandma to wake up, I would wander around the ward and just look. I got to know some of the staff, and even chatted with some of the other patients. The room two up from Mum's was a double, with a lovely view from the window. Martine showed it to me, you know, the girl who became a nurse?' Claire and Aaron nodded.

'There were two patients in that room, both confined to their beds, so neither of them could appreciate the view. Martine said I would always be welcome in their room, although they probably wouldn't remember me each time. Their dementia was so bad that they couldn't form new memories. Apparently they had stopped recognising their own children, which Martine said she only knew from their notes. She didn't remember them *ever* receiving a family guest.'

He paused, swallowing forcibly, as if trying to lubricate his throat against the pain of the words. 'I said to Ma...' and he stopped again, swallowing once more. 'I told her about them, about what Martine had said. I remember her response. She said, 'We can only hope and pray that their children learn something from it, even if it's not until their mother is gone. It's not that amazing, when you consider what a parent is willing to do for their children.'

Claire looked over at the corridor leading to the room where her two boys slept peacefully, and then back at Aaron. Tommy could see the love between the two of them, and was so very happy that his daughter had found such a good man to share her life. He could see her mind churning; and as she looked at her father she knew that he felt the same way about her as she did about her own kids. That her father would do practically anything for her, or for her boys. And that her Nan would've felt that way about all of her descendants. She had written in her journal about wanting the very best for her unborn children's unborn grandchildren.

'Are you saying that they made a choice? That some part of their mind is deliberately trying to teach their children a lesson by hanging on in such a state?' Aaron asked.

'No', Tommy replied. 'What I think she meant is... if they could have, they would have. I know that if I could somehow help you, or them,' he said, nodding toward the corridor, 'by enduring months or even years of senility and suffering, I would gladly accept. I mean, what is a couple of years of Earth time, compared to eternity, right? Compared to a billion years, a decade or even two is relatively nothing. Although, perhaps our resident stellar would care to clarify?'

Justin was still sitting there, leaning back in the chair holding the tea cup between his hands. He seemed to scatter his smile at the three of them, glancing with bemusement at their attempt to bring him into the conversation. 'No, you are doing fine. Please...' he said, inviting them to continue. 'Unless this is one of your questions...?'

'Questions?' repeated Claire and Aaron simultaneously. They looked at each other and giggled briefly, aware of how funny their speaking in unison would have appeared to their twins. Aaron clarified. 'You have questions? What do you mean?'

Tommy blushed, remembering that he had yet to actually explain that part of the bargain. 'Justin has agreed to answer three questions in exchange for the journal,' he said. 'And I'm afraid I've been off wondering what to ask.'

'You've been 'off with the stars', eh Dad?' Claire smiled, using an old family expression for wool-gathering. 'Three questions, just like the three wishes from a genie's lamp?'

'Yeah, kinda,' he replied. 'But I've been thinking about the possible consequences as well. As Justin here said before, sometimes ignorance is bliss. And the story of Pandora's Box figures prominently in my mind. And remember,' he prompted, 'you only ask a question...'

'...when you are prepared to accept the answer' she recited.

Tommy smiled to himself, proud of his daughter. He grasped that this expression was one his mother had taught him – and possibly had learnt herself from this man on his right. His smile broke through and he relished a strange feeling. The pride he felt was suddenly compounded, compressed and yet expanded, multiplied and yet simplified by the awareness that his mother was truly proud of him. In a way, his actions themselves honoured her, in having instilled her lessons in another generation. He was mulling over the beauty of this feeling when Aaron directed a question at him.

'Have you checked with him already,' he said, indicating Justin, 'that you or we are not in a time swallow as well, that our lives are not at risk? Because frankly if there's any risk to us, or the boys, then I say 'no deal' straight out. You know?'

Tommy looked at Aaron, prioritising his family's health so clear-headedly, and felt the strings of pride pull at him from new directions. 'Yes, I've asked. He assured me this is not a time swallow, and that we are all safe.' He turned his attention to Justin, who appeared to be trying to avoid answering the question. 'Right?' The silence was excruciating, and the three of them sat there around the table, waiting for an answer.

'What did he say exactly, Dad?' asked Aaron. 'What were his actual words, do you remember?'

Tommy slowly moved his tongue around his teeth, as if he could extract the memory out of the enamel. 'Back in Ma's lounge I asked him, and he said, um, let's see…he said, 'We are not in a time swallow, and as far as I know you are not about to die.' Those were his actual words, I'm sure of it.' Tommy looked at Justin quizzically, and the understanding dawned on him as Aaron spoke.

'That was you, Dad, back then. What about us, and now?'

The silence was broken as the wind whistled loudly outside, and the three of them stared at Justin. He looked lost in deep thoughts, as if he was unaware of the tension at the table. Tom could hear the tears in Claire's voice threatening to melt her calm exterior as she spoke to Justin.

'Our boys, Alex and Kyle are asleep through there,' she said, nodding at the corridor. 'And tonight, when they went to bed, Pop told them a bedtime story.' She was obviously choking up, and her eyes started to glisten as tears swelled. 'He told them that their Grand-Mama was now a star in the skies, because she had finished being a human. He told them a beautiful story about how baby stars go through six grades or forms, just like at school. That when they put on a first-form uniform, they become a plant, and forget they are a star.' She was struggling not to cry, and she had to stop and swallow before continuing. Aaron took her hand, and offered with his eyes to continue for her. She shook her head, and wiped the excess tears from her eyes.

'Those are Katherine's great-grandchildren in there. They now know that they are baby stars; that are now in the final grade of school and are wearing human uniforms that make them forget. Are you telling me…can you…?' Claire looked up directly at Justin, and with those words, another thought struck her. 'She wrote down something that you told her once. You said if you ever met her great-grandchildren, her 'unborn children's unborn grandchildren', right?' She looked at Tom for confirmation of her quote, and he nodded.

'You said that you were sure she would be proud of them. Well, that's them in there. Can you possibly tell me that their knowing they are in a stellar school, and that one day they'll be a star just like their Ma-Ma, that that can in some way undermine the lessons they need to learn? Can you really tell me that there is no other option? Why can't you just go home like *Native Diamonds* wants and leave us alone?'

The words were like a bucket of cold water over Justin, and Tom realised with a start that he'd completely forgotten the message that his mother had written on the last page.

Many of her journal entries had been addressed to Justin, but they may as well have been written to a journal with no expectation of response. But the final page message was different, it was the last thing she'd written. She'd sent him home to get the journal, taken him into her confidence because it couldn't wait, she'd said. And he'd forgotten about it. He reached out his left hand toward the book, asking wordlessly for Claire to pass it over. Meekly, she reluctantly relinquished her grasp on it, and he immediately turned to the last page. He re-read the message, but silently, refreshing his memory and wondering what these words meant to this man.

He spoke slowly. 'This...is obviously meant for you. This message. And I want you to have it. But this may be our only trump card, and unless you're willing to assure me that my family is not in danger...' To the sound of gasps to his left and his right, he tore out the final page, screwed it up and popped it in his mouth.

Justin's eyes blazed for just a second, before returning to his usual long-suffering parental expression. 'This is childish. And there's...'

'No need?' interjected Claire. 'No. You're right. There's no need at all.' She turned to her father. 'Dad? If we want this man's help, or even his forbearance, perhaps we ought to be working together rather than being on opposite sides of the table.' She looked down at the table, and then up to face the man sitting opposite her. She smiled, and simply kept on smiling till she got Justin to smile as well, which broke the tension in the room.

She turned back to address Justin. 'The message was from someone called something like *Native Diamonds*' she said. 'It said Zest needs to talk to an orphan about coming home. That was it, I think. All pretty clear, except for the strange name I suppose. Oh, and I didn't understand the orphan bit. Does all of that mean something to you?'

Justin abruptly stood up from his chair, and walked over to the sliding glass doors that led off the dining area onto their back porch. Through a Perspex ceiling they could see a spattering of stars overhead, and it was at these that he stared as he answered her question. He spoke as if preoccupied, and the dreaming quality to his voice made his response barely loud enough for anyone to hear.

'I need to talk to an orphan, eh?' he asked rhetorically, quietly. 'Maybe she did make it home then. Maybe they all did.'

'Justin?' Claire said. 'You wanna tell us about this orphan? Or about *Native Diamonds*?' He turned, and looked over the trio sitting at the table.

'Ok,' he said. 'A long, long time ago, *'The Orphans'* was a name we had for ourselves. Our little group. And Di...was someone I was very close to.'

'What does it mean?' Tommy asked.

Justin turned slowly as he answered. 'It means...I can probably go home. In fact, I have to go.' He looked like he was in shock, and he repeated his last word with a strange look on his face, as if the word didn't fit or tasted strange.

'Home' he said, again. Justin seemed to have turned pale. 'This probably needs some thought, but frankly I've had millennia for thinking.' He turned and looked at Tommy, Claire and Aaron with a cheeky grin. 'It's time for some action.'

Justin wandered back over to the chair he had been sitting in, and stood behind it looking at the faces gathered around the table. He could see elements of that young girl he had saved all those years ago. Katherine Amelia was still very much alive in her son and granddaughter. He remembered again the promise that he had made, all those years ago. He promised that he would look in on her unborn great-grandchildren, and he resolved to honour his word.

'If it's alright with you, before I do go home, I would like to do one thing,' he said, looking at Claire and Aaron. 'I would like to see the boys.'

Worried looks passed between the young parents, and he sighed bemusedly, before reassuring them. 'I'm not going to be bringing harm to anyone, least of all your little stars. I just want to see them. I...I made a promise once. One that I'd like to keep.'

Aaron squeezed his wife's hand, deferring to her as spokesperson for their family. She nodded, and stood up. With Aaron and Tommy following, she led her grandmother's great-uncle down the corridor to the twins' room. The nightlight cast a warm glow over the scene, and as she walked in, she could see that Kyle had kicked off his blankets. She bustled over to his bed and untangled his leg, covering him up again. She felt Justin standing beside her, and as she brushed Kyle's fringe back from his eyes, she heard this ancient man whisper.

'They are beautiful little stars,' he said. 'Katie was truly blessed; as are you.' She looked up at him, and was taken aback to see tears in his eyes. She stood there unmoving, taken aback with awe. 'There is nothing more precious in the cosmos than our offspring. Nothing has made my time here more bearable than being surrounded by the wonders of children.'

Claire murmured agreement, aware that she was sitting in the same spot her father had occupied earlier that evening as he had woven his mother's tale into a bedtime story. She wondered briefly if the room had absorbed the frequency of his thoughts. She looked at her precious little stars and hoped that while they took a break from dreaming they were human, that the energy of their imaginations would infuse the room.

She remembered reading that Justin had told Katherine that long ago he'd had a family, and sired children here on Earth, but had deliberately stopped reproducing long ago. She imagined that watching your loved ones dying off could only be experienced so many times, even for an eternal. Even with the knowledge that they were being born and now constantly shone down from the heavens, she imagined it would hurt.

Another thought struck her, about how Justin was an original stellar, back from before Death © had brought life to the cosmos.

'Did you ever have children of your own, as a star?' she asked quietly. He shook his head. 'And if you go home now, will you be able to?' she enquired. Justin thought about the widely scattered elements of the proto-galactic mind he had once inhabited as *Zest as Breccia*. He knew the destroyed cloud of gases would be now spread across many light-years, perhaps light-centuries. Those materials from his body would have contributed to subsequent populations of stellars, but he saw no reason to explain that he chose to see his offspring all around, in every single living thing on the planet. After all, it was possible that any lifeform here was at least partially comprised of particles created in the moment of that death.

'I don't know,' he whispered back. 'I hope so.'

He reached out and lovingly rested a hand on Claire's shoulder, like a family member. She stood up slowly, and as he turned to leave, she stopped him. With her father and husband looking on from the doorway, Claire opened her arms and bear-hugged Justin. Justin had not received a decent hug in a while by the looks of it, and the guys knew what a bear-hug cuddle Claire could give. She squeezed and rocked gently, waiting for him to relax and accept her embrace. It was almost funny, and they might have laughed if it hadn't been so poignant.

They stayed that way for a good thirty seconds. When they finally released, Tommy observed how that half a minute had taken years off each of them. Still wary of waking the boys, they all made their way back to the dining table. Sitting there in the middle was Katie's journal, protected only by teacups.

Justin looked at his hosts, the precious descendants of his dear old friend Lawrence. It had been Lawrence who had given Justin a job and a place to live when he rode into their small country town over a century ago. Back then, all he wanted to do was to get as far from the memories of New York as he could. His experiences there had left him disillusioned, and he needed the rejuvenation of manual labour.

A few years later young Sarah, the wife of Lawrence's eldest son Daniel, reignited his love of life when they brought little Katherine Amelia into the world. By that time he had already decided an extended and isolated retreat from human society was in order, and he had settled with the Coulston family on their farm. Many years later he had attempted to make a surreptitious exit after his faked 'death', young Katie had inadvertently been present and stumbled onto his true nature. Now here he was, generations later, still entangled with this family: tied not by blood, but by honour.

'Let me have a quick read, and I'll be on my way,' he said. Tommy nodded, and Aaron asked if anyone wanted another cuppa. Justin declined, but Claire, watching in astonishment as Justin starting flipping through the pages of the journal, announced that she was going to have a drop of something stronger.

'I think I could do with that too,' her father added, his eyes similarly transfixed to the quickly turning pages.

Aaron walked into the kitchen pantry to see what he could rustle up. Tommy started to collect the teacups onto the tray, while Claire stood at the end of the counter watching Justin. It had taken her a couple of hours to read the whole journal, but he was skimming it, turning page after page so quickly she imagined his eyes as scanners that were absorbing every drop of ink on the page in some cognitive digital array. She watched, entranced. Every now and then he would stop for a moment, as if relishing something on the page.

She noticed Aaron at her side, offering her a small cognac glass. She looked at him briefly, smiled thanks for the liquor and directed his gaze over to where Justin was bringing a new definition to speed-reading. Nearly at the half-way mark, she could see where the crumpled page stuck in the side of the journal indicated the end of her Nan's unbelievable tale. She noticed her father standing in the corner, similarly fascinated by the rapid intake of information being displayed in front of them. And then it was over. Justin looked up at his audience, his face a tumultuous cloud of emotions.

Tommy broke the silence. 'I have a question,' he said. 'Or actually, it's a request. I'm guessing that when you go 'home'…'

and he looked out the screen door at the stars overhead, 'that you'll get to see my mother again, right? Will you tell her how much we all love her, and miss her, and look forward to seeing her again one day?'

'Not planning on becoming a star just yet are you Dad?' joked Claire.

She had lost her grandmother that morning, but her father had lost his mother, just as he was meeting her afresh. She was struck with how much perhaps she didn't know about her own father, about this man who had helped bring her into the world and raised her. She and Jackson had surely been as much of a challenge for him and Gloria as her boys could be sometimes. She determined then to spend more time with her Dad, and to make extra effort to ensure that he had time to spend with her boys too.

'No, not just yet,' he laughed back at her. 'I've got a few more things to do.' He looked at his son-in-law, wondering if he would immediately recognise an old family maxim. 'Hurry?' he prompted, and was filled with happiness when not only Claire and Aaron, but Justin at the table all chimed in with the ritual response.

'No need!' They were all still laughing, perhaps a trifle too loudly, when they were interrupted by a sleepy six-year-old voice coming from the corridor. Claire turned to see Alex standing there in his pyjamas, rubbing his eyes.

'What's going on?'

'It's ok, baby. Sorry if we were making too much noise,' she cooed. 'Back to bed, ok?'

'Is Pop still here?' he asked, and Tommy leaned forward from the corner to wave and smile at his grandson. As he turned back he did a double-take. Justin was gone. Either he had made himself invisible again, or he had left properly this time. His sharp intake of breath drew Claire and Aaron's attention to the now empty chair at the table, and they both gasped.

'Dad. The book,' breathed out Claire. His mother's journal was gone as well. He hadn't had the chance to ask his questions. He didn't know whether to feel duped or not. Part of him felt relieved at the pressure being off. Wondering about the realities of God or the intricacies of the afterlife was one thing: having the answers provided was quite another altogether. He wasn't sure what he would have done with the answers once he had them, either. Such responsibility, yet to waste the opportunity on trivialities would have seemed irreverent.

The adults just looked at each other with incredulous expressions, their minds still boggling from all they had learnt that evening. As Claire took Alex back to bed via the toilet, Aaron suggested that Tommy sleep in their spare room that night. After saying one more goodnight to Alex, Tommy accepted and bade sweet dreams to Claire and Aaron.

Tom had already slept on the story, although the nap he had caught between his bath and the early morning phone call from the hospital felt like many days ago already. As he collapsed onto the bed, he realised how tired he was, and how much he needed to sleep. With the imminent prospect of a solid night of sleep came a wonderful thought: that with both Justin and the journal gone, there was no reason to think that anything terrible was going to happen.

Neither he nor the kids were in any danger. *At least, not in any more danger*, he thought gratefully. *Life was dangerous enough*. He looked over at the empty pillow, and imagined Gloria's loving eyes staring back at him. 'But I suppose it's meant to be', he said with a grin as he fell off to sleep, imagining her smiling back at him. 'Apparently, the whole thing is designed to be fatal.'

Tommy's whole family had always been early risers – not that you have much choice when you have young children. Tommy awoke to the sounds of the boys in the bathroom, and discovered that someone had removed his shoes and covered him with a blanket. *I must have really needed that sleep*, he observed as he performed his morning stretches. He wondered if this ritual was also something his mother had learnt in her dream, the importance of stretching upon waking. 'The only animals that don't stretch are human adults', she had impressed on them all. 'Kids know to do it. Cats know. Dogs know. But human adults seem to forget.'

The thought of his mother reminded him that had yet to speak to his sisters, and that his mother's garden and house were calling to him like a pet needing to be walked. It was an activity he usually enjoyed, but he struggled this morning. It was as if his mental skies had yet to clear; he didn't know if those phone calls would be an invigorating stroll through the sun or a begrudging, reluctant excursion into an emotional storm.

The thought of both his mother and Gloria watching him via the sunlight brought a smile back to his face, and he reflected on the potency of their lives. In every drop of light, on every mote of stardust was carried a dose of her happiness virus, and he could spread it, a constant memento of memory that could reach out and infect him anew, every time he opened his eyes and saw the light. The thought of his Ma generating smiles even after she had gone changed his smile into an outright grin.

He deliberately and consciously reached out and picked up an invisible hat, one that his mother had sewn out of magic for him as a child. His happiness hat. 'Every minute of every day, you make decisions and cultivate habits,' she'd said many times. She had also sewn bonnets and berets for the girls and a top hat for Thomas.

'Whenever you put on your happiness hat, it squeezes squillions of smiles down into your head and out your eyes and mouth and everywhere.' Tommy had watched his mother sew invisible hats of happiness for his kids, and for the children of his sisters. He remembered a couple of years back when she had tried to give her magic hats to the twins, only to be told that their mother had already made them one each. 'Well you can never have too many smiles, or too much happiness,' she had responded, letting her brief flash of disappointment be washed away in a wave of maternal pride.

The sky outside was gloriously clear, and it looked like being another beautiful sunny day. He politely accepted Aaron's offer of a ride home and they listened to the news on the car radio on the ride over. It was just the usual stuff. New proposed peace talks in the Middle East. Some celebrity bimbo, whose face he wouldn't be able to pick out of a police line-up, was newly-wed again; while the storms in Queensland were getting worse. A derided politician made a calculated speech about hard-working men and women of the country, people that he had nothing in common with. Then the announcer changed tone to include what was an unusual 'human interest story'. Astronomers the world over were puzzled by a strange phenomenon early this morning. Apparently all the stars had briefly vanished, although they were back now. The announcer laughed reassuring his audience that even without the stars, it looked like being a beautiful day.

CHAPTER 40

[Celebratory Song]

Of all the strange expressions Carols had encountered from her time amongst humans, one stood out in her mind. 'No man is an island'. It seemed so anomalous, so essentially wrong. Every stellar in the cosmos was in effect an island, but by no means did that isolate them from the community in which they lived. Although she imagine that if they lost the ability to communicate, how easily madness might indeed follow. Grateful for the beauty and bounty of life as it was, she gave thanks: a ritual action she performed religiously, a habit not needing thought.

Working together, she and Nat had managed to impress a message on her child's sleeping mind, and the excitement the two of them felt at seeing her write it down in her journal rivalled any celebration song Carols could think of. It was nice to see their efforts succeed; plus it felt nice to be communicating again with her midwife. It had become a little strange there for a while, and Carols was delighted to feel the camaraderie again, to be infected with her colleague's enthusiasm. Seeing someone so extraordinarily happy was an exquisite vision, and being part of making that happen left her tingling with vicarious anticipation and joy. Now it was just a matter of waiting and seeing if Nat was right about Zest returning to cover his tracks.

Watching the years accumulate for her daughter was like a countdown in reverse – every year was a step closer to her birth. Carols would soon accompany her via tangled photon to her new home, and the darkness would dim a little as a new star was born. She knew that the average semisent rarely survived as long as three billion seconds; as Tavi, her gestating stellar hadn't even reached three hundred million. *Far too short a time*, she thought again.

It was during these latter years of Katherine's life that Carols began to question the implications of what human society was doing. Tavi's community had been isolated and technologically simple, living under the generally beneficent eyes of various gods watching from the skies above. In Katherine's lifeworld, the sparks of light in the night sky had become stars; galaxies instead of gods. Some humans apprehended the holistic implications of sharing a star dust heritage, but those few that did trip over the truth generally dusted themselves off and interpreted the facts through the bifocal lenses of religion or science. Binaries refused to buckle, and the nature of life and death remained hotly contested.

In their birthing chamber at the Academy of Death ©, *Carols in Sequins* and *Nativity of Diamonds* also engaged with the material that Katherine was collating in her journal. Carols was pleased to discover, and a little relieved, that although Nat was ostensibly the only real expert, she was not a perpetual source of knowledge. Such honesty motivated her more, and her questions about the process of life and death became more intense.

Together they bounced around ideas and possibilities, and Nat also found herself enjoying the camaraderie, the bonding collusion found in sharing a passion. Together they wondered about the anomalous fact that there were more stars calculated in the skies around Earth than there were stellars in the cosmos. For the first time, Nat admitted that the hypothetical tipping point that *Demisting as Acapulco* had long ago once dismissed as unrealistic now stood a better than even chance of manifesting. If everyone used Light-Lite, if everyone stood in the shadows, their combined body heat would eventually brighten the area. If there were more stars seen around Earth than in stellar society, there was the slightest chance that the polarities might de-synchronise, permanently separating life from Death ©.

They knew that would drastically change reproductive dynamics in the cosmos, possibly even resulting in conflict. But as for what it would do to Earth and all the dreaming stars bound there, they couldn't even pretend that their guesses were close or not. They simply didn't know. Carols found it fascinating that Nat had been present in futures where humanity was almost extinct, and futures where they had spread off planet and reproduced like a virus. They were discussing the semisents' comprehension of the multiverse when Katherine fell and hurt herself.

Nat had warned Carols that the end might be fast approaching when Katherine was hospitalised. Carols had estimated that Katherine could still easily last another three hundred million seconds, but the odds changed significantly after she broke her hip. Although she'd seen Katherine's siblings and children recover from broken bones before, apparently the rate of healing was related to her chronological age. Carols accepted this as part of the inexplicable package that was human physiology, and puzzled again at the anomalous abdication these semisents made regarding control over their own rejuvenation and health.

The last notes that Katherine had written in her journal had been about births and deaths in her family, with the notable exception of the distress she had experienced when watching Krakatoa erupt. She hadn't known why this particular disaster had affected her so, but Carols and Nat knew. Krakatoa had actually been the remnants of what used to be the largest and most isolated volcano on the planet. Centuries ago, it had nestled at its base the tribal community of the Holotan people, the family into which Tavi had been born.

As Carols and Nat watched the words go down onto the pages together, Carols felt the tingles of excitement rise in intensity. She wondered if it was her own feelings or the osmotic contagiousness that either Nat or Katherine was emitting. It didn't matter.

Carols was more than eager. She was thrilled at the general feeling that this whole experience was nearly over. Nat had confided unofficially that there was no way that her gestate was not going to graduate, and knowing that the plan to increase her structural integrity and protect her precious menagerie was succeeding brought palpable relief.

As Nat had predicted, Katherine confided in her first born and delegated the responsibility for safe-keeping her journal, adamant in her belief that her Uncle Justin was going to return. Carols and Nat looked at each other with glowing pride as Katherine wrote the strange message down.

Sitting up in her hospital bed alone (apart from the Venus Fly-trap on her side table), she also wrote down the same five words that her Uncle Justin had spoken to her just before his alleged demise. Her careful cursive script etched onto the page, *'Never forget you're a star'*.

As she wrote, Carols could hear an alarm sound from Nat's panels, and in the background could feel the lights start to brighten back in the birthing chamber. She knew without being told that this was it. She couldn't explain exactly how she knew, except to say they'd been through it before. She had accompanied her baby through form after form, death after death, lesson after lesson. Carols understood then that by the very act of writing down those words, right on the heel of having shared her secret and delegated her duty, that her baby had effectively completed everything she needed for a full complement of skill-sets. She now had experienced the six forms, and acquired all of the sixty compulsory skill-sets, leaving her a comprehensive 360 degree ring of strength and connectivity. The final skill-set hadn't been so much the act of delegation, but the acceptance of the inevitable: Katherine's anticipation of a future and acceptance of letting go had rounded her out. She didn't need to die any more.

Connected to her gestate's mind, Carols couldn't tear herself away to see what happened with Tommy and the journal. She and Nat had already discussed what would happen during the seventh and final round, and she was confident enough to encourage her midwife to follow the journal and complete their task. Her baby had left her human body, and was moving through the layers of the immersive, destined for the birthing tank. Waiting patiently in front of them in the chamber was an agitating maelstrom of energies, a haptic simulation of the mindless Brown from her outer system, soon to be infused with the fires of consciousness, turning Brown into Red, and making her into a binary system.

Carols checked one last time that the entangled photon link from the chamber to her home was secure, and she inserted herself inconspicuously to watch the unblocking of the memory shunts. It was something she had been through herself, but like everything that happened inside Death ©, she wouldn't remember it until she engendered.

In an empty sphere that defied boundaries and relations, she listened to a muffled >clunk< as her daughter's most recent memory shunt was lifted. All the experiences she had accumulated in her brief time as Tavi were reinstated, and they swam together in the confluence of completeness. She could feel her child's happiness, her confidence, her excitement and anticipation. She wondered if her baby knew she was there, but Carols knew not to speak. She understood that first contact had to be initiated by the new-born.

There was another >clunk< sound, and another shunt arose. Carols visualised the appearance of a canal, releasing blocked-up waters of memory that flooded over and through them. They were moving backwards through the levels, and with each >clunk< another segment of memories was released. When the final (first) level washed over them, the sense of connection and belonging was more intense than any mere language could encompass. The words didn't even exist. They couldn't.

They were both back in the birthing chamber proper now, and Carols could sense the processes of transfer begin. The compulsion to move grew in her daughter, and she was swept along with it. Every molecule of their beings flowed with the same >*AWAY*< imperative, the universal gift bequeathed by Zero onto every particle of matter when his grand symmetry was dispersed, crystallised into a lower energy state. At an essential level, no matter what generation or temperature, they knew they were distant cousins, all lives were the star-dusted descendents of Zero. As they turned to leave together, she called out to Nat.

Overwhelming gratitude and best wishes suffused her voice as she saw the tangled links open. The memory shunts that had buttressed the levels of growth now moved to encapsulate their entire experience, fractally twisting those engraved atoms of memory into a compressed state neither of them would be able to access until they too compressed and engendered. The seventh level of review was complete, and with all of her memories accessed and assimilated, Carols recognised her baby was now ready to be born.

The direct channel to her new body effervesced wide in front of the new stellar, and as she moved into the tangle, Carols sang out in joy and pleasure. From her perspective, she immediately initiated her own tangle, and braced herself for the integration with her exo-ghost. Her memories of shepherding a new-born were entwined, absorbed and compressed into the foundation of the stellar she had been birthing. All the memories Carols had accumulated during the birth, she expected to remember when she engendered, billions of years in her future. What she would find instead would be the memories of her own parent or parents, marinated for millennia as atomic tattoos. Nat was long accustomed to this particular ruse that Death © played on parents, and as she ejected a colourful burst of good wishes, she quickly returned to focus on the events unfolding planet-side.

Carols in Sequins – sans any memory of the events – exited Death © only with the knowledge that she had succeeded. The kernel of consciousness had been germinated; a mind capable of coping with eternity was about to be born. She absorbed her exo-neural ghost, and the memories of her ghost's activities overseeing the physical aspect of the birth became predominate. Together as one she watched her baby Brown churn in silence no longer. The chain reaction she had initiated completed itself, and answering a congratulatory call from her sister *Berries in Cerise*, they both watched as the ever-compounding gravity well emanating from the kernel of consciousness acted to compress chunks of helium and hydrogen together.

Waves of heat and gravity and light rippled through banks of helium; and, ever-so-quickly, seemed to burst forth on the surface. Ripples intersecting and reflecting off each other, triggering new swirling waves of change to sweep further out, bubbling in complex yet recognisable patterns. All this activity, all this stretching and testing of energies: it was the most wonderful thing she could remember seeing in a long time. She heard her daughter's mind echo her joy, skating over the cresting symphony to join with her in a celebratory cry, a mutually magnifying roar. It was spectacularly, divinely good to be alive.

CHAPTER 41
(The Happiest Birthday)

Katherine thought briefly of all the stories she had heard about the afterlife, about cloud-laden harp players or tunnels of white light, and felt amused. She played with the thoughts, turning them over in her mind like physical objects. Connections sprang forth, and the fullness of her life appeared all around her, leaping outwards in vivid scenes. The images held her transfixed; mesmerised, she watched her daughters become mothers. She felt herself holding her first grandchild. She watched her husband George, beaming as he performed the service at Tommy and Gloria's wedding. Holding Tommy's hand on his first day of school.

The images came faster, and it soon became apparent that she was seeing her life flash before her eyes, but it was now running in reverse. It wasn't just in front of her eyes though, that was a vast understatement for what she was feeling and seeing. She felt her heart fill with elation as she relived the moment when she and George were pronounced man and wife. She watched herself with detachment as she threw a temper tantrum as a teenager. She wanted to reach out and grab the face of Uncle Justin as it appeared – but then it aged, and he was the old man her family knew him as. She relived the thrills of the rope swing down by the stream on the neighbour's property; she felt the shock of being left alone by her mother at school.

The memories and images were vastly clearer than anything she had ever dreamt or consciously recalled, but she could see now that they were all intrinsic parts of the patterns she had always swum in. She felt a comfortableness, a sense of implicit trust that imbued everything. The images started to fade, and a fog dispersed the remaining feelings and sensations.

There was a subtle >clunk< sound; one for some unknown reason she had quite expected to be a lot louder. For a moment she wondered if those expectations were actually her own, but then those thoughts elided as she completely remembered. She had been a little boy named Tavi. It felt like yesterday, and she remembered sadly that she – he – had experienced only a brief life, but it had been filled with wonder and experiences that contributed to who she was now. She knew his family and the island in every detail, as if it really was yesterday for her. His family in the forest; the catastrophic and tragically early death. But before she had time to reflect, she felt another >clunk<, and remembered her life from *before*, again.

She'd dreamt something of this, and the knowledge echoed like a mutant form of déjà-vu, a sensation there were no words for. She smiled as she recollected her life as a mammoth. A male again, possibly the last of its tribe, desperately seeking an escape from a brutally changing landscape.

There was another muffled >clunk< and she was flying! She was a dove; rather, she had been a whole flock of doves! She felt the wind in her feathers as she soared across the planet in a distributed consciousness, and experienced the combined thrill of living all parts of a lifespan at every single moment.

>Clunk< The disseminated nature of a gestalt mind increased in intensity, and for a second she remembered 'forgetting'. The joyous freedom of being a collective. She was – had been - a mass of krill, feeding and being fed upon, moving with the waves and cycles of the oceans.

>Clunk< So distributed now she is (or was) hardly aware of herself, she floated in a colour that has no word. She was breathing and living and dying as millions of ringworms, encircling the entire globe.

>Clunk< She smiles, feeling complete somehow, remembering that which she had forgotten the longest. She felt a sense of beauty at the synchronicity of life, and she remembered her first venture into the physical realm. She had been a Venus Fly-Trap, cut and transplanted and nourished and bred to exhaustion. She smiled at that, connecting all her pre-memories, and felt herself spread out and simply float in the beauty and balance of all the lives she had lived. She remembered it all, felt them all, and held them all together. She had her whole life – no, all of her lives, here in the palm of her metaphysical hand. She smiled again, appreciating that there really were no human words to encompass it.

Le mots n'existent pas, she said to herself. *But no 'zannen ne.' The words don't exist because they're not meant to, there's no need.*

She bobbed, floated, glided without thought. She swam through things she had done, things she had been, things she had not remembered. She relished her time as a plant; as a microscopic creature in the soil; her experience swimming in the ocean. She recalled again the thrill of flying, the disconcerting reduction involved in moving from a collective consciousness to an individual one. She relived the agony of knowing that you were the last of your species; the skills of self-sacrifice that parenting involved. She swam through her own history, touching on moments of joy, and some of pain. They had all gone into the recipe that had made her who she was now; each ingredient was worthy of acknowledgment. She felt obliged, that she owed a display of honour and fealty to herself, and all that she had been.

As she envisioned holding each of her lives, they began to compress. The memories twisted around each other, rainbow ribbons of colour that shrunk beyond her ability to distinguish individual aspects. There was no sadness in this: she knew nothing was ever lost. She felt no sense of loss, more a feeling of security, knowing that all those experiences were who she was, who she had been, and that they would in some way propel her forward. She held out her ghostly hands, and turned them palm down as if to grab hold of memories in motion. She envisioned grasping an invisible handlebar, and felt herself move. She was in motion, growing, she saw herself never staying still. There was nothing wrong with where she was, but she felt impelled to move, nonetheless. Subsonic motivation drew her, called her *>AWAY<*.

Steadily rising through absence, floating out of the absolute blackness, she encountered a blinding flash, a kaleidoscope of light and colour that vanished so quickly she wondered if she had imagined it. Despite any referential points, she somehow knew that she had travelled somewhere. It was the same, but distinctly different. She had arrived into what was definitely a somehow lesser shade of black, a softening of the void, cushioned in a moment of now. The only constant was her own self-awareness, her own old Descartian cognition. She possessed a vague feeling that since this place existed, space must therefore be. Other than that: nothing.

There was a vast absent sensoria that simply appeared to surround a solitary cognitive bubble. Inside she could sense no movement, no gravity or inertia or sense of force at all. There was a certain force behind the process of self-acknowledgement. There was some sense of personal responsibility or individual onus that could not quite be acknowledged yet, but for a moment it did not compel action. This was good, because she didn't want to follow that through. Not just yet. She was in no rush to assume the mantle of anything permanent.

The new blackness was an imperceptibly changed yet undoubtedly lesser void. While it was all encompassing and omnipresent, it did have a shape, and it was a pattern that seemed familiar. She observed the outline, the evenness of its distribution. She grasped that it could be artificial – something constructed. It was something that she was on the inside of; floating in. There was an edge to her new universe, a border that begged to be mapped. Putting aside questions of who made it, she decided the smartest thing might be to at least familiarise herself with where she was.

Feeling out the boundaries of the absence required her self-awareness to extend to the very edges. It was roughly a ball, but the entire axis seemed to stretch impossibly before somehow twisting again, and then merging and diverting into the timelessness that was somehow part of where she was now. Perhaps not having an inner ear to provide a sense of balance had been disorienting, but it might also have helped with the leap of association that followed immediately on her use of the word 'where'.

It was not a question of "where", but of "who", she realised. This void, this space, this potentiality, this all...not only was someone, it was *her*. All of her lives, every single one of her experiences were forever engraved on the vast inner screens, cellular walls coated in atomic memory. Stretching all around her, was all of herself. It was Katie, Tavi, the mammoth and all of the others. This little space where she existed looked like it was absolutely everything that was her, and all that was. She was not simply in a void, she was the void. A void that had shape: but it was merely an illusion, she could see the outline of the vacuum inside an egg.

There was nothing outside; there was no outside, because there was only herself. She was filled with a sense of awe: an overwhelming awareness that she was much more than she had ever dreamed. She had a history and a context far vaster than she had imagined. She was glad that Uncle Justin had been so elusive about the process. To have arrived in this experience with expectations, with words to describe or interpret it, would have somehow diminished the wonder, taken away from the astonishing sense of awe she floated in. She coasted and curled around herself, her memories and experiences laying clear for her a very personal history, one that only existed inside time.

Outside of time she could focus away from reminiscing and try to discern a 'now'. Without using sight as such, or hearing or taste – all impossibly limiting to a being without a body anyway, having no corporeal organs with which to sense - she took her awareness right to the edge of her bubble, tentatively exploring. 'Know thyself', she chortled. Clusters of activity and curlicues of energy were evenly dispersed, but obviously not evenly used. *"Obvious": really?* She questioned. *How do I know that?* Yet there was a definite difference between this arc and that section, but the means of defining or differentiating were, as yet, beyond her. There was an intangible yet undeniable sense of déjà vu about the whole pattern, the whole construct seemed like it was a very familiar apparatus. Something that was valued but not often used: an egg-slicer of a meme, stashed in a drawer and forgotten.

That's it, she thought with sudden recognition. *It's an apparatus.* It, or she, was actually the shape of some form of tool. Was it an egg, or tank of some kind? An immersion tank designed for...her. Somehow she was sure of that, that this tank was specifically hers, that this experience, that everything she had experienced and observed and learnt; it was all her. There was no bubble of consciousness measuring, assessing, floating or flying through an unidentified medium, no central control nodule that you could step out from.

Outside? She wondered. *Is there an outside?* As far as she could tell, she was the whole medium. Every swirl of photons, every cluster of carbon, each clump of iron, even the experiences of being a Venus Flytrap, or a krill or nematode or mammoth or even her time as Katie and everyone she had met there – all of that was a part of herself. There was nothing that was not her, not even the tiniest scrapes of nothingness. Not even the tank. She turned to it, enquiringly.

The tank seemed vast, yet it could have been microscopic for all she knew. Yet if it was that small, then it was a feat of engineering far beyond her ken. She found a myriad of vents, deeply embedded in the fabrics of the blackness. Identical in appearance, some had seen more use than others, the evidence of extended exhalations pouring forth could be evidenced deep in the etchings. They appeared to be jets of some kind. A staggeringly enormous number of miniature jets. There was no moisture, no mould or growth that she could see. They weren't jets for pressurised liquids, she somehow knew that. Nor were they for liquid, or gas either.

As she thought about it, the answer fell into her mind and she suddenly understood. They were vents of energy strings, notes for making music. The tank was - no, in fact *she* was – a musical instrument. The vents were for creating jets of patterns, solid symphonies of infinitely variable matter, wave functions configurable to order. Winds of thought and energy, incessantly vibrating on micro-atomic strings. They were all inter-laced and formed part of a pattern.

There *is* a larger pattern. The idea fell into and filled her mind with an overwhelming compulsion. She had to zoom out. To hear and to see: to feel the whole song. To retract perspective and appreciate the larger symmetry, to hear not the individual notes but the song in completion. She may be an instrument, designed to create music, but even so, she grasped that all of her efforts were but part of a larger whole. She was a music-making instrument, but without a doubt she knew she was also part of an entire orchestra. Her notes, her creations and energies, they were but part of a larger melody, a more encompassing creation that could only be fully appreciated in context. She needed to see the context, to feel the music, to smell and touch and swim through a song – a song designed to be played on hearts and souls. With this insight, she zoomed, retracted, expanded.

Although she didn't move physically, she knew that she was travelling faster than she had ever dreamt possible. She could feel herself being thinned, winnowed out. Her memories were becoming vague, although it didn't concern her. Everything that she had been, everything she had experienced, had all contributed to who and where she was now. It was *now* when things were important, and it was always a moment of *now*. Even without the details of her various lives and deaths, she knew that she had everything she needed inside her already. It was time to move.

With that awareness, her surroundings began to get lighter. And warmer. The tunnel of white light from her memories seemed to surround her. Quicker than the spray of sunrise lighting darkened skies, suddenly absolutely everything was brightening. Extremely bright, intensely light and invigoratingly warm. She was overwhelmed with beauty. Had she still tear ducts she knew she would be drowning in emotion. Swimming through the prelude to the elusive song, she realised that the light was coming from...herself. She was more than simply a note in a beautiful song. She was also light. All the colours of the rainbow were there, and many more.

A fire of intense light burst forth from deep inside her, pulsing through new beats and shining out to illuminate the neighbouring darkness. She could hear sounds of joy and happiness, and she eagerly aligned her energies to the noise. She erupted from the transfer, burst out filled with excitement and anticipation, thrilled by the wonder of life. No longer coasting, she had no need to be dragged anywhere. She felt the heat of the music sing. She felt the multiple harmonies of memories pulse, and at just the right moment, she stepped into her new life.

And then there was light.

CHAPTER 42

[Uncrossed Lovers]

From the comfort of distance, Nat would later conclude that she must have partially been operating under a state of shock during this period. She only vaguely remembered her client and new-born even leaving, but later when she reviewed the records of the session, she thankfully reflected that such distraction had only been apparent to herself. Once the gestate had finished her final lesson and accepted the responsibility of delegation, she'd been transferred to the seventh day of Death ©'s creation week. There she had successfully assimilated all her mortal memories, and as was customary had chosen her own name before those memories were locked away.

Although *Skating with Serenity* was now being born and had departed the immersive, there were still physical imprints left by her birth. Each child did that: every single stellar added a little something to the biosphere. Nat remembered how some thanotechs had wanted to eliminate the anachronism and maintain a steady state population. They had run numerous simulations, yet the only steadfast result was their lack of success in actually maintaining balance. When the unique consciousness-generating properties of Light-Lite had been found within the PreyData © gaming system, the open access opportunity for anyone to contribute data on a unique species (predator or prey) must have either imprinted a pattern, or magnified an aspect intrinsic to the Light-Lite substrate itself. Nobody had been able to determine for certain.

With physically-incarnate echoes from Forms One, Two and Four still sunbaking, wriggling and flying around the simulation, Nat could justifiably stay even after the mother and new-born had completely exited. Even considering the virtual instantaneousness of tangle-travel, the time differential between stellar society and the constrained four-dimensional construct of the Death © immersive only allowed her a limited period in which she could watch the journal. She gave thanks that it would be enough, and made herself comfortable while she waited.

She didn't have long to wait, and was pleasantly surprised to see Katherine's son use his imagination and intuition to call out to Zest. Her mind froze for a full microsecond when he made himself visible, and she had to restrain herself from making contact right there and then. Although they were by nature only semi-sentient, her constant stewardship gave her ample opportunity to appreciate some of their aphorisms. *'Out of the mouths of babes', 'Patience is a Virtue'* and *'Silence is Golden'* all sprang to mind.

As she eavesdropped on Zest/Justin speaking with Tommy, a reminder chimed on her control panel. She went to snooze it with a swipe to the side when a thought hit her with such force she was almost stunned. Her next birth scheduled was the last one she would ever midwife. For although most females (not the Blues, they were simply too massive) and most males (the mobility and multiplicity of Silvers outnumbered the vast conglomerate of Blacks, even disregarding the latter's general omnivorousness) could uplift and parent a new mind, only female stellars could midwife.

She wondered if she would participate in jokes about it being a 'girl's job' once she was a male. She couldn't imagine it, and she acknowledged that once she was a boy, the memories she carried might very well set her apart more than before. She'd be more of a loner than a short-lived Blue in a conservative and previously stable neighbourhood. Which was the unfortunate future allocated to her next and final scheduled birth. She'd almost forgotten - she was going out with quite a bang.

Nat knew that despite the memory shunt she had received as a midwife, her unique experiences as one of the Orphans was going to give her a special advantage. She could remember when she wasn't supposed to be able to, thanks to her re-birthing after the war.

None of the other Orphans had chosen to become midwives. Despite generous offers, she was the only one who had chosen to continue on with the newly formatted Academy of Death ©. She hadn't been surprised though, only seven of the Orphans had been involved with the bloodthirsty immersive PreyData © before their body loss; and one of those was still an Orphan. After all this time, one of their little group was still parentless and unborn; wandering around alone, surrounded by children.

She was enormously reassured to see that Zest hadn't gone mad. Sometimes the things the semisents did drove her a little crazy, and she wasn't even physically there anymore. She was glad she had tangled onto the journal rather than Tommy, or she might have lost them in the translocations. At Katherine's grand-daughter's house, her great-grandsons were sleeping, and she listened eagerly to the conversation as Zest/Justin had an impressively evasive conversation with Katherine's descendants. Nat wondered if Zest had become involved in human political affairs in the centuries that he'd managed to keep off her radar. Nothing would surprise her now.

As one of the young boys interrupted them, Nat had to focus carefully to determine whether he had phased out of vision or had translocated again. She smiled at finding Zest in the first place she looked: back in Katherine's lounge, sitting where he had first appeared to her son earlier that evening. They had always known each other so well. They had such an affinity, they often joked at their imaginary psychic powers. So when Justin greeted her as soon as her mind focused into the room, she wasn't surprised. But she was still touched, and an immensity of emotion threatened to bubble forth and reduce her composure to an ineffable and ineffective mist.

He subvocalized a whisper. 'Diana?' He looked around. 'That's you, isn't it?'

My dear sweet Zeus she replied, and solidified into a visual form. She wove a stable human-shaped quark lattice that was transparent but solid. Inside her outline moved a billowing overlap of energies, generated by folded quantum fields that gently circulated miniscule gravity wells around seven central orbits. It was a trick that Zest had originally taught her, ever so long ago. She was pleased to see him smile in recognition.

'What are you doing here, my darling one?' Justin asked, standing up and moving closer to her apparition. He looked at her with wonder, with pride and with love. She beamed back.

'I could ask you the same question' she replied cheekily. 'I understand you're the person I need to talk to about having a baby.'

Although she hadn't seen it in millennia, she could still read his human face clearly. His eyes: those sparkling, enchantingly blue eyes that acted as a bedazzled distraction from the enormous depths hidden behind those specks of gold. She could see worlds of possibility unlocking, dreams and frustrations long put aside being released and relinquished while other threads of potential thickened exponentially. She was overcome with emotions, and stuttered as she tried to get her words out.

'It's time for you to come home' she said, and remembered how Katie had felt when her Tommy had wrapped himself around her waist, tears falling from his eyes. She knew that she'd been right to hold on, that giving thanks had paid off and the cosmos truly had balanced. Her dedication and faith was finally bearing fruit, and she struggled under the unexpected weight of it. 'No arguments' she added, reaching out a hand to take Justin's face and lift it up. He shook his head agreeing with her, and she could feel his body shake.

He looked at her eye-to-eye. 'Before we go, I need to ask you. Is there something going wrong in here? Has the operating system changed? The population balance and biosphere integrity appear to be, let's say, malfunctioning.' He paused, hesitant to ask the next question. 'Is the system getting another reboot?'

She smiled at her beloved: always concerned with others, with the system, with immersive integrity. Far more than a reclusive artist, Zest had a passion for life that sometimes exceeded her own. Theirs had been a *simpatico*, one *par excellence*. Katie was right: no matter the language, sometimes words themselves simply cannot express an idea.

'I'm afraid I can't answer officially. I'm a midwife now. Senior midwife, mind you. It's kept me busy while letting me keep an eye out for a lost little orphan. But I do know what you mean. There's been no official announcement about a reboot, but there have been attacks directed at Death © via attempted Light-Lite frequency infiltrations. As for population balance, that's probably to do with all the males becoming parents. It's quite the trend amongst Population Three and Four boys.' She held back a smirk, barely able to contain her anticipation of the shocked look on Justin's face.

'Population Four….males? How is that possible? There have been less than a hundred billion humans, not enough to fill one galaxy. The very first Population Two females were only just being born when…'

'…when the war broke out.' She said, completing his sentence. 'And we were caught in here. Yes. My darling, darling Zest. The war was nearly thirty complete cycles of the cosmos ago. Have you forgotten? As above, so below? Death © is adaptive, it keeps up with life here, remember? How do you explain the 170 billion galaxies, each one now full of stars? Sounds to me like you've gone a little native, started thinking in limited human time-frames. You're only counting up until today, aren't you?' As recognition dawned on his face, her love was renewed all over again. 'My sweet little artist, what have you been doing? And why have you never answered my calls?'

Confusion spread over his face. 'Answer? Answer what? I never heard from any of you again. I thought…'

'You thought when we were rescued, that we were actually just transferred and trapped in another immersive. Am I right?' He nodded, mutely.

'I'm guessing that whatever you did to survive the reboot must've disconnected or damaged your communications, because trust me my darling one, we've been… I've been calling for you, looking for you ever since.'

Emotions and memories too deep to be embodied in words or expressed on a human face fought for ways to manifest, and the conflict Zest was experiencing was painful for her to watch. All this time, if only he'd called out, or made a sign – but then again perhaps he was wary of being corralled into a fate even worse than an inferior immersive, one which he couldn't bring himself to admit. At least, not at the moment. They'd have time for that yet. For now, she had to keep Zest safe and get him out of here.

When she'd been younger, it would have been no problem to translate Zest straight into her own Brown. Two aeons ago she had birthed that stellar, who had swung out of her heliosphere to safety, becoming her own system before Nat engendered. As it was now, with her own irreversible transformation already underway, even had she a spare Brown it wouldn't have been safe. Or fair, bringing Zest back only to be annihilated as she moved into her new state. She had less time left as a girl than a short-lived Blue.

The Blue! She remembered the massive short-lived stellar she was scheduled to midwife next. Her human-template mind raced at 60,000 km/sec, not fast enough to connect all the dots. She re-centred, momentarily un-inhabiting her human shadow, while she peered forward through the sludge of space-time. Holding the metaphorical hand of Lady Luck, Nat surfed the possibilities, calculating the almost impossible. She carefully sent a push into the material, changing the form of the conduits. Like a ripple in a heavy rug, a bow-wave once made will forever pull energy in to itself. Any stimulus response, once conditioned, never stops wanting to be pushed again. Even attempts at flattening invariably create more ripples. She knew the theory, and had the skills, but she'd never cared for future surfing. Here it was an unfortunate necessity.

The simulations showed promise, but such a devious thing had never been done. She outlined her idea to Zest, who pragmatically accepted this risky course of action as the only alternative. He would have to re-corporealize through the gestation process, but by going through the forms he could become the gestate she would soon be guiding to life. It was possible for a gestate to master skills exceptionally quickly, almost completely bypassing the usual time spent in each form. She felt a sense of urgency she couldn't explain, and attributed it to the stress of the situation. She couldn't see how time was relevant, yet she felt it laying heavily on her, as if all the time-keepers were ticking down to a very special deadline for her: one that she simply had to make.

Luckily a short-lived hyper-Blue like the final birth she had scheduled needed no parent present. In fact it was rare that one even could be. The nursery from which this gigantic stellar was even now coalescing into shape was actually a collation of numerous stellar remains. Earlier stars had dispersed seeds of their life into the family, from which the cycles of life would continue. Those minds were now elsewhere, as nothing was ever lost, and everything always balanced.

Justin gestured towards the journal, and she knew that his instincts would be to destroy it. Claire's passionate entreaty rang in her mind, and she stopped him, suggesting an alternative. She'd seen how Katherine's great-grandsons had accepted the truth so easily. She'd sat and listened as a Baptist and a Buddhist and a scientist had bounced around ratifying ideas, finding more in common than what they'd ever imagined.

It was all a matter of words and of perspective, and Nat had been pleasantly excited to see their responses. She thought there might be hope yet, despite all of her concerns about what was happening with all her beloved babies on the planet. Before he dissipated and while she prepared the birthing process, Zest took her up on the new idea. He seeped his story onto the unwritten pages in Katherine's journal, and left it on the coffee table.

Within a relatively short period of time, the hyper-Blue would also engender. Possibly, even before she completed her own process of transformation. The Blue's birth and dispersal would disrupt an entire neighbourhood, spreading compound elements for light-years even as her mental core twisted and compressed. They could both become boys together.

Blues almost inevitably became boys of Black, whereas although Nat's Population Two body was larger, she had assumed herself destined to engender as a boy of Silver. There was the slightest chance, an almost miniscule possibility that was almost ridiculous to calculate, that they could both transform into the rarest kind, the neutered time-keepers called boys of Grey. Such an unlikelihood made her smile, and filled her with confidence. The beauty and synchronicity threatened to overwhelm them both with emotion, and they embraced each other tightly.

They had been there together at the beginning of Death ©, and had experienced so much together in the human centuries they shared as Orphans. Now they would be together forever in the next stage as well. As tears flowed down Justin's cheeks, *Nativity of Diamonds* saw the drops undergo a phase transition as they turned into steam. She felt his entire body shudder; releasing the structural patterns relied upon for so long. Connected together again by freshly-instigated tangled links, they both dissipated into the air. Together they would begin the process of dying, all over again, for the first time.

POSTSCRIPT

[Every Day is a Good Day)

After being dropped off home, Tommy had quietly stood out the front, looking at his house. It had been *their* house for so many years. It was the home that he and Gloria had filled with memories. As he walked down the driveway he noted with satisfaction that his car was still there, and that although he had left by unconventional means and not locked up first, everything appeared to be in order. He walked up the garden path to his mother's unit, and was surprised to see the door ajar. He knew that it had been closed when they left; he had gone over it in his mind last night when considering whether or not to stay in Claire and Aaron's guest room. He remembered leaving the keys to his house and car on the coffee table in his mother's lounge-room.

He hurried inside and was relieved to see that everything was in order. His keys were right where he had left them, next to his tea cup. He picked them up and put them in his pocket, and had just decided to come back later and tidy up when he saw his mother's journal sitting on the armrest of her chair, as if Justin had returned here to read. He called out his name again, but the unit was empty. It suddenly felt very empty, intolerably empty, and he picked up the journal and scurried back out the door, locking it behind him. He checked the garden and pathways as he walked the ten metres to his own back porch, half expecting to see footprints in the dew. *Or crop circles in the grass*, he laughed at himself.

He put the journal on the bench, unsure what to do with it now. It sat there, and each time he looked at it, he thought it was taunting him. It had already turned his world upside-down and inside-out, a couple of times over now. And now it was back. He stood there, looking at it, head tilted sideways as if scanning a bookshelf. It wasn't right for it to just sit there, but he didn't know quite what to do with it now. He couldn't let anything happen to it, he knew that much. But he couldn't physically bring himself to move over and pick it up. It was as if his whole body refused to indulge the curiosity of his mind.

He'd done quite enough thinking over the last two days. With a forced exhalation, he broke the gaze he held with his Mum's most precious possession, and wandered deliberately into the kitchen. Making a pot of tea would force him into action, and sometimes, he knew, any action at all is all that is needed. He flicked on the radio and the kettle, but when it boiled he still just stood, staring out the window. He was a little overwhelmed by the events of the past two days, by how much his world had been turned upside-down.

The same catchy song that had started his adventure rang forth, but he couldn't sing along anymore. His mind was full of his mother's story: her impossible, beautiful story, which he now believed absolutely and completely. *How blissful was ignorance*, he mused, *and yet how alien in retrospect.*

He smiled at himself, grateful at having the pressures of asking those three questions removed. A line from a song danced around the edge of his consciousness, but the exact lyrics eluded his grasp. Something about deciding whether you would accept the chance to meet God, if the cost was becoming a believer? He couldn't focus, his mind was full of this fantastic story. He idly wondered what his grandfathers would say to that, and how they had come to deal with their fervent fundamentalist beliefs, now that they were truly living in bodies of light, *as* one of the many mansions of the heavens. The song finished, and he turned the radio back off. The aroma of the tea seemed to beseech silence.

He looked at the journal on the bench, and felt a shiver of shame that he had desecrated it by tearing out a page. He noticed then that he couldn't see the page he had crumpled; indeed the spine and pages looked in almost mint condition. He flipped it open to the middle, and casually strode through the words his mother had written. Page after page was filled with her careful cursive script, and he soon flicked to her final entry. The page didn't look as if it had suffered any damage, and he lightly ran his finger along the edge as if he could feel an invisible scar. There was nothing, and he left the page open as he turned to pour the boiling water carefully through the tea leaves waiting in the strainer.

Breathing in the refreshing aroma that wafted from the teapot, he fitted the lid and decided to sit in the morning sunshine, perhaps peruse his mother's journal once more, and to simply be grateful for the beauty and wonder of life. To reflect and give thanks that this treasured account had been returned to him; but also for having children and grandchildren that made the world a better place. For having had the opportunity to share in the mystery and marvelousness of his mother's amazing 'dream'. He looked around the room, over the bench to the dining table where so many Christmases and family birthdays had been celebrated.

'It won't be the same without you,' he said to his ghostly companions. But life goes on. He hadn't known how to deal with Gloria's death when it happened, and he wished that his mother had shared her secret with him back then. It certainly would have made his wife's loss easier to accept. He blew a kiss into the air, and imagined he could feel her kisses floating back through the air at him. *On a drop of light,* he thought happily, and smiled. *On every single drop of light, I'm forever immersed in your love.*

He tidied the tea tray, and grabbed a couple of pieces of fruit to eat as a belated breakfast. He turned to pick up the journal, and noticed that the breeze caused by his pottering about had turned the page. He stopped and looked more closely, and was astonished to see that there was a new journal entry. It was a letter written to him, from Justin. He flicked a couple more pages, and was amazed to see that all of the remaining pages were empty no longer, that every single page was filled with a tiny script.

He turned back to the first part of this new section, and wondered how Justin had found the time to write so much. Then he remembered who he was thinking about, and berated himself for his ignorance. He read the introductory letter quickly. In it, Justin apologised for not having lived up to his end of the bargain, and said that he was sure Tommy knew that he already had all the answers he needed inside himself. Nevertheless, he wrote, he hoped that by returning the journal and including his own story that Tommy would be satisfied.

Tommy re-read the paragraph again; unsure he could be astonished any more. Exercising enormous self-restraint, he closed the journal and propped it under his arm. He carried his breakfast tray out to the back porch, which got the best morning sun. Sitting down just under the shade, he opened the journal once more. Finding the start of Justin's story, he settled in to read, and couldn't stop.

Hours later, dusk began to settle, and in the gradually darkening skies overhead, the first stars came out. Tom knew the largest and brightest were actually planets, but the minutiae of reality wasn't as important as what those lights represented. It didn't matter that he couldn't see with human eyes the part of the universe where a brand new consciousness now prepared to awaken. It was not relevant whether it was a Brown Dwarf turning Red, or a massive Blue Dwarf forming from the gaseous graveyard of a nursery nebula. Somewhere, he visualised, new fires were coalescing, new minds were bubbling forth. Along with a large percentage of the neighbourhood in a distant arm of our galaxy, Tommy gave thanks, knowing that any time now a new stellar would burst into life.

With a slightly rueful grin, he looked down from the stars overhead. He almost felt guilty about having such a good way of thinking about death. He couldn't help it; no matter how hesitant he felt about admitting it, he knew that he really liked the idea of his mother being born. That she was a star, that Gloria was a star; that the hundreds of millions of souls that had ever lived now lit the heavens. *Bodies of light, inhabiting the many mansions of the cosmos*, he thought, and couldn't help but grin again. He knew Gloria would like that, as would his mum.

Tom glanced over briefly at his mother's unit, and her garden, before his gaze settled on the plant he'd brought home, the newest addition to his own garden. The Venus Fly-trap plant he had bought for her only a couple of days ago was still closed, digesting carbons as it dissolved the exoskeletons of its meal. He savoured the simple act of watching it bask in the abundant star-light. All it had to do now was to grow: to dream, to digest, to soak up the light.

‘*One day, little plant,*’ he murmured with a touch of love, ‘*One day, I tell ya, you’re going to have the most beautiful great-grandchildren.*’

THE END